SHADOW HEART

A PARANORMAL REVERSE HAREM ROMANCE

CURSED LEGACIES
BOOK 2

MORGAN B LEE

Copyright © 2024 by Morgan B Lee

All rights reserved.

No part of this book may be reproduced in any form or by any electronic or mechanical means, including information storage and retrieval systems, without written permission from the author, except for the use of brief quotations in a book review.

No AI was used in the creation of this book.

Important: If you are reading this anywhere except Kindle Unlimited or as a purchase from Amazon, it is a pirated version. The first book of this series was pirated widely, and it's still an uphill battle. Please help us authors keep our rights to our work and read responsibly!

SERIES PLAYLIST

Spotify Link

Darkside *by Neoni*
Can You Keep a Secret? *by Ellise*
You Put a Spell on Me *by Austin Giorgio*
Queen *by Loren Gray*
Play with Fire *by Sam Tinnesz, Yacht Money*
Savage *by Bahari*
No Mercy *by Austin Giorgio*
Control *by Halsey*
Make Me Feel *by Elvis Drew*
Who's Afraid of Little Old Me? *by Taylor Swift*
lovely *by Billie Eilish, Khalid*
Worship *by Ari Abdul*
you should see me in a crown *by Billie Eilish*

READ BEFORE YOU READ

Just so we're all on the same page, this book isn't wholesome or fluffy. Maven's background is dark-ish. This series, in general, gets darker after Blood Oath.

Trigger warnings are tough to gauge. Many readers won't consider this series dark at all, while others will be leaving not-so-happy reviews about how they needed a warning (P.S., this is the warning!).

If you're concerned **at all** about potential triggers, please feel free to reach out to me on Instagram, TikTok, Facebook, or wherever else and ask me to spoil anything you're worried about. I will 100% spoil possible triggers because reading safely is extremely important.

With that being said, here is the ~~check~~list:

- Death (on page)
- Death of a main character (don't worry, it doesn't stick)
- Drugs
- Female dominant/switch
- Group sex scenes (no M/M)
- Graphic violence
- Loss of a loved one (past tense)
- Mentions of childhood abuse

- PTSD
- Somnophilia (with prior consent given)
- Stalking (of FMC by MMC)
- Strong language
- Torture (on page)

PROLOGUE
EVERETT

Thirteen Years Ago

"I don't want to watch the executions," I tell my birth mother quietly, watching the raindrops trailing down outside the window to my right.

It's just the two of us in the back of the limousine. We're running late because she had to make sure my outfit was perfect before I could be seen in public. The rest of my parents are already inside the big courthouse we're driving to, where the Legacy Council and the Immortal Quintet meet to conduct official business.

At fourteen, I've already been to the courthouse too many times to count. I've hated it every time.

My mother reaches out to adjust my collar, muttering about wanting me to look flawless when we step outside. I can already see the horde of people holding cameras standing outside the massive front doors of the courthouse, and my stomach clenches.

I hate cameras.

Ever since my parents insisted I make my modeling debut in the human world last year, cameras have followed me everywhere I go outside of the Frost estate. My parents tell me I'm a child modeling phenomenon, but I can't stand looking in the mirror anymore. It doesn't help that I look so much like my father.

"You must learn to watch whenever this happens, son," Mother says. "Executions are uncommon but necessary. The council and the Immortal Quintet expect the strongest legacies to support their final decision, and what are we?"

"The strongest," I mumble on autopilot. I know there's no use trying to get out of this dread pooling in my gut, but I still look at her pleadingly. "Heidi never has to sit through shit like this. Why do I?"

"Don't use that language. And your sister isn't a real Frost. You know this."

I've heard it too many times to count, but it still bothers me. Alaric Frost is my father and the prestigious keeper of my parents' elite quintet, so they all took on the Frost last name. But Corbin, another of my parents, fathered Heidi with Daphne, my mother. Since Heidi isn't *biologically* a Frost from Alaric's bloodline, they had her take my mother's maiden name. She's only eight, but we've been raised so differently.

Heidi can't stand looking at me, either. I wonder if she will always hate me as much as I've forced her to. I've pushed her away for her own good, just in case my parents ever stooped low enough to try using her as leverage against me, but it still hurts.

"The gods have granted you power and beauty befitting a true Frost," my mother muses, checking her lipstick one last time as the limousine slows to a stop. She turns and levels me with a harsh look, slipping her compact mirror back into her purse. "But it's up to you to live up to our name. Which means in that courtroom, there will be no more whining, no grimacing, not so much as a *sniffle* if you don't like what you see. Frosts are not soft. You will sit up straight, observe, and say nothing. And if you embarrass us in any way, you know what will happen."

My stomach pain worsens, and I look away, tucking my hands into my gray overcoat so she won't see the frost prickling my fingertips.

It's true. I *do* know what happens when I disappoint my family. They punish me, but not by hurting *me*. Instead, they take it out on anything or anyone I remotely like.

Which is why I pretend to hate everything. Every gift, every hobby, every person.

It's safer for everyone that way.

Maybe one day I'll be able to love something, *anything*, without the fear that it will be ripped to pieces if I step out of line. Even my curse mocks me, reminding me that I'll ruin any chance at my own future happiness if I *care*.

"Yes, Mother," I mutter.

She opens the door. As we step out, I look straight ahead through the flashing lights despite the photographers screaming for me to look at them. By the time we make it through the doors and to our seats at the edges of the massive vaulted courtroom filled with legacies, my vision is spotted from all the camera flashes.

I sit with my parents' quintet. My father, as usual, sits with the rest of the Legacy Council. I can't remember a time when he wasn't sitting at the front of the room with them. He's completely focused on something another council member is saying to him. Even here, many legacies eye me from their seats, curious to see the heir of Alaric Frost. Members of influential quintets are here as representatives from each of the four Houses.

My attention lands on two Cranes sitting on the opposite side of the room, the only members of their quintet in attendance today. They wear all black, and their faces are chalky with dark circles under their eyes. I'm pretty sure that shifty-eyed blood fae is Silas Crane's birth father.

Mother sees where I'm looking and whispers, "Their keeper just committed suicide. Rumor has it that Somnus DeLune's bastard son got inside his head and drove him to it. Quite the scandal—needless to say, we won't be associating with any of them anymore. But pay attention. Even in mourning, even with their curses returning, the Cranes know to heed when the Immortal Quintet extends a call. We Frosts are just the same. Loyalty is everything."

She goes quiet along with everyone else when the large double doors at the head of the room open, and the Immortal Quintet strides in.

I've seen them in person before, but it's still hard not to shrink in on myself when their intimidating presence fills the room. It's impossible to forget that they have ruled legacies for centuries for a good reason—we legacies might be descended from the original monsters who escaped the Nether, but they *are* monsters who escaped it. They're frighteningly powerful.

Especially their keeper, Natalya, who calls the court to order before she turns to address the Legacy Council. When she does, I stare at the keeper emblems that are etched like a crown across her forehead, curtained by her copper-colored hair. Each emblem represents one of the Four Houses—one for each of her quintet members.

"Bring in the dissenters," she says.

Several uniformed legacy security guards drag two shifters and a caster into the room, all beaten to a pulp. I don't recognize any of their bloodied, bruised faces.

But then my eyes widen when a *human* is brought in, too.

He also looks like he took a beating, but he holds his head high despite limping from a mangled ankle. When they shove him forward to stand in front of the Immortal Quintet, he doesn't flinch back like the others do. Instead, he looks at the room and the crowd around him with a curious, dazed frown.

I'm not the only one surprised—after all, humans have never been permitted in legacy proceedings. Murmurs roll through the rest of the audience as an elemental council member stands to begin the address.

"Brought before us today are three of our own who have been captured and charged with unlawful casting of forbidden spells outside of the borders of the Divide, disturbing the peace among humans, and supporting acts of—"

One of the Cranes stands and interrupts him, looking down her nose at the human. I realize she's probably Silas's mother.

"Get to the point. Why is there a *human* in our midst? They're not permitted here."

Rumbles of agreement echo around me. The elemental looks nervous as he reads from the official document.

"Ah, yes...also brought before us today is one Pietro Amato, whose final hearing and punishment have been left to our discretion by the human government. Over the last seven years, he has been found guilty of multiple offenses, including fear-mongering among humans, spreading propaganda about the Nether, acts of violence against legacies—"

"That was in self-defense only," the human insists over the angry murmurs filling the room.

"And most disturbing of all, forming alliances with demons and other convicts of the Nether to...*willingly* volunteer in necromantic rituals on multiple accounts."

The court is in an uproar before the council member finishes speaking. I duck down into my seat, wide-eyed as I watch the powerful legacies stand and scream over one another. I've been here too many times, but I've never seen a hearing blow up like this. Even my father is standing, his cool demeanor replaced by disgust as he glowers down at the human.

Despite slurs and screeches from all around, Pietro Amato holds eye contact with the keeper of the Immortal Quintet. When Natalya speaks, everyone else goes silent, but the room is filled with tension so thick that I can barely breathe.

"So his final hearing begins," she announces in a bell-like voice. "Tell us of your crimes, human, and we will choose how you shall be executed."

Sick smiles of excitement spread on the faces of the legacies leering down at the man. But the longer I watch him, the more my stomach twists. He's been charged with a lot of severe crimes, but he doesn't *look* like a threat.

He looks...desperate. Distraught. Tears gather in his eyes as he takes a step forward.

"All that I have done, I did to rescue my daughter from the

Nether. Seven years ago, she was stolen away by shadow fiends, and I have been doing everything possible to try to get her back—"

My father's loud, condescending scoff interrupts him. "Insanity! Fiends don't *take* humans—they slaughter them. Your daughter is long dead."

"She is *alive!*" Amato insists, facing my father. The courtroom quiets as everyone's interest rests on the unexpectedly brave, bruised, bloodied human. "I know she is. The charges against me are true on one account—I *did* volunteer in necromantic rituals, but only to find her. Only to trace my bloodline in her to learn whether she's still alive. And she *is*. My daughter…"

His voice breaks as emotion clouds his face. He turns back to the Immortal Quintet. They all watch him coldly, except for the earth elemental, who frowns at the sight of the human with tears on his cheeks.

"My little miracle of a daughter was just two years old when she was taken from me in the surge that destroyed my hometown. Please, I have to get her back. I know in my very bones that she is still alive in the Nether. I need to rescue her. *Please*," he begs raggedly. "You must believe me!"

Somnus DeLune, another member of the Immortal Quintet, arches a lazy brow, observing the frantic father as if he's studying an injured ant.

"Even if I did believe that the Nether is spiriting away humans—which I don't, by the way…go on, amuse me. How could your little mortal runt have survived for *seven years* in that hell?"

It sounds so impossible that even I shake my head. I've never been to the Divide, but I've heard the stories. I know it's otherworldly and deadly, even for powerful legacies. And that's only where the Nether starts to seep into this world.

A child surviving in that lifeless plane of existence? Impossible.

But Pietro Amato seems to believe it with every fiber of his being. Why execute someone for choosing to believe his daughter is alive when he has nothing else to believe in? Can't they just put him in a cell so he doesn't do anything else against the law?

Watching these monsters judge a desperate human who has no power to fight back just feels...wrong.

I wonder if I can leave the room, but when my mother notices that I'm compulsively readjusting the same sleeve over and over, she shoots me a savage warning look that makes me go still.

Pietro looks at each council member and the unforgiving Immortal Quintet before straightening. Sudden confidence punctuates each of his words.

"My daughter is far more precious than you can possibly imagine. I don't know how she has survived, but she has. And if I am not permitted to pass through the Divide and fight to get her back...the wrath of the gods will be upon you tenfold. They will smite your kind with fury unlike anything you have ever seen."

Insulted gasps and outcries flood the room once again. One of the angry casters hurls a magic attack at Amato. The guards beside him do nothing to stop the flare of light, and I cringe when the human is hit by the spell, crumpling to the floor with a hoarse, pained cry.

Corbin, my other father, grips the back of my collar in warning. He doesn't like that I reacted. The courtroom is still filled with yelling and swearing, but Pietro gets to his feet again anyway, grimacing.

"Behold, the lies a desperate madman clings to," Somnus muses as things finally die down.

"A madman who dares threaten us with a pretended knowledge of the will of the gods themselves," Melvolin Hearst adds with a sneer on the other end of the Immortal Quintet.

Natalya holds up her hand, and everyone goes deadly silent. She slowly moves to stand right in front of the pleading human. Her words are soft as rose petals, as usual, but the look on her face has me shrinking into my seat even more. My hands are covered in frost inside my pockets now, and I'm getting increasingly sick as eagerness sparkles in the eyes of all legacies watching, including my cool, collected parents.

"All parents think their children are precious," Natalya says, studying Pietro with no empathy on her face. "That is not reason enough to get involved with demons. Yet you did. And before you die for your crimes, I will tell you the truth. The demons lied to you. They misled you so they could use you as a tool to stir up mistrust and violence among humans and our kind. You are nothing but an easily manipulated pawn for those who prey on the innocent."

He shakes his head. "No, I *know* the truth. My daughter is—"

"Dead. No human could survive in the Nether, least of all a toddler. The crimes you have committed far outweigh the insanity you claim to believe." She raises her voice slightly, circling him like a shark. "I call all legacies present to vote. Shall I put this mad human to immediate death for the atrocities he has committed against our law and our kind?"

Screams of assent permeate the air that I can no longer breathe as the dread in my stomach builds. I want to hide my face. I want to run out of the room so I won't have to see this. But showing weakness in front of my parents is not an option, so I force myself to sit still and watch.

I watch as the desperate father turns his pleading face to the rest of the room, his gaze connecting with mine momentarily.

I watch the hopeless tears falling from his dark gaze, his heartbroken, silent plea cutting into my chest until moisture wells in my own eyes.

And then I watch as Natalya rips Pietro Amato's head off in front of a room full of cheering, bloodthirsty sadists.

1

MAVEN

Growing up in hell, I was taught to appreciate a beautifully broad spectrum of pain. I was conditioned to have a high tolerance for it and learned it can be a great distraction. A tool.

Although right now, my world is nothing *but* pain—nothing but blazing agony emanating throughout my limbs and blurring every thought in my head until I'm paralyzed and delirious.

Which is why, at first, I'm certain I'm imagining things when I hear *them* shouting from some watery, distant universe.

"Maven!"

"No!"

An ear-splitting roar like a dragon's is cut off suddenly by the sound of an explosion. I wonder if that explosion damaged me in some way. If it did, I can't feel it over the agony encompassing everything else. There's more shouting before I realize two of them are at each other's throats.

"She's in pain. I'm healing her. *Move.*"

"She said *no one*. Lay a single finger on her, and I'll rip it off and shove it through your eyeball."

Their fighting blends into the background as I hear a soft voice above me. Cool fingers stroke over my face tenderly, the only pleasant thing I've been able to feel since coming back with this damned poison scorching through my system.

"I'm sorry. This is my fault. I was selfish with you. Dear gods, I'm so, *so* sorry."

His broken whisper turns into a prayer to Galene, the goddess of healing. Which is how I know I'm more delirious than I thought. Because *that one* would never pray for me. None of them would because I was nothing but the target of a bet to them. This must all be wishful thinking in my poor, pain-addled mind.

The voices blur together. Someone snaps that they have to get me out of the room, and someone else is swearing profusely. There's also nonstop screaming in the background…oh wait, that's just me in my own mind. I can't make my mouth move to make that sound, so I suppose I'm stuck with it echoing in my head.

Nightshade root powder is a bitch.

Finally, I reach my limit, and my mind starts to drift the way it always has when I've disassociated to deal with pain. I've been here many times—it's my own particular form of subspace, free of my harsh reality. In this oblivion, there's no looming, blood-oath-bound mission with a tragic end waiting for me. There's no ache in my chest from naively allowing four gorgeous legacies to fuck me for sport.

Right now, it's just me and my inner darkness.

So peaceful.

But when I rouse again, the excruciating pain is still coursing through me. The softness at my back must mean I'm lying on a bed, no longer in the headmaster's office. I keep my breathing even and listen carefully. For a moment, there's nothing, but then it sounds like a door opens.

There's a quiet shuffling sound as if someone is setting things down, and then a hand brushes hair from my forehead. That hand drifts down to press just below my clavicle, the touch so brief and methodical that it doesn't trigger my haphephobia.

Silas's hoarse voice murmurs, "I don't understand. You're breathing, so where is your heartbeat?"

It's obviously a question for himself, and I'm surprised by the raw frustration and vulnerability in his tired voice. Then he begins chanting in fae, and I know he's casting a potent healing spell because my hair stands on end. But otherwise, I feel nothing.

Because only one type of magic can heal me, and it's not blood magic.

That's why I've been hell-bent on avoiding any situation where this might happen—because it just raises more questions I can't afford to answer.

But he doesn't know that his magic is useless on a creature like me, so he tries and tries. Again and again and fucking *again*. It's a wonder he hasn't died of blood loss himself at this point.

"Why can't I heal you, *ima sangfluir*?" he whispers.

His desperation is…touching.

At least, it would be if my muddled brain didn't choose now to remember Everett's words at the inn.

We thought getting you in bed would be a challenge, but here we are. One day of fawning over you, and it opened you right up. Now we just have to decide who won their prize.

Assholes.

Someone else enters the room, and Silas's formerly soft tone turns razor-sharp. "You still haven't hunted today, therefore you're still a threat. Get the fuck out before you hurt her."

Baelfire's voice is guttural, unhinged. "I would *never* hurt my mate."

"As if your dragon leaves you with a choice. You were mid fucking shift when I hit you with that immobilization spell earlier. Between you and putting no less than *nine* hexes on that godsdamned DeLune to temporarily lock him in Limbo so Everett could get her back to this apartment for me to heal, my magic is annoyingly depleted. If you lose your shit again—"

"She looked *dead*." Baelfire chokes and then breathes out slowly like he's trying to diffuse a bomb in his head. "Of course, I lost my shit. I'm in control now."

"I'm not taking chances with her. Leave."

"If you think I'm leaving her in this fucking condition, you've lost more of your mind than you realize. Shut up and heal her already."

"I'm *trying*," Silas grits, and I feel his hand brush lightly over my hair again. "It's not working."

I'm perplexed. If I was just a bet to them, why the hell do they both sound so worried over me right now?

Guilt. That must be it.

They must somehow feel responsible for this happening, and even though they're descended from monsters, they can't handle the guilt. I cling to that reasoning, refusing to entertain any other possible reasons for their panic.

Because they hurt me. I can't let it happen again, so I carefully tuck all of my emotions away in a metaphorical cage in my chest.

Right now is about survival, not *feelings*.

"What the fuck do you mean, it's not working?" Baelfire demands. "You're a damn prodigy. I watched you turn raindrops into diamonds when you were seven. You just trapped Crypt fucking DeLune in Limbo—not even his immortal father has ever managed to do that. Why the hell can't you heal—"

"I don't know," the blood fae snaps. I hear more shuffling and then a savage swear. "I need to feed to boost my magic. Give me your blood."

Bael growls, but a chair shoves backward, scraping on the floor. "Fine—for *Maven*. But you are not fucking biting me."

Through the hallucinogenic haze of agony clouding my brain, I listen to the sounds of them leaving the room, presumably to find something to collect Baelfire's blood in. I find the fact that the proud Decimus is donating blood in such a fucked-up way kind of... morbidly sweet.

But that thought disperses as the familiar sensation of *leaving* tugs on whatever remains of my soul. The release is swift as I feel my body go cold, now completely incognizant of anything in the mortal world as I slip away.

Your first success is done.

Images flicker at light speed through my mind, a cacophony of randomly sickening scenes. Hordes of shadow fiends slinking through a maze filled with bloodcurdling screams. Rotting flesh. Green fire burning piles of corpses. Snow stained with blood and a dark throne made of bones—and, briefly, Lillian.

She's still alive but bone-thin as she weeps over a fresh grave. I can practically feel her sobs rattling in my chest, and I want nothing more than to stand beside her to silently offer comfort.

Move on quickly, my telum. Fulfill your purpose, and they will be spared.

Reviving is slow and disorienting because I force myself to keep my eyes closed. But I have to because I have no idea how long I was gone or what I'm about to wake up to. If Silas and Baelfire witnessed me slipping away…

But no. I hear them outside this room still, talking and snapping quietly at each other. Peeking one eye open, I realize I'm lying in the enormous bed where I first explored Baelfire and discovered his praise kink.

Just thinking of that creates a twinge of hurt in my chest—but also, to my horror, warm goosebumps scatter down my arms.

Stupid fucking body. It's been way too confused by them.

The pain is entirely gone now, which I find fascinating. From an objective standpoint, at least now I know that nightshade root powder isn't listed among the handful of ways to *actually* kill me, even if it hurts like hell.

My head lolls to the right, and I squint at the closed curtains. Faint gray light peeks through them, telling me it's nearly dawn. I've been under for roughly twenty-four hours, then. The bedside table next to me is crowded with every kind of spell ingredient known to the House of Arcana and several rags stained with drying streaks of blood.

Gritting my teeth, I try in vain to move again. My body is much weaker than it usually is after one of my episodes, probably thanks to the poison. I need to get out of here and disappear entirely so I won't be caught and suspected of the headmaster's assassination. I don't have to worry about the winter solstice deadline anymore—my first target is dead, whether or not it was by my hand. Now, I need to start tracking down the others.

But I freeze as the image of the changeling standing over me comes back.

Kenzie.

I can't leave. Not yet, not when I know that changeling got to her. I need to figure out whether she's dead or alive—and if she *is* alive, there's a very high chance that the changeling has her hidden away somewhere to use her as a feeding source.

Changelings are uncommon monsters. They're intelligent, but they lack emotion and loyalty. If they have time to observe a target, they can mimic that person down to the slightest mannerisms, but to survive, they must feed on other people's memories. So there's a high chance it has Kenzie stashed away, slowly feeding on her mind until she's nothing more than a blank slate.

Just a husk of who she was.

Unexpected emotion clogs my throat at the thought of losing Kenzie in that way. Still, I hope that's the case because at least it would mean the bubbly lioness shifter might still be alive. A surge of anger and bone-deep determination washes over me, finalizing my decision.

If Kenzie is alive, I'll find her. The rest of my tasks will wait.

Not to mention, I have to kill that changeling to cover my own tracks since it now knows what I am. I can't count on a faithless changeling not to tell the fucking Legacy Council that the *telum* is at Everbound University.

But first, I have to get the hell away from these legacies who hurt me.

2

MAVEN

WHEN I TRY to move again, I manage to sit up before my strength gives out, leaving me slumped against the headboard. But as my senses return, I tense. Because even though the room is empty, I don't *feel* alone.

The Nightmare Prince is here, watching me from Limbo.

He witnessed me slip away and revive. *Again.*

I glare at the spot on the bed near me where I feel a slight, indescribable pull. Silas said he temporarily locked Crypt in Limbo, so I'm running on limited time before the psychopathic, dreamy stalker returns. I wonder if he'll tell the others what he saw in the headmaster's office and in here.

I also can't help wondering how much of his stalking was motivated by their little bet. The thought makes my chest ache, and I frown. This shouldn't be bothering me as much as it is. Sure, they fucked me over. It hurts, but I should be able to get over it quickly and move on with my mission. It's hardly the first time someone hurt me when I was stupid enough to let down my guard, so why do I *feel* it so much more this time?

At long last, I drag myself from the bed. Glancing down, I see I'm still in the ripped black clothing stained with mine and the changeling's blood. That's a relief. Once I get more magic into my system, I'll need this dried blood for a ritual to track it down.

Quietly, I move to the door and take a deep breath as I prepare to leave. But then someone shouts from the direction of the kitchen down the hall. Something shatters. Slipping out, I approach on high alert. I can sense Crypt following me closely in Limbo.

Glancing around the hallway's corner, I see Silas and Baelfire grappling with each other. Silas's bleeding crystal protrudes from Baelfire's bicep, which keeps trying to heal around it. Baelfire is gripping the blood fae's hands with a snarl to keep them from encircling his throat. Shards of a broken bowl speckled with bright blood are scattered across the tile nearby, right in front of a decorative table filled with thriving potted plants.

"Snap out of it, Si," Bael barks. "It's all in your fucking head!"

I catch a brief glimpse of Silas's face, and the mindless panic mixed with fury I see there makes my throat tighten. Because he doesn't seem like Silas. He looks entirely out of his mind.

From his curse, I realize.

I clench my hands, torn between the desire to sneak out of this apartment and the bizarre urge I have to intervene. But even if I tried, I'm too weak at the moment to stop them from spilling more blood.

Silas starts chanting in fae, but Baelfire snarls as he loses his temper. He shoves Silas's hands aside, twists Silas's shoulder under his arm, and wrenches it violently in the wrong direction. The loud *crack* of a bone breaking makes me inhale sharply.

Silas hisses in pain, cradling his broken arm as he stumbles away, but Baelfire hears my gasp. His attention snaps up to me, and his eyes flare wide. In a blur of shifter speed, he's abruptly right in front of me, his hands coming up like he's about to try bracing my weak form against his muscular body.

"Don't."

I may be barely holding myself upright, but I can still use my *don't fuck with me* voice. The one I perfected in the hellscape I was raised in.

Baelfire pulls his hands away but doesn't move back, consuming me with his eyes like he's sure I'm about to vanish. He looks rougher than I've ever seen him—his T-shirt and jeans scorched and torn, his golden hair a mess, and dark circles under his eyes, which are a deeper shade of amber than usual. Blood is smeared on his hands and arms and continues to drip from Silas's forgotten crystal, still embedded in his arm.

"Maven," he pleads raggedly, scanning my face.

I forcefully keep it blank, even though my chest pangs. I have the most irksome urge to feel his warm arms wrapped tightly around me. My stupid, exhausted body can't seem to remember that I'd hate it if he actually did touch me.

His hands twitch toward me again, but he clenches them at his sides. "Fuck, baby, I know you must be pissed, but please just let me—"

I step around him. I need to leave before I have to face my emotions, which are bubbling to the surface, but Silas steps in front of me. His ruby-red eyes are now focused, but the blood fae looks as exhausted as I feel and even paler than usual.

"I tried everything. How is your pain suddenly gone?"

"It's not."

I'm not lying. It's painful being around them like this.

Silas's face softens. His gaze drops to my chest, where a hole torn by my dagger remains, but the only scar to be seen is the one I've had for five years.

"You had no heartbeat. I thought I lost you."

You can't lose what you never wanted in the first place.

"Heartbeats are overrated," I mumble instead.

When I try to step around him, he only moves closer, determination and something unbearably tender bleeding into his expression. Seeing that bit of tenderness sparks my temper. From some angry, petty part of my mind, Sierra's sneering face comes back to me along with her words.

They might even fuck you once or twice out of pity. But make no mistake, they're not yours.

My anger deepens, overshadowing the lingering hurt until I decide I need to get out of this apartment really fucking soon before I do something stupid.

Silas's voice is soft. "We should talk—"

"There is no we."

"Yes, there is," he says firmly. "I know you're upset—"

"You four used me as a dick-measuring contest, and you think I'm *upset*? That's cute." I arch a brow. "You can't lie, so tell me yes or no. Was there a bet about who would fuck me first?"

His mouth opens and closes twice in a row before he swallows. "Yes, but—"

"And prizes for whoever won?"

"Yes, but that was not—"

"Congratulations," I make my voice sickly sweet. "You won. Now go find a new plaything to fuck. I'm sure Sierra would happily volunteer to entertain the two of you. Again."

Baelfire flinches and snarls, "You were not a fucking *plaything*, and we are not touching anyone else. Ever. As far as I'm concerned, from now on, anyone who touches me is touching what belongs to you. We did make that stupid bet, but it was just a competition between rivals. We didn't mean for you to—"

"Find out?"

"Get *hurt*," he corrects vehemently, golden eyes pleading. He looks miserable. "I take it all back. Screw that fucking bet, okay? It was just a juvenile game. We're legacies, we're competitive, and we were being stupid. None of us gives a shit about those prizes now, anyway."

One glance at Silas tells me that's absolutely false. He looks away.

The hurt doubles in my chest, but I keep my face impassive as I turn to face the front door.

"You can't leave, *sangfluir*," Silas says quietly. "None of us can get out. The university is on lockdown."

I pause, irritation welling up in my throat. Or is that emotion? Oh gods, it is. I have to get away from them as soon as fucking possible because I can't seem to hide how I really feel around them anymore.

Steadying my voice, I ask, "Lockdown?"

"The headmaster was assassinated," Baelfire says carefully as if he's trying not to place meaning in the words, even though we all know they found me in the room with the dead mage. "We were barely able to get you out of there and wipe away all traces before the rest of the Immortal Quintet arrived. They've put all of Everbound University on a strict magical lockdown. No one can leave their dorms or apartments until further notice—except for the faculty, who are all being questioned as we speak. We've already been stuck in here for an entire fucking day and night. No one knows when they'll let up."

I process that without turning to face them. The Immortal Quintet is here?

How…convenient.

All my targets in one spot.

But it does complicate certain things. If we're on magical lockdown, they must know that someone here killed their quintet member. And I'm positive I heard Everett's voice in that office when they found me, which means he might tell them I was found in that room. I can't think of a single reason he wouldn't rat me out. After all, he heard my fake confession of being part of the anti-legacy movement.

I wonder how long I have until they realize the *telum* is here at Everbound. I need to come up with a new plan—one that will help me find Kenzie, kill the changeling, *and* pick off the rest of the Immortal Quintet one by one…

But my head is pounding, and my body feels sluggish from exhaustion. How aggravating. I've spent most of my life working my ass off to make my physical body into a honed weapon. I can't afford to be tired, not with so much danger on the horizon.

Baelfire must sense that I'm frozen in anxiety-ridden exhaustion because he murmurs, "There's no getting out right now, Boo. And I don't know what fancy caster shit happened to get rid of that fucking poison, but you need more time to recover. I'll make you food, and...we can talk about everything. All of us, all the cards on the table."

Hard pass. No way in hell am I about to *talk* with these assholes about anything, now or ever. So instead of acknowledging anything he said, I grumble, "I need a damn shower," and turn to leave the room.

But Silas's hand wraps gently around my shoulder to stop me.

"Agree to talk to us first," he demands.

Even though his touch is cautious, tension rackets up my spine. I'm too emotional right now, a dozen feelings warring inside me—especially hurt and anger.

I inhale slowly, trying to calm the angry hum in my veins. "No."

"Maven—"

My nerves jolt when his touch slips down to my bare hand in an attempt to turn me to face them. It sets off everything I'm feeling, demolishing my lockbox of emotions and my typical level of control.

So when I knock Silas's hand away, the sheer force that escapes my fingertips in a flare of dark tendrils takes all of us by surprise. He's sent airborne, smashing into the dining room wall hard enough that everything hanging on it falls to the floor with a crash. He groans, gripping his broken arm with clenched teeth.

When his blood-red gaze flicks back to me, it's filled with shock. His brow furrowed in both pain and confusion. My particular brand of magic hurts like hell, and he's obviously never felt something like that.

Briefly, I'm puzzled about how I even *had* magic to lose control of, since the ordeal with Headmaster Hearst and the changeling completely drained my power. But one glance at the nearby cluster of potted plants shows me they've withered to nothing, dead and gone.

Damn it.

I didn't mean to do that.

I deplore losing control.

It's dead quiet before Baelfire murmurs, "Maven?"

He steps toward me, but I stare him down, ignoring the tired throb in my head.

"Leave. Me. Alone."

But now that my emotions aren't under a tight hold, my voice wobbles. I internally curse the gods when I realize moisture is threatening to escape my eyes. Seeing that makes Baelfire go perfectly still with horror, and he swears softly.

"Boo...oh gods, *please* don't cry or I'll—"

As if the gods have finally decided to sprinkle some mercy into my existence, there's a cheery knock on the front door. I glance down at my incriminatingly bloody ensemble, as do Silas and Baelfire. Without a word, I slip back behind the corner of the hallway. Finally giving in to the lingering weakness from reviving, I brace myself against the wall and listen as they open the now-unlocked door.

I recognize Mr. Gibbons' voice. "Ah! If it isn't my two favorites of your most promising quintet—"

"Are we free to leave now?" Baelfire interrupts impatiently.

"Well, now, not exactly," the warlock hedges. "Until further notice, students will not be permitted outside the walls of Everbound Castle. There will be some rather heavy supervision and new rules, and some, ah...bold new changes to the school's schedule going forward..."

He trails off and then clears his throat. "But the wonderful news is that students may now leave their rooms. Classes are on hold for the rest of the day, but at eight o'clock this evening, we will be holding the mandatory Matched Ball—where the Immortal Quintet will honor us with their attendance!"

From his tone, he clearly expects them to squeal and clap at the news.

"Gee whiz, that's great," Baelfire drawls, his dry tone going right over Mr. Gibbon's head. "But what about us shifters? We don't like being cooped up. It's the animals inside us. Take it from me—this whole school will become a hunting ground if the House of Shifting gets cabin fever. Wouldn't want you to be dragon chow."

The underlying threat in his voice makes me tip my head.

Usually, Baelfire is exceptionally charming, but he's on edge right now. Is he also struggling with his curse in some way I don't know?

"Well...you're right," Mr. Gibbons agrees after swallowing loudly. "I suppose that will only add further excitement into the mix, eh? I shouldn't be telling you this, gentlemen, but seeing how you're a Crane and a Decimus...I'll let you in on a little secret. As of tomorrow morning, the no-killing ban will be officially lifted, and quintet rankings will begin."

Quintet rankings mean all matched legacies will be at each other's throats, intent on proving they're the strongest. It will be an absolute bloodbath.

At least I have that to look forward to.

"Quintet rankings aren't supposed to start until next semester," Silas points out. "After the holiday break."

"By order of the Immortal Quintet, the holiday break has been indefinitely delayed...as has First Placement," Mr. Gibbons explains, sounding nervous when Baelfire scowls. "You see, we'll begin next semester effective tomorrow on an expedited timeline. Rather different, but then one is not to argue with the Immortal Quintet. Well then! I have other students to whom I must deliver this news. Here is your official invitation to the Matched Ball—I'm sure your quintet will be the envy of all. Oh, and all food in the dining hall is complimentary for the rest of the day as an apology from our most understanding leaders. Have a good day, gentlemen."

The door shuts, and Baelfire scowls savagely again. "We're not allowed to leave for the holidays? My family is going to be pissed when I don't show up. What the fuck is going on?"

I know what's going on. The Immortal Quintet is keeping everyone trapped here while they search for the one who killed their mage. They're going to tear this place apart until they find their culprit...and they might discover me in the process.

Everbound is officially a ticking time bomb.

Pushing myself off the wall, I retreat because I really do need a shower. Then I need to get away from these assholes and start searching.

Please be alive, Kenzie. I'm coming for you.

3

SILAS

I GLANCE down the hall when I hear Maven shut the door to the bathroom.

What are you hiding, my blood blossom?

My entire life, I've studied magic. When I apprenticed with the Garnet Wizard, I learned more about it than most casters ever do. He was never a fan of how the Legacy Council monitors the craft, censoring certain types of magic and many potion ingredients and grimoires. Instead, he made it a point to teach me more about forbidden magics than the Legacy Council would ever have permitted, had they been aware.

So I *know* magic. Even the kinds I don't practice.

But my eyes slip back to the withered plants nearby, and I'm... captivated. I'm also in a great deal of pain, thanks to my broken shoulder and the lingering tendrils of pure anguish left behind from Maven's...curse? Hex? Malediction?

What the hell *was* that? And what happened to the poison she was fighting? How could it just vanish from her system?

"Sorry about your shoulder," Baelfire grumbles, drawing his hands through his hair and down his face as he paces like a caged animal.

He's been stuck in here with nothing to slay to appease his curse for an entire day and night, on top of missing out on hunting yesterday. I have no idea if he's ever been in a similar situation or how long he will be able to remain in his right mind without hunting, but I suspect his dragon is biting at the bits to get out.

I brace myself against the wall, babying my shoulder. "No, you're not."

He grunts. "You're right. You were out of your fucking mind. I'd do it again."

When his pacing increases, and he huffs in frustration, I arch a brow. "The door is unlocked. You could hunt another legacy if need be."

Baelfire grimaces. "See, that's the difference between me and you. That is my last fucking resort—I'd rather not murder someone in cold blood unless there's no other option. Besides..."

His amber gaze flicks toward the hall, and his voice turns rough. "She needs to eat. I know she's pissed at us right now, but I need to make sure she's taken care of. I just...fuck, I can't get that image out of my head."

I know exactly what image he's talking about because it's haunting me, too. Maven lying broken and motionless on that floor, covered in blood—*her* blood. We had been frantically searching for her and had just crossed paths with Everett on his way to his office when I'd caught the scent of her mouthwatering blood.

It's a sickening thing how much the aroma of her blood both terrorizes and entices me.

And walking in on her like *that*...

To take my mind off it, I drag myself into the kitchen, where I stashed a few of my spare spell ingredients over a week ago.

Uncorking a vial of chimera venom and grabbing dried moonflower petals, I prepare a healing mixture. It's not a commonly prepared mixture since it is painful to ingest, but I'm a fae. Between our mead and our wine, we have cast-iron stomachs.

Baelfire groans and drops into one of the large couches off the side of the dining room, burying his head under a pillow. I realize his shifter hearing must be picking up on the soft sounds of Maven in the shower, and I don't envy him.

This situation is hard enough without being *hard*.

I've barely had time to down the potent but disgusting concoction before the Nightmare Prince flickers suddenly into existence beside me, grips me by the back of the neck, and slams my face into the cold marble countertop. I feel the crunch of my nose breaking, and the sudden cutoff from oxygen has me choking for air through my mouth.

Crypt leans down to speak beside my ear, his voice a low, infuriated rasp.

"That's for trapping me where I couldn't reach her. And this—" He jams his elbow into my broken shoulder, which makes my brain white out for a second as pain overwhelms everything else. "Is for forcing me to watch that happen a *second* fucking time."

I don't know what *second time* this prick is talking about, but when I sense the warm trickle from my broken nose, I draw from that blood, forcing my depleted magic to lash out at Crypt any way it can. A violent burst of scarlet light flares around me. He's knocked backward with a satisfying crash.

I straighten and wipe the blood off my nose and chin, but when I glance over my shoulder, Crypt has already slipped back into Limbo. He returns a second later, and I tense, ready to overextend my magic a second time. But he just leans against the dining room wall and digs his lighter out.

As I slump into one of the dining room chairs, feeling the healing concoction hum through my veins and soften the pain, I watch the Nightmare Prince warily. He has dried blood crusted over one wrist, Maven's blood on his hands, and he looks…uncharacteristically fazed. Perhaps even as rough as Baelfire and I.

Bael says nothing but observes the two of us like he's waiting to watch a cockfight on which he's bet good money. He clearly enjoyed that little show just now.

My tired attention zeroes back in on Crypt and how he fumbles with his lighter as he pulls out a cigarette. His hands are shaking so slightly, it's almost imperceptible—but I notice it just like I take note of the tension slipping from his shoulders after he takes the first deep drag of the odd herb.

Interesting.

Is this a sign of weakness in him I never noticed before? Evidence of strain from being in Limbo? Aside from perhaps being unable to feel true emotion, I've never had a solid guess as to what his curse could be. Except now, he clearly feels strongly for Maven.

Or does he? a voice in my head titters.

He's faking it. He'll end up hurting her. You should kill him.

The incubus will end you like he ended your family. But first, he'll watch you go mad.

The voices have been even worse today, twisting my mind and constantly drawing my thoughts back to Maven's motionless body. They're making my spine twitch and my head pound.

When Crypt catches me watching him, his eyes flash with warning.

"If you've got something to say, Crane, you can shove it right up your ass. And never lock me in Limbo again, or I'll rip my way into your psyche and make the voices in your head seem like fucking saints."

My jaw clenches, and I glare at Baelfire.

But my suspicion that the dragon shifter is to blame dies when the Nightmare Prince scoffs, "I do my best work in mad minds, Crane. Of course I know that you're one of them."

He tips his head back to blow out a long exhale of sweet-smelling smoke, and Baelfire snaps, "Now is not the time to smoke, you creepy fuck."

"Smoke shouldn't bother a dragon."

"*Everything* bothers me right now. I need to fucking kill something, and it's about to be you."

The incubus's typical levity is gone as he ignores Baelfire to look at me. "If Frost tells the faculty or anyone else that Maven was at the scene of the crime, I truly will kill him. Don't try to stop me."

As a faculty member and not a student, Everett wasn't locked in this apartment with the rest of us. He went to a big meeting with the other professors and faculty, who are undoubtedly in a tizzy about Everbound being locked down.

It's never happened before. Then again, neither has an assassination within the Immortal Quintet.

I glance down at my hands, watching the fresh clusters of puncture marks from my bleeding crystal as they start to tingle and seal, thanks to the concoction. I lost track of how many times I drew my own blood while trying to heal her, but whether or not she killed the mage for some anti-legacy plight, I would do it all again.

At least, I would *try*. I have no idea why my magic refused to heal her.

"When I couldn't rely on either of you earlier," I mutter, glaring at both Crypt and Baelfire, "Everett is the one who snuck Maven to this apartment while I wiped away all traces of her from that office. I doubt he'll say anything to anyone else, but if he does, I'll help you kill him. Gods only know how badly I wanted to when he told Maven—"

"About the bet *you* suggested," Baelfire growls, cutting me off. "Fucking fae. You just couldn't help yourself, could you?"

Whenever we were forced to spend time together as children, we'd made plenty of bets about all kinds of juvenile things. Typically, to prove who was the best. This bet was meant to be a harmless competition between childhood enemies and nothing more—for the others, at least. I was serious about winning Baelfire's dragon scales, and I intend to collect them later for two good reasons.

But right now, my priority is to make sure Maven knows I wasn't faking anything for the wager.

I roll my eyes. "Don't pretend you weren't the first to jump on the bandwagon."

"Whatever. Unlike you, I don't trust that icicle prick to keep his mouth shut. Hell, he *just* screwed us over! What's going to stop him from telling the Immortal Quintet that Maven was in that room with their dead quintet member?"

I consider that quietly. The tingling in my limbs is softening, and my nose isn't drizzling blood anymore. I'm sure my shoulder will be fucking sore, but at least the concoction did much of the heavy mending of my broken shoulder for me.

Finally, Baelfire sits up on the couch, grunting as he pulls my bleeding crystal from his bicep. His bicep immediately heals, and he studies the fae-created mineral.

"Okay, are we going to talk about the fact that our adorable little keeper might've murdered the headmaster? It sounds fucking nuts, but why the hell else would she have been in there? I mean…even if she's part of the anti-legacy shit going on, she's just an atypical caster, so how would she—"

"She's not *just* an anything, so watch your mouth. We've all been underestimating her." Crypt exhales another long puff of smoke before tossing down the stub and stepping on it to snuff it out. I note that he's no longer shaking.

"Easy to do when we've learned frustratingly little about her," I mutter. Then my eyes narrow on him. "Were you watching her from Limbo when she was in that office? Do you know something I don't?"

"I know plenty of things you don't, Crane."

"If it's about Maven, tell us," Baelfire grits. "We could have lost her—"

He cuts off, and we all go quiet when we hear the click of the bathroom door opening down the hall. A moment later, my throat constricts violently when Maven steps into the room wrapped in nothing but a white towel. Her dark, wet hair drapes over one of her bare shoulders, and her boots hang from one hand. Water still clings to her arms, legs, and neck, glistening like miniature crystals all over her tantalizing body.

My cock is immediately demanding attention. I'm not the only one because Baelfire looks like his brain is malfunctioning, and Crypt is instantly at her side.

"Darling," he rasps so quietly I almost don't make it out.

Maven surveys each of us with a highly guarded expression. It takes intense effort not to adjust my erection, but she already has enough reason to be furious with us without me slavering over every inch of her like a starving wendigo with my dick in hand.

"I have no clothes here," Maven mutters.

"Take mine," Baelfire says quickly, hurrying from the room using his shifter speed to go to the bedroom he's claimed for his own.

A few seconds later, he reappears and eagerly offers our keeper an armful of shirts, hoodies, and other random articles of clothing. Maven begrudgingly selects a massive dark gray hoodie from the pile. Her attention drifts to my still-healing nose, but she has no outward reaction.

"Well, baby? You gonna tell us why you were in that room?" Baelfire asks bluntly.

"If you're wondering who killed the headmaster, I sadly can't take credit."

"Then what were you doing in his office?" I press.

Her dark gaze clashes with mine. "Besides bleeding out on the floor in agony after four idiots used my body to boost their egos? Not a damn thing."

Ouch, one of the voices in my head snickers.

She has a sharp tongue, but there's a faint undertone of hurt in her savage words that cuts even deeper. Baelfire is right. I was the one who suggested the very bet that hurt her. I'm no fool—I know Maven must be so completely closed off for a reason. Something made her like this. She won't talk about her past, but my blood blossom must have been hurt deeply.

And now she's hurting again, because of me.

I need to fix this. Immediately.

"*Sangfluir*," I begin gently, intending to smooth things over.

Her eyes flash as if my trying to cajole her has the opposite effect. "I'm not interested in your justification."

I continue anyway, determined. "The bet had nothing to do with us wanting you—"

"Stop talking."

"Maven, please just—"

I see it the moment her temper flares. But instead of snapping at me or storming away, she does the last thing I could possibly expect. She lifts her chin, drops her boots to the floor, and lets the towel fall away, leaving her gloriously naked.

I nearly bite my damn tongue off.

Gods above, her body is so fucking *beautiful.*

It's impossible not to recall just how tight and wet and utterly addictive it was to be inside my keeper. My eyes snag on a water droplet that traces slowly down the smooth, olive-toned skin of her neck before it drips between her breasts, its path veering slightly when it rolls over the pale scar there.

I want to lick away the water and then…sink my teeth into that gorgeous neck.

Fuck me.

I should not have thought about biting her. Now it's all I can think about—biting and drinking and finally finding out what her tantalizing blood tastes like.

Crypt exhales sharply, and Baelfire makes a strangled sound, gripping his own erection. Meanwhile, Maven holds my gaze as a very clear show of *fuck you* as she slips into Baelfire's hoodie, which reaches all the way down to her knees. She adjusts her hair, slips into her boots without bothering to lace them up, and brushes past three extremely aroused, stunned legacies before slamming the front door behind her.

It's quiet for one beat before Baelfire rubs his face. "Holy fuck. She knows how to shut us up."

Crypt vanishes, no doubt to follow her. But as Baelfire and I stand in mutually frustrated silence, my ears begin to ring. The voices in my head build in volume until their whispers drown out my own thoughts. I squeeze my eyes shut, trying to breathe through the cacophony of paranoia swarming in my brain.

What are you doing, letting her go out without your protection? You couldn't even heal her. How useless are you?

Your keeper will die, and you're powerless to stop it.

You'll lose her. It's for the best.

The taunting echoes in my skull reach a crescendo until I grip the sides of my head, snapping, "Shut *up.*"

When a low whistle breaks through, and the voices slink back into the corners of my mind, I blink my eyes open. I don't know how long I've been standing here out of my mind, but Baelfire stands in front of me with his arms folded and his eyebrows drawn down.

"Your curse has you fucked up more than usual. I can't believe I'm asking this, but should I be worried? What are the actual odds that your sanity will last through the upcoming semester, Si?"

It likely won't, a fact of which I am painfully aware.

I ignore him and his asinine concern, grimacing at the ache lingering in my temples as I make my way to the cabinet in the kitchen where I stored the good liquor. It won't stop the voices, but I don't care right now. I just need something to dull this before I lose control of myself and try to kill the dragon shifter again.

Baelfire is quiet as he watches me pour a glass of whiskey, but then he glances longingly at the front door. "Think she'll still go to the Matched Ball with us? I mean…it's mandatory, right?"

"I doubt it very much. She hates us," I remind him.

The dragon shifter huffs. "For now. She hates us *for now*. But we were making solid progress with her before Everett went all Frost on us and ruined it. Call me a fucking optimist, but I say if we ignore that stupid bet like it never happened and work on earning her trust, she'll finally start to open up to us. And once we all get our heads out of our asses, I think she'll love being our keeper."

"Fucking optimist."

He smirks, reaching into his pocket before tossing my red-stained bleeding crystal to me. "You're not gonna like this next part, but if we want Maven to start trusting us with all the secrets she's keeping in that pretty head of hers, we need to make the first move."

"Meaning?"

"Trust is a two-way street. Maybe we should all tell her what our curses are. Who knows? Maybe we'll start to trust each other more, too." He makes a face. "Except Everett. Fuck that guy."

I nod in agreement to the last part but carefully consider the rest of his words.

I don't give my trust away to anyone. Even when I was younger, my parents and their quintet taught me to fend for myself first and foremost. We all kept secrets from each other. I doubt they knew one another's curses before they were bound together to break them—speaking about individual curses is a taboo in the world of legacies, even among matched quintets.

But whether I like it or not, Crypt and Baelfire both already know my curse. I know so little about Maven that I can't possibly trust her yet in all the ways I want to, but her learning the state of my mental health wouldn't be the end of the world.

However, Baelfire's suggestion about forgetting our little wager entirely isn't an option. I'll need to get those dragon scales.

But first, I need to find a way to show Maven exactly how sorry I am.

4

MAVEN

After I knock, the door creaks open, and poor little Vivienne bursts into tears at the sight of me. She reaches out like she wants a shoulder to cry on, but panic shoots through me at the incoming touch.

Instead, I grasp her arms through her long sleeves and put on the softest smile I can muster.

"Can I come in?"

"K—Kenzie is m—missing," she hiccups, shaking her head hard. "We've l—looked everywhere, and I don't know if she's even still..."

She can't finish the thought and begins sobbing again, the tears rolling down her cheeks and dripping freely.

Fuck.

I'm *awful* at comforting crying people.

I blame it on my upbringing since showing any significant amount of emotion around others was an invitation to get beaten to a pulp and fed to nightmarish creatures. Someone shedding tears out in the open is an entirely foreign concept to me.

It's unbearably awkward for a moment as I let her go of her arms and glance behind her through the doorway. Morning sunlight shines through the windows in Kenzie's apartment, lighting everything with a warm glow.

"Is…anyone else here?"

Preferably someone whose face isn't leaking.

Dirk hears me with his shifter hearing and comes to the door. He's in just as bad shape as Vivienne, but he's not crying hysterically. Thank the universe for that. He invites me in, and I enter their shared living and dining room area.

For a moment, I'm surprised that I don't feel Crypt follow behind me—he's been trailing me ever since I left their quintet apartment fifteen minutes ago. But then I notice the dreamcatcher dangling beside the front door of Kenzie's apartment. There's another one beside the large window in their dining room.

"Kenzie hung up a bunch of those right after she met your, uh… DeLune," Dirk says, scratching at his neck. Then his face crumbles. "Please—you're her best friend. Do you have any idea where she is? We've looked everywhere. *Everywhere*. She just vanished without a trace and…"

His eyes grow moist, his cheeks ruddy. Oh, gods. If I don't start talking, he'll start crying, too.

It's like a fucking pandemic that I am entirely unequipped to handle.

"I can find out what happened to her," I say quickly. "I just need some of her DNA."

Vivienne's face lights up with hope, and she hurries into one of their other rooms, leaving Dirk and me alone. For a long moment, we're both silent. Possibly because I've barely gotten to know Kenzie's quintet since I didn't want them to think of me as a friend.

I already care about Kenzie more than I'm comfortable with. I'm not about to start doing *friends*, plural.

My eyes stray to the many erotic paintings hanging up in their living room. Kenzie's works. I've seen them before, but my attention lingers on an abstract water painting of a woman sandwiched between two masculine figures, her head thrown back in ecstasy and her hair swirling around them. It's a beautifully sensual painting, but I have to jerk my attention away when I realize I'm envisioning *myself* in that painting.

Between any combination of four particular gorgeous legacies...

Who I should *not* be thinking about like this ever again.

My face feels too warm as I subtly examine several other paintings. There's so much variety, so many positions I've never considered.

Because survival was my number one priority in the hellscape I called home, I kept any sexual urges under lock and key after I hit puberty. Except for the time five years ago when I let my curiosity get the best of me and decided to lose my virginity. But that experience hadn't been beautiful or erotic like these paintings. Instead, it led to the worst memory of my entire life, which then led to me becoming...well, this.

After that, I'd forced myself to become more of a thing than a person. Any urges or emotions were kept deeply hidden. It was safer that way for everyone.

It's still safer that way. You can't have them, and they never actually wanted you anyway, I remind myself.

And yet, my eyes keep straying to those damn paintings. Especially the one with a woman sucking off an abstract array of cocks. I've never had a cock in my mouth. The basic concept behind it doesn't *sound* enjoyable, but...is it?

Maybe I should find out. After all, I thoroughly enjoyed my first orgasms. I definitely want more of those. Who knows what other sexual experiences I might enjoy?

Bad Maven. Your purpose has nothing to do with enjoying things. Focus.

Finally, I shoot Dirk a sideways glance, needing to distract myself from my thoughts. He's frowning after Vivienne, still roughly scratching at his neck. And his arm.

Does he have fleas or something? He's a shifter, after all.

When he catches me looking, he stops and grimaces. "Uh...curses, am I right?"

Oh. Right.

I have no idea what Kenzie's matches are cursed with, but I'm surprised Dirk had the guts to mention it. Most legacies are extremely hush-hush about how the Legacy Curse affects them. But if his curse is itching all the time, that seems kind of mild.

I change the topic for his sake. "Did Luka leave you two to fend for yourselves? His jackassery must be chronic."

Dirk shakes his head, scratching one of his palms. "No, he just went to get food from the dining hall since we didn't have anything here during the lockdown yesterday. Actually, he's been the one holding us together ever since we realized Kenzie was…"

His voice breaks, and he clears his throat, looking away. "Look, I was pissed when I found out Luka was such a dick to her before, and I was all for it when Kenzie told me about you hexing him. But then I realized Luka is just like…really, *really* bad at expressing himself. He's not a bad guy. Definitely not nearly as bad as the rest of his family—I mean, his brother Levi was probably the most disgusting asshole in the world."

"Was?" I note. I'm only tolerating this small talk because chatter is infinitely preferable to him getting weepy again. "Is he deceased?"

"Yeah, he was found burned to a crisp less than a month ago. Even though they weren't close, it's been pretty brutal on Luka. He's still in mourning."

Well. This is awkward.

Now that I think about it, that vampire I killed when I first came to Everbound *did* have some striking similarities to Luka. Maybe I should come clean to Kenzie about that incident after I find her.

Please let me find her.

Vivienne returns and triumphantly holds up a plastic bag that contains one pale strand of long, curly hair.

"Will this work? I found it on our bed."

"Yes." I accept the bag from her, careful not to touch her fingers. I can't wait to get another pair of gloves from my room. Slipping the bag into Baelfire's sweatshirt pocket, I turn to leave.

But just as I do, Luka opens the front door and blinks at me in surprise. He's holding several bags of warm food in both arms. I don't miss that he glances over Vivienne and Dirk protectively as if he's worried I somehow hurt them in the brief time I've been here.

The fact that he's wary is good. Maybe Dirk is right, and he's not an unmitigated douchebag after all.

He sets the food on the nearby dining room table and glares at me. "You got a reason for being here? If it's to lift that damn hex you put on my dick, don't bother. The healers finally got rid of it, so fuck you very much."

I take it back. Douchebag is a mild term for him.

"Luka," Vivienne sighs. "Don't be rude."

He folds his arms. "Whatever. What are you here for, Minerva?"

"I just said don't be rude!" the petite air elemental chides.

"I wasn't," Luka huffs. "I was just asking a fucking question."

Dirk snorts, leaning down to scratch one of his calves. "Calling people by the wrong name on purpose is rude, man."

Luka looks so confused that I could almost laugh. But the longer I stay, the longer I go without knowing whether Kenzie is alive, so I hold up the bag to show him the single strand of pale, curly hair.

"I'll do a spell to look for her."

"We already asked another caster to try that shit," Luka gripes. "It did nothing."

Probably because they were using common magic, which I can barely use in general. Fortunately for Kenzie's quintet, I'm far more skilled at other types of magic.

Specifically, the forbidden kind.

"No harm in trying," I muse, turning.

But Vivienne grabs my arm to stop me from leaving. Even through Baelfire's sleeve, the familiar discomfort skitters over my body, prickling the back of my neck as I go stock still. She doesn't notice that I'm immediately desperate to escape her touch. This is Kenzie's most gentle match, who was just bawling her eyes out, so breaking her hand for touching me is probably not the best course of action.

"Wait! I just remembered that Kenzie and I got something for you. A dress. We went on a shopping spree a couple of days ago, right b— before she…"

Her eyes water again, and now I'm *really* uncomfortable. Trying to ignore the cold sweat breaking out over the back of my neck, I slip away from her grasp and retreat closer to the door.

"Thanks, but I'm good."

"But she said it was perfect for you for the Matched Ball, and that's tonight! I'll go get it. She was going to leave it in your dorm room as a surprise when you got back from Pennsylvania, so she wrote a note for you and everything," Vivienne adds before rushing out of the room again.

A note from Kenzie? I hesitate.

My skin is crawling from all the unintentionally nauseating touching I've been subjected to, but if I find out that Kenzie is gone for good…

I've never been sentimental, but suddenly, I want to read anything she left for me. After all, these may be her last words to me.

When Vivienne returns with a large pink shopping bag and a note, I accept the note first, trying my absolute hardest not to visibly flinch when her bare fingers brush against mine this time. I read quickly over the bubbly scrawl of words.

SURPRISE!

Okay, so I know I just bought you a dress a couple weeks ago, and you totally haven't even worn it, but this one is so freaking gorgeous, and you are going to SLAY at the Matched Ball in this. It's so your style, and it's going to show off how hot you are (yes, I said it, you hot little monk), so please, please, please wear it even if it's just to watch your guys' jaws drop (yes, I said it again, they're totally your guys even if you keep denying it).

Love, your favorite pale-assed bestie

P. S. I call dibs on doing your hair and makeup!

Let's get ready together while we watch that sexy human-legacy forbidden love drama I told you about.

P. P. S. Just wait til you see my dress... ;) It makes my tits look WOWZA.

I crack a smile. *It makes my tits look wowza.* Of course, these would be Kenzie's final words to me. Screw sentiment—this is much better.

When he sees my grin, Luka blanches. "You're smiling? That's fucking creepy. What did she even write to you?"

He reaches for the card, but I quickly slide it into the bag and take it from Vivienne, grabbing it from the bottom so as not to touch her again.

"Thank you," I tell the elemental sincerely. "I needed that."

Then I excuse myself and leave because it's time to track down some ingredients for forbidden magic.

It takes breaking into twenty-three locked storage chests in a forgotten archive of the eastern library before I find what I need.

Flinging open the top of the chest, I wave away the dust and thank the universe when I see a bundle of vibrant orange phoenix feathers. They're an annoyingly rare ingredient.

I grab the bundle and slip it into the bag thrown over my shoulder, which I grabbed from my dorm earlier. I also took the time to change into my own clothes, including a pair of soft leather gloves, so now I feel more like myself. Once again, it's just me on a mission.

Well. Me and the incubus who I can feel watching my every move from Limbo.

I can't see him, but Crypt hasn't left my side even once since I left my dorm. At least he's giving me the illusion of space, but something about his presence feels darker right now—as if he's on edge as much as the others, liable to snap any moment.

The threat of that is oddly thrilling.

Best not to linger on that.

Quietly shutting the wooden storage chest, I double-check that I left no trace, aside from disturbing the dust in this barely visited room. Satisfied, I ascend a long flight of winding steps to the main level of the eastern library. It's empty right now, with not even a faculty member in sight. No one cares about the library when the entire school is in an uproar over the lockdown and the Matched Ball tonight.

Fifteen minutes later, after avoiding all high-traffic hallways, I'm back in my dorm room, sitting on the floor with the lights off and a candle lit on my desk. I stare at the ingredients in front of me. Phoenix feather, Kenzie's hair, hag's root, onyx dust, a dagger, a bowl for collecting my blood…and all my thriving potted plants.

Which I'll have to sacrifice for this spell.

I sigh as I slip off my gloves and brush my fingers over their leaves. I don't like killing the plants I worked so hard to cultivate. Lillian is the one who got me into botany—at the time, she'd fussed over what she'd called the "barbaric, inhumane" way I was being raised, with no respect for the sacredness of life. She helped me build an indoor garden so that I would learn to appreciate the effort it takes to simply *live*, even for a plant.

But it didn't take me long to figure out that plants can fuel my magic, too. I don't get the same buzz of power as I do when I take the life of a monster or legacy, but it's enough to get by when I have limited options.

Like right now.

Raising my hands, I whisper a common magic spell that sets fire to the potted plants. They steam and shrivel, dead within seconds as the room fills with the scent of burnt herbs. Grabbing the dagger, I make a long, diagonal slice through the palm of my left hand. I keep my voice to a barely audible whisper since Crypt is probably still lurking outside my dorm room, and he's already overheard me through the door once.

"*Obsecro te pro anima huius sanguinis.*"

As I speak, the room darkens, chilling around me as the bitter tang that always accompanies necromancy fills my mouth. Of the three kinds of magic I can tap into, this is the most taxing—because only necromancers are supposed to be able to wield it.

I'm not a necromancer.

But apparently, all the rituals I had to go through to become *this* changed me in ways they never expected.

I chant the words again as I hold my stinging hand over the bowl, feeling a macabre thrill as I watch my blood splatter over the tendrils of the bright orange feather. Adding the onyx dust, hair, and hag's root, I whisper the forbidden words again to complete the illegal life-force-searching spell.

Malicious, lifeless power pulses through my body and swirls around the bowl in the form of black smoke. All color leeches away from everything in the bowl before the phoenix feather bursts into green fire.

I exhale a harsh breath and squeeze my eyes shut, ready to collapse from how taxing that spell was...but also from pure relief.

Alive.

The feather catching fire means Kenzie is still alive. Now I just have to find her.

And to do that, I'm going to find that godsdamned changeling and show it just how much it should *not* have fucked with someone I happen to care about.

The green fire fizzles out, and I glance down at my fingertips, which are now blackened and numbed from the necromancy. The cut on my hand is still bleeding, but I make no move to wrap it because the weight of that ritual presses on my chest like a frozen anvil. I overextended myself, and now my eyes can barely stay open.

But it was worth it. Now I know Kenzie is still alive somewhere.

Pulling myself onto my bed, I instantly pass into a fatigued sleep so deep that it's almost dreamless. *Almost.* The nightmares still catch up to me, and in the end, I'm trapped in their grasp, reliving old fears and past traumas that claw me to tatters.

When I finally startle awake, trying to catch my breath, my

muscles are wired, and cold sweat is beaded on my forehead. I sit up, needing to work off this tension but grimacing at my burnt, scabbed hands. I don't have enough magic to try healing myself right now—not to mention the spell I'll need to use to track down the changeling.

I need to refuel my magic soon.

Dragging myself from the bed to peek out one curtain, I realize I've slept for hours, and it's only a short time until the Matched Ball. From everything Kenzie told me about the Matched Ball, it's an excuse for quintets to dress up and show off their gods-given groups for the first time. The dance will no doubt involve posturing, preening, alcohol, small talk, and copious amounts of PDA.

I would rather peel off my own eyelids than attend.

But I hesitate, glancing at the pink bag sitting on my desk. Kenzie was beyond excited about this frivolous activity. She likely would have dragged me along and made me try the punch or whatever shit they'll serve. She would've tried to make me dance, too. It would have been pure fucking torture.

What a shame to miss out on that.

Plus, the Immortal Quintet will be there, so I'll have my first chance to analyze my targets and decide which to take out next. If the changeling is still on Everbound's premises, trapped here like the rest of us—which I hope is the case—then it might attend the mandatory dance to blend in. I can hunt it down to get answers and revenge.

Maybe I should go.

Except my matches will also be there.

The idea of facing them again has me kicking myself for flashing them before I left earlier. I only did it to stop Silas from saying anything else that would affect me. I've been unable to keep my emotions in check ever since I revived. Either nightshade root powder has emotion-enhancing properties I've never heard of, or all the years I've spent shoving down how I feel is coming back to bite me in the ass at the most inopportune time.

In an ideal world, I would have been long gone by now, which theoretically would have made getting over them easier. But if I'm stuck here, where the Immortal Quintet might sniff me out, then my top priority is blending in with the other legacies for now.

Which means…playing along with my so-called quintet.

Fine. But that doesn't mean I'm going to play *nicely*.

With a sigh, I reach into the pink bag and pull out the dress Kenzie believed would be perfect for me.

Oh, damn.

She was right. This is very me.

The dress is a gossamer black masterpiece, lightweight with a halter top that ties behind the neck and looks like a lace choker. The skirt is layers of shredded tulle ending in fluttering tendrils beneath a corset-like midsection. It's backless, but I'm relieved that the halter top means it will cover the center of my chest where my scar is.

I run my hands over the fabric, enchanted by its dark beauty. Rechecking the bag, I also find two black lace opera gloves, long enough to reach past my elbows. They'll hide my blackened fingertips and scab until I get the chance to heal myself later.

"So annoyingly thoughtful," I murmur, shaking my head.

Once I find Kenzie, I'll find a way to repay her for such a melancholically perfect gift.

But for now…

My so-called quintet has fucked with my head enough. It's time to settle the score.

5

MAVEN

When I step outside my dorm, Crypt is leaning against the wall beside my door, perfectly visible in the mortal realm in his regular attire. As soon as he sees me, he straightens. The last rays of sunset streaming through the windows across the hallway catch on the piercings in his ears and brow. His silver-flecked purple irises bore into mine, filled with a host of emotions so consuming that, for a moment, I can only stare back at him, transfixed.

"You look like pure sin," he whispers, drinking me in slowly. "And I've always loved sinning, darling."

Some horribly inconvenient part of me melts hearing the marvel in his voice. It's nice to hear after putting in the effort. I even put on a tiny bit of the makeup that Kenzie insisted on buying me when I first came here. I've never worn makeup before, but I watched Kenzie apply it on herself often enough that I just mimicked her methods.

I finally look away from Crypt, glancing down at two corpses on the floor beside him. They're dressed nicely as if they were on their way to the dance, but it looks like a wild animal got to them. Their dress and suit are soaked in blood, and their eyeballs have been scratched out.

Kenzie told me that most guys bring fancy corsages for dances.

This is much more my style.

"They made the mistake of lingering outside your door for far too long."

"So you mauled them?"

He's still distracted by my appearance. "Hmm? No, love, they did that to each other. Took only the barest dose of mania on my part. I am sorry you missed the show, though."

So am I. But I have a vendetta against my so-called matches tonight, so I feign disinterest.

"You clearly intend to continue stalking me."

"For the rest of this life and into the Beyond, yes."

For an incubus with a reputation for feeling nothing, he's so melodramatic around me. But the fact that he's here, shamelessly devouring me with his gaze, makes me wonder if his fascination with me was genuine after all.

I mean…he *did* try to keep Silas from healing me, just like I asked. And as far as I know, he hasn't breathed a word to the others about my little reviving-from-death parlor trick.

If Crypt's interest was real—

No. It's a moot point. All my original reasons for rejecting my quintet still stand, and I have more important things to focus on right now. Such as…

"Where's my dagger?"

I can't lose track of that. First of all, it's my favorite dagger, and I happen to be emotionally attached to it, considering that it was a gift from a once-upon-a-time friend. I even named it—Pierce, for obvious reasons.

But second of all and more importantly, it's made of adamantine, which is only found in the Nether. If someone found it in the headmaster's office, the Immortal Quintet will put the pieces together and begin looking for the *telum* here at Everbound. That would complicate my attempts to kill them off discreetly.

Crypt tips his head. "Your dagger?"

"The one you pulled out of my chest."

That casts a menacing darkness into his expression. "That was *your* dagger, buried in your heart? Tell me who put it there."

"It doesn't matter. Just tell me where it—"

"*Doesn't matter?*"

The Nightmare Prince vanishes for a fraction of a second. When he reappears, he's so near that I press back against the door to put space between us. But that's precisely what Crypt wanted, and he braces his hands on either side of me, so now I'm trapped looking up at him. Although he's careful not to touch me, his face is so close to mine that strands of his messy dark hair tickle my forehead.

His alluring gaze has me pinned in place. "It absolutely fucking matters. You died. Twice. And I was powerless as I watched it happen. *Twice*," he adds hoarsely. "So make me a promise."

This position, having him so near, smelling that sweet leather scent that's all him—it makes warmth thrum through my veins and turns my mind to mush. I can't stand that he has the ability to fluster me like this, so I fix him with a stony glare, even though my voice is less even than I'd like.

"I will not promise you anything."

His laugh is devilish as he dips his head to lightly kiss the hair beside my temple. I can't feel the contact, but my stomach flips.

"Oh, my dark little darling…yes, you fucking will. Right now."

He's never used this tone with me before. It's treacherous and fierce. I try to shove down the illogical urge to rub my cheek against his. My stupid, confused body isn't reacting to his proximity the way I'm used to.

I feel lightheaded. Restless.

I blame it on the fact that I now know what an orgasm feels like. My body is greedy in all the ways I've never experienced, but I refuse to listen to it.

"Crypt—"

"Promise me that I'll never have to watch you die again."

His voice breaks, and that show of emotion does something unexpected to me. It makes me want to…*reassure* him.

But I can't. Not with this, not if he expects me to be honest.

I study him as I pick my words carefully. "I don't make empty promises. If you can't stomach death, you should run now. It's...part of my nature."

His brow furrows as he puzzles out my words, and for a moment, I worry I've let too much slip. He's going to figure out what I am.

But finally, Crypt leans back down and whispers near my ear, his breath caressing my neck and sending a delicious shiver down my spine that I try to hide.

"All right. Keep your secrets. Just promise to keep me, too."

The gentleness in his voice kills me because deep down, I want that. I want to pull him closer for a kiss and forget about everything I've been through and everything I know will happen to me. I just want to fucking lose myself in the dream world that I know the Nightmare Prince can weave for me.

But it doesn't matter what I want. I made a promise, so whether or not Crypt's interest in me is genuine...I can't be selfish. Not when so many people are relying on me.

It takes monumental effort, but I keep my poker face intact. "If you value your testicles, step away from me."

His mouth twists up into a wistful yet flirtatious smile. "Now, darling. We both know you wouldn't dare hurt your chances of having little nightmares running around the house one day."

Before I can fucking unpack *that*, Crypt steps back and extends his arm in an offer to escort me. But the night has barely begun, and I'm already struggling with how I act around them. I need to steel my resolve, so I walk past him without looking back, knowing that, seen or unseen, he'll follow me whether I like it or not.

Ten minutes later, I step through the massive double doors of Everbound's vaulted two-story ballroom and gaze wide-eyed upon the societal horror to which I'm about to subject myself.

The sprawling checkered marble dance floor is dimly yet sensually lit by an array of warm mage lights. Illusionary displays of glittering magic swirl around the massive columns lining the room. Music pulses through the air courtesy of more enchantments, the bass of it just loud enough to cover much of the laughter and chatter.

The fringes of the ballroom are crowded with quintets and unmatched legacies alike, all dressed to the nines as they clink champagne flutes and parade about like deadly peacocks having the time of their lives.

A complimentary bar manned by faculty members is tucked into one corner of the dance floor. On the opposite end of the room is a cascading ornate grand split staircase.

I assume the Immortal Quintet will enter over there. Immortals like themselves are bound to have a flair for theatrics.

Couples on the dance floor writhe rhythmically while others blatantly grind on each other. Others look on from the darker corners of the room, enjoying the show as they drink, chitchat, or play tonsil ping-pong with their quintet members.

For a moment, my attention is arrested by all the grinding, swaying, and PDA filling the room. I wonder if I would have enjoyed things like this in a different lifetime. Not that it matters, because I can't help how my body reacts with a prickle of apprehension, my throat tightening and skin turning clammy.

I don't want to get closer to all of *that*, but tonight is all about blending in…and keeping an eye out for the changeling.

Changelings aren't too difficult to kill once they're identified. The real trouble will be finding it again without the aid of my magic since I haven't refueled it. In order to sift through other students and try to identify the changeling tonight, I'll have to get close enough to see other people's pupils.

I may even have to…mingle.

Ew.

I wander inside, sticking to the edge of the ballroom as I observe everything. I can sense the subtle hum of wards everywhere here—something only magic-users can sense. They're faint, likely put in place to prevent psychics, empaths, sirens, and others from superficially influencing other legacies in such a crowded extravaganza.

Just as I realize I no longer sense Crypt's invisible presence, the sound of glass shattering nearby draws my attention. Flutters break out in my stomach when I turn and make eye contact with two of my matches, both of them staring open-mouthed at me.

The shattering glass was because Silas apparently let his drink slip out of his hand, but he hasn't noticed the mess. His crimson eyes stay pinned on me, dark with hunger. Baelfire is checking me out just as thoroughly, biting his lip.

Gods. They clean up nicely.

Silas's tuxedo is pitch black and has a red rose in his breast pocket. Baelfire's white button-up shirt is untucked, and I can't help staring as he loosens his tie and rolls up his sleeves, revealing gorgeously tanned, muscular forearms. He prowls towards me with an animalistic gleam in his golden eyes.

"Drop dead fucking gorgeous."

I go perfectly still out of surprise when he leans forward and inhales at the crook of my neck. My cheeks warm when he groans raggedly.

"Gods, baby. You have no fucking idea how much power you have over me. I could come just from your scent alone."

It takes effort to swallow.

Focus. Don't be affected.

I can't afford to get hot and bothered by anything they say tonight. I need to show them I'm not someone to fuck with ever again.

Fool me once and all that.

Only the ugly truth is that this isn't the first time someone screwed with my head to screw with my body. To say that the one and only other time I dallied in romance ended badly would be an understatement.

Silas approaches, finally meeting my gaze as his tongue slips out to drag slowly across his lower lip. Despite the rest of his fancy getup, his normally-mussed curly hair is worse than usual. As if he's been unable to stop messing it up.

"*Thu mi le d'chal lei fhuil, ima sangfluir,*" he murmurs.

Which is fae for, *You drive me mad with your beauty, my blood blossom.*

And since I'm dangerously close to getting sidetracked by how unfairly gorgeous they are, I choose to be impish.

"Nach, ás mo esio chial na'mi cobhair," I reply smoothly in fae.

No, you are mad enough without my help.

His head rears back in surprise. "How do you—"

"Attention, everyone!"

The music softens to silence as Professor Gibbons climbs the first few stairs on the massive staircase, turning with a bright smile as a mage light settles around him like a spotlight. Using magic to amplify his voice, he addresses everyone present.

"Welcome one and all to Everbound University's prestigious Matched Ball! As you know, there have been some significant changes to our schedule going forward, which the Immortal Quintet wishes to reiterate. So, without further ado, let us welcome Iker Del Mar, Somnus DeLune, and the effervescent Natalya Genovese!"

Everyone applauds as he retreats. From opposite sides of the split staircase, those three members of the Immortal Quintet enter the room.

And unlike legacies, who look mostly human, these are clearly monsters.

Descending from the left staircase is Iker Del Mar, the immortal hydra shifter. His skin is a deep, mottled pattern of grays and greens broken up by clusters of scales. Several horns protrude back from the dark hair of his head, and his eyes are a pale yellow with snake-like slits for pupils. He wears an outfit that would have been tasteful a hundred years ago but somehow looks equally sharp now.

And on the opposite staircase, Somnus DeLune enters.

Crypt's father.

My eyes can't help seeking similarities between this suited monster and his mysteriously absent incubus son. His hair is dark, his face just as strikingly handsome, and they're similar heights—but that's where the similarities end. Instead of Crypt's vibrant, silver-flecked purple eyes, Somnus's are a beady black. Leathery, bat-like wings riddled with ragged holes extend from his back in mangled arches. A barbed tail whips back and forth behind him, and his sharp fangs gleam when he sneers down at the legacies below.

I admit, they're an impressive sight.

But the most impressive of all is their keeper, Natalya.

Her foreboding presence fills the room as she descends behind Iker Del Mar, dressed in a nude gown that clings to her curvaceous body and glitters with thousands of teardrop-shaped diamonds. Natalya's cinnamon-colored hair is styled perfectly, and though her blue eyes aren't glowing now, I know they will if she uses her psychic abilities—a trait of the original vampyr. Though she looks less monstrous than the other two, she is the last survivor of the psychic vampyrs, who led all of monsterkind in the revolution to escape their dark ruler in the Nether many hundreds of years ago.

And like a crown of runes etched into her forehead are all four of the keeper emblems. A line for Arcana, a circle for Shifting, a triangle for Craving, and a square for Elemental.

Those emblems manifest on keepers once their hearts have been bound to the members of their quintet. It's a symbol of unity— though they don't always manifest on the forehead in the vague shape of a crown as Natalya's did.

All three of the monsters scan the legacies below as if they expect to see one of us covered in their mage's dried blood, blatantly guilty for them to execute on the spot. But finally, Iker Del Mar's voice booms across the room, needing no magic amplification. His forked tongue flicks out on occasion as he speaks bluntly.

"Heirs of the Four Houses, your next semester starts effective tomorrow morning. The no-killing ban for legacies matched into quintets has been officially lifted."

Whispers fill the room as fresh tension vibrates through the air. From the corner of my eye, I see sneers and smirks pass between many of the matched quintets. Many of them move to better surround their keepers.

Silas and Baelfire also move to either side of me. Baelfire skims the crowd with a scowl on his ordinarily cheerful face. Silas looks one wrong look away from another psychotic break. He withdraws his bleeding crystal, twisting it restlessly between his long fingers.

Del Mar continues as if he doesn't notice the heightened tension. "All matched quintets, complete or not, must report their chosen emphasis to Professor Gibbons before the conclusion of this dance. Classes shall begin tomorrow morning. All students will arrive at their courses promptly and obey curfew. Anyone caught skipping classes or wandering the halls outside of designated hours shall be dealt with by me personally."

That makes another hush fall over the Matched Ball as the other students seem to catch on to what's happening. Typically, quintets have weeks to pick their classes, and Everbound is lenient with legacies—but not now. Now, we're being highly monitored by the Immortal Quintet themselves.

Watched. Studied. Vetted.

If I want to retain the element of surprise, I'll need to keep pretending to be an untalented wallflower. They can't know that I'm the *telum* whispered about in the underbelly of the legacy world.

"Several prophets and healers from Galene's nearby temple have arrived at Everbound to assist in the infirmary, which will no doubt fill quickly as quintet rankings unfold," the hydra shifter goes on, his pale yellow gaze flicking from student to student. "We look forward to observing you just as we observed your ancestors prove themselves worthy legacies. Be fierce and remember that weak legacies will only be a liability to our kind. Weed out the weak and bring honor to the Four Houses, be it in life or death."

The Immortal Quintet descends to join everyone else on the ballroom floor. Somnus and Iker flank both sides of Natalya as she sweeps toward the bar, the crowd of legacies parting effortlessly for her glittering form.

I track their movements. If they're mourning the loss of their mage, all three of them are excellent at hiding it. They look as if they own the world and everyone in it—the perfect picture of the ideal quintet.

I wonder which one I'll decide to kill first.

6

MAVEN

I LOOK AWAY from the immortal monsters and find that Silas and Baelfire have returned to consuming me with their eyes. Once again, it's inconvenient how much I enjoy that they obviously like what they see.

I've never had much reason to care about the way I look. Survival always came first. I didn't even see my own reflection until I was ten years old and caught a glimpse of what I looked like in a murky forest pond...right before someone tried to drown me in it.

All this to say, it's nice to feel pretty.

But I'm still determined to get over these gorgeous assholes, so I step backward to get out from between them—but cool hands gently grasp my bare shoulders from behind.

"Watch where you're going, Oakley," Everett says, his quiet voice almost lost to the music that has resumed.

I step away from the white-haired professor—though right now, he's not dressed like a professor at all. He's in a sharp, perfectly tailored dark blue suit that would make any fashion photographer cry tears of joy.

What a shame that someone so beautiful is an asshole.

The last time we spoke, he hurt me on purpose. I realize that now.

He was intentionally hostile, pushing me away and trying to make me hate him and the others.

And it worked. It stings, knowing they made a game out of fucking me.

I'm prepared to meet his cold, aloof stare, but when our gazes clash, I frown. It's difficult to make out in this lighting, but…is he blushing as his gaze sweeps over me?

"Get lost, Snowflake," Baelfire growls, moving to my side again as he glowers at the elemental. "I'm about to dance with my mate, and I don't need you fucking this up, too."

Anyone who expects me to dance is fucking delusional. I've never danced a day in my life. I wouldn't even know where to begin.

Everett adjusts his cufflinks. Three times. "Believe me, I don't plan on sticking around. But all five of us need to pick an emphasis for me to report to Gibbons." He pauses. "Where's Crypt?"

"Probably avoiding Daddy Dearest," Baelfire grunts.

That piques my interest enough that I tip my head. "Is Crypt scared of Somnus?"

He snorts. "Nah, that psychopath doesn't feel anything. He *should* be scared of Somnus, but instead, he riles him up if they're ever around each other. It's a huge pain in the ass—gets other people killed most of the time. The Legacy Council tried to enforce a restraining order to keep them out of the same room, but that didn't do shit."

I absorb that as I glance absentmindedly at Everett. Immediately, he looks down to fix his cufflinks *again*, obviously to avoid meeting my gaze. He wants nothing to do with me, and that sends another inexplicable pang of hurt through my hollow chest.

I force myself to shove down any emotion and focus on what's important.

"Tell Gibbons that our quintet emphasis will be combat."

They all stare at me. Silas looks like he wants to pry my head open and read my thoughts.

"*Our* quintet emphasis?" he says slowly.

"As in, you're finally admitting we're a quintet?" Baelfire jumps in to clarify, hopeful excitement brightening his face and bringing out his blinding smile. "You'll forgive us for acting like a bunch of stupid, immature fledglings and be our keeper?"

I need to blend in with the rest of the students here at Everbound. If that means training and taking classes with the four legacies who made me feel incredible right before they made me feel like shit, I'll endure it.

But I need to draw some hard boundaries first.

"Forgive, no. But I'll be your *platonic* keeper. For now."

Baelfire's face falls. "Come on, Boo-tiful—"

Boo-tiful? Okay, fuck no. Time to nip that one in the bud.

I hold up a hand to cut him off. "I'm vetoing that nickname."

"Okay, Boo—"

"That one is out now, too. In fact, don't give me any fucking nicknames. Including any in fae," I add, glaring at Silas.

His ruby gaze narrows. "Speaking of which, how are you so fluent in fae? Even your accent is impressive."

Lillian was once married to a fae, and their language was all she spoke for years before I met her. When I was growing up, she was the only living person I saw for weeks on end. She tried to help ease my isolation by telling me all about her past fae family, sharing their culture, and teaching me their language. We spoke English and fae interchangeably.

But Silas doesn't need to know that or anything else about me, so I offer no answer. "Back to the topic at hand. Combat."

"No, the topic at hand is the fact that you think we'll be fucking platonic," Baelfire grits out. "No way in hell is that happening."

"Lots of quintets are platonic."

"Not ours. You're my mate. I won't accept *platonic* anything with you."

I look heavenward, wondering if the gods are enjoying this shitshow they're putting me through. They're probably all laughing their godly asses off.

"For the last time, I am not your mate."

He growls and grasps my arm, pulling me closer to him and

ignoring Silas's warning scowl. There's a wild, animalistic gleam in Baelfire's golden eyes that I've never seen before.

"Yes, you are. You're mine, and I'm yours—end of the motherfucking story. The end. Get over it."

Excuse me?

I yank my arm away and give him my finely tuned death stare, slipping into the lethal tone I rarely have to use.

"Rephrase that."

Baelfire's glower softens. He blows out a breath and rubs his face. "Shit. I'm sorry. Fuck, I didn't mean to be so…I'm just…"

"Manic?"

He grimaces. "My dragon is a Grade A alphahole, and he's got one clawed hand on the wheel right now. Believe it or not, his temper is even worse than mine. Having you in this crowded-ass room without my mark or scent on you is already driving me up the wall—this is just making it worse. I am not getting fucking friendzoned by my mate."

"You're not," I agree. "Because we're not friends. We'll be work acquaintances."

Silas pierces me with a stare. "I've been balls deep in your perfect pussy, and we've all heard the delicious little sounds you make when you come. This will be no *acquaintanceship*, not when we all crave you so ardently."

Warmth prickles my neck and cheeks, but so does anger as I regard him. "Oh, I'm hardly what *you* were craving. Tell me, what prize did you win for being the first to screw me?"

"He's not claiming any prize," Baelfire says vehemently. "We're dropping the—"

"Dragon scales," Silas concedes. "And access to Frost ledgers."

Everett stiffens before glaring daggers at Silas. Baelfire looks equally put off. They each look as if they're about to rip him a new asshole, but we're interrupted by an all-male quintet approaching. All five of them have their heads held high as they face off with us, and the one I assume is their keeper greets us with a fake smile. His buzzed hair shows off his tiger-stripe-tattooed scalp.

"So this is the jackpot quintet, huh? I bet you guys will have the top ranking at the beginning since *most* of you are somewhat impressive." He nods with something like respect to Baelfire before looking pointedly at me, his green eyes turning mocking. "But a quintet is only as strong as its keeper. So, as far as I'm concerned, I'm looking at the weakest quintet in this room. Watch out, Oakley. They can't protect you forever."

Baelfire snarls, but I hold up a hand to stop him as I hold the rival keeper's glare, arching my brow.

"*Watch out?* That's all you've got? Let's hope your bite is worse than your bark because that was pitiful. I'd feel embarrassed for you, but that would be a waste of my time. Run along, Stripes."

Now he's pissed as he bares his teeth and steps forward, but to my surprise, Everett also steps up until they're nose-to-nose. I've never thought the professor seemed intimidating, but the penetrating stare-down he gives the other keeper has goosebumps prickling over my arms.

It's the same kind of thousand-yard stare I acquired through years of terror and terrorizing. I wonder how he acquired his.

"Brooks," one of the other quintet's legacies hisses. "Let's not get on *this* professor's bad side. Come on."

Stripes, who is apparently Brooks, casts me one last scowl before he and his posse move on. The moment they do, the tension left behind only grows.

"I'm not giving you a single fucking scale," Baelfire snaps at Silas.

"And forget about the ledgers," Everett adds. "My father would have you killed if he knew you even asked."

"Who cares about your stupid father?" Baelfire huffs. "We're not paying up because the bet was a bullshit idea from the beginning, and we're dropping it. End of discussion."

Silas scoffs. "Of course you're bitter. Decimuses always have to be the best. You just can't bear losing."

"I didn't *lose*. We were all in that bed."

Yikes.

"And yet I was the only one in *her*. Like it or not, I won fair and square—"

Okay, fuck this.

Deciding to ditch the four assholes who I was stupid enough to catch feelings for before getting stabbed through the chest with a dose of reality, I turn and march through the crowd of mingling, chattering legacies.

The hurt I've felt since learning about their wager to fuck me simmers under my skin. It's irritating to know that all those stupid feelings I fought so hard were one-sided. They were only motivated to be with me for the sake of their fucking egos.

I want to repay how they made me feel. I want to punish them.

Reaching the relatively uncrowded bar, I glance around. The few legacies mingling here seem to be having a great time, though some eyeball me. When I notice a handsome, dark-skinned siren leaning against the bar, checking me out with a drink in his hand, I approach him.

I've never tried to flirt before. Sweeping my gaze over his tall form, I try to simulate Kenzie's carefree, flirtatious smile. I'm pretty sure it looks deranged instead, but I'm working with what I've got.

"Hi."

Yes, hi. That's the best I have in this department.

How bleak.

But his face splits into a grin. In this dim lighting, I can just make out that his pupils are round, an assurance that he's not the changeling I'm looking for.

"Damn, you're hot tonight. I probably shouldn't say that when you've got a quintet of your own panting after you, though, huh?"

"We're platonic."

He sets down his drink while eye-fucking me. "Really? In that case, can I get you a drink?"

"Only if it's strong."

I haven't imbibed very often in my life. Probably because by the time Lillian decreed that I was old enough for alcohol, I had already become *this* and discovered that it takes a ridiculous amount of booze to feel even the slightest bit tipsy. Hence why Silas's fae mead didn't demolish my stomach.

Stop thinking about him.

The siren steps nearer to hand me the drink from the bartender, and I try to ignore how my body rebels against the idea of getting any closer. My nervous system breaks out into metaphorical hives when I picture touching him.

But I'm genuinely curious about what things I might enjoy if I can just get over my stupid conditioning. Once I'm over this hurdle, maybe I can learn to actually enjoy physical pleasure so I can get more of those fantastic orgasms.

And since I'm going to keep things platonic with my damned quintet, I might as well force myself to give it a try with someone I find passably attractive.

Someone like this guy.

"Care to dance?" he asks in his rich, lilting siren's voice.

"Depends." Battling internal horror, I reach out with my free hand to straighten his bowtie, trailing my fingers briefly over his shoulder. "Will this dance lead to something more…fun?"

"It will if I have any say in it."

He covers my lace-gloved hand with his, and even though I try to hide it, needles of hysteria scatter through every inch of me. And it's not just my customary panic because of someone else touching me—it's mixed with a surprising aversion to touching anyone who isn't… *them.*

It just feels wrong.

And not in the good way.

I pull my hand away, reminding myself to breathe as I drink the too-sugary cocktail. Touching this guy more tonight is officially out of the question, but still…I don't have to get touchy to flirt. Maybe if I get used to him over time, my body won't freak out so much.

The siren hasn't noticed my inner struggle. He's all smiles as he says, "Actually, what are you doing after this? Collins invited me to a secret orgy in his dorm. It's a pretty fucking exclusive group going tonight, but I bet he'll let it slide if I bring you. I mean, everyone is talking about the mysterious Maven Oakley. If you're platonic with your quintet, why not come and have fun? I'll make sure you enjoy yourself. And I know I'm not the only unmatched dude who's dying for a shot at your ass—"

Ice seals his lips together. Frozen crystals bloom all over his dark skin and clothing, sealing together and thickening until less than a blink of an eye later, I'm staring at a siren frozen in place like a statue. His faint, muffled grunts of panic at his inability to move show that he can still breathe through his nostrils.

I'm abruptly so cold that I'm sure my nipples will show since I opted not to wear a bra. With all this chill, I'm not surprised when I hear Everett's voice directly behind me.

"Enjoying yourself, Oakley?"

His voice is easygoing, as if he's perfectly unbothered. Yet when I turn around with my poker face intact, his jaw is clenched, a muscle ticking.

It's satisfying to get a reaction out of him. I decide to push it further.

"I was until you interrupted my first choice for getting laid tonight. Kindly unfreeze him."

The professor's gaze drops briefly, and this time, I know I'm not imagining the way his cheekbones darken when he notices my hard nipples through my dress.

"I saw you touch him. That's not happening ever again."

"Why the fuck do you even care?"

"I don't," he says at once. "I was just…concerned. Just like any elemental would be for their gods-given match. Don't mistake it for *caring*."

My chest hurts, and I'm starting to lose my patience and my temper. I step closer to him, looking up into his pale blue eyes so I won't be mistaken.

"I need you to do something for me."

All of Everett's anger seems to liquefy at my proximity, and the temperature around us returns to normal. His eyes study mine fervently.

"Anything," he whispers, his tone nearly throwing me off because it's bizarrely soft.

I give him a saccharine smile. "Take your concern and shove it up your ass so your head can have some company."

He wilts. And this time, his reaction is somehow not as satisfying. I don't know the reason for that, but before either of us can say anything else, Baelfire plants a hand on Everett's shoulder and shoves him away from me with a growl.

"Get the fuck away from her, asshole. She wants nothing to do with you."

Everett lifts his chin, donning his characteristic aloof sneer. "She wants nothing to do with any of us, which is why she was all over that siren."

All over is an exaggeration, but I don't bother correcting him when Baelfire's nostrils flare and Silas looks equally pissed off.

I should leave them and look for the changeling since I don't know how long the Matched Ball will last. But this tiny, petty form of revenge is too wickedly entertaining to stop now.

7

BAELFIRE

Silas steps up beside Maven, looking as possessive and pissed as I feel. He's gripping his bleeding crystal, gaze darting about mistrustfully at anyone nearby. Though we're out of everyone's earshot, that doesn't stop them from staring. The tension in the ballroom is thick enough to taste since everyone is on edge after the Immortal Quintet's announcements.

"Were you just flirting with that legacy, *sangfluir?"* Silas demands.

Maven shrugs one shoulder nonchalantly, but the expression on her face as she lifts her glass back to her perfect lips is full of warning.

"I can flirt with anyone I want."

"Like hell you can," I grit.

She takes a sip, and I bite back a groan as I watch the muscles of her throat work.

When I spotted my mate across the dance floor earlier, I thought I had accidentally wandered into my own personal wet dream. The dress she's wearing shows off her shoulders, back, and most of her legs—though she's still wearing her kick-ass black combat boots, which is cute as fuck. Whoever did her makeup added sultry touches around her enchanting eyes and dark lipstick that I'm fantasizing about having smeared all over me.

The result is that my dick doesn't stand a chance. I'm rock-hard gazing at this dark queen.

Mine, mine, mine, my inner dragon growls.

Yeah, she is.

Except she was just fucking *flirting* with someone else.

Everett starts to say something, but Maven downs the rest of her drink and cuts him off, skirting around all three of us.

"If you're done with this caveman performance, could you point out who Collins is? I'd like an orgasm or two, and apparently, that incubus throws a lot of orgies."

Blistering wrath scalds my insides at the idea of anyone outside our quintet giving Maven pleasure. Before I can get myself under control, I grip the back of the choker built into Maven's dress and use it to turn her around, snarling, "Don't even think about it."

Instead of the fury that I expect to flash across her face, Maven's dark eyes glitter, and she smirks.

Fucking *smirks*.

Oh, shit. My sadistic little wet dream is doing this on purpose. This is her way of putting us through the wringer and getting even.

My heart pounds as I twist my grip in the back of her dress tighter, need for her making my cock hard as fucking steel in my suit pants.

"You enjoying this, baby? Tell me, how wet does it make your panties knowing you're torturing us?"

"Hard to tell when I'm not wearing any."

Fuck. Me.

Knowing I could lift up her fluttering skirt and find her pussy bare and ready makes me groan. Silas looks equally tortured from where he stands behind her. His hand slips up to tangle in the back of her hair until we're both gripping our cruel little caster to keep her in place.

When he tugs on the dark hair at the nape of her neck, Maven's eyes grow slightly hooded as she gazes up at me. I catch a hint of her addictive, delicate scent and wrap my other hand in the top layers of her skirt, swallowing tightly as the needy tension hums between us.

Gods, I want her. I want to get her alone, rip this damn dress off of her, and see how she punishes me for it.

"No panties, huh? Sounds like you want my tongue between your pretty thighs instead. Say the word, and we'll show you just how fucking real this has always been, Mayflower. No bets or games."

She blinks. "Mayflower?"

"You said Boo is out," I shrug. "Had to find another one."

"And comparing me to a delicate little *flower* was your second choice?" She shakes her head as much as Silas allows her to. "I said no more nicknames."

Silas presses his lips against her hair. "Let us apologize to you the way I know you're craving, *sangfluir*. You've resisted long enough. Admit that you want this, and stop fighting us."

His quiet words break her out of this intoxicating moment. She moves away to glare at all three of us since Everett is lingering. If looks could kill, we'd all drop dead at Maven's feet.

"I'll make this crystal clear. I'm temporarily playing along as your keeper because I have limited options. This is only an act for me, just like it was an act for you four to see who could fuck me the fastest. Consider this an allegiance of convenience because I want nothing to do with any of you. Now leave me alone. There's someone I need to track down."

Our keeper storms away, leaving me reeling and my inner dragon snarling in rebellion at her words. The last thing I want is for her to track down that fucking incubus and try to join his orgy.

Silas murmurs, "That was a lie. When she said she wanted nothing to do with us, she was lying."

"How do you know?"

He smirks. "Maven has a tell that I just figured out. Come on."

All three of us weave through the mass of dancing, talking legacies as we follow after her. I ignore the stares following us. My entire life, I've been paraded around as the miracle golden child of the last line of dragon shifters, so I'm used to drawing attention.

But my teeth clench when Iker Del Mar suddenly steps in front of me, stopping me from following after Silas.

Damn it. This won't be good.

"I've always wanted to meet Brigid Decimus's youngest son," he rumbles.

I dip my head respectfully, slipping on a charming smile even though I'm well the fuck aware that the Immortal Quintet can't stand my mother. Actually, as revered as my family is for how useful we are at the Divide, we Decimuses get into a shitload of trouble with the Immortal Quintet and Legacy Council all the time. It's because they like to keep such careful control of everything, manipulating the other high-profile legacy families by pulling on their strings, but we dragons are stubborn as hell.

My mom's always said that she'd rather we all be dead than blindly obedient.

All four of my older siblings have warned me that if I ever meet any of the Immortal Quintet, they'll automatically try to establish dominance over me because they love the idea of finally getting a Decimus to roll over and show its belly.

Not fucking happening.

"It's an honor to meet you, sir," I lie. "But if you'll excuse me, I really need to catch up with—"

"Not so fast," he cautions.

This monster gives me the heebie-jeebies. His pupils are like pinpricks in the pale yellow of his irises, and the horns and scales don't help him look any better. My inner dragon tenses, snarling as the hydra sizes us up.

Even though I'd love to flip him off and race after Maven, I stay polite. "Something I can help with?"

His smile is without warmth, showing off his pointed teeth. "More like something *I* can help you with. A gracious warning, if you will. Know that any students found stepping out of line will be severely punished. Pedigree and family pride will not excuse them. Dragons are only valuable assets if they can heed direction. Remember that."

Okay then. This fucker just threatened me and insulted my family all at once.

I bare all my teeth with my next smile. "Noted."

Then I turn my back on him and stalk toward the edge of the ballroom, keeping my eye out for Silas or Maven. When I catch a whiff of coppery burnt herbs that is unmistakably Silas and not some other blood fae, I follow his scent out of the Matched Ball completely, into one of the empty grand hallways.

A moment later, I turn into another dim corridor and find Everett standing with his arms folded and a scowl on his face, watching Maven and Silas in the middle of a heated argument. They would be nose to nose if it weren't for the fact that Silas is almost a foot taller than her.

"Then *ask*," Silas snaps in reply to whatever she said before I walked in. "Fucking ask me if it was all a show, Maven. You know I can't lie."

As I approach, her gaze darts to me, but she shakes her head stubbornly.

"I don't care if it was a lie. This isn't just about the bet. I already told you back in Pennsylvania—"

"What, that you're trying to protect us?" I growl, recalling her confession about her blood oath and claiming that she was rejecting us to keep us safe. "I want *you*, Maven, not your motherfucking protection. I'm a grown-ass dragon, and I can handle myself. So what if the anti-legacy movement says we shouldn't be together? If that's all you're worried about—"

She cuts me off with a harsh scoff. "*All* I'm worried about? You think the anti-legacy movement is the worst thing out there? Not even fucking close."

"Then enlighten us," Silas hisses angrily, pressing forward. The closer he gets, the more Maven looks torn between backing away and holding her ground. "What *exactly* is keeping you from accepting that we want you? Why are you fighting this so hard? What is the big, terrible secret that you think we can't handle? Tell the gods-damned truth."

Maven's temper flares as she looks between all of us. "Fine. You want to know why I'm fighting this so hard? It's not because of your juvenile bet. That hurt like hell, yet for reasons only the assholes in Paradise understand, I still want you—all of you. But I'm literally a fucking dead end for you four idiots, so get it through your thick heads that I just *can't*."

She wants us.

She wants *me*.

Now that I know that, I'm not holding back. Fierce determination sets in.

"Yes, you can," I growl, moving closer to her. "You want us, baby? We're already yours. Our hearts will be bound to yours, and it's that fucking simple."

Helpless anger colors her voice. She shakes her head like she's at the end of her rope and is desperate to make us see what the problem is.

"This is not *simple*. You're not getting it. We can't be bound, and I can't break your fucking curses because I don't have—"

Abruptly, she cuts off with a pained gasp, her hands flying to her chest. Terror has me forgetting all about the no-touching rule, and I immediately pull her against my chest when her knees collapse and her face twists in pain.

My mate. *In pain.*

I go into full panic mode.

"Maven? Fuck, what's happening, baby—is it the poison? Is it back?" I ask, my hands going to cover hers where she's clawing at her torso.

Her eyes are squeezed tight. "Gods. Not right now. *Please*, not right now," she gasps, sounding strangled.

"What's happening?" Everett demands sharply, crowding closer as the temperature around us plummets. "Maven?"

Silas cradles her face and tries to catch her eye, his eyes wide. "Is it that you can't breathe? Baelfire—"

Before he can even finish the order, I rip open the front of her dress, desperate to help her get air into her lungs. But it's useless.

All it does is show us that there is nothing visibly wrong with her perfect chest. The jagged, pale scar between her breasts is unmarred.

"I'm fine," Maven tries to insist, but the strain in her voice is pure agony. She clenches her teeth and tries to bat our hands away but suddenly goes limp.

"Maven?" I shout, my dragon beating on the inside of my head as horror overwhelms me. "Maven!"

Silas pulls out his bleeding crystal and slashes it deeply across his palm. The red flare of blood magic, combined with more smell like burnt copper, fills the dim hallway, illuminating the harsh planes of his face as he tries to heal her chest. I hold my breath, staring at my gorgeous mate motionless in my arms.

For the hundredth time in the last twenty-four hours, that horrible image comes back to me: my mate lying in a pool of blood, the scent of her tinged with poison and pain.

No, no, no, no—

While I'm still spiraling, Everett swears and takes Maven out of my arms before rushing down the hall.

"Where are we taking her?" I demand, keeping up. If it didn't feel like my entire world just turned sideways, I would beat the hell out of him for holding her when he's the last person in a never-ending line of people she wouldn't want touching her.

"To the healers," he mutters. "Because Silas is fucking useless."

Silas scowls as he catches up. "I don't understand. My magic absolutely refuses to work with her. It's almost as if—"

He cuts off, looking like a train of thought has taken him to a dark place. I don't bother asking what his new theory is because I'm too busy noticing how pale and cold my mate looks.

A minute later, I burst through the double doors and stride into Everbound's lengthy infirmary. Hundreds of years ago, when this castle was first built, it was a chapel devoted to the gods. Now, gone are the pews and priests. Instead, the intricate purple-and-white stained glass windows serve as a backdrop for dozens of empty sickbeds, counters filled with spell ingredients and medicines, and two chattering casters dressed in white. They jump in surprise as we walk in.

Everett is cradling Maven like he's afraid the air around us will hurt her, and I notice the frost climbing up to his elbows. He's losing his shit over this, just like the rest of us, which makes no fucking sense.

"What's going on?" one of the healers chirps in surprise.

"Heal her," Silas demands as Everett lowers Maven onto one of the sickbeds, adjusting the blanket with shaking hands to cover her naked upper half. "Now."

The healers exchange glances but quickly gather around Maven to look for signs of injury. Their proximity to my mate sets off my dragon's temper, and he lashes out against my control, wild and savage.

Mark her. Claim her. Covet her.

I grip the side of my head as splitting pain rocks through it, trying to fend off the shift he tries to force. The stupid lizard doesn't understand that now is *not* the fucking time to pin Maven down and mark her as mine. I really need to kill something before he strong-arms me into crossing her lines even more than I already have. Or worse, if he forces me to shift when I'm too close to her and she ends up getting hurt.

When the agony of refusing a shift finally recedes from my muscles, I see one of the healers reaching towards Maven and snap, "Don't fucking touch her. She doesn't like to be touched."

"We have to check her vitals. I promise we'll be very careful with her."

That promise doesn't help. I'm still filled with distress when the healer checks for her pulse, a frown pulling at his lips. He then leans down as if to press his ear to her chest, which has my dragon seeing red.

But before the healer can make contact with Maven, the Nightmare Prince emerges into existence beside us, grabs both healers by their necks, and vanishes in the blink of an eye. So do they. And when Crypt reappears from Limbo, both healers are dead. One still has his eyes frozen wide open in acute horror as if before he died, he saw shit that broke him. The other looks like he was slashed to threads and bones.

It all happened so fast that I'm still processing. Everett looks equally stunned, but Silas snarls, "What the fuck are you doing? We needed them to help Maven, you psychotic bastard!"

Crypt kicks aside one of the corpses, his face murderous as he stalks toward Silas.

"No, what are *you* doing? Where's your overdeveloped sense of paranoia when we need it? She told me to let no one heal her. It wasn't a polite suggestion, Crane. She must have a reason to avoid the healers here, so I don't fucking trust them. You shouldn't have, either."

"I wasn't *trusting* them. If they made a wrong move, I would have killed them just as quickly," Silas seethes. "But now look at her. She's not *breathing*, Crypt—she has no godsdamned pulse! My magic refuses to interact with her, so what are we going to do now? Did you think of that before killing people who could have potentially helped her?"

I go numb. Maven isn't breathing. She has no pulse. Which means...

"He made the right call," a gentle voice says, interrupting their furious argument.

We all look over as a familiar white-veiled figure steps forward, entering the old gothic chapel from a concealed entrance near the old pew. I blink at the sight of the prophetess who was at the Seeking, realizing she must be one of the people from Galene's temple that Iker Del Mar had mentioned would be here.

What was her name again? Pay-Pay? Pie?

"Prophetess Pia," Everett greets her, his tone formal but guarded. He glances at the dead bodies on the floor. "About this—"

She waves off his concern with an elegant, white-gloved hand. "As I said, your incubus made the right call. I fear they would have learned something about your keeper that would have been reported to the Immortal Quintet right away. Now, step away from her. I will take it from here."

It's odd not to see her face under all that white fabric. But even though I'm wary as hell about this mysterious prophetess, my inner dragon goes uncharacteristically quiet and calm as she approaches, as if he has no problem with her being around our mate.

Fine. I'll trust the asshole's judgment for now. But if she harms a single fucking hair on Maven's head, there will be one more corpse bleeding on the ground.

Pia laughs lightly, her head turning in my direction. "A guard dragon, are you?"

Fuck.

She's a mind reader—or a seer. Something like that.

The others must come to the same conclusion because Silas grips his bleeding crystal tighter, and Everett stiffens. The Nightmare Prince's eyes narrow as he watches Pia sit on the bed beside Maven, her hands hovering over my mate's chest but making no contact. A faint light radiates around Pia's hands, but otherwise, there's no obvious magic happening.

"You have no aura," Crypt notes in a precarious tone. "Every living thing has an aura."

She doesn't reply, moving her hand over Maven's head. We all watch in tense, perplexed silence. Finally, Silas rounds the bed to see Maven's face better, and his brow furrows.

"You said the healers would have learned something about her and reported it to the Immortal Quintet. What did you mean?"

Pia's tone is gentle. "You already have your suspicions about her nature. And the incubus is much closer to the truth."

My gaze darts to Crypt. "What the hell is she talking about? What do you know?"

Crypt doesn't even acknowledge my question. Clearly, he's not about to tell us anything.

Silas studies Maven at length before speaking slowly, hesitantly. I can practically see the gears turning in his paranoid head.

"She has no heartbeat. She didn't earlier, either. And when I was trying to heal her of the poison, I found a bottle of nightshade root powder in one of her pockets. That substance is all but impossible to get—the Legacy Council has made it entirely illegal. Why would a human-raised atypical caster go to the trouble of getting that?"

The question hangs in the air as Pia finishes healing Maven and straightens. I stare at Maven hard until I see her chest rise and fall, and relief hits me so hard that I have to sit down on one of the other empty beds.

Thank the gods. She's breathing.

Silas rubs his jaw as he goes on. "The dagger we found in Headmaster Hearst's office was made of adamantine."

"So?" I ask.

"Do you know how rare that metal is? It's what the weapons of the most powerful shadow fiends that make it into the Divide are made out of. Legacies don't use adamantine, and no one in the mortal world knows how to forge it, so how did that dagger end up in that office?"

I pull a face, but Everett seems to be catching onto whatever I'm missing because he abruptly looks even paler than usual.

"You think that dagger is Maven's?"

"Who cares if it is?" I snap. "Look, maybe one of the anti-legacy cultists who raised her picked up the dagger in the Divide or something. It doesn't matter."

Silas glares at me. "Yes, it does. If Maven's weapon is from the Nether, she's on a mysterious mission, and she doesn't have a godsdamned *heartbeat*…"

I stare at him long and hard. "What the fuck are you saying?"

"You know exactly what I'm saying."

Everett stares down at Maven again, his voice barely audible even by my standards. "Do you remember, years ago, when several humans were put to death by the Legacy Council?"

That had been huge news in the world of legacies because they kept why they did that classified. Even I heard about it and I was eight.

"Yeah, so? I don't see what that has to do with—"

"It was because they claimed the Nether was taking in humans and keeping them alive."

He looks between the three of us meaningfully, and even Crypt frowns.

Immediately, I shake my head. "No. That doesn't make any fucking sense. Maven manifested as a caster a few weeks ago, and she's part of some kind of anti-legacy cult. She told us that herself."

Silas pins me with a look. "Did she, though? She never said it outright."

I open my mouth to argue and then hesitate, realizing he's right.

"Damn it. She was just trying to deter us again," Everett murmurs. "That's all she's tried to do since we met her. I should've figured that out sooner."

I'm still shaking my head in denial, but then certain things click into place. Maven being so technologically impaired. Her delight in anything macabre. The way she had stared wide-eyed at everything in that cozy little town in Pennsylvania like it was from an alien planet. How hell-bent she has been on pushing her matches away, trying to get us to appeal for another keeper, insisting that she was all wrong for us.

The momentary confusion that had been on her face when Crypt had asked if she was part of the anti-legacy movement, right before she nodded.

You guys have no fucking idea how bad it would be to be bound to me. I'm protecting you idiots.

I refuse to drag you four down with me.

I'm your enemy.

All her past words swim in my head until I cover my face. "Holy shit."

My mate is from the Nether.

8
EVERETT

BAELFIRE, Silas, and Crypt stare at Maven as they think. But I can't think. In fact, I can barely get my voice to work as I glance at the prophetess, the dread and guilt eating me alive.

"You managed to heal her. Thank you. But...can you tell me what was wrong with her?"

I already know this was my fault, but I still have to ask. It's like I just need that extra stab of self-loathing to convince myself to get the hell out of this room and stay as far away from Maven as I can until graduation.

Dear gods, I should have stuck to the plan and kept my distance from her at the Matched Ball—but the moment I'd seen her hand on that siren, all bets were off.

Now, here we are, with my curse rearing its ugly head. I should have been stronger. She deserves so much better. I can't fucking stand myself.

Pia's head tilts toward me. Her voice is unexpectedly warm and gentle. "This was not your fault, nor was it your curse's. Be kinder to yourself."

I flinch when her words unintentionally make three pairs of eyes swing in our direction, and then Baelfire frowns. "What is she talking about? Why would this be your curse's fault?"

"It's nothing."

Crypt is watching me too closely, as if he's putting something together, so I change the topic quickly, once again addressing the white-shrouded prophetess.

"But how did she survive if she came from the Nether?" I ask. "Unless…"

Oh, dear gods. Maybe she *didn't*. Silas said she'd had no heartbeat. She could be…

"Unless what?" Pia asks.

Unless she's one of the Undead.

I can't bring myself to say it out loud because it's so damn outlandish. I've been exposed to hundreds of pictures of the Undead, and they're revolting creatures that look absolutely nothing like Maven.

But then, it's also outlandish that she could possibly be from the Nether. No living thing can survive there.

Silas adjusts Maven's hair away from her face, his brow furrowed deeply. Then he faces Pia with determination. "You can read people. Tell us what you read about our keeper."

Of course, he has no problem demanding answers from a prophetess. He's a blasphemous asshole.

She's quiet for a moment before sighing. "It is true. I am blessed with the ability to see nearly anything in this mortal realm. Thoughts, feelings, memories, truths… But there are places of darkness that even Galene cannot see. Places that have been claimed by the Nether. It consumes everything it touches and turns it all to shadow, just as it has done to your keeper's heart."

Crypt's attention snaps to Pia. "Explain."

"I can see only broken pieces of her past, all shrouded in darkness. But that degree of darkness only exists in the Nether, and it seems her heart still remains in that realm of death."

…What?

"I'm confused. If Maven has no heart, then…how is she alive?" I ask.

Looking like his mind is a thousand miles away, Silas murmurs, "Damn it. A shadow heart."

Very unhelpful since I don't know what that's supposed to mean.

"Hang on. If she's from the Nether, is she still human?" Baelfire asks, looking equally out of his depth here.

Pia adjusts one of the white drapes hanging from her arms. Her voice is deeply sorrowful. "That is hard to say. I only know of her purpose and her blood oath."

"Care to share?" I manage.

It sounds like the prophetess is smiling when she speaks. "If she ever wishes to share the true depth of her nobility with you, she will. But that will be her choice. Now, let her rest, and please dispose of the bodies before anyone else comes in."

Pia's head dips as if she is checking on Maven one more time, and then she leaves the room as sagely and silently as she entered. The door clicks shut softly behind her.

The silence is deafening. It stretches on far longer than it ever has between me and these three legacies as we watch Maven sleep deeply. Some of the color finally returns to her face. She's so pretty it hurts my chest, and it's difficult to breathe as I try to convince myself to leave the room now that I know she's all right.

I can't make myself leave her.

But I need to.

Fuck, I hate this.

"What happened?" Crypt finally rasps.

Silas wipes the dried blood from cutting his hand earlier onto his pants, obviously not caring about ruining the poor suit. "We were arguing, and then she collapsed outside the Matched Ball. It happened out of nowhere."

I reach out and feel the back of Maven's hand. It doesn't feel warm to me, which is how I know she must be freezing cold. "Baelfire. Warm her up."

He gives me a testy look, smacking my hand away from our keeper before he walks to the other side of the bed.

"Hold her without permission, and your mate will be down to three matches," Crypt warns.

Baelfire shakes his head, mumbling something about being stuck with a bunch of psychopaths as he gently adjusts Maven to one side of the mattress, grabs an extra blanket from a nearby bed, and tosses it over both of them. At least now his obnoxiously excessive body heat will transfer to her, though it looks like half his ass is hanging off the bed. I guess it's his fault for being roughly the size of an ox with basically the equivalent in brain power.

I catch Crypt staring at me again, but now one side of his mouth is pulled up into a smirk.

"What? Why are you making that face at me?" I demand. "Stop. You're fucking creepy."

"You're just as far gone for her as the rest of us. Aren't you."

It's not a question. He's stating this accusation, and I immediately shake my head.

"The gods assigned her as my keeper, so it's not like I want her to fucking *die,* but I don't care about her. Not like that."

"Bullshit," Silas snorts. "Look how red his face is."

I resist the urge to cover my cheeks, which have always been annoyingly blush-prone, and feign aloofness once more. "You three can believe whatever you want, but Maven is nothing to me. I don't feel—"

I cut off when Crypt's hand is suddenly wrapped around my throat, bruising me as he pins me to the nearest wall. His eyes gleam with malicious threat.

"Your feelings don't interest me, Frost. But that prophetess insinuated that you believe your curse could hurt Maven. Anything that concerns her concerns me, so spit it out."

I'm getting really fucking tired of these jerks going for my throat. My anger quickly turns into ice crackling up the wall behind me. When I focus my power, Crypt lurches away just as fatally sharp ice spikes explode into existence, surrounding me like a shield.

I allow them to melt instantly and snap, "Leave me the fuck alone."

But Silas is a persistent asshole and takes a defensive stance, his bloodied crystal in hand. "Much as I hate admitting it, he's right. We need to know if you're a risk to Maven. Don't share all of your curse if you don't need to, but tell us any way it could hurt her."

I rub my face. Godsdamn it. They're not going to let this go.

And maybe they're right not to. After all…I *have* been putting her at risk. No matter what Pia thinks, I know it's my fault she's been bedridden twice within the space of twenty-four hours. It correlates too much with how spectacularly I've been failing at fighting my emotions.

"Fine," I mutter, breathing out a puff of frigid air before I regard all three of them. "But you can't kill me."

Baelfire snorts derisively. "Is that a challenge? Because I definitely could if I wanted to."

"Shut up, dragon. I'll tell you three about it, but there better not be any more trips to Limbo," I say pointedly, glaring at Crypt.

"As if I'd kill you in such a mundane way. Spit it out already."

I swallow and look back down at Maven. She looks so peaceful in her sleep, with her hair sprawled across the pillow and her dark lashes settled on her cheeks. My chest aches as I imagine seeing her like this every morning, safe and warm in silk sheets with the promise of nothing but pleasure and comfort ahead for her.

Cherishing her would be as easy as breathing.

But…

"My curse will kill anyone I fall in love with," I confess quietly.

They all absorb that for a moment. Then Baelfire opens his big, fat mouth.

"Damn. That sucks ass. Especially for your past girlfriends."

I just sigh. Fucking idiot.

He blinks. "Wait. *Have* you had any past girlfriends? Or boyfriends? Casual flings or one-night stands? *Anything?*"

"If he knows he'll be the death of anyone he accidentally catches feelings for, even from a one-night stand, then willingly putting someone in that position would be akin to secondhand murder," Silas muses.

My thoughts exactly.

Baelfire props himself up slightly, his mouth hanging open like he just unearthed treasure. "Hold the fucking phone. Don't tell me no one has ever hopped on your popsicle before. You're a virgin?"

Even though I'm sure my bright red face gives away the answer, I decide now's the perfect time to move this conversation along.

"*Anyway*, I've tried keeping my distance from Maven. I worried that if I was too obvious about pushing her away, it would make her pursue me out of curiosity, or you guys would pick another fight. But honestly, I never should've gone to the inn with the rest of you because no matter how much I try to ignore it, Maven makes it so...it's impossible to not..."

I'm struggling so much with my words that Silas finishes for me. "To not care for her."

My shoulders slump. I expect another wise-ass comment from Baelfire, but to my utter shock, he looks almost...*sympathetic*.

"I'm guessing that's why you decided to be an even bigger asshole than usual and tell her about the bet," the dragon sighs.

I start fidgeting with both cufflinks before stopping myself. My parents always hated that I had compulsive, nervous ticks growing up. These days, they only reappear when I'm anxious or when I'm stressed as hell.

Like right now.

"When we found her in the headmaster's office, I thought...I thought I'd killed her." My voice is dangerously close to breaking, so I clear my throat. "And when she passed out tonight, it's because I got close to her at the Matched Ball. It's my fault—my curse. I can't let anything like this happen again. Maybe you three can help me stay away from her as much as possible. At least until we can break our curses."

Silas says nothing as he considers everything I just said. Crypt's face is unreadable. Baelfire doesn't look at me, instead reaching out to adjust Maven's pillow slightly.

"Are you *sure* that's your curse, Snowflake?" he prods. "If you had a long track record of dead ex-lovers, I'd get it, but how do you know for certain if you've never…you know? *Fallen* for someone and all that gooey shit."

I rub my neck. "When they couldn't figure out what my curse was by the time I turned four, my parents took me to Arati's temple."

Arati is the goddess of passion, fire, wrath, war, and love. She's also the queen of the gods and the sister of Galene, the goddess of prophecies.

"The high prophet there divined a personal prophecy for me and revealed my curse. That's how I know for sure."

Once again, they're all quiet for a while before Silas sighs.

"I'll help you maintain distance from Maven."

Baelfire nods. "Never thought I'd feel bad for a fucking Frost, but yep. I'll help cockblock your heart or whatever."

I really hate him.

Crypt is oddly quiet, staring at one of the stained-glass windows. Before I can ask if he's going to bother joining us on Earth anytime soon, Silas sighs again and scrubs his face.

"Before she collapsed, Maven was trying to tell us that she can't break our curses because…because she has no heart for us to bind ours to. That's why she was trying so hard to reject us."

Dear gods.

I swallow hard as my stomach sinks. Here I was, holding out hope that my curse could be broken at graduation so I could finally let myself adore Maven. But if there's no chance of that…

I really should leave, but I can't seem to make myself move.

"Well?" Silas sighs. "What do you bastards have to say about it?"

I consider it for a long moment. The truth is…I never thought the gods would ever bless me with a keeper. Until I met Maven, I assumed I would remain lonely until I finally passed into the Beyond.

But now, I think of myself as Maven's. And I think of her as mine, even if I can never actually have her. Even if my curse separates us forever.

"The gods made her my keeper, and I won't question them," I murmur.

Baelfire nods. "Not having my curse broken is going to fucking suck. But whether I'm cursed or not, she's my mate. So nothing changes for me."

Crypt says nothing. Whatever his curse is, he doesn't seem bothered.

Silas is quiet for a long moment, and then he sighs. "If the gods chose her to punish me even further, they couldn't have picked a more frustrating, heavenly demise. Nothing changes for me, either. She's *ima sangfluir*."

Whatever the hell that means.

But at least we're all on the same page.

"Here's the plan," Silas goes on. "We won't say a word to Maven about knowing where she's from."

Crypt finally reacts, leaning against the wall and pulling out his lighter to fiddle with it. "Speak for yourself. You three fucked up last time by omitting your asinine little wager, so now I will keep no secrets from our keeper."

"I'm with Stalker Boy. No more keeping shit from Maven," Baelfire agrees.

Silas hesitates. "We all know how secretive she is, and now we know it's for good reason. I doubt she feels she can trust us right now. What if we tell her we know, and she goes back to thinking we'll kill her? If she wakes up and we assault her with questions about her past and her so-called noble purpose, it will make our standing with her far worse than it already is."

That's all true. We need time to absorb this, anyway.

"We'll ease her into knowing that we know," I suggest.

"Suit yourselves," Crypt rolls his eyes. But then he looks at me with an expression more serious than I've ever seen on him, which is fucking weird. "I don't think Maven was harmed by your curse, Frost. I have my own theory. But if any of you asks follow-up questions about what I'm about to share with you—"

He halts, and his face darkens as he glances down at Maven. As if on cue, her brow furrows, and she makes a soft sound of distress in her sleep that has frost prickling the tips of my fingers.

"What is it?" I demand.

Crypt says nothing. He just vanishes, and a moment later, Maven relaxes, returning to a deep sleep. Silas, Baelfire, and I exchange glances. He obviously just helped her with a nightmare.

Having a lot of nightmares makes sense for someone who's experienced the terrors of the Nether firsthand. I really hate that thought, but there it is.

The Nightmare Prince returns, acting as if he didn't just drop everything to soothe our keeper.

"As I was saying, there will be no follow-up questions regarding what I'm about to share with you. But Crane, you may find a way to make this information useful for Maven thanks to your knowledge of plants, no matter how broken your mind is."

Silas's face twists bitterly. "Thanks a fucking lot, bastard."

"Compliments are my specialty." Crypt pulls out one of his strange cigarettes, handing it to Silas. "I smoke *reverium* from Limbo to ease the strain of passing between planes of existence. It's quite potent. Dulls much of the pain. Plane-walking takes a heavy toll on the mind and body."

Hang on. "If bouncing back and forth between here and Limbo causes you pain, then why do you—"

The Nightmare Prince's purple glare is piercing.

Right. No follow-up questions.

"Why are you sharing this?" Silas asks, turning the cigarette between his fingers as he studies it with genuine interest.

"According to that prophetess, Maven's heart is somehow in the Nether while she's here in the mortal realm. That means she's caught between planes just as I sometimes am, which may be why she collapsed earlier. I doubt *reverium* would do her any good since it's Limbo-specific, but perhaps there is something…"

Silas's eyes light up with understanding. "There might be another substance or plant that could take the edge off for her. Something native to the Nether."

Crypt nods.

I stare at Maven's profile. If Maven is from the Nether, it raises a thousand and one questions. How did she survive? How did she escape? Was she all alone? What kind of hell has my beautiful keeper been through?

"No wonder she didn't even know what ice cream was," I mutter.

"Or how to drive," Crypt agrees.

Silas goes very still. "What are you talking about? She drove herself to Pennsylvania."

"That she did."

"Are you telling me that you let her drive all the way there *knowing* that she'd never driven a fucking car before?"

Crypt grins. "She made it in one piece. Our girl is a quick learner."

The blood fae pinches the bridge of his nose. "One day, I'm going to kill you."

"Better make it soon since your sanity's expiration date is quickly approaching."

They continue bickering quietly, but I back away from the bed, still staring at Maven's sleep-softened face. More than anything, I want to be here when she wakes up so I can make sure she's all right. But despite Crypt's doubts about this being caused by my curse...I'm not taking any more chances with her.

No matter where she came from, I'm going to protect my keeper. Including from myself.

Before I leave the room, Baelfire catches my eye. And instead of the glare or disgust I usually see on his face, he nods once in begrudging understanding before I close the doors behind me.

9

MAVEN

"I've got you, Mayflower. Whatever you've been through, you're safe now."

I frown softly into the darkness of my closed eyes as my senses return to me. This feels…off. Normally, when I wake up after one of my episodes, I'm freezing and feel like shit.

But right now, I feel good. No headache. No lingering pain.

What bizarre witchcraft is this?

And I'm warm. *Really* warm. So warm that I can't help sighing because it feels so damn nice. I've never experienced a heated blanket, but Kenzie once told me they were a gift from the gods straight out of Paradise. Now, I'm pretty sure she wasn't exaggerating.

Wait. *Mayflower?*

I open my eyes and find that Baelfire's handsome, smiling face is only a few inches away, his irises like warm honey.

"There she is. Prettiest eyes I've ever seen."

What the fuck? Why am I in bed with him?

I sit up, taking in my surroundings quickly. I'm in Everbound's infirmary, which is mildly alarming. But I don't see anyone here trying to heal me or running away screaming that a convict of the Nether has infiltrated Everbound, which is promising.

Baelfire sits up, too. His warm body is so close to mine that I get tingles in my stomach, which I dutifully ignore. Silas is upright on the sickbed beside ours, his ruby irises soft as he studies me.

But why the hell is he looking at me like that? Weren't we just fighting?

I feel like I'm missing something.

His gaze drops, and he bites his lip. "Mmm. I much prefer this view, but I'm obligated to let you know that your very lovely tits are on display."

I glance down and frown. Oh, my gods. These barbarians ripped the dress Kenzie gave me.

"You couldn't breathe, and I panicked," Baelfire says quickly. "But I'll get you any dresses you want, anytime. Or better yet, we can make Everett buy you a few million dresses. His treat."

I squint at him for a long second, still disoriented as I gather my thoughts. "You're avoiding a serious conversation. I know you two witnessed my...condition. Tell me what happened after I lost consciousness."

They exchange a glance, and then Silas sighs. "We brought you to the healers, but Crypt killed them before they could examine you. Then the prophetess, Pia, healed you."

Impossible. "What really happened?"

"I can't lie," he reminds me, his attention slipping down to my bare upper half again.

Oh. Right.

I frown, realizing that must explain how I don't feel like shit. How the hell did Pia heal me? It couldn't have been through common or blood magic. I did pick up an odd feeling from her at the Seeking. Maybe I should corner her and demand some answers.

But that will have to happen later. I have a clock in my head, slowly counting up the time that Kenzie has been missing, and when I glance out the stained glass windows of this room, I grit my teeth to see that a couple of hours must have passed.

"So, about this condition of yours," Baelfire interrupts my train of thought, tugging gently on a loose strand of my hair.

The familiarity of sitting topless in bed so close to him has my face warming. I finally pull up a blanket to cover myself, which makes Silas sigh.

"It's harmless," I lie, checking to make sure I'm still wearing my gloves out of habit. "I just pass out sometimes."

"How often?" Silas demands.

"It's happening more frequently."

That is not a lie. Each episode has been getting closer together and more severe, which is inconvenient.

"But it's nothing I can't handle. It won't get in the way of me being a decent keeper. A temporary, *platonic* keeper," I add pointedly, looking between them to let them know I haven't forgotten about our argument.

Baelfire snorts. "Yeah, no. That ship has sailed. Unless you want to offer a concrete, honest-as-hell reason for insisting we can't be together, accept that we're yours to keep, Boo."

I give him a sharp look.

"Mayflower," he amends, winking. "Mate. Cutie Pie. Raincloud. Take your pick."

"I pick fuck off."

"I'm not going to call you Fuck Off," he teases. "That's just rude. 'Fuck Me,' on the other hand, could definitely be worked into the mix. Especially if you moan it."

Oh, my gods. This dragon is something else.

Silas examines me like his mind is far away. "You need more sleep."

No, what I need is to find Kenzie sooner than later. And as painful as it is to admit to myself, I'm struggling to progress there. In order to track down the changeling alone, I'd have to find a way to fuel my magic, perform a ritual on its dried blood, hunt it down, probably fight it again, torture it for information, find some brutally imaginative way to kill it…

All great fun, except for the time crunch.

But Silas doesn't need anything to fuel his magic except blood. I may need to swallow my pride to speed this process along. For Kenzie's sake.

I take a deep breath. "I want your help."

His brows go up, and then a wicked grin curls his lips. "Absolutely. I'll gladly help you get to sleep, especially if you need to be worn out first."

I open my mouth and then close it. Then I rub my face to hide the warmth blooming there.

"That's not what I was talking about, and you know it."

"Do I? You said it yourself that you want an orgasm or two. I'll give you plenty."

Baelfire leans close to my ear to whisper. "I'll double whatever he's offering. All the orgasms you want, as long as you come on my face and make me beg for it."

Oh, my fucking *gods*. What the hell has gotten into them?

I can't hide the flush on my face as I shake my head at their matching grins. Clambering from the bed with the blanket still wrapped around me for modesty, I stomp toward the door.

"Forget I mentioned wanting *anything*. Fucking legacies."

But my exit is cut off by Crypt, who appears directly before me. His smile twists as he scrutinizes my appearance.

"Fashionable."

"Quilts are all the rage," I deadpan, then tip my head. "You missed the Matched Ball."

That sobers him. "Am I too late for a dance, love?"

"I don't dance. Were you avoiding Somnus?"

If Crypt is bothered by the mention of his father, he has no reaction. "No. I was held up."

"By?"

His lips twitch. "My, my. Aren't you curious tonight? One would almost think you missed me."

It's a marvel of nature that they manage to stand upright with heads so big. Obviously, the Nightmare Prince has no intention of telling me where he was. He couldn't have left Everbound Castle, so what was he up to?

"The bodies?" Silas asks Crypt as he stands and joins us.

"Disposed of."

Baelfire joins us, too, wrinkling his nose as he folds his brawny arms. The seams of his poor shirt look ready to pop under the strain of those muscles. "Do I want to ask?"

Crypt's smile is one hundred percent psychopath. "Absolutely not. Your delicate lizard stomach couldn't handle it. However, our beautifully morbid keeper might enjoy the details. Care to hear, love?"

Yes. Disposing of bodies in mysterious ways is a fascination of mine.

"Later," I say, meaning it. "Perhaps when I'm wearing real clothes."

He hums. "Or no clothes."

Clearly, their hive mind is active right now, and it's focused on one thing. Unfortunately, so am I—I keep recalling Kenzie's erotic art and the newfound fantasies I've been having. I wonder if jumping headlong into a blazing sex romp would help me get over my haphephobia...

"I'm on a mission," I blurt to keep myself from doing something stupid, like asking one of them if I can try sucking their cock to see if it's as enjoyable as people make it out to be.

Crypt nods. "We know. You've told us of your blood oath."

"No, I have another far more time-sensitive mission. A rescue mission, to be precise."

Baelfire frowns. "Rescue mission? For who?"

My throat tightens. Even though I try not to let my emotions show, I know the worry I've been trying to keep at bay seeps into my voice.

"Kenzie."

All three of them exchange glances, and then Crypt leans down to meet my eye better.

"If you believe she may be somewhere within this castle, I can find her quickly."

"How?"

"I read auras."

"He does," Baelfire confirms. "Bragged about it constantly when we were kids. It was fucking annoying." Then he tips his head. "I've always wondered, what's my aura like?"

"Just as obnoxious as you are but a hundred times as bright."

They glare at each other, but Silas ignores them completely as he studies me. "Crypt can go looking for her aura, but if there is another way you believe I can help you, I will. On one condition. Come to my private dorm with me."

"You're not fucking me," I say immediately. "I still hate all of you."

He huffs. "Believe me, I'm painfully aware of that. This isn't about getting you in my bed. I need to speak with you alone, and in return, I'll help you however I can."

I consider that before nodding. It's convenient that Silas can't tell bald-faced lies. It means I can trust his words even when I don't know where I stand with him.

Crypt blows me a kiss before slipping into Limbo to look for Kenzie. I'm tempted to pray to the gods that he'll find her, but I learned my lesson about praying to them a long time ago. So, instead, I hope the universe is looking out for her. If anyone deserves cosmic good luck, it's Kenzie.

Baelfire, Silas, and I leave the infirmary and trek through the castle halls, following Silas's lead toward his private dorm. Baelfire's eyes sweep the dim hallways, and he steps a little closer to me with every turn as if he expects someone to pop out of the shadows and grab me. Silas is equally bad, gritting his teeth at every tiny echo in the hall.

"Is the chill pill a real thing?" I ask.

Bael blinks down at me. "What?"

"Kenzie once told me that I'm far too intense and need a prescription for a chill pill. If that exists, you two also need a prescription."

The dragon shifter throws his head back on a laugh. "See, it's adorably out-of-the-loop stuff like this that should've tipped us off."

I don't know what he's talking about, but Silas gives him a warning glare. "You're not coming into my private dorm."

"Nope. I'm just escorting my mate. I trust your ability to protect her about as far as Everett could throw you. Which can't be far at all, by the way. Have you seen that professor? Scrawny as hell."

"Indeed."

Everett is far from scrawny, but I find myself fighting an unexpected smile at the shit talk. I still don't fully understand the dynamic of their shared past or why my matches dislike each other so much. But there's a familiar ease with which they hate one another that's almost...brotherly.

But saying that out loud would probably start another bout of the Great Wars, so I keep my mouth shut.

Finally, we walk up a staircase that ends with a single door. My hair stands on end as I sense the ripple of magic guarding this space.

Damn. How many wards does Silas have on that thing?

"I'll see you later at our quintet apartment," Baelfire says, tugging gently on the corner of my blanket to get my attention.

"No, you won't. I'm sleeping in my own dorm."

He frowns. "But you agreed to be our keeper."

"*Temporarily.*"

"Temporarily, my ass. Did you not hear that horned freak, Del Mar? Quintet rankings are beginning, and we all know you'll be at the top of the godsdamned kill list along with the rest of us. You're a walking target. Even with the patch job Silas did on your door, your dorm isn't nearly safe enough for my dragon to rest easy."

I open my mouth, but Silas speaks first. "Sleep in my dorm. It's the most secure place in the entire castle. I doubt even the Immortal Quintet could get in here if they tried."

"Here's a thought. I'll sleep wherever the fuck I choose to sleep," I tell them both firmly.

Baelfire relents but gives me one more warm look. "I'll see you in class in the morning. Get enough rest, and if you have any nightmares—"

He cuts off, ducking his head when my eyes narrow. Did Crypt tell them about my nightmares? I feel strangely betrayed.

Bael clears his throat. "When you were sleeping off your, you know…"

"Episode," I supply.

He nods. "You weren't sleeping very peacefully for a bit. So if you keep having trouble sleeping, my bed's always open. I'm not a blanket hog. I don't even use a blanket, actually—it's too fucking hot at night. Also, I sleep in the nude most of the time. I know that's a massive selling point for you because you check me out whenever you think I'm not looking," he smirks.

I shake my head, allowing myself the smallest smile. "Careful. Your ego may smother you in your sleep."

"I'd much rather *you* smother me with that sexy ass of yours. I dream about that all the fucking time, actually."

My thighs clench at the rousing mental image that paints, and Baelfire's nostrils flare as he picks up on my arousal. Before he can finish turning my insides to goo, I turn and slip through the dorm door just as Silas opens it with a low chuckle at my expense.

Once I'm inside, I pause and take in the space. It's very…Silas.

The dorm is a large studio perfectly balanced between cozy, rustic, and luxurious—and very decidedly of fae design. An antique-looking burgundy fainting couch sits on a plush rug in front of a hearth that flickers to life with a wave of Silas's hand as he steps up beside me. The kitchen is small but clean, with one entire counter filled with various liquors and another fully stocked bar cart in the living room. A big bed is tucked into one corner by a window, topped with dark red blankets.

Most of the walls are lined with overfilled bookshelves, and a coffee table near the fainting couch is covered with papers and all kinds of spell ingredients. Off to one side is a carved wooden door leading into a bathroom.

Silas's dorm is busy but not messy. When I glance at him, he's analyzing me as thoroughly as I was his personal space.

"Do you like it?"

"That's not important. It's your dorm, not mine."

He hesitates, rubbing the back of his neck. "It is important, actually. I want you to be comfortable here. No one else has ever been in here since I made it into my own months ago."

"Not even Sierra?"

"Who?" Silas frowns.

I admit it. Deep down, some petty part of me is satisfied that he didn't bother retaining her name. I'm a bitch like that.

"The fire elemental you fucked a few weeks ago," I tell him as if I couldn't care less. "According to her, at least."

He grimaces. "I don't remember details about anyone I've been with. Typically, I had to get myself fairly drunk to get through the paranoia before I could even get into bed with someone, and then I'd get out of that bed as soon as it was over just to be safe. I've certainly never brought anyone into my own dorm room." Then he pauses, frowning. "Wait. What do you mean, *according to her?* Was this girl goading you? When was this?"

He's so up in arms, it's almost amusing.

Still wrapped in the blanket from the infirmary, I venture deeper into the dorm before stopping in front of the hearth to examine the crackling fire.

"It doesn't matter. What did you want to talk to me about?"

He moves behind me, brushing some of my hair over my shoulder. We're near enough that I can smell that mild bourbon and spice aroma on him.

"I need to apologize. The wager we made was my idea. I take full blame for it."

Damn it. If I'd known this chat would be about their stupid bet, I wouldn't have agreed to come here at all. Some people believe talking about problems will lay them to rest, but I prefer the old-fashioned way—with a rope and shovel. I'd rather sleep in a coffin than talk about this ever again.

"Just forget it, Silas."

"No. I will never brush something under the rug if it has hurt you. We're discussing this."

"For the last fucking time, *drop it.*"

He pushes on anyway. "You think we were only after the prizes, but that isn't—"

I spin to glare up at him, ready to be done with this. "Look, it's not the first time someone manipulated me into bed and fucked me to get what they wanted. It's shitty, but I'll get over it, so let it go."

Silas stares at me for a solid seven seconds, unblinking. Then he snarls, baring his teeth, and—

He has fangs. Huh. Those are new.

"*What?*" he roars.

I tip my head. "Do all blood fae have retracting fangs? That's—"

"What do you mean, someone *manipulated* you into bed? Who the fuck did that to you?"

In the flickering firelight with fury and shadows dancing on his face, with pointed ears, eyes red as blood, and gleaming fangs, he truly does look like the descendant of a monster, primed and ready to kill.

Utterly gorgeous.

But such a hypocrite. As if he has the right to get mad on my behalf.

"You did," I point out coldly. "*Scútráche.*"

That's a fae insult that Lillian accidentally taught me when she was ranting about my father one day. She was scandalized when I repeated it later. It's quite a severe insult regarding overdrinking and the size of one's penis, plus a sprinkling of family shame that the fae abhor.

That takes Silas aback. He drags both hands through his hair, tugging and mussing the curls as he takes a deep breath to calm down. When he speaks again, the fangs are nowhere to be found.

"No. I wasn't manipulating you. None of us were." He looks at me, vulnerability replacing the fury and softening his features. "I made that bet because there's something I needed. It only hinged on you because wanting you is the only thing we four have ever shared."

I recall what he mentioned in the Matched Ball and arch a brow. "This thing you needed. Was it the Frost ledgers or the dragon scales?"

Silas opens his mouth, closes it, and looks away with a sigh.

He's probably not sharing because he doesn't trust me. That's understandable, but it's still irritating that he won't tell me why it was crucial for him to win a bet where nailing me was the determining factor. So although his help with tracking down Kenzie and the changeling would be great, I decide I'll handle shit on my own instead of putting up with this.

I turn to leave, but Silas holds up an arm to stop me.

"Stay."

"Make me."

Silas's jaw clenches, and then he does the last thing I expect.

He gets on his knees.

10

MAVEN

Seeing Silas on his knees immediately does something to me. Something that heats my entire body.

"I'm not letting you go anywhere until you know how truly sorry I am that you ever had reason to doubt my motivation for being with you," he murmurs, gazing up at me. "I need you to forgive me, Maven."

It's far too warm in here. I can't seem to think straight as I stare down at the sharply dressed blood fae in front of me, whose intense, blood-red, pleading focus is all on me.

It's...heady.

"You want my forgiveness?" I whisper. "Fine. Beg for it."

"Please—"

I drop the blanket and slide my lace-gloved hand over his mouth to muffle him, tingles spreading as I feel the warmth of his lips through the thin fabric. Something has come over me—I'm mad, but...I also need this. This power over him. I want it enough that I ignore the shiver down my spine at touching someone else, even through lace.

"No. Your mouth can do better than that. Beg me without words, Silas."

His red gaze flares with hunger, devouring my body and

lingering on my toplessness before stopping at the apex of my thighs. A thrill spreads from my hand to my chest when he licks his lips slowly, his tongue brushing against the fabric on my palm. I remove my hand, feeling nearly lightheaded when Silas immediately presses me back until the backs of my knees hit the fainting couch—and then I'm seated, and he's kneeling between my legs.

His eyes arrest mine as he places a lingering kiss against the skin on the side of my exposed knee, sending more goosebumps rippling.

"Are you all right with me touching you like this, *sangfluir?*"

"I will be if your apology is impressive enough," I murmur as a challenge, reaching out to tangle my fingers in his soft curls.

When I decide to fist his hair, twisting hard, Silas's eyes slip shut, and he grunts softly. One of his hands pushes up my dress, but he pauses when he feels the strap around my thigh where two particularly fun daggers are sheathed.

When he sees them, his lips quirk up. His eyes meet mine, shining with dark pride.

"So vicious. *Naen mahk.*"

In fae, that means good girl. I am most decidedly *not* a good girl.

Yet, for some reason, hearing Silas call me that in his husky, low voice makes heat curl down my spine.

His head disappears beneath the skirts before his hot tongue drags roughly in precisely the right spot. I gasp, and my eyes slam shut.

Gods. That feels so good.

But that sharp pleasure recedes as Silas takes his time exploring me with his mouth, gentle and methodical in the way he licks and sucks. It's such a slow, thorough approach, and it turns me hot all over as I continue tugging at his hair, panting as I try to direct his head where I want it.

When I tug his hair more insistently, frustrated that his tongue keeps swirling teasingly close to the spot near my clit that drives me wild without ever touching it, he hums and gently nips at my clit with his lips. That drives another spike of pleasure through me, and I curse. I want to fall over that glorious edge that I've only experienced twice in my life, and at this rate, it will take too long for him to get me there.

"Do that again," I demand breathlessly.

And the asshole blood fae...*doesn't*.

Instead, he returns to his languid pace, his tongue sliding ever so slightly into me before he kisses all around. Frustration and need course through me. But when I try to grind against his face, Silas pulls away just enough to deprive me of the friction I want.

This time, my swearing is more creative as that pleasure recedes again.

And I realize he's *teasing* me. Taunting me. Showing me that he can give me what I want, but only when he chooses to. He's in control. Abruptly, it makes all that hot need feel somehow... humiliating.

I hate it.

I've never felt sexually embarrassed before. Hell, I've never explored *anything* sexually before, but for reasons I can't explain, I suddenly just want to get out of here and never talk to this asshole again.

I push at Silas's head to try to get away from him.

"Never fucking mind," I huff angrily.

But his hand locks around my knee to keep me in place as he lifts his head from under my dress. His brow furrows deeply when he sees my stormy expression.

"Did I do something wrong?"

When I once again try to close my legs to get up and leave, Silas braces his hands on my thighs, a determined expression taking over his face.

"No running this time. Talk to me. Is it that you dislike edging?"

"That's what that was?" I make a face. "Never do that again."

"If you're thinking of *again* with me, I must have done something right. Tell me why you disliked it so I can do better."

My body is starting to hyperfocus on his hands on my bare thighs, and I squirm. Recognizing my discomfort, Silas removes his touch but waits expectantly.

I look away, trying to find the right words and choosing to keep them honest. "Pleasure is a luxury I haven't had until recently. Now I'm curious about things I've missed out on, but...I want to experience them on my own terms, I suppose."

Silas's expression softens, and he nods. "I think you dislike not being in control. We're similar in that way. But right now, you call all the shots, *sangfluir*. So, if you're frustrated, take it out on me. Tell me exactly what you want."

Take it out on me.

I debate for a moment, getting over the urge to leave and instead standing as my curiosity gets the best of me.

"Strip for me."

Silas stands, too, shrugging out of his suit and unbuttoning his shirt as he holds my gaze. He doesn't question how much to take off, instead getting wholly naked and casting his clothes and shoes aside. For a moment, I feel a flush of pleasure seeing him completely nude like this. It's almost mesmerizing the way the firelight highlights his beautiful, lean muscles and the subtle throb of his stiff, eager cock.

The cock that looks kind of too big for my mouth.

Only one way to find out.

I clear my throat. "I want to try something. Sit."

He obeys, his eyes tracking my every movement. "What do you want to—"

He cuts off in a sharp groan when I kneel and drag my tongue against the tip of his cock. It's warm and surprisingly...*nice* to feel in my mouth. When I pull away and see a bead of liquid well up, I wrap my lips around the tip, swirling my tongue to taste him.

Silas tries to muffle his next moan by biting his hand, his thighs flexing and his head falling back in pleasure. He slips into fae as he moans that it feels incredible.

I like that reaction far more than I expected.

Curious to see what else I can do to this man just by licking and teasing his glistening erection, I bob my head, humming at the strangely pleasant sensation as his hardness glides against my tongue. It's not like anything I've ever experienced. It doesn't set off any anxiety about his skin on mine because I have nothing to compare it to. As I take more of him into my mouth, I feel a steady throb between my own legs.

Mystery solved. I now understand why people suck cock.

"*Sangfluir*," he breathes raggedly after another minute of my content exploring. "I'm...I'm supposed to be the one begging for your forgiveness, but—godsdamn it, your perfect, filthy little fucking *mouth*..."

Sliding off with a soft pop, I stand. The needy ache between my thighs is now so strong that, for a moment, I'm tempted to straddle him, shove his cock inside me, and ride him until I come undone.

But I meant it earlier when I told him he wasn't fucking me tonight.

And he's right. This is about his apology.

"Scoot down to the floor."

Silas does as I say, sliding down the couch until he's sitting on the floor, but his head is still on the seat. Perfect. I straddle his head, my knees on either side as I grip the back of the fainting couch.

"You can go back to apologizing now," I whisper breathlessly, grinding against his face slightly.

"Gods above, forgive me," he growls against my entrance.

And then he fucking *feasts*.

I cry out, my hips reflexively bucking away from the onslaught. But Silas grips my hips and pulls me back to continue mercilessly eating me out, licking and sucking and attacking that *perfect* spot. In between making me scream, he groans his apology again and again, both in English and in fae, groveling between my thighs as he slowly unravels me.

He's so ravenous that for a few long minutes, my mind blanks out as all the delicious sensations wash over me. And then, out of nowhere, a powerful release slams into me.

I go breathless, squeezing my eyes shut in agonized pleasure as my insides clench and tingles sweep down to my toes. I lose track of time, of space—and of my mouth, since I'm pretty damn sure I'm swearing up a storm, but I can't be sure since my head is floating.

"Fuck. *Gods,* stop, Silas—it's too much," I whisper finally, my nerves sparking with every flick of his tongue in a way that I can't handle anymore.

He kisses my clit one more time before letting me go. Immediately, I fall sideways onto the couch, trying to catch my breath. He sits up and licks my wetness from his lips, his scarlet eyes predatory as they drag over me.

"Gods above, how I crave you," he murmurs. "You have no idea."

I glance down at his still-leaking cock. "You'll change your mind when I offer you no relief."

He smirks and stands, bracing one hand on the back of the couch behind me so I'm looking up at his face.

"Keep your eyes on me, *sangfluir.* That's all I need."

And then he wraps his hand around himself and strokes roughly. My mouth parts as I watch him, the way he works his hard cock, his breathing increasing as pained bliss crosses his face. It's so fucking erotic that I hold my breath, wanting to see him fall over the edge.

When he does, it's with a shudder as he groans my name—and I gasp as his come paints my tits again and again while he continues pumping himself.

Gods. Why did I like that so much?

Finally sated, Silas surprises me by dropping back to his knees and pressing his lips to mine. The kiss is luxurious, and when he pulls back, we gaze at each other.

But my curiosity is building again, and without looking away from him, I swipe my index finger through his release and raise it to my lips for another taste.

Silas's gaze turns searing, and he groans brokenly.

"You'll be the death of me," he whispers in fae, closing in for another kiss.

That's what I'm afraid of.

But our kiss is interrupted when someone knocks on the door, startling us both. Silas huffs and stands, grabbing a dark bathrobe from its spot on a hanger by the door to his bathroom.

I go from feeling dazed in an afterglow to battling amusement.

Because of course, he has a bathrobe like any melodramatic fae on the brink of madness might. It somehow makes perfect sense for him.

Silas ties the front of it and throws the door open, snapping, "What is it?"

"Oh! Mr. Crane, I d—do apologize," Mr. Gibbons sputters.

I'm sure the bushy-browed legacy must be turning ten shades of red, realizing he's interrupted Silas's *extracurricular* activities.

Even though I know he can't see me, I grab the blanket from the floor and wrap it back around myself. As I do, my attention moves back to the wetness still left between my thighs from Silas eating my soul out.

And touching me.

The events of the last half hour start to sink in, and my body breaks into a cold sweat as I shut my eyes.

Safe. That touch was safe. Don't freak out.

My nervous system doesn't get the memo, and now all I can think about are maggots. Those corpse-eating worms terrorized me when I was younger, and so they were incorporated into my conditioning—especially when it came to avoiding physical touch. I feel like their wriggling phantom bodies are all over me again, trying to burrow into my flesh.

My stomach clenches dangerously.

"What couldn't have waited until the morning?" Silas seethes.

"W—well, it seems that no one in your quintet reported your chosen emphasis during the Matched Ball...and you see, at the end of the celebration, I was—"

He starts rambling about how he searched for Silas during the dance to get our emphasis because he wants to ensure we're put in classes with the best professors. But I'm not paying attention as I start swallowing repeatedly to try to keep bile from rising in my throat.

Damn it. I need *something* to distract me.

A shower. I need a shower.

I stagger to my feet. Silas is still standing with the door barely ajar so the interim headmaster can't see inside, but he glances over his shoulder at me and immediately tenses.

"Combat," he snaps at Mr. Gibbons before slamming the door and rushing to my side.

"Damn me to hell. I forgot that you have…" He shakes his head, changing whatever he was about to say. "Tell me how to fix this."

Shaving my skin off would be a good start.

But since I doubt he'll take me up on that, I sidestep him to hurry into his bathroom, locking the door. As soon as I'm alone, I strip and stumble into the shower, turning it on and breathing out a sigh of relief when the sharp cold of the spray eases my body out of the fight or flight mode that was crippling me a moment ago.

Several minutes later, I'm no longer nauseous. My eyes feel heavy as I wrap myself in a thick towel. When I emerge from the bathroom, I find Silas sitting on the edge of the fainting couch, a bottle of hard liquor in one hand as he glares into the fire. His bleeding crystal is clutched tightly in his other hand.

"Tell me why you can't stand touch, *sangfluir*. I just need to know."

I change the topic without batting an eye because there is no way in hell I'm about to give him a post-coital sob story. That's way too intimate, and already, I'm having a hard time not taking the bottle away from him to try and soothe his inner demons myself.

"Something happened during my episode," I surmise. "Something the three of you were eager to keep me from noticing. Tell me exactly what I missed."

Silas's attention flicks down to the scar on my chest that's just visible above the top of the towel before he looks away. Yet even that tiny movement makes me tense.

What does he know?

"If you're not answering questions tonight, neither am I," he mutters. "But now that you've forgiven me, tell me what you wanted my help wi—"

"I never officially forgave you," I point out because a little lighthearted torment never hurt anybody.

He lifts the bottle to his lips and takes a swig before rubbing his face. "You are the most stubborn creature in existence."

"You have no idea."

My stubbornness is what made me what I am today. That, and my sense of focus, which is why I quickly get back to business.

"I need you to perform two tracking spells. One to find Kenzie and one to find the person who poisoned me. You can use their dried blood from the clothes I was wearing."

He examines me curiously. "You can't cast the spell yourself?"

"Not at the moment."

To my relief, Silas doesn't ask follow-up questions and instead nods. "I can track them. As long as I get to drain the life out of the one who poisoned you."

Intriguing. But as much as I'd like to see how Silas uses those surprise fangs, I give him a dark smile.

"No. But you can watch me kill them. Deal?"

The corner of his lips twitch. "Very well."

"I'll go get the bloodied clothes," I tell him, turning toward the door.

"You want to do the spells tonight?"

He's surprised. That's understandable since it's now well past midnight. But every minute that ticks by is another minute where that changeling could spill my secret. And even though I know Kenzie is alive, I don't know what condition she's in or where she is. I need answers, even if my limbs feel heavy and my stomach is starting to complain that I forgot to put anything in it today.

As if Silas sees how tired I am, he moves quickly to step in front of me when I reach for his door handle.

"We'll do the spells first thing in the morning."

"I told you this was time-sensitive."

His crimson irises are unbearably tender. "It wasn't a suggestion, Maven. You're tired. That episode clearly took a toll on you. Rest so you'll be better able to help Kenzie once we track her down."

He's annoyingly logical.

"Fine," I grumble, reaching for the door handle again.

"Sleep here tonight," Silas blurts. When he sees me start to shake my head, he adds on quickly, "You'll have the bed to yourself. I sleep on the couch most of the time, anyway. Besides, the Immortal Quintet made it clear that those violating the curfew will be caught and punished. And..."

"And?"

Vulnerability returns to his face. "I just...want you here. Please."

Godsdamn it, this cutthroat blood fae needs to stop showing me his soft side. It's too endearing.

He has a point about the Immortal Quintet, though. I don't like the idea of being brought to them in the middle of the night, half-naked in a ripped-up dress for interrogation if I'm caught.

The solution? I'll simply not get caught.

Because there's no way I can sleep here. I'm supposed to be platonic with them. No matter what Baelfire said, I can't *actually* be their keeper and have the things they think they want with me.

I slip around Silas, open the door, and give him a genuinely apologetic half-smile over my shoulder before he can stop me.

"See you in the morning."

Kenzie isn't at Everbound.

But the changeling is, somewhere.

That's all we managed to get out of Silas's efforts since, according to him, the changeling is utilizing an amulet that throws off any tracking spells. He still doesn't know it was changeling blood he was casting with, but at least now I know that the monster I'm hunting is still trapped inside the castle. Which means I just need to hunt it down.

The trouble is finding the time to do that since classes have started.

We found our class schedule posted outside the dining hall earlier. Now Silas, Baelfire, and I are on our way to Fiend Studies

101, with Crypt trailing behind us in Limbo. The halls of Everbound are filled with the stares, whispers, and tension of legacies on edge. They stick to groups, both matched and unmatched, and size each other up at every chance. The air is thick with the possibility of death at any moment.

It's positively sinister. I wish I could enjoy it more fully, but I'm drawing too much attention.

Dozens of pairs of eyes track my every move since I'm supposed to be the keeper of four of the most powerful legacies here. I'm a target for all the competitive monster spawn here, and it's making Baelfire and Silas look like they want to stab someone.

Which reminds me.

"After class, I want Pierce," I mutter quietly enough that no other legacies will overhear.

Baelfire shoots me a sharp look already tinged with jealousy. "Pierce? Who the fuck is that? Is some other guy trying to—"

"My dagger," I clarify.

Silas pauses, and I don't miss their shared glance before he responds. "You had other daggers strapped to your thigh last night. Just use those."

I clench my jaw. Why would he keep my favorite weapon from me?

Meanwhile, Baelfire misses a step, his golden eyes darting between us. "Back the fuck up. Her thigh, *last night*? As in, after I left? Did you two...?"

I don't bother acknowledging the question he was about to ask since my face already feels warm enough remembering a certain someone's ridiculously talented tongue. Silas just looks smug as hell.

"You fucker. You could've at least invited me to watch," Bael huffs, pouting.

"I didn't take you for a voyeur."

"Normally, no. But it's *Maven*. You think I'd willingly miss all those sexy sounds she makes when she comes?"

"They were delectable," Silas smirks. "As was she. I now fully understand your desire to be smothered by Maven. If we hadn't been interrupted, I would have kept my face between her thighs all night."

Holy fucking gods. Are they seriously having this conversation in broad daylight?

Baelfire swears harshly, shoving Silas's shoulder. "You're a godsdamned asshole."

"You're *both* godsdamned assholes," I inform them, pretending like my neck and face aren't currently on fire. "And we're still platonic."

They both snort at that, which makes me sigh heavily. I don't get it. They were furious with my antics at the Matched Ball. I came so close to telling them about the inconvenient little fact that they can't get attached to my heart because it was ripped out of my chest years ago.

But then my episode happened, I woke up, and they were suddenly full steam ahead.

I glance tentatively up at Baelfire, who immediately winks and mouths, *Tonight, it's my turn.*

They figured something out about me. I'm sure of it.

So why the fuck are they acting like *this?* Like they…want me? They can't possibly, not if they know the truth.

Right?

I shake my head at myself. Even if they could get over what I am, where I came from, and my purpose, it doesn't change the fact that being with me would be gambling everything about their futures. I can't promise them anything because I have to look out for my own first.

And even if walking through the halls with them at my sides like this feels so right…they're not mine. I can't let them be.

We pass a roped-off corridor where faculty members use magic to lift blood out of the stones, a sign that other legacies have already started picking off their competition. Finally, we round a corner and enter the massive auditorium-style classroom with a vaulted ceiling where our first class as a quintet will be held.

Since our emphasis is combat, we have a very straightforward schedule. There are two classes in the mornings—Fiend Studies and Advanced Combat Theory. After that, it's all physical combat training. Alternating at the end of every other week, we'll have Field Testing, which, as I understand it, consists of tossing legacies into an inescapable maze deep in Everbound Forest, where we'll be left to live or die at the mercy of some of the Divide's most fearsome creatures.

It's supposed to be brutal.

I can't wait.

But my secret excitement fizzles, and I stop dead in my tracks when I spot the gorgeous ice elemental sitting in the upper left corner of the auditorium. His stark white-blond hair makes him impossible to miss as he sits in his typical, tasteful professor's clothing, watching the snow fall outside the window.

I was just concerned. Don't mistake it for caring.

Yet I can't unsee how shattered he'd looked when he saw what his words did to me in that inn.

I don't want to sit anywhere near him. But...I also do.

Ugh. This is why feelings should be locked away indefinitely.

Silas is giving a death stare to anyone who passes too close to us as they enter the classroom, but Baelfire catches my eye with a warm smile.

"We don't have to sit with that ice-shitter if you don't want to, baby."

Professor Crowley, my old Introduction to Runes professor, strolls through the door and makes a beeline for the whiteboard at the front of the room. Over his shoulder, he calls out, "Take your seats. All quintets must sit together. Quickly, now."

Bael makes a face. "Damn. Spoke too soon."

I keep my face blank as I start up the stairs toward where Everett is sitting. But my focus is on the wrong thing because as we pass another quintet's row, a smirking legacy kicks out her leg to catch me in the back of the knee just as I take a step. I lurch forward and manage to catch myself on my hands, but not before my head smacks loudly off the corner of another desk.

Other legacies break out in gasps, laughter, and whispers.

The bump on my head hurts, but what hurts more is the fact that I was too focused on Everett to see that coming. What an amateur mistake. It's a good thing that blunder just plays right into the quiet, weak wallflower reputation I've crafted for myself.

Only a second has passed, and I fully plan on getting up and walking it off without drawing more attention.

But Crypt abruptly materializes, grabs the girl by her ponytail, and vanishes with her. In the next second, she reappears—at the height of the very tall ceiling, screaming in abject terror before her body hits the stone floor at the front of the classroom with a loud crack.

11

CRYPT

THE SOUND of her skull cracking on the stone is immensely satisfying.

Maven and I appear to be the only ones of that opinion. From Limbo, where I float high above the other legacies, I glance over and catch the tiny smirk on her face that she quickly hides as she gets to her feet, brushes herself off, and ignores Crane and Decimus fussing over her.

Everyone else is either still in shock or shouting. The quintet who just lost their idiotic match has gone pale and sickly at the sight of the blood quickly pooling around her broken head.

"DeLune," the professor says sternly, his brow furrowed as he scans the air as if I'm also about to drop myself from this height.

When Maven sits, with Crane and Decimus sitting between her and Frost, I drift over and take the aisle seat beside her. I'd like to stay unseen longer to continue terrorizing the legacies who are scanning the room in acute panic, but severe pain wracks my bones, and I quickly slip out of Limbo while hiding my grimace. The effects of moving back and forth between planes too often feel far worse in Limbo, and I'm out of *reverium* to take the familiar edge off. So, I suppose I'll be attending this class in the mortal realm.

Gently, I brush some of Maven's hair aside so I can examine where she hit her head, feeling a wave of satisfaction when she doesn't push my hand away. She doesn't acknowledge me, either, as if choosing to pretend nothing happened as she watches the flummoxed professor below.

My keeper isn't bleeding, but I'd still like to resurrect that bitch and kill her again for good measure.

"DeLune," the caster says again at the front of the room.

I look at him. "Problem, Professor?"

"Killing is prohibited while classes are in session."

"Oh, dear me, whatever have I done?" I drawl.

He's exasperated. Of course, he is. After all, he may be able to punish these legacies, save perhaps Frost, but there is no controlling me. All manner of harsh forms of punishment were attempted when I was younger, but I made sure everyone knew that nothing and no one could discipline me. Whenever they applied pressure, I merely stopped caring or got even.

"Perhaps I should have your keeper clean up your mess alone as punishment," he suggests, raising a brow.

Although the threat doesn't seem to bother Maven, Decimus growls, and the sharp chill that fills the air tells me Frost is equally annoyed, even if he's feigning disinterest.

"She hurt our keeper before you explained the classroom rules," Silas points out. "He just responded to the threat. I highly suggest dropping this matter and moving on, Crowley."

Good gods. Now *Crane* is defending my actions?

This newfound camaraderie is too strange. I much prefer getting his eye to twitch and watching him descend further into madness.

Oh well.

I blow Crane a kiss to try to get a rise out of him, but he ignores me as the professor rubs his face, appearing eager for this class to be over.

"Fine. Just get the body out, someone."

The dead girl's quintet quickly gets to it, their faces ashen—except one of them, who glares viciously in our direction. They carry the body out, and I take the time to survey the rest of the room. I spot a few quintets side-eying me, but they look away if I look at them directly.

"There will be no *more* violence, maiming, killing, or, gods forbid, *cell phones* in this classroom," the professor snaps. "I don't care that communications are under a magic chokehold, just keep those damn contraptions out of my sight."

"Amen," Maven mutters under her breath, making me laugh quietly.

Crane and Decimus also look amused, and I note that even though he acts bored, Frost's gaze keeps flicking to our keeper as if her presence draws him as intensely as it calls to me.

Poor, pitiful tosser.

Still, if he ever hurts Maven again, unintentionally or not, I'll tear him to shreds.

The professor moves on quickly, announcing that for the first two weeks, he will cover all the monsters and creatures we will be fighting at the Divide if we survive until graduation. Typically, I would tune it out and observe Maven to my black heart's content.

But now, I share a small glance with Crane and Decimus as the professor starts his lecture on Nether creatures. Anything about the Nether is worth learning about twice over because now we know that Maven, against all odds, came from that cesspit.

"Now," the professor begins, looking over the class. "Let's see how many types of shadow fiends you can list off the tops of your heads."

Immediately, students offer their input. Wraiths, ghouls, the Undead, banshees, phantoms. A tall shifter sitting two rows in front of us raises his hand.

"There are still demons in the Nether, right? Do they get into the Divide?"

The professor nods. "Quite frequently, unfortunately. Many of them find ways to slip into the mortal realm and blend in amongst humans. Not many other full-blooded monsters or shadow fiends can do that—save changelings, perhaps."

Maven huffs so slightly that it's almost unnoticeable.

Another student raises their hand. "One of my moms died in the

Divide, and they told me it was because of a shade. What the fuck is a shade, anyway?"

The professor scratches his bald head, his gaze moving to me briefly. "Ah, yes, well…those are fairly rare, as are wisps. They're quite dangerous, but they aren't actually classified as shadow fiends because they are native to Limbo, where they are typically guarded."

"Guarded by who?" the same legacy asks.

When the professor's gaze slips to me again, I promise him a slow, brutal death with my eyes if he draws any attention to me. The unique nature of my curse isn't widely known, but he is clearly too in the know for my liking.

He clears his throat and transitions easily, giving a non-answer before moving on, but I notice Maven studying me. She's sharp, my dark little darling, so I'm not surprised she picked up on that nonverbal exchange.

"How's your head, love?" I ask quietly, only for her ears.

"Better than hers ended up."

I smile, and my heart stops when she grins back, pure mischief and morbid humor sparkling in her eyes. It's fast, and she quickly composes herself before tuning back into the professor's lecture. But I keep staring at her because gods above, every tiny piece of herself that she drip feeds me only fuels the obsession.

I need more—all of her, every haunting puzzle piece, and I must find a way to make her need me just as badly. So badly that she'll let me into her head and her bed every night.

I pause. There's a thought. Maven was clearly frustrated with her body's reactions to physical touch, but phobias are in the psyche. Which, for me, is somewhat malleable. Maybe I could offer her some reprieve from whatever makes her fear skin contact.

Subconscious therapy, if you will.

The idea consumes me until class ends. As students begin rising from their seats, I decide I'll pull Maven aside to discuss this with her. I also must let her know that her friend's candy-floss-colored aura was nowhere to be found within Everbound when I searched last night.

She'll be disappointed, but I can offer her comfort however she likes. I've never attempted to comfort someone before outside of weaving pleasant dreams, but I imagine either an orgasm or a random act of violence will cheer her up.

Both things I am more than happy to provide.

But before I can lead her to a private alcove somewhere, a profound silence sweeps across the classroom as Engela Zuma steps through the door, her gaze locking on mine at once. Of all the members of the Immortal Quintet, she's the one I've interacted with the least throughout my life. She motions for me to follow her.

"Uh oh. Someone's in trouble with Daddy," Decimus mutters. "This can't be good."

I reach around Maven to flick the shifter's eyeball hard enough that he yelps before I descend the stairs to see what Engela wants. It's satisfying how the other legacies part for me, eager to get out of my way. When I reach Engela, she motions for me to follow her down the hall.

I suppose this means I'm about to have another not-so-pleasant chat with her, just as I did during the Matched Ball. She's the one who had held me up after finding me smoking in one of the school's hidden alcoves. She'd turned much of my body to stone so she could interrogate me about the peculiarly topsy-turvy state of Melvolin's office when they'd arrived. She hadn't mentioned his death but said it looked like my handiwork in there. I'd lied easily, insisting I knew nothing about it but sincerely hoped Melvolin was pissed about the mess, whoever caused it.

As we pass through the halls, I sense slight tremors in Limbo and know it's because of all the wisps.

Most people don't understand much about the nature of the little balls of light. They're ghosts of dreams, echoes of a dead person's subconscious that linger in Limbo long after the spirits they were once attached to have passed into the Beyond. Wisps are also carrion eaters, which is rather convenient whenever I have a body to dispose of without a trace.

But in large groups, they pose a significant threat to the mortal realm.

All day and all night, I've observed more and more wisps pop into existence inside the walls of Everbound. With the no-killing ban lifted, legacies have been whittling down weak competition, and the wisps that remain can't leave the castle thanks to the powerful wards the Immortal Quintet placed even in Limbo.

It's only a matter of time before the amount of wisps starts causing trouble for everyone here.

Engela is as taciturn as usual as she takes me to the headmaster's office, and when the doors close behind us, all of them are here. Including Somnus, who lounges on Melvolin's sofa while Natalya taps her fingernails against the desk. Iker broods in the corner, his forked tongue flicking in and out as if he's agitated.

Engela locks the door behind us, and it promptly turns into an indestructible stone under her touch.

"Ah, so this is one of *those* meetings," I muse. "Lucky me."

At least Melvolin is no longer around to paralyze me with his magic. I detest each monster in this room, but aside from Somnus, Melvolin had been by far the worst.

As always, when we cross paths, Natalya wrinkles her nose as if she has never seen anything so offensive in her nearly thousand years of existence.

"Let's make this short, mongrel. Duty calls, so you will leave Everbound long enough to clean up the mess."

By *mess*, she must mean a Limbo-caused massacre that paints them in a bad light. Otherwise, they wouldn't bother calling me here and demanding that I leave my keeper.

But leaving Maven's side is out of the question, so I fix the vampyr with a cold smile. "Have your neutered servant take care of it."

Somnus's lip curls in contempt at my description of him. It's always a joy getting under his skin. "Don't speak to her like that, whoreson."

I roll my eyes. "Don't pretend to give a chimera's scaly ass for her. I know the truth."

The truth is, Somnus loathes Natalya. Perhaps she cared for him at one point, but after learning of his long history of unfaithfulness and my existence, she threw a tantrum and permanently maimed his wings before she killed my mother.

All my life, I've witnessed them make each other miserable. It would be poetically sweet, except it's mostly obnoxious.

Somnus's nostrils flare. "Watch your tongue—"

"Or else what? You'll kill me?"

Thanks to my curse, he won't, and he knows it. My smile widens as his face darkens in anger. But Natalya's voice is cold as she stands, her gaze penetrating.

"Or else I'll kill your keeper."

My smile fades.

Never before has there been a weakness they could take advantage of. They could twist my arm and break my bones as many times as they liked, but for all the threats and curses, their attempts to command me were as effective as trying to bottle starlight.

But *Maven*...

I can't let them anywhere near her, or they may figure out she's from the Nether. Thank gods that Natalya's eyes haven't glowed since I stepped through that door. I can't have her picking the truth about my keeper straight from my head.

Pushing all thoughts of Maven aside just to be safe, I tuck my hand into my jacket pocket and fiddle with my lighter, wishing I had *reverium* on hand to take away the aching throb of my joints.

They're choosing to play hardball, so I make a final attempt—because being parted from my obsession, even to tend to the necessities of my curse, would be torturous. It's already aggravating to be away from her for the length of this meeting.

"You don't want me anywhere outside these walls," I warn. "After all, I doubt the Legacy Council sanctioned any of the changes you've made at Everbound, let alone the lockdown. They're already growing wary of your tyrannical ways. I know you love your political games, but what do you suppose they would do if I spilled on your little tantrum?"

My guess that the Legacy Council has no idea they're here proves to be correct when they all growl and snarl at me. Well, all but Engela, who remains silent as a rock behind me.

Iker blurs to my side faster than I'm prepared for, slamming me against the stone wall hard enough that I taste blood. As a pure monster shifter, he's far faster than most.

Natalya prowls around Melvolin's desk like a lioness closing in for the kill. "You dare threaten me, mongrel? When I could snap your weak little keeper's neck with barely a flick of my wrist?"

I grit my teeth as Iker shoves me against the wall again, his forked tongue flicking up to wet one of his pale yellow eyes. When I slip into Limbo to get away, Somnus is already waiting there and drags me back into the mortal realm, baring his fangs in pure hatred.

I'm strong, but I'm not a pure monster. They are and always have been frustratingly stronger than I am, especially when they're working together like this.

"Give us permission to kill his little bitch. It would teach this wretch a lesson for once," the monster who fathered me hisses.

I go still at that. Natalya's lips curl up triumphantly as she slinks to a stop just in front of me, enjoying the sight of me pinned by her quintet members.

"Not yet. Just look how pliant he is with her at our disposal! Now then, *Nightmare Prince*. If you do as I say, keep your mouth shut, clean up the mess, and return promptly so we can keep watch on you, I give you my word that you won't return to find your keeper's head moldering on a spike for all to see. Are we agreed?"

That visual makes my mood quickly veer towards murder, and Limbo starts to seep into this room as it reacts. Natalya just scoffs at the sight of our hair and clothes starting to waft as gravity loosens its hold.

"Agreed," I smile thinly back, even though I've fantasized about killing her more times than I can count.

Unfortunately, killing any member of the Immortal Quintet is outside of my wheelhouse. Now and then, highly trained, hired assassins even stronger than myself have tried and failed spectacularly at dethroning the monsters who reign over the Four Houses.

Which makes it even more impressive if Maven did, in fact, kill Melvolin. I'd like to kiss her for ridding the world of him. And if she didn't kill him, I'd still like to kiss her.

Natalya tuts and pouts at Iker, her favorite. "I don't believe him."

"Prevent him from speaking, just in case," Iker suggests without missing a beat. "Call it a punishment for daring to threaten you, my sweet Natalya."

I roll my eyes so hard it hurts my brain. The words *sweet* and *Natalya* should never be uttered in the same room. To say she's a bloodsucking, mind-leeching hyena with the emotional intelligence of a screaming, tantrum-throwing toddler would be more accurate but still an understatement.

Her face lights up as she giggles and practically prances back to Melvolin's desk. I grind my teeth and resist fighting. The more I fight, the more they'll continue to threaten Maven.

Resigning myself to the fact that I'll have to be parted from her out of necessity, at least for a couple of days until I can get back, I quickly form another plan. One that will hopefully give my beautiful keeper a semblance of peace at night until I can tend to her nightmares myself. All it will take is nimble fingers and a moment of Somnus being distracted.

That moment comes quickly enough when a very gleeful Natalya returns with a wickedly sharp knife and a vial of brightly glowing liquid. My muscles tense as I recognize it. Liquid bronze. A potion Melvolin perfected long ago and thoroughly enjoyed using on me.

Just as fae are weak to iron, vampires fall to oak, and all types of shifters can't heal from silver, bronze is every siphon's weakness. Our accelerated healing is put in a chokehold when bronze is involved.

This is about to hurt like fucking hell.

Though I tell myself to hold still to get this over with quicker, I can't help instinctively struggling as Engela helps Natalya pry open my mouth to cut out my tongue—and *Syntyche's scythe*, it's painful. Iker and Somnus are still pinning me tightly to the stone wall. Just before Natalya pours Melvolin's potion into my mouth, I swipe what I need from Somnus's front suit pocket without his noticing and tuck it up the left sleeve of my leather jacket.

Pickpocketing has always come easy to me.

But then the fucking *agonizing* liquid gushes into my mouth and down my throat, halting the way my body is trying to mend my tongue, and I momentarily black out from the pain. When I come to, I'm slumped on the floor, coughing up blood. I immediately sense the lack of tongue in my mouth and grimace.

It stings like hell. It also stings that all remaining members of the Immortal Quintet are standing above me, leering, watching me struggle to get to my feet. Natalya giggles and tosses my tongue over her shoulder. Somnus looks like this is the best day he's had in a long while. I flip him the bird for good measure as I finally stand.

Thanks to the liquid bronze, my tongue is going to regenerate painfully slowly—something siphons can do with missing bones, skin, muscles, and ligaments. I suspect it will take a full two days to recover enough to speak, which is precisely why Natalya did this. She knows I won't waste time outside of Everbound reporting them to the Legacy Council once I heal, not when I need to return to Maven to make sure she's safe.

Speaking of which…

I glare at Natalya, willing her to read my mind for once.

Her eyes glow blue just as I push the thought at her. *Let me leave a note.*

Asking this immortal bitch for any favors sits like acid in my stomach, especially when she giggles and reaches up to pat my head condescendingly.

"A note? How utterly soft you've gone over such a weakling!"

I certainly wouldn't describe myself as *soft* when I'm thinking of Maven. My stunning keeper makes me hard all the damn time without even being the wiser.

Hearing my thoughts, Natalya wrinkles her face. "I saw her at the ball, and I'd hardly describe *that* as stunning. But then, there's no accounting for taste. Except in this case, I suppose it makes sense—she did look rather corpse-like. Like father, like son."

It takes a miraculous level of self-control to keep my thoughts in check. But when miniature fissures in Limbo appear in the room, and everything begins to float, I know I'm dangerously close to letting my fury get the best of me.

Comparing me to Somnus has always been Natalya's favorite button to push. It's the one thing that sickens me more than anything.

But I would do *anything* for my dark little darling, so I ask Natalya again, this time politely.

After Natalya's eyes stop glowing, they "grant me the privilege" of letting me use Melvolin's stationery to leave a letter that Engela surprisingly offers to deliver. I write quickly and discreetly slip Somnus's stolen item into the envelope before sealing it. I then write three more letters addressed to the other members of my quintet.

Because if I'm going to be forced to leave Maven for any amount of time, those clueless wankstains are going to need a reminder of what I'll do to them if they let our girl come to harm.

12

MAVEN

ADVANCED COMBAT THEORY WAS A BORE. Not a single cracked skull to be found, just a petite water elemental professor giving a long-winded lecture about her favorite defense strategies. She openly glared at me several times, which I found odd until I saw the stars in her eyes whenever her gaze lingered on Everett. Which happened to be for most of the class period.

For reasons I have yet to determine, that bothered me.

Not that I blame her for staring because *everyone* stares at the gorgeous ice elemental.

He ditches our quintet immediately without looking back as soon as the lunch break starts. Silas and Baelfire say nothing about it. Come to think of it, there's been an uncharacteristic lack of barbed comments from either of them toward the ice elemental all morning.

But it's clear that, outside of necessary training, Everett wants nothing to do with me.

I remind myself that the feeling should be mutual.

I'd hoped lunch would allow me enough time to search for the changeling. Instead, we're given fifteen minutes to eat in the awkwardly silent dining hall under the watchful eyes of big, burly legacies. They were clearly brought here to act as the Immortal Quintet's muscle whenever they can't be bothered to show up. These unofficial wardens are full-fledged legacies—I even see keeper emblems on a couple of the strangers' necks or peeking out from their sleeves.

Their presence is making all students equally antsy. I notice Kenzie's quintet at a nearby table, and they're all glaring at the newcomers. Even Vivienne looks like she wants to use her elemental wind abilities to blast them out of this room.

Luka catches my eye and raises his eyebrows, silently asking if I've found anything about his missing keeper.

I hold up a finger to indicate I'll need more time. In return, he flips me off and goes back to his blood bag.

Baelfire scowls down at the plate in front of me. "You need to eat more than that."

All entrees for lunch today included copious amounts of meat. I'm fine with my bread and steamed vegetables, plus whatever this wobbly green substance is. I poke it tentatively with my fork, certain it isn't meant for consumption.

Silas's lips twitch. "It's called Jell-O."

"What is it made out of?" I ask, bewildered.

"Food coloring and happiness. Here, try some," Bael encourages, offering me a spoonful.

"This will shock you, but I possess the mystical ability to feed myself," I inform him.

"Come on, Mayflower. Humor me."

Damn it, his smile is too charming. Deciding to just get this over with, I slurp the wobbly block of green off his spoon and immediately choke on it, eyes watering as I splutter and shake my head.

Ew. What the hell? They actually *like* this?

"That is revolting," I decree.

Baelfire laughs at my reaction. "Good to know. I'll add it to our long, growing list of mortal enemies."

Silas also seems amused for a second before his gaze skims over the room around us, and his eye twitches. Suddenly, he winces and grips the side of his head, his breathing growing erratic.

"Silas?" I tense.

He drops his forehead to roll it back and forth on the table, muttering under his breath in nonsensical fae. Bael grimaces, glancing around as he gives the blood fae a shake.

"Not a good time to lose it, Si. People will notice. Focus on Maven."

I blink. "Why me?"

"Because you're his sunflower or whatever."

It takes me a moment to piece that one together. "*Sangfluir?*"

"Yeah, that."

Silas bangs his head on the table, growling something at no one in particular. When nearby legacies glance in our direction, a surprising wave of protectiveness sweeps over me. I quickly tangle my gloved fingers in Silas's hair and tug on the dark, wavy strands until he's forced to look up at me. His scarlet eyes are wild as they bounce around my face without recognition.

His curse really is corroding his mind away.

"*Eireach chial, thiga ais thu'ganh,*" I murmur in fae.

Come back to me, handsome lunatic.

Silas's pupils slowly dilate to normal. He stares at me, looking steadily more like himself until he reaches out to trail his fingertips over the hair beside my temple. He opens his mouth to say something, but we're interrupted by the magical tolling of the bell that tells us the lunch break is over.

Baelfire grumbles unhappily about me not eating enough as we leave the dining hall along with dozens of other legacies on their way to combat class. The class schedule indicated they would be held outside in the training fields, so everyone is murmuring with excitement at the prospect of finally setting foot outside after being cooped up for three days.

As we wait in the large corridor to be let out into the training fields, I stare down all nearby legacies one by one. They meet my gaze with varying levels of wariness, irritation, contempt, or outright offense—but it allows me to check their pupils for any signs of the changeling.

But my staring contests end too early as Coach Gallagher steps into the hall where we all wait, scratching one of his ears as he studies the group.

"The wards locking down Everbound have been extended, so now they encompass the courtyards, training fields, and all of Everbound Forest," he announces.

Several legacies clap or cheer.

"Yeah, yeah, don't get too excited," the instructor huffs. "Doesn't change the fact that we're still under lockdown and can't contact the outside world, but whatever. Today, you'll be training with the unmatched legacies who picked combat as their individual emphasis. Your quintets will each be assigned a specific location to reach within Everbound Forest. The goal is to get to your location alive as a unit, while the unmatched legacies' goal will be to pick off every matched legacy they can. Not to mention, watch out for other quintets, and I suggest guarding your keepers at all costs. Especially the weak ones, like atypical casters."

Coach Gallagher tosses me a meaningful look, which makes a few legacies laugh despite Baelfire's warning growl. The loudest chuckle comes from Brooks, the buzzed-headed, green-eyed legacy who approached us during the Matched Ball. He's standing nearby with his all-male quintet, sneering at me.

I've worked hard to be perceived as weak, so as far as I'm concerned, this is a win.

But then the temperature drops as Everett strolls into the corridor to join the rest of us, his hands in his peacoat pockets. He casts a cold look at the coach, who he clearly overheard.

"You were saying, Patrick?"

Coach Gallagher rubs the back of his neck uncomfortably. "Hey, relax, Frost. It was nothing. Just giving some friendly advice about protecting your keeper."

"That advice really isn't yours to give, considering you let your keeper get devoured by Undead within the first week you were deployed at the Divide. So watch your fucking mouth and stick to coaching."

Someone whistles low while the coach winces at the painful

memory. Other legacies subtly shuffle away from the icy professor, who stops next to me. But right away, Silas steps in between us, issuing a crimson glare that makes Everett take another step away from me with a sigh.

Odd. Is it just because he's still mad at Everett for telling me about their bet, or is this something else?

The coach gets over his verbal spanking and uses a fae charm to open the massive double doors leading out of the castle. As we approach the training fields closest to Everbound Forest, I see that the unmatched legacies who will be training with us are already out here—including Sierra and three guys who are all fawning over her as she flirts with them.

When she catches my eye, she glares savagely and draws a finger across her neck.

I smile back darkly and mouth, *How's the knee?*

Sierra's face turns red before she promptly turns her back on me.

There are a few dozen unmatched legacies out here stretching and eyeing everyone else suspiciously as they prepare for combat. As we come to a stop, I find that yet another legacy is glaring at me—Angry Girl. The silver streaks in her dark hair are vibrant in the cold winter daylight as she wrinkles her nose at me before stalking to the other side of the group.

Silas sees her retreat and arches a brow. "Do you know Amelia Lykoudis?"

I look at him sharply. "Her last name is Lykoudis?"

"Yup," Baelfire pipes up. "Her dad is the Northeast Pack alpha for wolf shifters. He was in a platonic quintet and had Amelia with a sorceress who died at the Divide a few years ago. So even though she's a caster, she was raised in a pack. Pretty fucking cool, huh?"

So *that's* why the name sounded familiar.

Damn it. First Luka, now this girl. I need to break this habit of killing off my peers' relatives.

Then again, Lykoudis was scum. I have no regrets about taking his heart, but I realize Amelia might not even know she's an orphan yet. They cut off all communications with the outside world not even twenty-four hours after I killed that shifter, so it might be days before the news of his death reaches her. She'll miss any funeral held for him.

Even though I'm the one who ended her shitty father's life, I feel kind of bad for her.

Which is fucking weird. *Why* do I keep having so many feelings? I need to get a grip. I can't afford to go soft now, not after everything I've been through.

Baelfire's attention drifts to the forest with an eager expression, as if he can't wait to get in there. "Hey, what are the odds I can go hunt something before training starts?"

Silas shakes his head. "Just hunt *during* training."

"Most of these legacies are friends of mine, you know. I'm not looking forward to having to kill them if they decide to attack," Bael grimaces, rubbing his temples. "Not that my stupid fucking dragon is going to leave it up to me."

"Your fault for bothering to make friends in the first place," Everett drawls, appearing insanely bored as he observes the coach talk with a faculty member beside a large, locked wooden chest.

Baelfire grunts before reaching out to twist the end of my ponytail between his fingertips. "Can't believe I'm saying this, but you might want to tell Crypt to stop hiding in Limbo and come out to play. We could use that psychopath, for once."

I frown, realizing I haven't sensed his presence since Engela Zuma came to get him earlier. Now that I notice his absence, it irks me.

"He's not here."

All three of them frown, too.

"Damn that impulsive fucking incubus," Silas huffs. "He's probably off eating daydreams."

I don't think that's it. I've gotten used to Crypt stalking my every move, so the fact that he isn't here right now doesn't sit right.

But he's the Nightmare Prince. He'll be fine. I'm sure he'll pop up sooner than later.

Finally, the coach turns to address everyone. "All right, we've been instructed to use weapons during this training session. In an orderly fashion, each of you needs to come pick out *one* weapon only. These aren't the best weapons in the world, but they're more than enough for practice. A little overboard if you ask me, but then, I'm not about to argue with the Immortal Quintet's requests."

If they're handing out weapons for combat on day one, it's safe to say that they want to cull the weak as quickly as possible. They're most likely expecting to find whoever killed Headmaster Hearst among the stronger, higher-ranked legacies at Everbound.

As we wait for the other excited legacies who swarm around the wooden chest, all this talk of weapons has me giving all three of my matches a serious look.

"This is the last time I'll ask nicely. Which one of you has my dagger?"

Silas makes the same face he did the last time I asked about it. Baelfire looks away, and Everett pretends like I didn't even speak.

"Use other weapons, or perhaps use your magic. That was more than potent enough when I felt it," Silas hedges.

"Why the fuck are you three acting weird about this? It belongs to me."

Baelfire gives me a pointed look, his golden eyes coaxing. "Yeah, but…we don't want anyone else here knowing that, right?"

Silas elbows him hard, and Everett looks heavenward like he's asking the gods why he has to deal with two morons.

I stare at them, putting it together as they each refuse to meet my gaze. I knew something had changed when they witnessed my last episode, but now my stomach clenches as I realize why they don't want me to have Pierce back.

Because they figured out where it's from.

Where *I'm* from.

Before I can process that, the faculty member who was just speaking to the coach approaches with a cautious smile.

"I have your location assignment. Your quintet must find the ancient cemetery on the far west side of Everbound Forest. You will find a circle of light there, and when you step into it, you will be transported back here. Please stick closely to your quintet, as we anticipate losing many legacies in this exercise. The other legacies will be quite aggressive, I'm afraid. And...I regret to tell you that we ran out of weapons already."

Silas clenches his jaw, but Everett nods. "Thank you, Shayla."

"O—of course, Mr. Frost." She blushes furiously before moving on to the next group.

"Damn it," Baelfire huffs, turning to me. "You're not leaving our side, understand? My dragon and I are both already pissed as hell that people will be after you. Going in unarmed—"

"I'm always armed," I reply coolly, brushing past him to stand with everyone else at the forest's edge. "So, as Kenzie would say, calm your tits."

The coach makes his final announcement. "I'll be seeing a lot less of you by the end of this practice. Stay focused, prove your strength, and pray to Syntyche that she won't be reaping your soul today. Ready, set—"

He blows his whistle, and immediately, we all plunge into the darkness of Everbound Forest.

13

MAVEN

THE DARKNESS IS FILLED with shouts and screams, and the ever-present mist barely conceals the bloodshed that has already begun in this haunting forest. I can sense death nearby, thick and potent, as it awaits hungrily for more victims.

If I closed my eyes, it might feel like I'm back home.

But closing my eyes would be stupid since an incomplete quintet is already rushing through the trees towards us. One has a sword, one wields the wind, and the shifter is already in bear form as she leaps through the air.

My hand slips into a concealed pocket on my pants. I'm ready to grab the dagger there and end anyone who comes close, but a blinding flare of red magic has my hair standing on end.

The bear drops dead from Silas's spell, blood gushing from where it's been split clean in half at the torso. The wind elemental is also knocked backward, slamming into a tree trunk with a sharp cracking sound.

When the legacy with the sword lunges forward, a wickedly sharp rapier made of ice forms in Everett's hand. He moves with the sly, practiced speed of a fencer, his ice blade piercing through the gut of the legacy. Immediately, they're encapsulated in solid ice, just like that cheeky siren at the ball.

It all happens so quickly that it takes me a moment to realize Baelfire is tensed in front of me like a massive shield of muscles, scanning for the next imminent threat with his eyes shifted into the slitted pupils of a dragon. Admittedly, he actually looks pretty terrifying when he's on edge, especially with the faint glow under his skin, like there's fire trapped inside him that wants out.

No wonder they're considered top-ranked legacies. They're not bad at this.

I mean, they're sloppy, but I would be lying if I said the frigid deadliness in Everett's movements didn't do something for me. It also affects me more than it should when Silas lifts up his hand, licking away his own blood with a drag of his tongue, the barest flash of his fangs reminding me that those appear when he loses control.

I wonder what they'd feel like buried in my skin. I bet it would hurt so deliciously.

Pulling myself out of my moment of distraction, I clap slowly. "Brava. Now follow me. The cemetery is this way."

I turn to lead them, but Silas interrupts me.

"First, Baelfire should end that wind elemental. A kill will give him more control."

Baelfire hesitates, glancing at the tree where the wind elemental is collapsed unconscious in a wheezing pile, probably with several broken ribs.

"No. Leave him be," I say immediately when I read the apprehension in the set of Bael's jaw.

Silas gives me a stern look. "If you're worried about sparing Bael's innocence, don't be. He's killed plenty—all of us have. But if he doesn't end a life soon, he's liable to shift out of control, which puts *you* in even more danger. That's not fucking happening."

He tries to turn away like that's the end of this discussion. But I grip the front of his shirt and yank him down to meet my eye again, not bothering to hide my true strength or the anger on my face. It makes his eyes widen fractionally.

"No, what's not fucking happening is making someone take a life that they're not sure about taking. I get it. You're a cutthroat asshole with no qualms about ending a deserving opponent, no matter what condition they're in. We're similar in that way," I parrot his words from last night with an eyebrow raise. "But Baelfire's dark side isn't quite as pitch black as ours. So if he isn't comfortable killing a defenseless enemy, then I get the final say, and I say leave him the fuck alone."

Roughly releasing the front of the startled blood fae's shirt, I start toward the ancient cemetery. I've been there plenty of times in my wanderings through Everbound Forest. It will take us at least twenty minutes to get there, which doesn't leave much time to refuel my magic to perform a search spell for the changeling.

Baelfire catches up to my side. "Damn. You're fucking hot when you're bossy. Do I need to step out of line to get my turn? You know I love being good for you, baby, but I can try being a brat."

Unexpected heat blooms in my neck, and something pools low in my stomach. The thought of punishing any of them sexually makes it really hard to think straight.

Baelfire inhales sharply, and I know he's scenting my arousal. "Fuck," he groans.

"Keep it in your pants," Everett snaps.

Bael grumbles something about frozen blue balls that I don't fully catch because an agonized scream splits the air of the forest nearby. We all go silent and still as we wait for the potential threat to emerge from the dark mist.

All that emerges is a baby manticore, which hisses and scales the nearest tree.

"Disappointing," I sigh.

Silas tips his head. "Is it? Do you enjoy watching our more monstrous sides in a fight, *sangfluir?*"

Apparently, I do.

But I haven't been in a good fight in ages, and I'm itching to spill blood. Of course, I only want to hurt people who truly deserve it, and I still don't want other legacies to catch on to the fact that I'm stronger than they are. That would draw the attention of the Immortal Quintet before I'm ready to start picking them off.

So, I'll have to temper the darker urges that were ingrained in me. For now.

Suddenly, another scream sounds much closer, and I sense another wave of death just before a cluster of legacies steps out of the trees. All seven of them are on high alert, with one of them bleeding heavily from their side.

I realize with a start that the heavily bleeding one is Monica—the empath atypical caster I met at Harlow's sadly-not-a-murder-rendezvous the other night. She slumps slightly onto one of the guys, who bares his teeth at us.

"It's the lottery quintet!" he snarls. "Take them out, and we'll eliminate the highest-ranked legacies at Everbound!"

That's enough for the rest of the legacies to launch forward with shouts and flares of blinding magic. These legacies don't seem to be matched together, so I assume they've formed a temporary allegiance as many legacies do.

Silas takes on two casters at once, Everett is attacked by a water elemental and a vampire, and Baelfire begins wrestling with a wolf shifter. The guy supporting Monica releases her and simply runs away, abandoning her to stumble backward in terror. I can already tell that the gushing injury on her side is fatal. But hearing her cries as she disappears through the trees calls to my human side—the often-dormant part of me that drove me to make the blood oath for those who needed it.

Monica might be an atypical caster, but she's far more human than I've been in years. I'm not part of their fluffy asscaster support group, but I can't just let her die in these woods.

The fight distracts all my matches as I take off after the atypical caster.

"Monica!" I shout, jumping over a fallen log and sidestepping a smoldering corpse as I continue in the direction she ran.

She ran fast. Really fast. Was she using magic to try to get away?

Finally, I stop in a clearing, taking in my surroundings quickly to avoid any nasty surprises. But I'm still taken off guard when I see Monica sitting on a nearby rock…with a smile on her face.

I'm just close enough to see that her pupils are square.

Fuck. I really hate this changeling.

Immediately, I whip out a throwing knife, but I barely have the hilt in my leather-gloved hand before blinding light smashes into me, sending me careening. Hitting the ground hurts, but I can usually take hits like no one's fucking business and walk it off.

But this time, I can't move.

And it dawns on me. That was a paralysis hex just now—a potent one. If I had magic in my system, I could rip the hex apart in the blink of an eye, but I haven't refueled. So now I can't turn my face away from pressing into a surprisingly green section of grass.

No matter how hard I try, I can't fucking move.

If I had my heart, it would be crashing in my chest. But even though I can feel my thundering pulse and breathe and bleed and *feel* like any living thing, my shadow heart is undetectable, a reminder of the monster they turned me into.

Except right now, I don't feel like a monster. I feel…helpless. It's been a long time since I felt this way. Trepidation claws at my chest.

Sierra titters, "See? Told you it wouldn't be hard to get her alone."

A guy's voice snorts. "Nah, that was fucking easy. Thanks for your help, Mon—didn't expect you to volunteer to help us like that."

"It was nothing. We all want to get rid of the lottery quintet, after all," the changeling says sweetly in Monica's voice.

I'm going to fucking kill it once I get out of this.

"So *this* is the unmemorable little bitch everyone got so worked up over?" another of Sierra's guy friends scoffs, and all of my senses are thrown into panic when I feel hands turning me over.

At least now I can see, but it's not a pretty sight. Sierra stands over me with a victorious sneer on her face, with two guys leering alongside her and the changeling off to one side, smirking in a nasty way I'm sure the real Monica never could.

"Damn, she's a butterface," the taller guy with dark hair says, and the panic doubles when he reaches out and squeezes one of my cheeks hard enough that it might bruise.

The other guy, a blond, frowns. "You think? I think she could be really cute if she put in more effort. It looks like she's wearing a fucking tarp, though. And what the hell is with the gloves?"

"She's a germaphobe," Sierra says confidently, and fire flares to life in one of her hands. "Let's see how well asscasters burn, huh?"

Fire.

Fuck.

I'm going to actually die. *Shit, shit, shit.*

But I can't even formulate a plan of how to stop this from happening because this asshole is still touching my face, and it makes it feel like every nerve in my body was just submerged in acid.

Stop touching me.

"Not so fast," the douchebag holding my face grins, showing off his fangs. A vampire. I should've guessed. My track record with vampires is abysmal. "I wanna see her cry."

"You always like to play with your food," the other guy grumbles.

Sierra beams. "No, Jace is right. This fucking bitch cheated in a fight just to take a cheap shot at me and stole my entire future from me. She deserves to suffer for everything she put me through, and I know how to make that happen. Get her gloves off."

My stomach careens. Once again, I try to move, but I'm completely locked in place by the spell the blond caster must have thrown at me. Jace, the fucking prick, grins with excitement…and his other hand slips up under my shirt to caress my stomach.

I'm going to puke.

Panic is now beating in my veins so hard that I start to acutely disassociate before I can feel them stripping my gloves off me, cackling as they rip up grass and dirt to shove in the "germaphobe's" mouth. But even though I try to check out as fast as possible, I can still feel when Sierra laughs and spits on my face.

And when the blond caster licks my neck, laughing uproariously.

The vampire's hands are on my arms, my face, my throat…

Disassociating isn't working, and hot tears start to gather in my eyes as bile crawls up my throat. I can't move to puke, so I might choke on it. I hope I do so I don't have to feel their skin on mine anymore.

Stop fucking touching me. Get away from me.

From the corner of my eye, I see the changeling approach. It's no longer bleeding, so it must've been healing itself just now. Its fingers brush against my temple, and a sharp, painful surge of memories rises to the surface, drowning out everything else and forcing me to relive the hell that conditioned me to hate all of this so much.

I can see it all again—myself at eleven years old, screaming and crying as I pounded on the thick wooden door of a dungeon, so desperate to get away from the maggot-infested corpses surrounding me that I left bloodied handprints on the wood. I can feel the fucking maggots that wriggled against my skin, trying to get inside to eat me alive from the inside out.

Then I see myself at fourteen, biting down hard on a strip of fabric so my teeth wouldn't break from clenching them in pain. But it wasn't enough to muffle my screaming as another one of the necromancers' never-ending, agonizing rituals seared through every muscle.

And finally, I see my own tear-streaked face when I was seventeen, reflected in whiteless black eyes as my heart was ripped out.

This one is not to be touched. She will be my masterpiece, Dagon's oily voice echoes in my head from so long ago. *If anyone lays a finger on her, tear them to shreds and send her back to me for conditioning. She must learn that she is nothing more and nothing less than what we make her. I will ensure she becomes the* telum.

Telum.

Scourge.

It's true. That's what I am. I'm the scourge—a living weapon. And I've been through shit that these three assholes can't even fucking imagine. They never would have survived a single day of my life in the Nether, so why am I holding back?

I snap back to myself as the changeling draws away with a smirk.

I can tell it ate no memories, but it's smug that it got inside my head. It probably saw far more memories than I just re-experienced.

But right now, I don't give a fuck what it saw.

Their hands are still on me as Sierra mocks me, the blond one laughing as he rubs dirt on my face. They're preying on my trauma, enjoying my tears and horror. My panic hasn't subsided, but now it's just white noise as I draw energy out of the grass beneath me and give in to the life-devouring magic that flows through me.

Dark magic explodes out from all around me, finally shattering the paralysis spell. A shrill scream cuts short as Sierra slams into one of the nearby rocks and goes motionless. But I know she's not dead yet because I don't get the familiar buzz.

I want that buzz.

Letting my temper and the bloodthirst thrumming in my veins take the lead, I grip the blond caster by the throat to fling him aside. Jace yelps in alarm and tries to back away, but I'm already on my feet as I stalk toward him, spitting out the taste of grass and dirt and enjoying the shocked terror on his face.

"Calm down! Look, I could've killed you just now, but I spared you, so you should—"

"What? Repay the favor?" I ask innocently, letting my lips curl into the sick smile that used to make even Lillian flinch. "Don't worry, I will."

He tries to dart away using his vampiric speed, but I move faster than he thinks I can. Immediately, I have him pinned to the ground as the boiling rush of hatred and lingering horror pumps through my limbs.

They touched me. Mocked me. Fucking *licked* me.

I'm sure this vampire would have done far worse if I had never broken out of that spell, which only increases the turbulence in my stomach. I'm either going to throw up or kill him.

Either way, I want him to suffer first.

I'm so far gone that I don't hesitate to draw more life from the grass beneath Jace's back, and then I dig my fingertips through his shirt into his chest and unleash a flare of power. He jolts and lets out a bloodcurdling scream so shrill that his voice gives out, his limbs twitching and spasming.

Music to my ears.

I do it again. And again. And I enjoy every second of it. Every scream and sob fills me with a sick, intoxicating thrill.

I may be fucked in the head now, but I didn't always enjoy killing. Actually, taking an innocent life is something I avoid at all costs. Even surrounded by the horrors I was raised with that would rip me to shreds if I showed weakness, I drew the line at killing anyone who didn't truly deserve it.

This one? He deserves it.

I pause for a moment to relish the agony on the vampire's face as he chokes on his own tears and snot. "W—what the f—fuck are you?" he sobs, too weak to push me off of him as his eyes flutter and roll helplessly.

"I'm what happens when the Undead experiment on the living."

His next scream is particularly satisfying as I force more lethal magic into his system. But finally, the fever pitch of fury starts to die in my head. The inescapable yearning to kill and maim and fuel my magic with death lulls. I'm abruptly dizzy as I pull my gloveless fingers out of his chest and glance around the small clearing.

The blond caster and the changeling are nowhere to be seen, and Sierra is still out cold. Part of me is tempted to end her life, too—to end all of their pathetic lives. It would be so fucking *easy*.

I was made for this. For death.

But as usual, when I'm on the verge of losing myself, Lillian's gentle voice is like the brush of a feather inside my mind.

Death is not your destiny. Everything you have gone through gives you a choice—the ultimate choice. Whenever you think of ending a life, remember how hard you have fought for your own. It's too precious to destroy so heartlessly. Rein it in, Little Raven.

Rein it in. Right. I should do that.

I finally shake off the last of the killing rage. But Jace is no longer breathing, his eyes frozen open as a fresh wave of buzzing magic lights up my entire system.

Oops.

Oh, well. Like I said, this dick deserved it.

I get to my feet and stumble away, my boots crunching over the now-lifeless grass. Nearby trees are equally drained. As I lean over to pick up the gloves they stripped off of me, another flare of nausea hits me hard, and I drop to my knees to heave until I have nothing left. My nerves are still burning, and it feels like my skin is crawling with thousands of invisible maggots, biting and burrowing little bodies.

I would give anything to fix how my body reacts like this.

Now that the vengeful outburst is out of my system, the panic catches up tenfold. I'm going into total panic. I can't be here.

I have to get their fucking touch off of me, so I run.

14

SILAS

I RIP my mouth away from the throat of yet another legacy who was foolish enough to attack, tossing aside their carcass as I storm after Baelfire. He's tracking Maven's scent, but if he doesn't find her soon, I expect to descend into madness instantaneously.

My freshly boosted magic prickles at my scarred fingertips, desperate to be set free. Everett is in the middle of verbally tearing Baelfire a new asshole when I catch up.

"...don't know what the hell you were thinking. How could you *not* shift and burn this entire godsdamned forest to the ground when you realized she was gone?"

"I *can't* shift right now, or the dragon will be fully in control, and he might hurt her, asswipe," Baelfire snaps back, shoving the ice elemental aside as he continues to track Maven. He pauses with frustration and swears viciously, rubbing his face. "Her scent is so fucking faint, even though it can't be that long since she passed through here. It's *always* faint. Why the hell is it so hard to track her?"

I imagine it has something to do with what she is and the shadow heart in her chest. I only know about that particular form of highly forbidden, unforgivable magic since I read about it in one of the Garnet Wizard's banned ancient grimoires.

A shadow heart can serve many purposes, but primarily, it keeps something alive that's…well. Not.

But Maven isn't Undead. I'm certain of that.

It doesn't make any godsdamned sense, but that's hardly the problem right now. The problem is that our keeper vanished in the middle of a deadly combat training, and I'm losing my mind, thinking that every corpse we come across is hers.

She's dead.

You lost her.

As it should be, the voices in my head taunt.

My ears start to ring, and my vision blurs. But finally, Baelfire stops in a clearing, and we all stare.

The grass is utterly colorless. Not like dead, yellowed grass—it's pure white. Nearby trees are in grayscale. It's as if any vestige of life or color has been drained away, including from a legacy corpse nearby.

"S—Silas! Baelfire! Professor Frost, you have to help me. *Please!"* someone wails. "It hurts!"

We all look over to see a redhead crawling towards us from a cluster of rocks. She's bleeding profusely from her head at a rate that tells me she won't live long. She slumps to cry into the grass.

"She was just supposed to be a w—weak little asscaster," she sobs. "Please heal me—you have to heal me! I can't die this way, I don't deserve this…"

She dissolves into nonsensical weeping. I crouch beside her.

"You're talking about Maven. You saw her cast?"

The redhead rolls over as well as she can, nodding quickly and brushing tears and blood off her hysterical, wide-eyed face. "Listen to me. Listen. You can't fucking trust her! That bitch has been lying this entire time. You have to believe me, her magic wasn't normal! I think she was using—"

I reach out and twist her head, snapping her neck.

Everett flinches and scowls at me. Baelfire swears and rubs his face.

"Couldn't you at least let her finish whatever she was trying to fucking say first? Or you could have tried to heal her enough so she could tell us what happened here and what direction Maven went. Fucking merciless cutthroat."

As if being merciless is a flaw.

"She was past the point of healing. I was putting her out of her misery efficiently," I mutter.

It's a partial truth. I was also keeping the redhead from saying anything more about Maven's casting. If she saw Maven cast, then I couldn't leave her alive. I know my blood blossom is hiding something about her magic, and I can't have rumors about it spreading around Everbound.

Baelfire calls me a dick before inhaling deeply and leaving the clearing, following Maven's scent. Everett and I follow.

The coach blew the whistle outside of Everbound Forest several minutes ago, but none of us give a fuck about not completing this stupid training. We were attacked so frequently that this was less of a structured exercise and more of a free-for-all shot at trying to kill our quintet off, which only led to us leaving a trail of bodies in our wake as we searched for Maven.

Finally, we burst out of the edge of the forest. Coach Gallagher sees us and storms over, barking that the training isn't over and we can't go back inside. He's still mid-sentence when Everett flicks his hand in the coach's direction and freezes him solid, pushing over the frozen instructor as we pass.

"There goes your chance at being the teacher's pet," Baelfire mutters, still leading the way.

"He's my coworker and a dick. Always has been."

I glance at Everett. "When we get inside, we'll keep searching for Maven. You should go to your office or whatever the hell it is that you do here. Just keep yourself and your curse well the fuck away from her."

Never before have I felt bad for the privileged, famous heir of the Frost fortune. What was there to feel sorry for? Even if he was a brooding, arrogant grouch, by all appearances, he had everything.

But the look of stark misery on the elemental's face as he halts to let us go on alone actually makes me pity him for a fleeting moment. I despise my curse more than anything, but at least my mere feelings can't put Maven's life at risk. She's taken center stage in my life so completely that I can't imagine having to resist her for her own good.

As soon as we step into the castle, Baelfire turns right down the hall that will take us to our quintet apartment. I'm surprised Maven would go there since she's avoided it so heavily.

I keep up easily, still clutching my blood-soaked crystal as I look around for anyone who might try to catch us unawares. Although our mere appearance seems to be enough to turn most legacies off from the idea of approaching us. Blood still drips down my chin and neck, drying from the last person I drained. I'm sure I look as mad as I feel as blood magic swirls around my fingertips.

Meanwhile, Baelfire snarls at anything that moves into his line of sight, and his eyes are still partially shifted. He's also covered in blood and dirt from a fight with a griffin shifter that didn't end well for the griffin.

As soon as we step into our quintet apartment, Baelfire drops to his knees and clutches at his head with an infuriated roar. The fire flickering under his skin and smoke rising from his nose as he barely resists a shift confuses me until I test the air and realize what set him off.

It smells like Maven's blood. Again.

Even though I'm gorged on the blood of our enemies, my mouth waters and my fangs ache at the fragrance. Gods above, nothing in the world should have the right to be so enticing.

Leaving Baelfire to wrestle with his inner dragon, I try to get myself under control as I approach the bathroom door. There are two bathrooms in this apartment. The bigger one is attached to the main bedroom that we all view as Maven's, but she's in the smaller bathroom connected to the hall right now.

The door is locked. I rest my forehead against it, gritting my teeth against the urge to break it down. "Maven?"

She doesn't answer.

Something is dreadfully wrong, another voice in my head snickers. *Perhaps she's bled out completely. One can only hope.*

I ignore the voices. "Are you hurt? Answer me."

There's a soft sound of distress, and that's my breaking point. Sending a hex through the wooden door that makes it cave in like paper, I force my way inside the bathroom—but I freeze when I see the nude silhouette of Maven behind the glass, scrubbing feverishly at her skin. The entire bathroom is filled with steam as I round the corner, anxiety curdling my insides.

Normally, Maven would be angry that I violated her space like this. But she doesn't even look up at me as I approach her, ignoring how I'm getting drenched in the shower spray as I reach for her.

She just keeps scrubbing.

"Stop. Maven, *stop*."

As gently as I can, I grasp her elbow and turn her to face me, but she flinches back immediately.

"Don't."

Misery fills me when I see tears in her eyes and streaked over her cheeks. But it's immediately eclipsed by unadulterated horror when I spot the steel wool clutched in her trembling hand, the scarlet blood running into the shower drain from where she's literally scrubbed the top layers of her skin off.

My blood blossom is typically so composed and practical, but now she's shaking and in a blind panic as she scrapes herself raw.

I can barely get the words out as I put the pieces together. "Who touched you?"

She lets out a shaky breath and throws the steel wool to the ground, grabbing the soap instead and slathering it over her arms, neck, and stomach.

They touched her stomach.

Red creeps into my vision as my throat burns.

"Maven. *Who the fuck touched you?*" I whisper.

She makes a gagging sound and drops the soap to cover her mouth, squeezing her eyes shut. Seeing her like this is ripping me to shreds. I want to pull her close and heal her damaged skin and beg for names so I can find whoever did this to her and paint the castle red with their blood.

But when Maven finally manages to speak, she whispers, "It's nothing. Wait outside for me."

She stoops as if going for the steel wool again, but I swipe it off the ground as I leave, refusing to let her touch it again.

In the quintet's entry room beside the kitchen, Bael is still gripping his head in residual pain, but he looks over as I storm into the room.

"What's going on? Is she—"

I left the door to the bathroom ajar, so we both hear the faintest sniffle from the shower.

That has him on his feet immediately, but I put up a hand to stop him and nod to the dining room table instead. "We're going to wait here for her."

"But—"

"You do not want to argue with me right now, Baelfire," I warn.

Any other day, he'd see that as a challenge, but the youngest Decimus looks utterly defeated as he slumps into one of the dining room chairs, frowning impatiently at the hallway. I sit, too, and rub my temples as I try to rein in my lingering fury and bloodlust from witnessing Maven in that state.

It's ten minutes before the shower shuts off, and another ten minutes later, Maven emerges from the hallway. She's wrapped in a white bathrobe that conceals the scrapes I know cover much of her body, and otherwise, our keeper is composed again. She holds her head high as she sits at the end of the dining room table, regarding us both in solemn silence.

Even Baelfire doesn't disturb the quiet as we wait for what she has to say.

Finally, Maven clears her throat. "It's come to my attention that I have a weakness that can too easily be extorted. I want to fix that, so I'm asking for your assistance."

Bael studies her. "Assistance? What do you—"

"Exposure therapy," she clarifies. "I need to get over my fear of touch."

I stare at her before looking down at the sticky, red-coated crystal that I still hold in one hand. "No. I didn't realize how severe it was until now, but I am not putting you through more of that."

She lifts her chin. "I'm asking you to. Fixing my haphephobia will be torture and not the fun kind, but it's a necessary evil. Also," she adds, cutting off another of my protests. "If you agree to help me, I'll offer some answers."

I want to understand my keeper more than I want anything, save breaking my curse, so I carefully ask, "You'll answer our questions?"

Maven watches us as if bracing herself for a strong reaction. "Yes. Considering you two already know I'm from the Nether, I think some transparency is in order."

I nod, but the wariness doesn't leave her shoulders. My *sangfluir* still expects us to attack her for being a Nether escapee.

Incomprehensible.

Baelfire perks up. "Finally! Like I already fucking said, we need to put all cards on the table. Our quintet needs it." Then he pauses and makes a face. "Although, I guess only half our quintet is here, which is pretty damn inconvenient."

The fact that Crypt hasn't turned up is mildly concerning. I could never miss that murderous fucking bastard, not in a million years, but his absence might be a sign of something malicious going on.

Everett's absence, on the other hand, is for the best.

Maven drags her damp hair over one shoulder. With her dark hair and olive complexion, she looks stunning in white. I try to focus on what she's saying and not that she looks positively edible when wet like this.

"They'll join us later, or they won't. Either way, let's establish a few things. I know both of your curses. Silas, you hear voices, and you're going insane. Baelfire, your dragon starts to take control if you don't hunt. Is that right?"

I grimace in agreement. Unfortunately, mine is becoming impossible to miss. I *could* share that the voices tormenting me are none other than those of my deceased family members or how they taunt me with the promise of peace if I just put myself out of my misery. But those are dark truths I doubt anyone cares to know.

Baelfire nods, worn out from fending off his dragon earlier. "Yeah, I have to hunt and kill something every day. If I don't, I'll lose my marbles bit by bit, Silas style."

I scowl at him, but Maven tips her head. "And that makes your dragon stronger?"

"Something like that. My curse didn't really set in until I was five. When my parents saw me losing control constantly, shifting without being able to shift back, throwing dragon-sized tantrums, and basically being a little shithead…they realized I must have the same curse that my uncle did. He was never given a quintet and never got to break his curse. He could hunt to appease it, too, but when he stopped doing that, he ended up shifting into a dragon. *Permanently.* He was completely replaced by the beast, and my asshole of a dragon wouldn't fucking hesitate to do the same thing to me."

Maven absorbs that for a moment. "What happened to your uncle?"

"He was put to death by the Legacy Council. They didn't like the idea of a dragon flying around outside of their control. Said he posed a risk to humans. Which he did," he shrugs.

I remember when that happened. Gruesome as it is, that was the last time a large batch of dragon scales was harvested, but those ones are all but gone now.

Hence why I need Baelfire's.

"Your turn, Mayflower," Bael urges. "Give us an answer about you. Tell us why you were in the headmaster's office."

She doesn't miss a beat. "To kill him. But a changeling beat me to it."

He blinks. "Oh, shit. How the fuck did a changeling get into Everbound? And why did it take out Hearst?"

"Changelings in the mortal realm are mercenaries only motivated by money and feeding on memories. It must have a master somewhere who wanted Hearst dead," Maven shrugs. "But now it's trapped here with the rest of us and the Immortal Quintet hunting for it."

Things click together in my head. "That's who poisoned you. The one you're looking for."

"The one I'm going to kill tonight," she nods as if she's describing taking a stroll.

Baelfire's jaw clenches. "Not without my help, Mayflower."

"And mine."

I expect Maven to refuse immediately, so it's a pleasant surprise when she studies the two of us for a long moment before sighing.

"How strong are your stomachs?"

"Why do you ask?"

"Because I'm going to torture this changeling, and oddly enough, not everyone enjoys that."

For nine years, I observed the Garnet Wizard torture anyone who attempted to trespass in his sanctuary without authorization. His punishments were brutal, and he occasionally asked for my help conducting magical experiments on those trespassers.

I'm no sadist, but I am well-versed in things like this.

"I can handle it," I say, smirking across at the dragon shifter. "Baelfire is far too soft, though. He should sit this one out. He once fainted watching a horse give birth on my parents' estate, back when they were alive to have one."

He kicks me under the table. "I was *four*, you motherfucker. When I saw your parents' keeper reaching into that thing, I thought he was stuffing his hand up its butt. What kid wouldn't find that shit appalling? But that was forever ago, and I can handle anything you can."

I look at my keeper pointedly. "As you said earlier, his dark side isn't nearly at our level. If he even has one."

"Everyone has a dark side," she mutters as if to herself.

"Look, I'm not a blatant asshole like Silas most of the time, but this fucker hurt my mate, so watching her torture it is going to be an absolute fucking treat," Baelfire huffs.

Maven nods, then frowns. "Come to think of it, that changeling got into my head earlier, so it might start spouting off shit about my past that it has no business sharing. I should do this alone."

I set my bloodied crystal on the table, shaking my head. "You've decided to be transparent with us. Consider this a part of that. Nothing it says will sway us from your side."

She openly grimaces at that before meeting my eye. "Don't be so sure."

"What will it take to earn your trust, *ima sangfluir*? Should we make a blood oath promising to take your secrets to our graves?"

"No. Besides, that would hardly be comforting. In my experience, graves aren't permanent."

Baelfire and I exchange a look before he asks, "Wanna expound on that, Mayflower?"

She opens her mouth, but someone knocks on the front door, interrupting our first half-official quintet meeting. Baelfire looks haggard as he bares his teeth. He's still liable to shift and kill if any threat presents itself, and there is no way in the world that I'm letting someone outside of our quintet see Maven in a bathrobe, so I'm the one who answers the door.

Engela Zuma regards me, barely blinking at the dried blood on my chin, neck, hands, and clothes. I'm so taken aback by a member of the Immortal Quintet at our door that I immediately step out and shut it behind me, ensuring she has no chance of glimpsing Maven.

Of all members of the Immortal Quintet, I know the least about Engela. Everyone knows Natalya is a spoiled, overpowered bitch, and that none of her immortal boy toys should be crossed because they're all equally powerful and inhumane.

However, the second female monster in the Immortal Quintet is a relative question mark, even by her appearance. I know she can transform objects and even people to stone at the touch of her finger, but with her deep brown skin, dark eyes, and black hair shorn close to her head, she could pass for a human. She doesn't look nearly as monstrous as the others in her quintet.

I dip my head slightly, a sign of respect I don't entirely mean because I respect no one in the Immortal Quintet. "What brings you to—"

She cuts me off by holding out four sealed envelopes without a word.

I don't want to take them. What if they're dangerous?

Of course, they're dangerous, a voice in my head scoffs. *The Immortal Quintet must know the truth about Maven. They're after her.*

When you open those envelopes, deadly hexes will emerge.

You'll be powerless as usual. Useless boy, my father growls among the voices.

My eye starts twitching, and I realize I'm breathing heavily and retreating backward. If Engela notices, she doesn't care. She drops the letters on the floor and walks silently away, rounding the nearest corner.

I wait several seconds to see if some kind of trap springs forth, but when I hover my hand over the envelopes, I sense no malicious magic.

I pick up the envelopes and return to our apartment, frowning when I see one each for Maven, myself, Baelfire, and Everett.

"What is it?" Baelfire asks, approaching. Then he wrinkles his nose. "What's that smell coming from Maven's letter?"

That intrigues Maven, who walks over and leans up and inhales near her envelope at precisely the same time I lean down for a whiff.

"*Calea ternifolia*," we say at the same time.

It makes me blink, and then a smile threatens to tug the corners of my mouth. "I almost forgot. You're quite the botanist. Odd that you should have that hobby, though."

With our faces close like this, I have the luxury of studying the dark kaleidoscope of colors in her irises as she arches a brow.

"Why, because I come from a lifeless void?"

"Precisely."

She shrugs. "Everyone needs a hobby, even in hell."

She slips the envelope from my hand and opens it. Baelfire and I lean in to study the small object that falls into her palm. It's a circular glass talisman. At the center of it is a golden eye closed in sleep while the outer edges of the glass bracket a pattern of swirling dried leaves—the *calea ternifolia* that, when spelled, becomes so pungent.

Although it's simple, it's incredibly well-crafted and appears to be very old. If this is a gift from Crypt to her, it's impressive.

Maven reads the note that came with it, and as she does, Baelfire and I both read the letters addressed to us. It doesn't take me long to skim, and I must finish at the same time as the dragon because he lets out a harsh scoff and shakes his head.

"Fucking Nightmare Prince."

Maven glances over. "What did he say in yours?"

"Mostly a grotesquely detailed threat of extreme testicular torture if we let harm befall you while he's away," I reply. I don't mention the part where Crypt added that he would search for anything at the Divide that might ease Maven's ailment, as *reverium* does for him.

"Same," Bael grunts, tearing up his letter. "How about yours, Boo?"

He tries to lean over to read over her shoulder, but she slips it into her pocket and glares at him. "No more Boo. Boo is dead. Put that nickname on a fucking gravestone and move on."

"My bad, *Mayflower*."

My attention moves back to the talisman in Maven's hand. "That must be a dream totem. An incredibly old one. I don't know where Crypt found it, but they're supposed to keep nightmares at bay, among other things."

Her lips curve into the slightest smile as she studies the talisman, and just like that, I'm fiercely jealous. I want to give her something she likes, too. Baelfire looks equally envious as he huffs and folds his arms over his chest.

"Doesn't change the fact that he fucking left. He should be here helping to protect our keeper."

Maven rolls her eyes and pockets the talisman before fixing us with a look. She no longer desperately clings to her poker face whenever we're alone, so right now, it's purely Maven, with that intoxicatingly dark, dangerous flare in her eye that makes my cock twitch in my pants.

"Let's get one more thing out of the way. You two have no idea what I'm capable of. I'm sure the last day or two of close calls has made you both think I'm fragile, but trust me. I can handle myself. Now come on, it's time to hunt a changeling."

15

MAVEN

I WOULD NEVER SAY it out loud, but I'm starting to miss my unseen stalker.

As I redress and wait for Silas and Baelfire to clean up and get ready for changeling hunting, it feels odd not sensing Crypt's dark presence lingering at the outskirts of my senses.

Even though Baelfire grumbled about it, the plan is to skip dinner and use that time to find the changeling. But before we leave, I can't resist skimming my letter again.

> *There never has been and never will be anyone but you for me. Twisted souls like ours can't help belonging together, will of the gods be damned. Quintet or not, bound or not, I was always going to be yours, darling.*
>
> *Wherever you rest your pretty head, keep this under your pillow until I return to you. And please dream of me, for if I could dream, it would always be of you.*

Gods. Why does he have to be so…*poetic*?

This kind of sweetness normally nauseates me, but for some reason, my stomach decides to flutter instead. My face feels warm. It's unclear why Engela Zuma herself dropped off these notes from Crypt, but I know one thing: there must be a good reason he had to leave Everbound if someone in the Immortal Quintet was involved.

It only stokes my curiosity about the Nightmare Prince.

"Ready, baby?" Baelfire asks, cutting into my thoughts as he emerges from the hallway, his dirty blond hair even darker when wet.

I nod, but when Silas joins us barely a second later, having also showered, I pause and tip my head, unable to keep the curious words from escaping.

"Did you shower together?"

Silas recoils in disgust. Baelfire gags.

"Hell to the motherfucking no. The only way I'm ever going to be naked near this jackass in a shower is if you're naked between us. That, I could get behind. Or in front of. You'd get to pick, of course."

My neck heats, but I do my best to ignore that sensual visual as I ask the natural follow-up question. "Would any of you go for each other?"

"I'd rather lop off my left testicle than play with any of their pricks," Bael says decisively.

Silas grimaces as if I asked them to lick mold. "Agreed. Are you asking because that thought excites you, *sangfluir?*"

I hadn't considered it until this exact second, but the more I think about it, the more I can't picture any of my matches wanting to fuck each other. They'd all much rather get in a bloody fistfight, except they seem to be begrudgingly buddying up for our temporary quintet.

"Not really. But what would you have done if the gods had put you in an all-male quintet?"

"Remained platonic."

"What about Everett? Or Crypt?"

Baelfire does a theatrical full-body shudder. "No idea, and I'm glad. I take it back when I said all cards on the table—I do *not* want to know about DeLune's previous love life. I didn't even want to know about Snowflake's, but here we fucking are."

I'm tempted to ask what that means, but then I glimpse a large, decorative clock hanging nearby and realize dinner won't last much longer. Either the Immortal Quintet or their legacy minions will be keeping a close watch on all students, and curfew is laughably early, so we don't have much time for what I have in mind.

And killing this changeling is essential. On the off chance that the changeling plans on targeting any more of the Immortal Quintet, I really need to kill it before it puts that plan in motion and robs me of my mission. Not to mention, I plan on torturing it until it tells me where Kenzie is.

Killing it might give me enough boost in magic to tear through Everbound's magical wards to find her. Fingers crossed.

"Come on." I lead them out of the apartment.

The halls are mostly empty since most legacies are in the dining hall for food after a long, danger-and-death-filled day. However, we still pass a couple of other groups and the occasional unmatched legacy. Anytime we do, Baelfire bares his teeth at them, and Silas's eye starts to twitch.

When the blood fae starts muttering nonsense under his breath again, I brace myself and briefly brush my fingers along his jaw. Even that tiny contact sends a wave of both tingles and chills down my arm, but he snaps to attention and blinks down at me.

"You touched me."

"Exposure therapy," I remind them.

Baelfire frowns down at me as we turn into another hall. "You sure you actually want that, Mayflower? Don't get me wrong, I'd touch you and hold you every fucking second of every day if I could, but if you don't like it—"

I stop to look up at him. Maybe I'm being too vulnerable, but I want them to understand this part of me clearly.

"It's not that I don't like it. I was conditioned. It's psychological, and I need to get over it. I *want* to enjoy touch, and more than that, I can't let anyone use it to fuck with me again."

Baelfire's expression hardens, and his pupils shift into a dragon's. His shifter emotions swing so fast that I'm taken off guard, and suddenly, he's shaking with fury.

"You were *conditioned?* What, like some fucking *lab rat?* Is that what you're telling me?"

Oh, my gods. Their curses are turning them into toddlers on the verge of a tantrum about every little fucking thing. How am I supposed to get anything done?

I spot a cluster of legacies coming closer on the opposite side of the hallway and don't want them to overhear. "Baelfire. Relax."

His sharp, angry breathing doesn't calm. "Who conditioned you, Maven? Tell me. Tell me right the fuck now, or I'm—"

"Calm down," Silas snaps, also noticing that we're being watched, but that just earns him a sharp shove and a snarl from Bael.

The other quintet is looking our way now, and I realize it's tattoo-headed Brooks and his matches. The last thing I need is for that moron to think our quintet is having a weak moment and decide to waste more of my time, so I push myself onto the very tips of my toes and plant a kiss on Baelfire's lips.

He's so *warm.*

Immediately, his trembling stops. His big hands naturally clasp my waist to hold me against him even as I pull my mouth from his. It's difficult to breathe since I can't seem to think about anything but those big, warm hands on me, but I force myself to give him a small smile.

"Be good for me and rein in your dragon, and perhaps I'll reward you later," I whisper quietly enough that only his shifter hearing will pick it up.

He swallows thickly, looking torn between frustration and want. "I need to know who hurt you."

Plenty of people. Especially people I was stupid enough to care about.

But instead of saying that out loud, I squirm, all too aware of the apprehension curling down my spine from being pressed against him like this. Baelfire notices and quickly releases me. Brooks' quintet has already moved on from this hall.

Silas studies me before sighing. "I do want answers about you, but not as much as I want you safe. So let's change the conditions. I agree to help with this *exposure therapy* if you really insist on it, but only if you move into the quintet apartment."

I consider that. Earlier, when I was desperate to get the lingering sensation of ghostly maggots and invasive hands washed from my body, I'd wound up at the quintet apartment without thinking about it. I hardly need protection, but I can admit that it feels more secure and comfortable in the quintet apartment.

Plus, legacies might gossip about a keeper not staying with her much stronger matches. I don't want more attention than I'm already getting.

"Fine."

Silas opens his mouth as if he's prepared with another argument but pauses when he registers my answer. "Really? So easily?"

"Would you rather I keep putting up a fight?"

"No," he says quickly, one corner of his mouth lifting. "You've put up more than enough of a fight in all aspects of this quintet. I'm just pleased to win, for once."

"Fuck, yes. I'll help move your things from your dorm," Baelfire offers, his smile dazzling. How shifters can handle bouncing between strong emotions all the time is beyond me. "I mean, I can help after we finish breaking this changeling's kneecaps or whatever. Speaking of…how the hell are we finding this thing?"

Making sure no one is watching, I lead them to one of Everbound Castle's most private alcoves. It's the same one where I tried and spectacularly failed at rejecting them the first time.

I slip my gloves off and tuck them in my pocket but then hesitate, realizing I'm nervous.

It's a foreign feeling.

Furtively, I glance up. They're both watching, waiting to see me truly cast for the first time. They know where I came from, and against all odds, they're still behaving like they want me, even without a stupid bet in place.

But what if they get to know the real me and *then* opt to hate me? *Get over it. It shouldn't matter to you anyway.*

But it does. I was an absolute bitch to them, trying to make them hate me and move on, but they never did. But if they grow disgusted with me now...

Silas's face softens, and he leans to catch my eye. "You're worrying, but there's no need. I already know your magic is different. I felt it."

Baelfire looks between us curiously. "Different how?"

Better get this over with.

Taking a deep breath, I step back and make a twisted symbol with my fingers, breathing out a short string of forbidden words. Dark, cruel magic surges to the surface, boiling in my veins as my fingertips blacken and tendrils of shadow swirl around my bare hands.

Silas's eyes widen infinitesimally, but I can tell it's from intrigue and not alarm. Baelfire looks concerned as the dark tendrils climb up my arms, circling and twisting until they encompass me. I shut my eyes and hold my breath, focusing entirely on the shadow heart in my chest.

It magically keeps my blood running, but it doesn't beat. Amadeus crafted this heart for me to replace the one he ripped out. But even with all his foresight, he didn't realize that pouring his magic into this heart would give me the ability to tap into his precognitive abilities in a tight pinch.

My "father's" foresight only encompasses death, misery, and future battles. It's not always accurate, so I rarely glean from it.

But right now, it comes in handy. My body starts to go numb just as images flicker in my mind—a dorm number, blood pooling on a stone floor, the changeling screaming in agony, and a blood-streaked vial of powder.

"Mayflower?"

"Don't get close to her," Silas warns. "Some spells are delicate. It might rebound and harm her if you interfere."

My head spins as I finally break out of the trance-like spell, catching my breath and blinking up at them. But even though Baelfire still looks worried, Silas appears fascinated by my display of the forbidden arts.

I grin. "Follow me."

Minutes later, we wind up at the door to a private dorm marked with the same dorm number I just foresaw. I can only assume the changeling killed to have this space.

Setting my bare hand against the door, I use another small burst of magic to corrupt all wards or protective spells, and then I try the handle. It's not even locked. This arrogant piece of shit puts far too much faith in its own lesser form of magic.

Opening the door, I waltz in to find the changeling posing in front of a full-length mirror in what I assume is a freshly stolen outfit. When it sees me, it hisses in a very un-Monica-like way and launches toward its sword propped against one wall.

Before it can touch the weapon, a flare of Silas's blood-red magic sends it crashing into the wall. A circle of powerful runes emblazons itself into the floor around the monster to keep it from exiting.

He's efficient. I don't mind that.

I also don't mind when the changeling hisses and snarls, flinging itself against the invisible ward as it glowers at me. Seeing it trapped and furious like this makes me smile.

Baelfire locks the door.

I approach the sneering changeling. It's strange to see it do that with the sweet empath's face, but things only get more bizarre as it smirks at me before its entire appearance ripples and changes. In the blink of an eye, I'm once again staring at myself.

"Would you look who it is?" it snaps in my voice. "Took you long enough to find me, *telum*."

"Scourge?" Silas translates with a frown. I'm surprised he knows even that much in the Nether tongue. "Why is it calling you that?"

The changeling peers over my shoulder at my matches and

smiles flirtatiously, batting its—*my*—eyelashes and blowing a kiss. Changelings don't experience human emotions but are great at affecting human qualities.

"Hello, pretty boy toys."

Baelfire makes a face. "Okay, that's fucking weird. I can't unsee that."

"We both know why I'm here," I say, drawing the monster's attention back to me. I slip one of my concealed daggers from its place and twist it in my hand, admiring it before I smile thinly at the creature. "You know what answers I want. So tell me. Are we going to do this the easy way or the fun way?"

Fake Maven wrinkles its nose and clamps its mouth shut stubbornly.

I grin.

Looks like this will be fun, after all.

16

BAELFIRE

Holy fuck.

Maven is enjoying the hell out of this.

I'm a seasoned hunter who deals with blood and gore daily, but I still grimace as my mate twists her knife under the skin at the back of the changeling's mutilated hand. Its scream is piercing, so it's a good thing Silas did some caster shit to soundproof this room. Maven also did something to this monster to keep it from thrashing around. It can only move its head and face.

I don't know shit about magic, but I do know that the smirk twisting up Maven's lips is both cute as fuck and terrifying.

My sexy little raincloud has been enjoying the screaming for the last twenty minutes. But since the changeling currently looks like *her*, I'm just…silently panicking.

Logically, I know that freak isn't Maven, but it looks just like her as it wails and shrieks. If it's bothering Silas, he's hiding it well, but it's making my inner dragon even more of a pest to deal with. My veins pump with fire and fury at the thought of anything like this happening to our mate, ever—it doesn't matter that this isn't her because the visual really isn't fucking helping.

"Let's try that again," my mate taunts smoothly when it stops shrieking. "Where is Kenzie?"

The changeling tries to spit at Maven but misses. Its head lolls to the right to pout at Silas and me. "You're really going to just watch as she tortures me like this? I'm an innocent who's just trying to hide from those awful bounty hunters! My situation is no different from hers—we're both from the Nether, after all."

It says it as if it's dropping a bomb. When neither Silas nor I react, it scowls, annoyed to learn that we already figured that out.

Maven tuts in disappointment and uses the tip of her dagger to languidly pry another vein out of the back of the monster's hand. Its squealing starts again, growing more frantic the longer she toys with it.

And yes, I know that thing isn't Maven.

But fucking gods above, it sounds *exactly* like her.

Finally, even though my mate seems satisfied to be getting back at the creature that took her friend, I can't take it anymore and snap, "Just answer the fucking question already!"

The changeling whimpers. "K—Kenzie is dead."

"No, she's not," Maven sighs, grabbing the creature's other mauled hand and lifting it to study the wrist. "You're taking too long to answer my questions on purpose. You're probably hoping we'll get caught and punished for missing curfew. But if you want to waste time, two can play that game. Have you ever seen an amputation with a dull knife? It takes forever, but it's beautifully unbearable."

Damn, she's brutal. I like that.

But when she pulls another weapon from out of her boot—this one a blunt blade—I start to feel queasy. Not because gore bothers me, but because I don't think I can watch even a fake Maven lose her arm.

The changeling appears to be panicking, but then it sees me and sneers. "Of course, you don't care how *they* feel about this. You never cared how Gideon felt about things, either. No wonder he decided it was better to strangle you and be done with it after he popped your cherry."

Back up.

What?

Heat sears through my body, and my very bones shiver under the wrath of my dragon, who is losing his shit over this just like I'm about to.

"What the fuck is it talking about?" I snarl, my voice barely understandable through my dragon's rage.

When Silas speaks, I catch a glimpse of fangs. He never loses control enough to sprout fangs unless he's royally pissed off. "Is that the bastard who *manipulated* you into bed? Explain. *Now.*"

I almost black out as my vision bows under my dragon's attempts to get free. It wants to burn everything to the ground, and when I smell smoke, I know I'm close to combusting.

I can't let that happen, though, or I'll hurt Maven.

Her jaw clenches in annoyance, and she doesn't look away from the changeling. "I told you it might share things it has no business sharing. Ignore it or get out."

"I am not fucking ignoring this, and we're not leaving you here alone," I snap. "You promised answers, so tell me all about this *Gideon* motherfucker."

"Now is not the fucking time for this," Maven warns.

That's the wrong thing for her to say because Silas loses his patience and scoops up the changeling's sword. Pressing the edge of it against the monster's neck until it draws blood, he glares at Maven.

"Enough games. Talk, or its head will roll before you get your answers."

Is he seriously going to keep Maven from finding out where her friend is? I scowl at him. "Don't fucking threaten her. Put down the sword right now, or I'll—"

"It's fine," she cuts me off, surprising me. "I would do the same thing if our roles were reversed. It's only practical."

Sighing like we're ruining all her fun, Maven stabs the blunt knife into the thigh of Fake Maven as she turns to face us. The changeling wails and shrieks about the pain, but Maven ignores it as she blows a strand of dark hair out of her face, as perfectly composed as ever.

"Fine. If you must know, I was taken to the Nether when I was little. But I wasn't the only one. Thirteen human children were brought there to be raised to…compete."

"Compete for what?" I ask.

"The chance to become the *telum*. Amadeus's chosen weapon."

Silas frowns, setting the sword aside. "Amadeus?"

Maven looks away. "You know him as the Entity. Although he made me address him as Father."

I stare at her.

And stare.

But it doesn't sink in, so I continue to gawk. The Entity. As in… the living world's worst enemy.

"Holy fucking shit. So when you told me you were adopted, you meant by the literal king of the Undead? The same asshole that the original monsters rebelled against over a thousand years ago when they escaped the Nether? *That's* the guy who raised you?"

"More or less. Still want me as your keeper?"

Silas is in an equally useless level of stupefaction, so it's up to me to cough out, "And…what about this *Gideon?*"

"He was another one of the kids there. We were each kept separate and isolated as we were trained for years. Necromancers ran tests and experiments on each of us to determine the strongest. I was ten years old the first time they finally allowed us to mingle. I stupidly thought it was so we could finally socialize and make friends, but I realized the real goal when one of the other kids tried to drown me."

I wince. What the hell? She was fucking *ten*.

Maven's expression turns both wistful and bitter. "Gideon saved me. He was the oldest kid taken from the mortal realm and decided to take me under his wing, so to speak. We all knew we were rivals since Amadeus made it clear that only one of us would survive to be his weapon. But he also started to make it clear that he favored me. As you can imagine, the other children didn't like that."

"Gideon didn't like that, either," Silas surmises, his face dark with anger.

She hesitates as if she doesn't want to share this next part. I'm tempted to pull her into my arms, soothe her, and tell her she doesn't need to talk about this. Even though she's trying to keep her face neutral, she clearly hates talking about all of this.

But I need to know.

"I cared for Gideon and had no idea he harbored resentment for me. Years later, when he claimed he was in love with me and began imploring me for affection in secret, I let my guard down. It wasn't love of any kind, and by that point, they'd already been conditioning me against physical touch for years. But everything Gideon told me about intimacy made me...curious. I just wanted to know what it was like."

Maven clears her throat and looks away, trying to hide the moisture in her eyes. "I didn't even feel human anymore. I needed to feel something. *Anything.* Gideon finally wore me down, and I gave in."

"And then he wrung your pathetic neck," the changeling taunts.

I ball up my fists, trying to steady my breathing. I want to kill that bitch for mocking my mate's horrifying tale—but any sudden movement right now, and I might lose it and shift.

Maven rubs her arm, still not meeting our eyes. "Yes. I woke up when he was trying to strangle me. I could have killed him right there if I'd tried, but I just...didn't try. I was too shocked. And then Amadeus broke down the door and dragged us both out to his throne room. He rarely exhibits emotion, but he was outraged. His chief necromancer had strict rules that I wasn't to be touched by anyone under any circumstances. So to find me in that state..."

She grimaces. "In defense of himself, Gideon accused me of being too soft-hearted to ever be the *telum*. He said only one of us could make it, and he was giving me a merciful death instead of letting them break me like they broke the others. He must have thought Amadeus would be impressed by his ruthlessness. Instead, it gave *Father* the bright idea to rip out my 'soft' heart and replace it with something more befitting of his chosen weapon. But first, he made me watch the Undead tear Gideon apart. We were the last two survivors of the kids taken from the mortal world, so I became the *telum*."

She quickly swipes away a tear before it can roll over her cheek.

Oh, gods.

I don't even know what to say. I knew Maven's past was dark, but…*that?* My stomach churns as I realize that my tight-lipped mate is probably leaving out plenty of other horrors I don't want to even imagine.

"*Sangfluir,*" Silas whispers hoarsely.

I watch as Maven forces her poker face back on. It's like she can't stand shedding a tear in front of us. But then, with a hellish background like that, there's no way she ever felt safe enough to be vulnerable about her feelings.

"There, you got some answers. Don't bring that part of my past up again. And you." She turns back to the changeling, which has been slowly working on getting its fingers to move to its command. "I'll only ask one more time. Where. Is. Kenzie?"

"Wouldn't you like to—" it begins in a whiny voice.

Maven moves far faster than I expect, ripping the knife out of the changeling's thigh and plunging it into one of its shoulders. It screams, but she does it again and again until—

"Halfton! The lion shifter is in Halfton!" the changeling chokes out. "Room 17 of the Black Wing Inn! I—I left her suspended in a stasis spell so I can go back and finish off the rest of her memories—"

Maven uses the flat side of the dripping knife to turn the changeling's face toward her. "Next question. Who sent you?"

It hisses instead of answering.

I brace myself for hearing more of the monster's screams in Maven's heartrending voice. But instead of losing her temper, Maven straightens and looks around the private dorm. It's a mess in here with a horde of stolen items, trash, clothing of all shapes and sizes strewn about, and a bizarre number of sex toys.

"Keep an eye on it," she mutters before rummaging through the filth.

Silas and I obediently glower down at the blood-drenched

changeling. It pouts its lower lip at us in an expression Maven has probably never made.

I flip it off.

There's a soft swear behind us, and then I hear Maven digging through the dorm's small kitchenette. She's far enough away that she won't overhear, so I look at Silas and whisper, "What are we going to do?"

"To this monster, for poisoning our keeper? I'm still weighing the options."

"I mean about Maven. You heard it all, too. She went through hell to be turned into the fucking *Entity's* weapon, and she tried to kill the headmaster."

His crimson stare locks onto me. "Baelfire Finbar Decimus, if the *doing something* you're suggesting involves harming Maven in any way, I will shred you to pieces, turn you into jerky, and feed you piece by piece to Everett's pet dogs."

Seriously, *why* did my quintet have to be made up almost exclusively of violently unhinged psychopaths?

I rub my face. "For being a brilliant prodigy, you really are a fucking dumbass. Why on earth would I suggest hurting my mate? I meant, what are we going to do to help her—should we tell the others all the horrible shit we just learned? How are we going to convince her to let us help her? Do we need to find a therapist she can talk to?"

Before Silas can respond, Maven returns and victoriously holds up a tiny bottle of bright reddish-pink powder, the outside of it streaked in dried blood. To me, it looks like any other random caster ingredient, but Silas is shocked.

"More nightshade root powder? How did it get that?"

"It must have talked to the same dealer I did," Maven muses, glaring down at the changeling. "Or at least, your master did. You used this on your sword to kill Hearst, but who gave it to you?"

The changeling clacks its teeth together in a show of inhuman annoyance. "You won't get more answers out of me. I know you'll just kill me anyway, so why drag this on?"

Maven's smile is chilling. "Because aside from sharing time, this has been the most fun I've had in weeks. So, what will it be? More fun for me, or a merciful end for you? You'll never see a single payment from whoever hired you, so why feign loyalty?"

The monster scowls viciously. But when Maven picks up the blunt knife again and trails it up Fake Maven's chest, settling over the creature's heart with a ghastly smile of excitement, the changeling flinches.

"*Fine!* I was hired by the Remitters."

Maven looks over her shoulder at us curiously.

"The anti-legacy movement," Silas offers.

"That's just one faction of it," I add. "I've heard about them. My mom's dealt with a lot of Remitters trying to raid the Divide in huge groups to demand that legacies return to the Nether. They're the idiots who think that if we monster spawn return to that plane of existence, it'll stop trying to spread into this world."

"Idiots," Maven agrees before addressing the changeling again. "Why did you take Kenzie's appearance? You could have mimicked anyone you came across. There had to be a reason you picked her."

"I was told to."

"By?"

"Carter," it spits impatiently, angry to be answering so many questions.

"Harlow Carter?" I guess. I don't know her well, but I met her last semester because my wolf shifter friend Cody had a huge-ass crush on her.

Maven frowns as if she also recognizes the name, and then she picks up the sharp dagger and presses it against the side of the changeling's neck. "Final question before I send you to the Beyond. Answer without a fight, and I'll make it fast. Where is the petite blonde asscaster you were mimicking?"

The changeling snorts. "I took her appearance and clothes and left her passed out in a courtyard. She wasn't worth killing—she's so weak, she's practically a *human*. Her memories would have been too bland to enjoy. Someone probably found her unconscious and finished the job, or maybe they decided to use her naked body while she was—"

Maven's eyes flash with revulsion, and that's the only warning before she expertly slits the monster's throat so that it dies in a matter of seconds. As soon as it stops gurgling and convulsing, its appearance ripples once again like thousands of minuscule scales flipping over, until suddenly we're staring down at a hideous creature with ghastly white skin protruding with dozens of spikes, no eyes or nose, holes for ears, and a gaping mouth full of dozens of tiny, pointed teeth.

"No wonder it wanted to look like anyone but itself," I huff. Then I glance at Maven, and the lingering horror and nausea from the emotional roller coaster starts to calm inside of me. "You know, Mayflower…you're kind of a softie."

"I suppose you're right. Slitting its throat was far too kind."

"No, I mean because you're worried sick over Kenzie, and you asked about that other girl. You care a lot more about others than you're willing to show. But I see what you're really like, baby. You're so fucking adorable."

She looks appalled. "I am not. Take it back."

Damn, I want to kiss her. Is that allowed with this exposure therapy thing? Cautiously, I lean down and press my lips against her temple instead. She ducks her head and clears her throat, and I can't help melting a little bit on the inside because my mate is obviously flustered.

So. Fucking. Adorable.

Silas studies the dead changeling. "I should harvest its spikes before we go."

So. Fucking. *Weird*.

"You're messed up," I inform him.

To my surprise, that makes Maven fight back a laugh, her dark eyes sparkling with humor as she glances up at me. "Actually, changeling spikes make a great spell ingredient. I'll help."

Why did I have to end up with *two* casters in my quintet? Or at least one caster and…whatever Maven is now. She implied that she's no longer human, but I don't know what that means.

I also know that I don't care.

Whatever she is, she's mine. Getting used to knowing about her gods-awful past will take time, and I'm not sure I can handle learning what she swore to do with a blood oath. But whatever it is, she's going to have to get over the idea of being a *temporary* keeper to us.

There's nothing temporary about this, and I'm going to prove it to her.

17

MAVEN

I wake and stare at the ceiling for several dazed minutes. Gods, it is remarkably difficult to shake off deep, quality sleep. Who knew? The totem under my pillow worked. I can't remember ever going a night without nightmares, and it's bizarre to wake up without my pulse pounding and terror-induced sweat drying on my forehead. Finally, I yawn and rub my face, rolling over.

A gentle knock sounds on the door of the big bedroom that is now officially mine. "Mayflower? I made breakfast if you want some, but we should go soon."

Right. Classes.

The Immortal Quintet is breathing down all students' necks to ensure there's no playing hooky so they can keep a close eye on us. The universe was merciful last night, so we weren't discovered sneaking back after curfew by the Immortal Quintet or their lackeys, but I know that missing class would result in some kind of severe punishment.

But this bed is so damn soft, it might just be worth it.

Have beds always been like this? I have only ever slept out of necessity before, but now I want to pull the covers over my head and return to that sweet, relaxing nothingness.

Then again...today is the day to see if I can break out of the wards and rescue Kenzie. Stasis spells are finicky, and I can't be sure if the changeling's spell will last past its death. And after I get Kenzie back, I need to prepare to take out another member of the Immortal Quintet.

Because if I take too long, Amadeus will begin threatening Lillian again.

With a sigh, I pull myself out of heaven and open the door to peer up at Baelfire.

His face breaks into a blinding smile at my sleep-rumpled appearance. "Aww. Good morning, Sleepyhead. You're so fucking cute."

I open my mouth to inform him that I am many things—a liar, a monster, a stone-cold killer, a convict of the Nether, possibly a sociopath—but I am definitely *not* cute. Except I forget to say any of that because my eyes drop to his gloriously naked upper half.

The gods might as well have chiseled him from gold.

Is it weird that I want to lick his abs? I'm entirely out of my depth.

Kenzie has way more experience with sexual attraction. She would know if that's an unusual urge. I'll ask her about it once I get her back.

Baelfire's smile grows wicked. "You don't have to limit yourself to just looking, baby. You wanna expose yourself to more touching, and my body is all yours."

Mine.

Gods, I want that.

Part of me wants to plaster myself against this unfairly sexy dragon shifter and ignore what will follow.

But it's hard to forget that I spilled my guts to him and Silas yesterday. They know more about my past than anyone else in the mortal world, and it feels fucking strange. What's even stranger is that they have yet to kick me out of their quintet or report me to the Immortal Quintet.

Maybe...

Maybe they're serious about wanting me despite everything.

But even though that thought makes my chest feel incredibly warm, it would be too selfish of me to keep them. This has to be temporary because they want to break their curses. Hell, *I* want to break their curses.

But that can't happen if I don't have a heart.

"Nope. Stop it. I can tell you're about to try pushing me away again," Baelfire growls, leaning down to catch my eye. "How can I prove that I'm not fucking going anywhere, Maven?"

I look at him. Really look at him, without any of my walls up.

"You shouldn't want me, knowing everything you know. And I assure you, you don't know everything. If my little sob story yesterday made you feel bad for me, don't. I'm not the soft-hearted girl I once was. They took my heart, but I *chose* to become the monster I am now. I'm an extremely all-or-nothing person, and that isn't going to change. You've been warned."

Baelfire examines me for a long moment. "Okay."

"Okay?" I repeat with a frown, feeling like that warranted more of a reply.

He places the softest, warmest kiss on the top of my head. "Yeah. Okay. I've been warned."

I tense when one of his big hands cradles my jaw, tilting my face up toward him. His voice lowers, and his golden eyes burn me.

"Here's my own warning, Maven. You're my keeper. My mate. You could tell me to swallow a fucking grenade, and I'd do it. But the one thing you will never tell me again is that I shouldn't want you. You don't get a say over that. You're all I want, and that's not changing, so learn to fucking deal with it."

He lets go and steps away, but the tingling heat of his touch lingering on my skin makes me swallow hard.

"Now, you should really eat something before class because my dragon will lose his shit if I hear your stomach growling. He's constantly bitching about me not taking good enough care of you. Come on."

Breakfast is a quick affair—sliced tangy fruit inside another new food substance that Silas explains is yogurt. They both watch as I try it, clearly hoping I'll enjoy it.

I quite literally don't have the heart to tell them that most food I've eaten since coming into the mortal realm has been worlds better than anything I was fed in the Nether. Of course, I like it because it's not the cold porridge with a side of pickled greens I ate most of the time growing up. They served meat sometimes, too, but after a certain sickening incident, I decided to never eat meat again.

"Well?" Baelfire asks, raising his brows.

"It's good."

When I hear Silas groan, I realize his attention is pinned on my tongue as I begin licking the spoon clean. He rubs his face, muttering something about another cold shower as he heads down the hall.

Baelfire winks at me and leans forward to lick the rest of the yogurt from my spoon. "Gotta remember you're surrounded by horny legacies, Mayflower. That poor fucker's already going insane enough without you trying to seduce us."

"Licking a spoon isn't seductive."

Or is it? I'll have to ask Kenzie that, too.

"Tell that to my boner," Bael laughs before offering me his orange juice.

Thirty minutes later, I'm strolling down the hall with them flanking my sides when Everett rounds a corner ahead of us, pausing at the sight of us. His glacial blue eyes zip to me before he quickly looks away with a scowl, straightening his blazer.

"I take it you three ate at the apartment instead of the dining hall. Would've been nice to know. I was just about to start looking for your bodies. There's been a few in Everbound's halls this morning."

"Did you hear that, Si? Snowflake was worried about us," Bael croons.

Everett rolls his eyes. "Die all you want, but don't be late to class."

"How professorial of you," Silas snorts as we descend a long flight of stairs. "Speaking of which, why *did* you return to Everbound as a teacher? Everyone knows you loathed your time here as a student. And you're hardly an academic."

Everett flips him off, clearly having no intention of answering. I'm only half-listening to their conversation as I watch for other legacies in the hallways we traverse. But as we pass an unfamiliar passageway, I sense that the air is thick with fresh death. Backing up and pausing, I tip my head at the sight before me.

Several mutilated corpses are lined up in a row. As I watch, a door opens, and a faculty member drags another lifeless legacy out to line him up. This corpse has pointed ears. They all do, I realize.

I don't realize my matches have joined me until Silas swears creatively and mutters, "Of course, they're going for the fae first. They love that we can't lie. Those *scútráchae*."

The faculty member glances up, and her brow furrows. "Please hurry along. You can't be here."

"What the fuck is going on?" Baelfire demands.

She grimaces. "Things have...escalated. The Immortal Quintet has commenced interrogations among students. These legacies all said things which were found to be, uh...treasonous, so they were executed."

I glance at a nearby corpse which looks like it's been drained of blood. By *treasonous,* she probably means too honest.

"Executions may only take place with the full vote of the Legacy Council," Everett says coldly.

The faculty member wrings her hands. "Y—yes, Mr. Frost, but... as I said, the situation has escalated. I highly suggest getting out of here before you catch the attention of—"

"Who do we have here?"

We all turn to face the voice, and I find myself looking up at Somnus DeLune. His black eyes settle on me, and his perpetual sneer deepens into disgust. I keep my poker face perfectly intact.

Silas's hand settles gently on my waist, eager to get me out of here. "We were just on our way to class."

Somnus ignores him. "If it isn't his pathetic little slip of a keeper. You're somehow even less impressive up close. But then, that whoreson deserves to be stuck with something so worthless."

"Are you the whore you're referring to? Crypt is your son, after all."

Silas tenses, Baelfire casts me a *don't-piss-off-this-guy* look, and Everett continues to frostily regard the incubus.

Somnus sneers, showing off his curved fangs. "It was nothing but a few bland pumps in a sub-par cunt, and yet for the rest of time, I'll be plagued by having that unmanageable abomination, that *mistake*, referred to as my son. He's nothing but a punishment sent by the gods themselves."

An influx of emotion swirls in my gut, so sharp and sudden that it takes effort not to sneer back at him. I'm not used to this emotion, but I think I'm…offended. Deeply offended that he would talk about Crypt like this.

Does he verbally abuse his son to his face, too? Has it always been like this for Crypt?

It's decided. I can't wait to kill this one. He's next.

"I would offer you my condolences at having him as a match, but it would be a waste of my breath since a filthy human-born like you can't possibly survive much longer." He passes by us. "Get to class before I decide to kill all four of you."

The door shuts behind him, the faculty member scampers away, and at the gentle urging of Baelfire, I finally unclench my jaw and follow them down the hall.

"Should I be concerned that Crypt has been gone this long?"

Baelfire snorts. "Wherever his keeper-abandoning ass is, I'm sure he's fine."

"He's like a cockroach," Silas agrees, making a sound of distaste. "My parents consistently tried and failed to hunt him down after he killed their keeper and my uncle. The human government hired bounty hunters to go after him two years ago after he slaughtered an entire courtroom of humans, and he was never caught or punished for it. Wherever he's run off to, he'll be back. Unfortunately," he adds spitefully.

I knew about the courtroom thing, but hearing that Crypt killed

Silas's family members makes their apparent hatred toward one another much more transparent.

In Fiend Studies, Professor Crowley discusses the Undead, discussing their aversion to sunlight and fire, inability to speak, shocking speed, craving for flesh, etcetera. It's all shit that I learned firsthand by the time I was seven years old, so I spend most of class plotting how to get Kenzie back.

Class ends, lunch passes as uncomfortably as the day before—except this time, I refuse to touch any mystery foods—and finally, it's once again time for combat training. All four of us trickle out into the training fields along with dozens of other legacies.

The air is thick with tension. A fair few legacies died during combat training yesterday, so everyone is more on edge than ever.

"Super cheery out here," Baelfire says sarcastically.

"It's only going to get worse." Silas shoots me a look. "There will be no repeats of what happened yesterday, *ima sangfluir*. Stay close to us."

I make a noncommittal sound before scanning the jumbled crowd for signs of the real Monica. I need to find out what happened to her. I'm also planning on tracking down Harlow to learn how the hell she was connected to that changeling. Her emphasis isn't combat, so I'll have to find her outside classes.

"The coach is late," Everett notes unhappily.

"Maybe they're still trying to thaw his frozen ass after your stunt yesterday," Bael shrugs.

Everett froze Coach Gallagher? I want to ask why, but then I spot a legacy storming towards us and square my shoulders.

It's the blond caster asshole who licked me yesterday. I'd hoped he had been picked off by some other legacy during training, but apparently, he's alive and hasn't figured out that I'm going to kill him if he gets anywhere near me.

"Oakley! What the fuck was that yesterday? You're not an asscaster at all, are you?" he demands. "You almost snapped my neck, and I saw Jace's body. What the fuck did you do to him? What kind of magic was that?"

Nearby legacies are turning their attention to this new scene. Silas steps in front of me, Baelfire moves to my left side, and weirdly, Everett also moves to guard behind me without touching me.

Silas's voice is deadly. "Walk away, Chase."

The caster, whose name must be Chase, scoffs. "You didn't see it, Crane. There's something fucking weird about your keeper. Sierra said she was a germophobic, quiet little asscaster, and at first, she was totally helpless under that paralysis spell but then out of fucking nowhere, she just—"

"Paralysis spell?" Baelfire repeats, his tone simmering. "Maven, what is he talking about? Did this asshole put a finger on you?"

Chase leers. "I put my whole *tongue* on her, you huge fucking moron. That's why I'm saying it makes no sense. If she was so completely powerless, then how did she just—"

"You *licked* my *mate?*" Baelfire roars.

And I mean, he literally roars it. His voice is no longer human-sounding.

I sense an alarming explosion of heat from my left just before Everett tackles me from behind, rolling us both away just as Baelfire loses control and shifts.

Legacies scream and scatter as blue fire erupts around the Decimus—but everything becomes muffled as a thick shield of ice forms out of nowhere, arching over Everett and me to protect us from the nearby flames.

The fact that Everett's ice can hold up to dragon fire is impressive. I blink up in surprise, finding that I'm lying on the cold ground as he covers me protectively with his body.

Everett's soft, cool mint scent envelops me in this enclosed space. He keeps his head turned to one side, jaw ticking as if he's still determined not to look at me—but I can feel his heart crashing inside his chest pressed against mine.

Without thinking, I squirm against him because this moment of proximity has thrown me for a major loop. When I do, the ice elemental groans brokenly.

Oh, shit.

178 | SHADOW HEART

That is a very hard erection pressing into me.

But the moment ends when the ice around us finally starts to melt. Everett swears under his breath, and a second later, the ice is entirely gone. He rolls to his feet and reaches down to pull me up, but now that I have a clear view of what's going on, I stay on my ass and stare.

Baelfire's dragon arcs through the air overhead, a glittering, golden masterpiece whose sprawling wings pummel the air, blasting everyone below. The beast lets loose a skull-rattling roar. Where Bael lost control, the field is scorched and smoking. All nearby tufts of snow are melted.

Silas is off to one side of it, and when his scarlet gaze collides with mine, he looks relieved. But my stomach lurches when I realize he didn't get out of Baelfire's way fast enough. His clothing is singed, and one of his arms and shoulders is charred and smoldering.

Damn it. I hate seeing him hurt.

Other legacies race back toward the safety of Everbound Castle. But in one graceful loop, the dragon flips around, opens its mouth, and spews molten royal blue fire, leaving a wall of blinding flames that cut off anyone trying to escape.

Then the dragon swoops down, wraps one massive clawed hand around Chase, and launches into the sky, climbing higher and higher. Finally, in a surprisingly smooth movement, the dragon flings the screaming legacy into the air, cranes its long neck, and roasts Chase with a column of brilliant sapphire flames.

And then the dragon looks down, directly at me.

Everett swears as the massive beast tucks its wings and dives, catching the flaming corpse in its mouth. It looks like it's about to crash into the ground, but at the last moment, those majestic wings fan out so that a tremendous gust of wind blows the hair back from my face.

The ground shakes as Dragon Baelfire lands. I watch its long tail snake back and forth on the charred ground restlessly as it stalks toward me. Even in this form, Baelfire is incredibly muscular. As it stalks closer, I can't help admiring the wickedly sharp horns that curl around the top of his draconic head like a deadly crown.

Gods. What a beautiful beast.

Everett is putting himself between me and Dragon Baelfire—but I abruptly realize that if Baelfire hates the professor, there's a good chance his dragon is about to kill him without blinking.

I jump to my feet and move to stand in front of Everett.

"Oakley," he hisses, grabbing my hand to try pulling me back.

But when he touches me, the dragon lets loose another roar unlike any other creature I've ever heard. This close, the deafening volume makes my ears ring. When I hear Everett swear violently behind me, I glance over my shoulder and find that he's clutching one of his ears, which is bleeding.

Silently, I wave at Everett to step back. He glowers at me for a long second before moving back so minutely it would be comedic in any other situation. But that seems enough to appease Baelfire's dragon because it lowers its large head, opens its mouth, and drops the still-smoldering corpse on the ground before me.

Like a...burnt offering.

Aww.

I peer up at the beautiful creature. "Thanks."

It huffs before nuzzling its snout against my stomach. The dragon is a little overly warm to the touch, but in pure fascination, I run a hand over the smooth, glistening golden scales along its cheek. When I do, the beast makes a sound deep in the back of its throat. At first, I think it's a growl, but as I listen more, I realize it's…purring.

All other legacies watching this scene look terrified. Silas is trying to subtly edge closer to me without pissing off the dragon. I can practically feel how tense Everett is behind me.

But I'm smiling.

"So you're the Grade A alphahole he warned me about?" I laugh quietly so only he can hear. "He obviously just doesn't know how to handle you. But I bet you'll be a very good boy for me. Won't you?"

The dragon nuzzles me more aggressively, the purr in his throat growing louder. The play of light on his golden scales is captivating, his sheer size staggering. But when Everett gets antsy and steps closer again, the beast's eyes flash open, its pupil narrowing into a slit as it bares its teeth and hisses.

"Fucking oversized lizard," the elemental mutters. "Back away slowly, Oakley. It might be acting like a puppy right now, but everyone read about it in the news five years ago when Baelfire lost control. His dragon slaughtered twenty-four legacies assigned to fight at the Divide under his mother's command."

"Those legacies were plotting a coup to kill his mother. Brigid Decimus had enough evidence to prove that to the Legacy Council in court," Silas intercedes.

Everett shoots him a fierce glare. "Whose side are you on here? My point is that she shouldn't be petting the damn thing. It's deranged."

The dragon puffs a breath of warm air at me playfully, tipping its head as if insisting on my petting the other half of its face. I've never had a pet, but I officially wouldn't mind a dragon.

"Magnificent *and* deranged. Just my type," I grin.

But then I frown, remembering what Baelfire said about his dragon trying to replace him. I've seen Baelfire shift before, and he remained in control. Right now, he's very clearly not. This is just his inner animal, and I wonder if Baelfire can even hear me right now.

"Hey," I say, getting the dragon's attention again. I rub my other hand against its snout. Nothing about this touch bothers me— perhaps because of the pleasantly warm scales and the obsessive golden eyes watching my every move as if I'm the highest form of treasure. "Are you going to give me back Baelfire?"

Its head tips as it continues watching me. Its tail curls, slipping between Everett and me to drag me a little closer. In the distance, I hear shouting and know more people are headed toward us.

But I don't look away from this exquisite creature.

"Let him go," I insist firmly.

This time, it does growl. Scarlet magic flares in Silas's hands as he prepares for a worst-case scenario, but I just lift my chin, staring it down.

The voices are getting closer, and when Everett looks over and swears something about the Immortal Quintet, I know we're about to have company of the monster variety.

I arch a brow, deciding to use words that Baelfire's dragon will probably understand better. "My mate. Give him back. *Now*."

The dragon's wings flex, and somehow, it looks incredibly pleased with the endearment. A moment later, the massive beast shrinks and morphs, muscles condensing and bones rearranging until suddenly, Baelfire slumps against me with a violent shudder.

Oh, fuck. He's heavy.

I suppose it only makes sense with all that muscle.

Silas shoves the shifter off of me with his good arm. Baelfire is disoriented—and very, very naked—as he straightens to get his bearings. His golden skin is beaded with sweat. When his attention finally lands on me, his eyes flare wide in panic.

"Fuck. *Fuck*. Did I hurt you, baby?" His frantic voice is like gravel.

"Not me." I look pointedly at Silas's seared arm. It looks painful, so I'm not surprised when he pulls out his crystal and pricks his hand to begin a healing spell on himself. "You put on quite the show."

Baelfire's expression turns mournful as he looks down at the big lump of charcoal that used to be Chase. He glances behind us at all the legacies standing a far distance off, glaring. Water elementals are working together to put out the fires, casters are trying to heal their burnt friends or matches, and sure enough, Iker Del Mar and a few of his older legacy hirelings are crossing the field toward us.

I admit, the hydra shifter has a decent long-distance glare.

"Shit," Baelfire mumbles.

He turns back to me, not at all focused on the fact that he's completely nude. I wish I could say the same for myself. It's taking significant effort not to glance down at his cock.

Baelfire grimaces. "Guess you've seen my dark side now. Sorry."

He's apologizing? Clearly, I'm doing a great job of hiding my newfound love for dragons…and naked dragon shifters.

Focus on his face. No looking down.

I allow my smile to come back. "Don't be. I thoroughly enjoyed it."

His face lights up. "I love your smile. I'd kill to see it more."

"You just did," I point out.

Bael ducks his head, rubbing his face. "Yeah…not proud of that. But at least that took the edge off my curse. I can finally think straight for the first time in days. Thank the fucking gods."

"Must be nice," Silas drawls bitterly, twisting his arm to heal his bicep.

"Decimus," Iker Del Mar booms as he stops a few yards away. His pale yellow eyes are trained hard and fast on my match, and his forked tongue flicks out repeatedly like an angry twitch. "You will come with me."

The image of all those dead fae in the hallway comes back to me, and I step forward without thinking, ignoring Everett's hissed protest.

"We still have combat training. You made it clear we're not to skip classes."

He doesn't bother sparing me a glance. "Your match will be back in time for training."

All the combat-emphasis legacies who previously ran from Baelfire's outburst are warily trickling back into the field, their curious eyes darting between our quintet and the immortal shifter. Brooks and his matches are nearby, and he sneers at me, drawing a line across his neck.

Seriously. When will people come up with a more original threat?

"Well?" Del Mar demands impatiently, baring his sharp teeth at Bael.

Baelfire glances at me one more time with lingering worry but follows the hydra and his legacy escorts off the scorched field.

18

MAVEN

Moments after Baelfire disappears into Everbound Castle with Del Mar and the others, Coach Gallagher storms outside, surveying the still-smoking field with distaste as he approaches. The other legacies have regrouped, though some of them have some burns. Plenty of them are giving my quintet dirty looks.

The coach stops and glares directly at me, opening his mouth. He's an easy one to read, so I'm anticipating he'll make some histrionic statement about atypical casters being unable to lead highly-ranked legacies.

But then he sees the frigid stare Everett is cutting him and apparently thinks better of it.

Turning to all the other legacies, he snaps, "Training will begin in fifteen minutes, burns or no burns, so get yourselves patched up and prepare for one-on-one quintet combat."

I glance at Everett, noting that his ear is still bleeding.

"Hold still," I tell him, slipping off one of my gloves. My healing capabilities with common magic are pretty shitty, but I can handle a burst eardrum.

He rears away from me and brushes dirt off his clothes, determinedly not looking at me. "For the last fucking time, Oakley, leave me alone. I don't want you anywhere near me."

I arch a brow. "Tell your body that. Most people don't pop a boner when tackling someone else out of harm's way."

Everett's cheekbones turn pink, and he mutters something under his breath that I don't catch. For whatever reason, my comment also makes Silas snap to attention. He gives Everett a death glare as he finishes healing his own shoulder. The skin is still raw and red, but the worst burns have faded.

"A word, *professor?*" he snaps, grabbing Everett by the arm and pulling him out of earshot.

I watch them, noting that while Silas is furious, the ice elemental looks frustrated and chastened. Is Silas this mad because Everett got close to me? None of my matches have reacted like this about me getting physical with the others, so that seems unlikely.

Curious.

At the thought of Crypt, I glance out over Everbound Forest, trying to gauge how far away the wards are. I'll have to get through them to get Kenzie, but I wonder if Crypt will be able to get through the wards when he returns.

Fine, I admit it. I miss my invisible stalker more than I thought possible.

My attention is arrested when I spot Baelfire returning to the field, now clothed. Relief hits me. I must have been far more worried about what Del Mar would do to him than I even realized.

Yet, as Baelfire gets closer, I see that his face is twisted in anger. His ears are bright red as he joins everyone else on the field. I can't figure out why he looks so pissed off until sunlight catches on the shiny buckle of a leather collar around his throat.

I know plenty of things about shifters, but one thing especially: collars are considered far more degrading in their culture than they are to any other beings. It's seen as a severe insult to their inner animals. Utterly humiliating.

I'm not the only one who notices Baelfire's new accessory, as another nearby shifter gasps.

"What the fuck? Dude, what the hell? Did they actually—" he begins.

"*Shove it*, Keith," Baelfire snarls before stopping beside me and folding his brawny arms.

I press my lips together, studying the collar. While some unexplored part of me finds this look on him bizarrely hot, I don't like what it stands for.

I don't like that *they* put it on him.

"Take it off."

"Can't. Tried already," he grits out, staring straight forward like he's too mortified to make eye contact. "It's enchanted to keep me from shifting."

Anger washes over me. He's a fucking *shifter*. He's supposed to shift. They took that away from him over a little outburst?

When Silas and Everett rejoin us, I note with surprise that Silas healed the ice elemental's ear when I wasn't looking. That seems out of character for the ruthless blood fae, but I choose not to draw attention to it. I'm just glad Everett's ear won't be a weakness to factor in during combat.

Both of them also frown at Baelfire's collar.

"About damn time," Everett mumbles. "I'm surprised they didn't add a muzzle to rein in your big fat mouth, too."

Baelfire glares at him, tugging at the collar. "You're a dick."

"At least you won't be putting Maven at risk by losing control again," Silas adds.

"He also won't be able to defend himself if things go to shit in combat," I point out. "Everyone here has taken notice, which means whatever quintet we're assigned to fight will see this as a new weakness and target Baelfire."

They all consider that before Silas shakes his head. "No, their first target will still be our keeper. Protecting you will remain our top priority."

I glare at him. "I'm a barely-ranked atypical caster. Baelfire is a Decimus, a dragon, and a highly-ranked threat with a temporary handicap. He's a far bigger prize. Enemies will want to take advantage of his inability to shift while they can. I'm the keeper, I pick the priority, and I'm telling you: watch Baelfire's back."

Bael stops tugging at his collar and smiles like he thinks I'm being adorable. "Look, I fucking *love* that my mate is worried about me, but you have nothing to worry about. I've made it through tons of combat classes without shifting. They usually tell me not to, anyway, remember? It'll be fine."

"The lizard can handle some extra heat," Everett agrees.

Silas nods.

I look between them, irritation brewing. They're not taking me seriously.

Maybe it's because they still see me as a weak asscaster, or perhaps they're just used to being the biggest, baddest threats around—but I've seen them in action now and as impressive as they are, they can be careless. They don't know how to work as a team yet, and it's going to bite them in the ass.

The coach calls everyone to attention and announces that each quintet will be assigned a rival quintet to hunt down and fight in Everbound Forest. No unmatched legacies are participating in today's combat training. He explains the point system and starts rattling off assignments. When he finally gets to our quintet, he nods at Brooks and the four guys standing around him.

"Maven Oakley, your quintet will be facing off against Brooks Benson's. And that's everyone, so line up and prepare for the whistle. Remember, maiming, torture, and death are all on the table, but today you're going in bare-handed. No weapons allowed."

Thank the universe. It's been too long since I had a good hand-to-hand fight.

We move to the edge of the forest. I'm sure that, as usual, the faculty's spells will transport us and our rivals into separate parts of the forest.

"Stay close, *sangfluir*," Silas reminds me, cradling my jaw gently as he gives me a pleading look.

I know it's part of the exposure therapy, but goosebumps scatter down my arms at his touch.

"Watch out for Baelfire," I fire back.

The whistle blows, and we all take off into the woods. Transportation magic twists and pulls us, and when my feet hit the ground running, we're in an area of spaced-out trees that I recognize as being near the small pond I occasionally visit.

We slow to a stop and follow training protocol, checking our surroundings. It's cold and quiet in these twisted woods, the darkness encroaching as the mist drifts past like a haunting cloak.

Everett steps further away from me and almost trips over a skeleton. He grimaces. "It's like they enchanted this forest to be eternally creepy. The shadows, the deadly creatures, all the bones and hideous trees…"

"Isn't it wonderful?" I grin.

That earns a snort from Baelfire before he tips his head. "Does it look anything like what you're used to? You know…back home?"

"A bit. Mostly because there isn't much sunlight or color," I muse, studying our surroundings. "It's nearly colorless there. When I emerged in the mortal world, my eyes hurt for days."

However, I've grown to like certain colors—gold, red, purple, icy blue…

Damn it. These legacies really have gotten under my skin, haven't they?

Silas frowns. "I'm curious about that. When *did* you come into the mortal realm? Did you escape it all alone?"

I hesitate. My leaving the Nether was an entirely formulated thing. Once Amadeus decided the stars had aligned and it was time to send out his weapon, my emergence was disguised under a massive surge in Maine. Once I managed to make it out of the Divide unseen, a demon with connections in the Nether gave me fake human records, modern clothes, and money. She was supposed to introduce me to the human world and help me blend in.

Of course, that demon was arrogant as fuck and decided instead to try her hand at killing the rumored *telum*, just to see if she could. I had to dispatch her and move on alone, giving myself a crash course into modern human shit to supplement everything I learned from Lillian previously. Finally, I reported myself as a "newly manifested" caster to get to Everbound and gain access to Melvolin Hearst.

But I don't enjoy talking about this. Even though Baelfire and Silas have gotten a snapshot of my past, it still feels weird as fuck to talk casually with *anyone* about it...especially when a particularly frosty professor is present.

Everett sees me cast him a brief look and grumbles, "I know where you're from, too, Oakley."

"If that's true, I find it strange that you haven't reported me, *professor*."

His jaw flexes. "It's not that strange. I didn't report you being in the headmaster's office, either. Believe it or not, I'm not trying to insult the gods by ripping apart my own quintet just because one of us was spirited away to the Nether as a helpless toddler."

I pause. "How did you know I was a toddler when I was taken?"

Everett rubs his neck, looking away. "It's nothing. I...I don't know if it was you. I guess I just assumed—"

"Company!" Baelfire shouts. "On our left!"

Thank the universe for shifter hearing.

We take defensive positions just before the ground rumbles, and a wave of rocks and earth sweeps toward us. Silas hits it with a deflection spell that sends dirt raining all around. Through that dust explosion, a vampire dives forward, leaping toward Everett.

Another blade of ice is in Everett's hands before I can blink, and he impales the vampire just as two casters and Brooks charge toward us. One caster launches an attack spell at me. I deflect, drawing on my reserve to use common magic because using either of the other two magics I can use might lead to another Chase situation.

Brooks shifts into a tiger and pounces toward Silas. I'm distracted with fending off three more magical attacks in quick succession since it's difficult to remember to limit myself to weak, common magic. Baelfire tackles the earth elemental before they can send another wave of rocks toward me.

But while Everett and Silas are both distracted, flanking my sides in an attempt to keep the vampire or tiger from getting close, I catch the movement of a powerful spell in my peripheral vision and realize that the second caster isn't currently engaged in combat—and he's targeting Baelfire.

Swiveling, I dig deep into what's left of my reserve, throwing a defense charm at the second caster. But my aim is off because Caster One's spell slams into me, making me faceplant hard into the forest floor.

My charm only barely grazes Caster Two. He stumbles, but most of his spell still slams into Baelfire—

And my dragon shifter's scream of pain rings through the forest.

My stomach plummets when Bael collapses to the ground, blood gushing from multiple injuries.

No.

"Baelfire!" I shout, scrambling back to my feet and ignoring the new, stinging scrape on my cheek as I race toward him. When I reach him, he's groaning, writhing on the forest floor as if every position causes immense pain.

And I can see why. That was a fucking silverblend spell.

His clothes are shredded, and dozens, if not hundreds, of tiny, thistle-like barbs of magically-formed silver are protruding from his arms, legs, stomach, shoulders, neck—everywhere. They're shaped so that they'll hurt worse coming out than going in, and *gods*, he is bleeding so much.

His shifter healing won't work with the silver embedded in him like this.

The other quintet planned ahead. Even without weapons, they cheated and brought in silver to kill off any shifter they came up against.

I hear an explosion of some kind nearby, but I can't seem to look away from my gorgeous match's face, contorted in agony as he bleeds too freely from too many places. I try to wipe the blood so it doesn't drip into his squeezed-shut eyes, but I realize my hands are shaking.

All of me is shaking.

How dare they hurt what's mine?

I'm…mad.

No. I am fucking *livid*.

All my life, no matter what brand of hell I was trying to survive, I have known one thing to be true: to protect what's mine, I have to be brutal. There is no such thing as taking it too far if the people I care about are at stake.

It's why I took beatings for Lillian without her knowing.

It's why I made a blood oath.

And now, it's why I decide that I don't fucking care about all the reasons why these legacies would be better off without me. All that matters is that they've become undeniably important to me—and now that I've decided they're mine, I'm not holding back anymore.

I'll be heartless for them.

"Maven!" Silas shouts, rushing to my side.

Everett isn't far behind. Ice spreads from each footstep he takes as he backs away from our enemies while keeping an eye on them. They're regrouping, too. This tiny lull in the fight must mean that our quintets are somewhat evenly matched.

But only because Baelfire is hindered, and I was tempering myself.

It's time to fucking change that.

"Heal him," I demand, standing.

Silas reaches for me, his brow deeply furrowed, but I push his hand away and give him the withering glare I perfected in Amadeus's arena.

"I said watch his back. I said they'd go for him. You didn't listen, but now I'm fucking telling you to *heal him* before he dies of blood loss. And don't *you* dare get in my way," I snap at Everett.

I stalk past them and directly into the miniature stalemate between quintets. Everett shouts my name, but I tune him out. I tune everything out and focus on the five assholes who just tried to kill my dragon shifter.

They have no idea what they just pissed off, but they're about to find out.

The caster who hit Baelfire with the silverblend spell sneers at me. "Offering yourself up as a sacrifice to win our mercy, Oakley?

Too bad this isn't even a fair fight. Our keeper is going to rip you to shreds."

Almost like they coordinated it, Brooks the tiger roars and leaps toward me. When he does, I let my instincts and training kick in. As always, during a fight, my senses sharpen almost to the point of pain. Everything seems to slow down.

Calling on the magic rushing eagerly inside me, I grab the tiger by the throat midair and twist, slamming him into the forest floor using his momentum and the unnatural strength I'm always so careful to hide.

Before he can do anything but snarl, dark magic flares around my fingertips before I plunge my hand through his rib cage, grab his heart, and rip it out. The tiger shifter goes slack as I turn back to the others and toss their keeper's heart aside, the hum of a fresh kill flooding me with pure, thrilling adrenaline.

The more lives I take in a fight, the more the urge to kill grows into a fever pitch and takes over. It's been that way ever since I was turned into this. Lillian was the one who always brought me back if I lost control, but now…

I hope I can keep myself in check while I end these idiots. Otherwise, I'll be a mindless, blood-crazed weapon until I'm killed and revived.

Either way, what fun.

The rival quintet is shocked by how quickly I just snuffed out their chance at a curse-less future. I smile and twiddle my bloodied fingers at them before flipping them off.

"You're right. This isn't a fair fight at all."

19

BAELFIRE

When I was eleven years old, my older brother Aidan was accidentally hit by a silverblend spell while serving at the Divide. He got an emergency magical transport back home, and I couldn't even recognize him under all the gore.

I'd asked my caster dad if Aidan was going to die, and he had quietly admitted it was very possible. All night long, I'd heard my brother's bloodcurdling screaming as they had to dig tiny pieces of silver shrapnel out of his entire body.

Turns out, he was handling it like a fucking champ. Kudos to him.

Because *holy motherfucking hell*, this hurts.

I'm starting to lose consciousness, probably because I'm leaking blood like a faucet. But I fight against blacking out because, as far as I know, we're still under attack, and that means I need to make sure Maven is safe. I just have to get through this searing agony and ignore my inner dragon, who's throwing a fit inside my head with no possible way of getting out to get revenge.

I guess I should be grateful that Silas is some kind of prodigy because suddenly, all the silver puncturing my skin starts vibrating. I blink my eyes open and vaguely make out that he's crouched beside me, his brow beading with sweat as he chants some shit I can't understand and makes a weird-ass shape with his hand.

There's a moment where, against all possibility, the agony gets even *worse,* as if the metal is reshaping itself inside my skin—and then hundreds of silver needles slide out of my skin and drop to the forest floor.

The moment the silver is out, I gasp with relief as my body starts to mend. Thanks to my weakened state, it's far slower than usual, but I'll take it. After several seconds, I prop myself up on one arm, wiping blood off my face and panting as I try to get over that traumatizing little brush with death I just had.

Everett is also next to us. What the fuck? Why isn't he fighting? Then I realize that both of their gazes are glued to something nearby.

When I crane my neck to see what's going on, I nearly have a heart attack.

Maven is dancing.

I mean, she's actually slaughtering our enemies—but every deadly move she makes is so lithe and graceful that it looks like a macabre, perfectly choreographed dance.

The earth elemental launches at her, but she does a back handspring to land directly behind the vampire. He whirls, trying to grab at her, but she breaks both of his arms in one brutal movement before dropping down and breaking both of his knees, too. He screams and collapses, and my mouth drops open when she…pulls out his heart.

Plucks it right out and tosses it aside without batting an eye.

"Oh…shit. Dear gods above," Everett breathes as we continue to watch Maven run circles around the fuckers we were collectively just barely staving off. "She's…"

"A badass," I declare.

"The *telum*." His eyes track her movements. He starts fidgeting nervously with his sleeves on repeat. "She's…the scourge."

Silas shoots him a suspicious look. "We know. She told us. But how do you know about that?"

"There was a prophecy about the Entity's weapon a long time

ago, and some legacies never forgot about it," he mutters. "I just caught wind of the rumors stirring. That's it."

He's definitely hiding something, but I don't bother trying to get the honest answer out of him as I watch my mate move with deadly speed, cracking one of the caster's skulls on her knee before rolling out of the way of another attack. She moves faster than a human can —maybe even as fast as a shifter. Reacts faster, too.

It's like seeing her in her true element for the first time, and I can't look away.

The earth elemental sends a barrage of sharpened stones flying toward her. Maven uses the vampire's corpse as a shield before taking off into a dead run at the elemental. I tense, worried she's about to need help, but Maven leaps up, twisting midair to wrap her legs around the neck of the elemental. There's a loud *snap*, and he drops dead before she lands and rolls back to her feet.

"Did...did she just snap that guy's neck with her thighs?" I manage.

Silas is just as mesmerized. "That she did."

"Fuck."

I wouldn't complain if her thighs did me in. What a way to go.

Finally, Maven faces the final rival—the caster who hit me with the silverblend spell. I can practically smell the fear rolling off of him as he sends attack after attack at her, all of which she deflects with swirling blasts of dark magic. I don't know what Silas meant about our keeper's magic being different, but it does seem to shatter anything in its path.

When the caster gives up and turns to run, Maven catches up and quickly pins him to the ground from behind, one knee on his back. She's far enough away that even I can't hear what she bends down to say in his ear before shadow-like magic flares out from around them.

He screams.

She beams.

Fucking gods above. My stunning little mate is kind of a sadist, isn't she?

I try to sit up more, grimacing at the pain. "Crypt was right. We've been underestimating her."

"She wanted us to." Silas shakes his head, a gruesome smile playing on his lips. "Our vicious little minx has been far underplaying her own abilities so she could escape all attention here at Everbound. Clever, but it makes me curious how strong she really is."

I hear a garbled cry and realize Maven killed off the last of Brooks' quintet. When she stands, she scans her surroundings in a trance-like state, almost like she's hoping to find another target to take down. There aren't any.

After a moment, she shakes her head to clear it and stalks back to us, splattered in the blood of our enemies with a smile on her beautiful face.

Terrifying.

But in a really hot way.

Mate, my inner dragon growls hungrily. *Mine.*

I clear my throat, which is still hoarse from all the screaming. "Is anyone else turned on right now, or is that just me?"

Everett looks at me like I disgust him while Silas hums in agreement.

Maven stops in front of us, and for a moment, she observes us warily with her hauntingly beautiful eyes as if expecting *us* to attack her next. A few days ago, I would have been frustrated that she still doesn't believe me about wanting her no matter what.

But now, knowing about some of her past...I don't blame her. It'll take time to earn her trust. Especially because we fucked up with that stupid bet.

I notice Silas hardcore staring at the small, lightly bleeding scratch on our keeper's cheek. Maven seems to notice, too, because her lips twitch.

"Fang me later. Now isn't the time."

The blood fae swallows hard before snapping out of it. "Here, allow me to—" Then he pauses and swears. "I forgot. My magic won't heal you because you use necromancy."

Everett's eyes get hilariously round. "What?"

"Necromancy and other magics mix like oil and water. They refuse to interact. Common and blood magic will not mingle with necromancy, which in turn will not—"

"Who the hell cares? That's not what I meant," the elemental snaps, turning to our keeper with a furrowed brow. "You're a necromancer?"

Ignoring him, Maven kneels beside me, lips pressed together unhappily as she studies my skin that's still healing each puncture wound slowly. Some of them are still bleeding. When she reaches out to gently test a couple of areas, I pretend it doesn't hurt.

Even though it absolutely fucking does. Now that I'm not distracted with seeing my keeper take names and kick ass, everything fucking hurts. Silver injuries heal slowly and sting for days.

But I want to soothe my mate. "I'm fine, Mayflower. All good here."

Come to think of it...she's right. Now that I've seen her in action, she doesn't strike me as a *Mayflower*. I'll have to find a better nickname for her.

"You could have died," she mutters. "I should have killed him slower."

"Aww. You do care," I grin.

Maven's gaze arrests me. "More than you know. Now apologize for letting yourself get hurt like that."

My heart starts pounding. I swallow and nod like a good boy because that's what I'll always be for her.

"I'm really sorry, baby."

She glances at Silas and Everett like she's looking for any more signs of damage to our quintet. The lucky fuckers are both roughed up but fine, so she tells them to check this area for signs of any other threats before we leave the forest. It's an excuse to talk to me alone, and we all know it, but they still give us space.

I have no idea what she wants to say to me alone, so I'm shocked when Maven uses one of her oversized sleeves to try wiping some of the blood off my face.

"For the record, I'm sorry too."

I'm getting distracted by her scent and nearness. "What…uh, what for?"

"As I understand it, shifters look forward to the day they get matched to a mate with even more excitement than any of the other Four Houses. You didn't deserve to get matched to a bitch."

A snarl rips from my throat. "Don't call yourself that. You're not a bitch."

"I punched you," she points out.

"So what? I probably deserved it."

"I mistreated you on purpose, which you didn't deserve. Also…" She meets my eye, her expression softening. "I liked those flowers you got me. I just couldn't let you know that, or you'd think I was encouraging you."

My heart is soaring. Seriously, I'm too lightheaded for this. Is she actually saying all of this, or is my head just fucked up from losing so much blood?

"Are you saying you're encouraging me from now on?" I ask, praying to all six gods that I'm reading this situation right.

Because I think my spooky little mate is trying to express her feelings but doesn't know how.

"I'm saying…" She hesitates, studying my eyes, and then peels off one bloodied glove to place her hand on my jaw. "The gods are cruel, but I can't resist anymore. So fuck it all. You're stuck with me until the tragic end."

The moment her soft lips press against mine, I can't think straight. Desire and desperation for my mate burn through my veins alongside the residual pain. I groan, deepening the kiss so I can stroke her tongue with mine.

I want to push further and explore her mouth until she crawls into my lap. I need to feel her perfect body all over mine. I just fucking *need her*.

But Maven pulls away far too quickly, leaving me panting.

"Come back."

She shakes her head, but her lips twitch.

"I'll beg if I have to," I try again.

"I'm not going to make you beg right now."

She sounds a little breathless, which makes me fucking proud. I pout as playfully as I can while looking like a bloody mess.

"Why not? I'll beg so fucking good for you."

Maven's gaze heats, and for a moment, I'm sure she's going to indulge my raging newfound kink. But then her attention lowers to the rest of my body, and her lips press together. "You're still healing, Baelfire."

"Your magical pussy would heal me faster."

"My pussy is not magical."

I smirk. "You're a caster. So it totally is."

"Am I?" she arches a brow quizzically.

I hesitate, thinking about it. She uses magic. She was once a human, and then she lost her heart, so that makes her...I have no idea.

Mine, though. Always mine.

Everett rejoins us. His face is stormy, and one cheek is noticeably red like he's been scratching at it.

"We should get going. I froze Silas."

"Seriously?" I scowl at him. "You're like a godsdamned toddler. Why the fuck would you do that? He's going to be so pissed when you thaw him out."

"Maybe, but let's hope he's pissed and *sane*. He was trying to claw my eyes out."

Maven stands, slipping her glove back on. "His curse is eating his mind."

"Oh." Everett looks away. "I guess graduation will break him out of that. Until then, I'm going to freeze his ass if he goes for my face again."

I roll my eyes and try to get to my feet despite how the world spins around me. "Protecting your one and only asset, huh?"

To my complete shock, Snowflake moves to support me on one side so I don't topple over, even though he looks like he wants to gag, touching all this sticky blood.

"Shut the fuck up, dragon."

"Shrimp dick."

"Asshole."

Maven snorts, which makes our attention snap to her. She's smiling as she turns to walk away in the direction Everett returned from.

Gods above, I love her smile.

I follow her, ignoring Everett's grumblings about how heavy I am and how I smell like a terrarium. We find Silas frozen in a thick cluster of trees, his face a mask of mindless anger and his hands stretched like talons. Everett unfreezes him, and the blood fae sags against the nearest tree, shaking his head until he's coherent again.

"Damn it," he grits. "I'm sorry, *sangfluir*."

Everett scowls. "Hello? I'm the one whose face you wanted to rip off."

"That hasn't changed. But I hate that I'm becoming such a liability. Had that happened during the fight earlier…"

"I still would have handed you your asses," Maven says so matter-of-factly that it makes me bark out a laugh. She regards the three of us like she analyzes chessboard pieces. "Speaking of which, you three need some serious training before they reschedule First Placement."

That wipes the smile off my face. "My mom's trained me since I was twelve."

"I had private combat tutors," Everett tacks on.

Silas stops leaning on the tree. "The Garnet Wizard handled my training. I could defeat his most seasoned acolytes by the time I turned eighteen."

"Then his acolytes must have been invertebrates because while your magic is decent, your physical combat needs help."

Shots fired. I barely smother a laugh as Silas's mouth drops open.

"Decent? *Decent?* I'm far more than—"

Maven cuts him off, glancing at Everett. "You're the opposite. Your skill with a blade is passable, but there are elemental children who can control their power with ten times the accuracy you have."

His face flushes.

"And Baelfire?"

Shit. My turn to be roasted.

I duck my head. "Yeah, I know. I got hit by a motherfucking silverblend spell because I was too focused on my target. My bad."

"No. You lack strategy completely."

Ouch.

I forgot that she doesn't pull punches. I guess that's a good trait for a keeper, but it makes my inner dragon downright petulant. I huff and fold my arms like a toddler. I want to impress my mate and make her happy, not hear *this*.

"My point is, you're all sloppy. I'll have to fix that, so we need to find somewhere to train for additional hours, away from other legacies."

Silas looks as disgruntled as I feel, but he looks away and sighs. "There are large rooms in the lowest level of Everbound Castle that can be reserved. They used to be dungeons, but they've been refurbished for exercise and training. If you really think it's so necessary," he tacks on.

"*Very* necessary. We'll start tomorrow."

"Because you're worried about me and want me to have time to heal?" I guess. I'm shamelessly milking this injury to get more of Maven's sweet attention.

"And because I'm leaving Everbound's wards to get Kenzie back after midnight."

She says it so nonchalantly, like she's announcing she's going to take a nap.

Everett immediately scowls. "No. Even if you can somehow get through the wards, anyone meddling with them will be sensed by the casters who the Immortal Quintet hired to put them up. They'll go looking for you. What if they figure out where you came from? It's way too dangerous, Oakley. You're staying."

I don't envy him the ball-shriveling look Maven sends his way.

"Oh, really? Make me."

He looks exasperated, turning to us for backup. I can't stand the idea of Maven putting herself in danger or getting anywhere close to the Immortal Quintet's radar. But I'm starting to understand my mate better, and it's pretty damn obvious that whatever she sets her mind to, she accomplishes.

Silas, on the other hand, starts to back up the ice elemental. But he's interrupted by the whistle blowing outside of Everbound Forest, signaling the end of combat training. That means we only have a small window for dinner before we're cooped up in our apartment until morning while the stupid-ass henchmen of the Immortal Quintet patrol the castle to look for anyone breaking curfew.

Maven makes her way toward the forest exit. We follow, with Everett right behind her and Silas and I bringing up the back. I grit my teeth when I notice that Snowflake can't keep his eyes off Maven when she can't see him.

It's not that I'm jealous. I totally get wanting to stare at her deliciously round ass.

But if he catches feelings for her and his curse hurts her, my dragon has full permission to eat him. Or roast him. I'm good with whatever.

"You still owe me scales," Silas mutters beside me, low enough that only I'll hear.

I do a double-take. Is he fucking serious?

He is. This asshole really thinks he's entitled to my dragon scales. As if that's even important—I know he wants them for fancy spells or some shit, but how the fuck is he even still thinking about that bet when we all saw how it hurt Maven?

"Not happening, dickhead."

"So, you're openly admitting that the word of a Decimus means nothing?" Silas snarks.

Irritation prickles over me. I can take a lot of shit, but not jabs at my family. My family is anything *but* dishonest. I bare my teeth at him.

"I said it's not. Fucking. Happening. You should have already groveled your ass off for Maven's forgiveness for ever suggesting that bet in the first place, you insensitive prick."

"I did." He pins me with scarlet eyes. "Fine. If you refuse to honor the first agreement, name another price."

Name my price?

Wow. He must be really desperate.

That gets my attention, and I glance ahead to check that Everett and Maven are still out of earshot. We're almost out of the woods as we pass a smoldering, charred section where a fire elemental or fire spell got out of hand. We skirt a couple of lumps of charcoal that might've been legacies at one point.

"Why the hell do you want them so bad?" I demand.

"That's my business."

"Does it have something to do with your curse? Maven? Some random spells you want to try? Just spit it out."

Silas clenches his jaw and looks forward. "I can't."

"Because you're a shady little prick," I huff.

"Because I swore I wouldn't, and I can't tell a lie."

I flip him the bird. "My scales, my rules. I'm not giving you jack shit until I know what it's for."

"I hate you," he mutters.

"Right back at you."

20

MAVEN

It's difficult to ignore the fresh wave of intoxicating, destructive magic humming through my veins while Coach Gallagher begrudgingly awards us points for winning against the rival quintet.

Other matched quintets emerge one by one from Everbound Forest, most heavily injured and exhausted and some missing entirely. I'm aware that my blood-splattered appearance is earning some suspicious looks, just as I'm aware of how Silas subtly steps in the way to block me from their sight. He's clearly put together that I don't want other legacies to know how dangerous I am.

Finally, combat class is over, and everyone limps back to the castle. Some are carried or dragged by their quintet members. As they do, I spot the real Monica with her quintet out of the corner of my eye. She leans heavily on a fae girl with lavender hair and cries quietly.

Whatever happened, I'm just glad she's alive.

I still need to track down Harlow and get answers, but that will have to wait until tomorrow after I've safely gotten Kenzie back.

As we step back into the vaulted stone hallways of the castle, Baelfire flags, pausing to brace himself against the wall like his head is spinning. Seeing him weak from the attack makes my fists clench. The puncture wounds all over his skin have healed, but he makes for a gruesome sight, with shredded, red-soaked clothes and blood all over. When a couple of legacies passing by take notice and approach, trying to talk to the overwhelmingly popular Decimus, my dragon shifter snarls at them, and they scamper away.

My dragon shifter.

I glance at Everett, who has been scowling since I mentioned leaving tonight, then at Silas, who quietly hisses at Baelfire to keep walking and not make us look vulnerable. Ever since I lost my temper and decided to stop fighting this, a sense of rightness has started seeping into my bones.

It's incredibly fucking selfish of me, but they're mine now.

Even Crypt, despite his bothersome absence. I'm starting to detest the fact that I don't feel him stalking me from Limbo nearly all day long.

When Baelfire finally insists he's okay, we return to our quintet apartment. Bael mutters that he needs a "long-ass fucking shower" and heads down the hall. Silas starts rummaging through random spell ingredients in the kitchen, and surprisingly, Everett follows him inside and checks the fridge.

He catches me observing him and grumbles, "You need to eat dinner, and I highly doubt your pet lizard can manage cooking tonight."

"There's a dining hall," I point out.

"The one full of legacies who would try to kill you in a heartbeat? Yeah, that's not happening."

I give him a deadpan look. "I just gave you all a front-row seat to the fact that I excel at homicide. Shocking as it may be, picking up food is well within my wheelhouse."

But when I turn away, a foot-thick sheet of ice crackles into existence, blocking the front door. Everett hasn't even looked up from digging in the fridge.

"There you go. Accuracy. Now you should go and get that cut on your face cleaned."

I open my mouth, ready to tell him to—

"Fuck off," Silas snaps before I can as he levels Everett with a surprisingly savage glare. "You shouldn't have even followed us in here. Get out. *Now*."

"I can at least be allowed to make sure she's fucking *eating*," the ice elemental grits out.

"Those who *care* about her will do that. So get. The hell. Out."

Everett's jaw flexes, and he slams the fridge closed as he turns to face Silas, but it's like someone opened the freezer instead because abruptly, my breath comes in white plumes in front of my face. For a moment, Silas and Everett go toe to toe, looking equally pissed off as icy flurries drift through the kitchen. Then Everett's expression transforms into the same miserable, defeated one he was wearing earlier…when Silas chewed him out for getting aroused after tackling me.

I study the interaction until things click together. "You guys think Everett is somehow a danger to me. Why?"

Everett winces and turns toward the front door. "Forget it, Oakley."

He storms out, the ice block shattering at his fingertips before he slams the front door behind himself. Such a strong reaction…but then it's slowly becoming clear that he's putting up a facade where I'm concerned.

I'm going to make his facade shatter just like that ice.

Silas mutters something in fae about Everett being a selfish ass and turns to me. "Here, *sangfluir*."

"You can't heal me, remember?"

"I know. But you can use your own magic now," he says carefully, studying me as if he's worried I'll react badly. "After you ended the others, you were able to use potent magic on that last rival. Perhaps you're more a siphon than a caster because, to me, it seems as if you…fed."

By killing.

He doesn't say that part out loud, but it's just as true unspoken.

When I don't deny it, he gently takes one of my gloved hands, presses the healing ingredients into it, and then places a kiss near my temple. I tilt my face up toward him. For a moment, he seems captivated by my eyes and the cut on my cheek. Then he steps away, giving me space to breathe after all that nearness and...touching.

"Heal yourself, *ima sangfluir*. I'll return later."

"You're leaving?"

"If you're intent on leaving the wards tonight, I insist on crafting an extremely potent concealment potion to mask our scents and magic footprints. I'll be back soon."

Placing one more feather-light kiss against my temple, Silas leaves. I hear the shower running down the hall as Baelfire washes away all the gore. Otherwise, it's silent as I sit at the dining table and crush moonflower petals. Twisting the tiniest amount of necromancy into healing magic, I create something that will actually work on me.

By the time my face is healed, Baelfire reemerges from the hallway with nothing on except the leather collar and a black towel around his waist. His cuts have healed, leaving nothing but golden skin and endless muscles.

Very smooth, lickable muscles.

My face heats. He's too damn attractive for his own good.

The sexy dragon shifter stops in front of me, and that's when I manage to draw my attention away from his incredibly cut muscles and notice the strain on his face.

"Are you hurting?" I ask, frowning as I stand.

"I'm fucking dying."

"What—"

He steps closer, and—oh, gods. His erection is hard and huge, pressing against my stomach through the towel. Baelfire's eyes are molten when I meet them, edged with that same animalistic obsession I saw in his dragon's eyes earlier.

"You said the rescue mission is after midnight, right? That gives you a few hours to grind that gorgeous pussy of yours all over my face until I can't breathe. *Please*."

Heat builds under my skin. As usual, there's no sensation in the region of my heart, but I can feel my pulse picking up as I gaze up at him. He's right—I have hours to kill.

And I want him, too. Badly. As if touching him now will erase the fact that I could have lost him today before I even let myself have him.

But...

When Baelfire sees my hesitation, he squeezes his eyes shut and takes a deep breath as if to anchor himself. "Okay. Got it. I won't ask again tonight. If you don't want it—"

"I told you, I *want* to enjoy touch," I remind him, feeling a flush crawl over my skin as I brush my fingers down his beautifully toned body.

Baelfire exhales sharply. "Thank gods. Then...can I wash you?"

Oh. Right. I'm splattered in blood. While I don't mind, it's probably not the best way to set the mood for Baelfire.

I start to pull my hand back. "I'll go shower—"

He catches my hand, shaking his head as a dazzling smile breaks over his face. "Hey, no getting self-conscious on me now. I'd fuck you six ways to Sunday right this second if you told me to cut to the chase, but I'm fucking *dying* to take care of my mate. Please, baby?"

Once again, my attention snags on the collar around his throat. Relying on the intoxicating instincts that seem to come so naturally around Baelfire, I reach up and tug on his collar until he's at my eye level. His golden eyes widen.

"Fine. Wash me. And then I'll decide whether I'll still punish you for getting yourself hurt."

He swallows hard, so I feel it against the collar. "*Fuck*. Please punish me, baby. Holy shit, I want that so fucking bad—"

I tug again more gently to stop him. "You can beg after you've washed me."

Without another word, Baelfire scoops me up and rushes to the massive bathroom connected to my room like his ass is on fire. Pausing to set me down gently, he reaches into the sizeable glassed-in shower. He turns on the spray, testing it until he decides it's the right temperature.

I reach for the hem of my shirt, but his hand covers mine.

"Let me. I want to do everything for you right now."

That idea is oddly pleasing, but I raise my brow expectantly and wait.

"Please," he adds ardently, his face pleading.

"Good boy."

Baelfire visibly shivers, swallowing again as he gently strips off my bloodied gloves and my shirt before unlacing and removing my boots and socks. When he moves behind me to ease down my oversized pants and plain black panties, he moans.

"Do you have any idea how much I daydream about this perfect ass? Your body is so fucking mouthwatering. All it takes is you breathing near me, and I'm so hard I can't even think."

Feeling impish and daring, I lean forward, reach back, and spread myself for him.

He swears viciously, and then I jolt when he drops to his knees, and his hot tongue drags through my pussy. Baelfire moans and presses in deeper, clearly forgetting about the shower filling up with steam in front of me. Before I can get too lost in how incredible it feels, I step away, moving into the warm spray.

After all, I really am gross from combat training. It's borderline embarrassing how fast the water going down the drain turns dark with blood and dirt.

Baelfire joins me without bothering to remove his towel, and the next few minutes are…confusing. Because even though he's gentle and soothing in all his touches as he covers his hands with soap to lather up my body…they're still hands.

On me. Skin on skin.

That familiar prickling feeling starts to crawl down my neck.

He starts washing my hips and thighs, but I step away, shutting my eyes to breathe. "Wait. I just…I need a second to—"

"You know you don't have to explain anything," Baelfire murmurs, giving me the time I need to keep my thoughts from spiraling. "I fucking love touching you like this, Maven, but if it's getting difficult for you, tell me and we'll stop."

I arch a brow and look pointedly at the raging hard-on that's barely concealed under his wet towel. Because of our height difference, it's impossible to miss right in front of me.

"He'll calm down once your addictive scent isn't burning me alive from the inside out," he moans dramatically.

My lips twitch. I step closer to him, putting his hands back on my hips. "I don't want to stop. I want you to wash me and then fuck me. But only after you've begged," I add, because I think I want that just as badly as he obviously does.

Baelfire's breathing turns staccato. "You'll let me actually…?"

"Not until you finish washing me. I want to be nice and clean before you try to fit all of *that* inside me."

"Oh, fuck."

After that, Baelfire washes me in an almost fevered state, his rasping breath and molten gaze working together with his large hands to make me wet as hell as he cleans me thoroughly.

When he shampoos my hair, his fingertips massage along my scalp. My mouth drops open, and I shut my eyes.

"Enjoying it, baby?" he asks, his voice thick.

No one has ever washed my hair for me before. Besides Lillian, and that was only when I was very young. But bathing out of a bucket was nowhere near this pleasant.

"It feels amazing."

"I'll do this every fucking day for you if you want."

He's done with my hair, so I tip my head back to glance up at him. "Right now, all I want is the sweet sound of your begging."

His eyes are pools of amber heat as he turns me to face him just outside the shower spray. Then he drops to his knees, buries his face between my breasts, and licks my scar there. That sends a jolt of both shock and need through me, and reflexively, I twist my fingers in his wet hair to wrench his head back.

He moans.

"You really do want to be punished, don't you?" I breathe, tracing the wet collar around his throat with my fingertips. "You look so good on your knees like this. I just wish I'd put this collar on you myself. Only for when we're alone, just for me to see, because we both know you're my good little pet."

Not that there's anything little about him.

Baelfire is panting now, and he reaches down to squeeze his hard cock through the towel still wrapped around his waist. "Oh, *gods*, yes. You have no idea how much I'd fucking love that."

"Good answer."

I lean down to sprinkle kisses on his face. He shuts his eyes and basks in it, not caring about the water dripping on his face. It's fascinating, pressing my lips all over him like this. I've only kissed lips until now.

Finally, I straighten, and when he opens his golden eyes, there's nothing short of worship in them.

Take it from me, Baelfire loves to watch a girl's expression when he's railing them.

Sierra's nasty words crawl up from some bitter recess of my mind. But somehow, being here with Baelfire right now, in this intimate moment, I feel nothing but curiosity about how I can use that.

"So damn handsome," I sigh.

"So fucking gorgeous," he breathes, leaning in against my chest again. He places kisses against my nipples and starts to tease one of them with his deliciously warm tongue. I bite my lip at how good that feels but step back, amused when he lets out a low growl of protest.

"I know a way to punish you. Come on."

He eagerly follows me from the shower to the bed, both of us ignoring that we're sopping wet as I tell him to take off the towel and lie down. He does, looking pleased when I can't keep my eyes off his cock, because…fucking gods.

Am I really going to try and fit that thing inside of me?

Yes. Yes, I am.

"Are you gonna tease me until I explode again, baby? That's still one of the fucking hottest things I've ever experienced, right after that shower."

I shake my head, smirking as I check the drawers of the room I've only half moved into. Finding a strip of cloth that will work perfectly, I return to the bed and straddle Baelfire's chest. He perks up at the sight of the fabric.

"Oh, *hell* yes. Tie me up, Boo."

I roll my eyes because it seems that nickname won't stay dead. "It's a blindfold, actually. I was told you have a major thing for watching the faces of all your conquests. Hence why this makes for a better punishment."

He blinks, and then his temper flares hot and fast. "You're not a godsdamned *conquest*, and please don't fucking remind me what a man whore I was before I met you. Thinking about being with anyone else makes me physically sick now, Maven. Who the hell told you all that? Were they giving you shit? I swear I'm going to fucking—"

I cover his mouth, shaking my head as my lips twitch. "You shifters. So emotional. But I really don't fucking care about girls in your past anymore, Baelfire. You're mine. I decided that, and for me, there's no going back. Now lift your head."

He bites back whatever else he wants to say and lets me slip the blindfold behind his head, circling it around his eyes before tying it on one side.

This time when I straddle him, I move further up his chest until my pussy is much closer to his face. I hear his breathing hitch as he scents how turned on I am, and he grips my thighs, lifting his head.

But before he can lick me again, I grip the side of his collar and use it to press him back down into the pillow. "Bad dragon. You'll only get what I decide to give you. Ask nicely first, and don't you dare move your blindfold."

Baelfire is breathing hard in anticipation as his fingertips press into my thighs. He swallows hard. "Let me taste you. Please."

I reach down to slide my fingertips through my own wetness, biting my lip at how good it feels. "Since you asked nicely," I whisper, bringing my fingers to his lips.

Baelfire jolts and immediately cleans up my fingers, moaning as he does. "More," he pants.

I touch myself for another long moment, toying with my clit before plunging my fingers into my pussy. Baelfire's fingers dig so hard into my thighs that I gasp. I can feel his hips buck behind me on the bed.

He groans. "Godsdamn, I can hear how wet you are. That's so fucking hot, baby. Give me more. Fucking drown me, Maven. Fuck, I need you so bad. Need my mate."

Mate. Hearing him growl that word does things to me. I move to straddle his face, hot arousal pulsing between my thighs.

"Be a good boy and lick this pussy until I come on your face."

Baelfire moans against me, and the vibrations tickle before he begins licking and sucking so ravenously that I squeeze my own eyes shut, the burning heat of arousal dancing low in my stomach. The sounds of pleasure Bael makes as he feasts are absolutely filthy, and I can't get enough. Finally, I refuse to wait any longer and move down his body, adjusting on my knees until I can rub the leaking head of his throbbing erection against my entrance.

He gasps my name brokenly, his hands fisting the sheets on either side of us. "Maven. Fuck, baby. Are you wet enough? I really don't want to hurt you. Let me just—"

"I'm not waiting anymore, Baelfire," I say breathlessly.

"Damn it, I...I need to see my mate when she takes me for the first time. *Please* let me see your face. Please."

The rough gravel of his voice is absolutely addictive. It's even more addictive when he says *please*. I've decided that's the sexiest sound—the sound of begging. I like it so much that I continue to tease him, doing my best to keep myself from moaning as I rub against his tip. By this point, I'm fucking soaked, and he's leaking so much pre-cum that we're a mess.

Baelfire is a mess, too. He's groaning and begging so fervently now that I can hear a wild edge in his voice. He desperately wants to see me when he's in me for the first time.

And even though I'm enjoying this...I want to give my shifter what he wants.

So, just as I sink the first inch of his impossibly thick, hard length inside of me, I push the blindfold off his eyes. My mouth drops open at the sensation of being stretched as I take more of him. Baelfire's eyes turn into a blaze of hunger as he watches me sink almost halfway onto his cock.

"Fuck, yes. That's it, baby. You can take it—take all of me." His eyes are hooded, and he grimaces with pleasure, sliding his hands back to squeeze my asscheeks. "*Gods*, you're so fucking tight."

When I feel him hit something deep inside me that simultaneously slightly hurts and throbs with need, I moan and take a second to adjust. He continues praising me, massaging my ass as he gazes up at me like I hung the sky itself.

I glance over my shoulder at the full-length mirror in the corner of the room—which gives me a perfect view of his cock buried deep inside me. It's so overwhelmingly erotic that I rock against him, and he swears again.

"Feels so fucking full," I manage, looking back down at him. "You're such a good mate for me."

It's my fault for using the *m* word.

Because the moment I utter it, Baelfire loses his mind. The next thing I know, he's flipped me over and is pounding me into the mattress, snarling and moaning as he ruts me like he can't stop himself. It's so rough and desperate, the sensations all so much, that my orgasm slams into me before I ever feel it coming. I cry out, clinging desperately to him as I ride out the mind-numbing pleasure.

Baelfire thrusts into me harder and moans. "Fuck, Maven. Gods, I want to bite you so fucking *bad*."

"I like biting," I manage through breathless gasps. "Make it hurt."

Baelfire's tongue drags up the crook of my neck, his pace increasing. "No. No, baby, I mean I want to *bite* you. Mark you. Claim you as my mate, because you're fucking *mine*."

I'm...his.

That sends another wash of emotions through me, and I squeeze my legs tighter around him as he continues to fuck me like he'll die if he doesn't.

"Please," he whispers against my throat, his pace growing

uneven. At first, I think he's asking to mark me as his mate, and I wonder if it's too soon to say yes. But then he chokes out, "Please, can I come?"

He's...waiting for my permission?

Oh, I *like* that.

I kiss him, biting his lower lip. "Come for me, Baelfire."

He shudders and groans like a dying man as he comes, burying his face against my neck. My mouth drops open again when I feel just how warm his release is inside of me—a dragon shifter thing that I failed to expect. He sucks and nips, leaving a couple of love bites on my neck as he finishes thrusting. When his orgasm leaves him winded, he slumps to one side and pulls me close to his chest.

I catch my breath as the lingering pleasure fades slowly from my system. After a few blissful moments, Baelfire gently turns my chin and kisses me sweetly.

He pulls back with a reverent, serious look. "I was right. Your pussy is literally fucking magical."

I can't stop the laugh that escapes. "Or it's your cock that's magical."

"Yeah, but I already knew that. That was never in question," he grins, kissing both my cheeks and down my neck. "But what you've got between your legs? That's pure paradise, Mayflower."

"So, did we cross off anything on your list?"

I can feel him smile against my skin. "Why, Maven Oakley. Are you asking to know about my *Ways to Fuck Maven Senseless* list? Because I'll absolutely fucking show it to you as long as I can eat your pretty pussy while you read it out loud so I can taste which ideas turn you on the most."

Oh, *gods*.

He starts nibbling and teasing my neck and clavicle, and I jolt in surprise when his fingers move between my legs, slipping through my pussy to push anything that has escaped back inside of me.

Is that something people do? It's fucking hot. Maybe that's another thing to ask Kenzie about.

But when Baelfire starts grinding gently against my side, my eyes pop back open, and I sit up, blinking down at his rigid cock.

"You already came."

"Harder than I've ever come in my entire fucking life," he sighs happily, his eyes sparkling as he sits up and kisses my jaw. "I'm so damn excited for round two. Need some water or something first? Or another shower?"

I abruptly remember a very brief conversation with Kenzie on my fourth day at Everbound. It was only so brief because I'd insisted she stop talking or I would shun her. She had been telling me that most legacies have very short refractory periods compared to humans—especially shifters. Which means that they usually spend hours, sometimes *days,* in bed thanks to their insane sex drives.

"Round two," I echo slowly.

Now that I'm not incredibly distracted, my stomach is turning, and my nerves tighten in apprehension. I'm still getting over the overwhelming orgasm, so I feel torn between two extremes and glance down when I realize I'm unconsciously scrubbing my arm hard enough to scratch the skin.

Baelfire notices, too, and catches my hand, pressing it to his lips. "Nope. No more."

"But I enjoyed all of that," I huff. "A lot. I want more. Ignore my stupid body. If we go again, I just need to be distracted—"

He cups my jaw, his gaze like warm honey. "I'm not fucking you when the only way you can enjoy it is by not thinking about it. What we just did was perfect and the best fucking thing that's ever happened to me, and we're not going to push it any further today. Okay?"

I sigh petulantly. "Fine. Enjoy blue balls."

Baelfire throws his head back in a sharp laugh. "You're so fucking cute. And not to ruin this moment by bringing up the elephant in the room, but…" He ducks his head and shoots me a surprisingly bashful look. "You…called me your mate."

Now, outside the heat of the moment, knowing I said that makes my neck heat. It just sounds so official and *intimate.*

I just shrug, pretending it's nothing. "I thought it might turn you on."

His smile is blinding. "Fuck yes, it does. You have no idea."

Actually, I do, I almost say.

Because the idea of him being mine is a siren call, something I know I should tune out...but I'm not going to anymore. As I said, I'm done resisting. The gods tempted me too far, and now these legacies will get a front-row seat to my bleak ending.

But I'm going to give them my everything right up until the end. I'll fight for them every fucking way I can.

Speaking of fighting...

"So, where exactly did you hide Pierce?"

21

SILAS

When I come to, I stare down at a bloodied knife clutched in my right hand. I'm standing in my private dorm, and for a moment, unadulterated panic swirls in my gut because the only person I have ever let in here is Maven. So if I stabbed someone in here—

But then I feel the pain scorching through me, emanating from my right upper thigh. Swearing, I drop onto the seat beside the fire, clutching at the wound to keep the blood from gushing while simultaneously drawing on it to send healing magic deep into my leg.

Stabbing myself is a new and rather unpleasant development to my curse.

He snapped out of it, one of the voices in my head complains.

Finish the job, my father's voice hisses.

Another one of them cackles at my pain.

My head throbs, my ears ring, and for a moment, I can barely focus on healing my own leg as an overwhelming wave of paranoia has my gaze darting about my dorm in alarm.

"Who's there?" I snap when I hear a sound come from my kitchenette.

It's the one who stabbed you.

Here they come.

Ignoring the laughing voices in my head becomes impossible.

Finally, I limp into the kitchenette, still clutching the bloodied knife, my breathing quick and labored. But all I find is a pot boiling over from when I started on the concealment potion for Maven...which, according to the clock on the stove, was hours ago.

I swear again. Slumping to the floor, I set down the blade and cover my face with trembling, bloodied hands.

I'm losing it.

How much longer do I have before my curse takes hold entirely? It can't be long. At this point, I likely have days or weeks left. Perhaps this could have been avoided had I come to Everbound immediately after my twentieth or twenty-first birthday, as is standard...

But then, no. Maven wouldn't have been here, anyway, and I have always been destined to suffer without my blood blossom.

The Garnet Wizard is the one who insisted I wait an additional year before enrolling at Everbound University. The Legacy Council was furious about it, but he'd dared them to try entering his sanctuary—which is more of a glorified death trap—and retrieve me themselves.

When I asked why the delay, he gave me a vague answer insisting he had an extremely valuable source who instructed him to keep me at his side for another year. I didn't ask follow-up questions, but now I wonder if he somehow knew that Maven wouldn't be here for me until this year.

Maven.

It's already nearing midnight. I need to finish the concealment potion and return to my keeper as soon as possible. But before I've even finished healing my leg, there's a knock at the door of my private dorm.

Immediately, my nerves are on edge.

It's someone with a knife. They'll attack the moment you open the door.

Gritting my teeth against the voices that refuse to leave me alone, I answer the door and go perfectly still. Because instead of Maven or any other legacy, Somnus DeLune waits with a sneer.

"Follow me, young Crane. It's time for your interrogation."

Damn it. This is going to end badly. And now that I know about Maven's past, if they ask questions about her...

I can't lie.

"Awfully late for an interrogation," I note, trying to keep my voice light.

The incubus monster bares sharp teeth at me. "Please do continue stalling. I'm to execute any who resist on the spot, and it would be immensely pleasing to kill any of your quintet."

My heart hammers in my chest. I glance over my shoulder at the cacophony of spell ingredients on my coffee table. "I won't resist, but allow me to finish bandaging my wound."

His black, soulless gaze drops to my leg, and he snorts. "Attacked, were you? Excellent. A weak quintet is fitting for him."

He must mean his son.

I nod absentmindedly because nodding isn't an explicit lie. Then I move quickly to the coffee table, leaving the front door barely ajar so he can't see inside. I grab a bandage soaked in bergamot poultice and wrap my leg until I can fully heal it later.

I also grab a talisman and slip it into my pocket. I crafted it before the Matched Ball after hearing that the Immortal Quintet was at Everbound. It will keep Natalya out of my head.

I hope.

Somnus DeLune escorts me through silent hallways, which are dimly lit by fae or mage lights occasionally. No one dares step foot outside curfew, not when the number of legacies at Everbound has been dropping at an alarming rate over the last few days. The Immortal Quintet's hired hands keep a close watch at night, ready to pounce.

As we enter the faculty hall, Somnus scoffs, "Let's hope you're found guilty."

"Of?"

"Anything. You've no idea how I longed to kill you and be rid of your bloodline after your parents fell prey to that son of a bitch's meddling. Amusing that you now share a cunt with the one who murdered your family, don't you think?"

Hot anger floods my veins, and I feel the prick of my fangs as my temper pushes me into my hunting state. As much as I loathe Crypt DeLune—which is *immensely*—I hate his father more.

Until recently, I'd only seen Somnus up close one other time. When I was eleven, he came to my family's house in the countryside unannounced to commission my father to make a powerful potion for him. My father wouldn't tell me what the potion was for, only that it was for unsavory purposes. When the time came for the concoction to be delivered, my father sent one of our house's human staff members. They came back in pieces in a blood-soaked body bag, and I decided not to cross paths with Somnus DeLune ever again.

Yet here we are.

"I'm not the last of my bloodline," I mutter through the anger, correcting his earlier statement. "There are other Cranes."

"None that are blood fae." Somnus stops in front of Headmaster Hearst's old office. He motions at the door as if I should go in. "Let's get on with it. Your inability to tell a bald-faced lie should make this rather quick."

I brace myself and walk through the doors. The room is spotless compared to the last time I saw it, but I'm still careful not to look at the place where we found Maven lying in a pool of her own blood. Instead, I stare straight ahead at the three monsters in the room.

Natalya, Iker, and Engela.

They're going to kill you immediately, a voice in my head snickers. *Make the first move. Attack them.*

That would be suicide, and the voices know that damn well. I resist the urge to slip my hand into my pocket where my crystal waits.

Playing my cards close to my vest, I sit across from them and tip my head curiously. "Is Hearst engaged elsewhere?"

After all, no one but my quintet knows that he was killed. Hopefully, this will give them less of a reason to question me. But if they're grieving, none of the Immortal Quintet shows any sign of it as Natalya snorts softly and folds her hands on the desk between us.

"It hardly takes all of us to get the answers we want."

Her blue eyes begin to glow. I hold my breath, sending a silent prayer to Koa that my concealed talisman will work. He's the god of invention, lies and truths, and magic, among other things.

Natalya's lips pinch, and her eyes stop glowing. "I see you have a buffer to keep me out of your head. Something to hide, fae?"

I shake my head no, relieved that I can at least lie with body language. "I prefer to be the only one inside my head. It's not a pleasant place to be, courtesy of my curse."

Typically, I would never overshare like that, but I remember well the lessons my father taught me at a young age. He'd explained that we blood fae are at a disadvantage, being unable to fib—but that there were ways to bend the truth even without a bald-faced lie. Nonverbal actions, asking questions instead of answering, redirecting attention…and offering information freely, so long as it isn't what is truly being asked of us.

My abrupt truthfulness regarding such a taboo topic has Del Mar raising an eyebrow. It looks odd on his semi-scaly face. He exchanges a brief look with Natalya, and I wonder if they're communicating telepathically, as some powerful quintets can. No one knows if the Immortal Quintet has that ability. I imagine anyone who has ever asked didn't survive to share the answer.

"Interesting," Del Mar muses. "I've heard some curses are hereditary, as it appears to be with you. Your parents' deaths were unfortunate. I always liked the Crane family of Arcana. Such a loyal lot."

Somnus scoffs as he stands beside Engela Zuma. "They proved quite useless in the end, ripping each other to bits like that."

I keep my eyes forward, pretending to ignore their conversation. But in my head, I can still hear the screaming and shouting as my parents turned on each other. I'd hid in the nearest coat closet so they wouldn't spot me and turn on me, too, and listened to the sickening sounds of them fighting to the death. They were the last of my parents' quintet after two died at the Divide and the Nightmare Prince drove Omar, their keeper, to suicide along with my uncle and several other random legacies.

I will never fucking forgive Crypt for his part in that.

"Very well. We shall be frank in our questions," Natalya says, her voice like a bell as she toys with the ends of her ruddy brown hair. "Where were you at dawn on the day of the Matched Ball?"

"My quintet and I were returning from a romantic getaway to a cozy small town," I reply, tipping my head. "Why do you ask? I've wondered what inspired the Immortal Quintet to grace us with your presence."

"Our business is our own," Del Mar replies coolly. "Don't presume to question us."

"Could it be a family visit?" I suggest, glancing innocently at Somnus.

His glare is laced with warning. "Say anything else bordering on impudent, and I'll gladly kill you to weaken that unmanageable prick's pathetic so-called quintet."

Evidently, he hates Crypt as much as he always has. I understand the sentiment.

"You were apprenticed to the Garnet Wizard, were you not?" Del Mar asks.

"I was."

"He's in good health, I hope?"

"As curmudgeonly as ever," I say breezily, avoiding a real answer.

That makes Del Mar chuff in an inhuman show of amusement before he nods. "I expect he's going to continue ignoring any correspondence we send his way. Natalya would have killed him decades ago if he hadn't proven so useful with charms and spellbinding."

I nod. Natalya is their keeper, and the Garnet Wizard cursed her name daily when I was under his tutelage. He made it no secret that he wanted the Immortal Quintet removed from power—but not killed. He never told me why leaving them alive was important, but he was very creative with his swearing when describing each of them.

"Moving on, then," Natalya hums as if bored by this small talk. "Do you know the real reason we're here at Everbound? Answer yes or no."

Yes or no questions are the bane of every fae's existence. My pulse picks up as I realize they're trying to back me into a corner. If they know that I know of Hearst's death, I'm fucked.

So, instead of answering, I feign deep thought as I study each of them and redirect to the most distracting topic I can think of. "Is it because the anti-legacy movement is growing more severe? Were they targeting the five of you, so you came here for shelter?"

Somnus snorts, and I thank the gods as he falls for the bait. "As if their little movement won't blow over in a few measly decades. We seek a far more pressing threat."

I try to channel Maven and keep my expression blank because it's not difficult to work out his meaning now that I know there's a prophesied *telum*...as in, Maven. She's the Entity's weapon, and I can only assume she's a danger to the Immortal Quintet.

So they're no longer looking for Hearst's killer at all.

They've started looking for *her*.

My theory is confirmed when Del Mar studies me keenly with his pale yellow eyes, his pupils slit like a hydra's, even in his more humanoid form. His forked tongue flicks out briefly to wet his lips.

"I heard your keeper is human-born. Odd that a mere atypical caster has survived so long in such a brutal semester, is it not?"

"She has strong matches, and we will continue to protect her no matter how brutal things become," I reply smoothly, holding his gaze.

"Where is your keeper from, pray tell?" Natalya hums.

I hate that they're asking about Maven, but I hate even more that I'm incapable of lying to protect her if it comes down to it.

You're going to betray her. They'll be after her now, a voice in my head snarls.

She's not strong enough to protect herself from them, and neither are you.

Just let her die already. We hate her. She's going to end us.

My left eye starts to twitch, but I finally manage, "She wasn't raised in the world of legacies, so I'm afraid her time at Everbound has been quite the adjustment period."

"That's not what I asked, fae," Natalya pouts dramatically, standing to walk around the desk.

The immortal wears a semi-sheer dress better suited for clubbing than interrogating students. She perches just in front of me, her blue eyes penetrating as they start to glow again. She's trying to pluck the truth from my head, and I pray the talisman holds up. I can feel it heating in my pocket.

"Let's try this again. What plane of existence did your keeper come from?"

My pulse is racing with alarm, but I recall that Maven told us she was taken to the Nether as a child. So the *absolute* truth is…

"The mortal realm, of course. Where else?"

"And has she always been in the mortal realm?"

My palms grow damp, and I keep my wording careful. "Where else would she go? Although technically, I've heard we all venture into Limbo when we're unconscious, so I suppose she's been there in that way."

Natalya's hand bolts out lightning-fast to wrap around my neck. I have no access to oxygen as her face twists into a hideous snarl, all that old-world beauty now ugly with anger.

"Don't dare to play games with me. Answer yes or no only. To your knowledge, has your keeper ever crossed through the Divide?"

She flings me back into the chair so I can choke for air and offer an answer, but I will never answer this. I can't. If I do, they'll know the truth.

But if I remain silent, they'll assume the truth just as quickly. There's no way to bend this. My voice will cease to work as it always does whenever a lie tries to pass through my lips.

So, instead, I feign absolute shock. "*Through* the Divide? As in, into the Nether? How would that even be pos—"

Del Mar moves so fast I don't see him until I'm flung across the room, slamming into the wall. Somnus is there an instant later, fisting my hair to drag me to my feet. He drives a knee into my fresh thigh injury. It's so unexpected and painful that, shamefully, a sharp cry of pain escapes.

Obviously, I've pissed them off. And as Natalya prowls toward me, that same hideous scowl twisting her features and her eyes glowing ominously, I know I'm about to be tortured for information.

Then they'll kill me.

And all I can think about is everything I won't get to experience with Maven if I die here. I won't get to wake up beside her in the morning, taste her mouthwatering blood, or watch the way her dark eyes flash with mesmerizing anger whenever she's angry. I won't get the answers I still desperately want about her. I'll never again get to listen to the intoxicating sounds my beautifully vicious *sangfluir* makes in bed or watch her expression turn soft just before I kiss her.

I wonder if she'll weep for me.

Somnus is still pinning me against the wall. But as Natalya bares her fangs and sinks them into my wrist, pulling an excruciatingly long draw of blood from me, there is a soft knock at the door.

"We are not to be disturbed," Del Mar booms angrily. "Who would dare—"

"It is Pia, sir."

The prophetess from the temple of Galene? I'm too dizzy from suffocation and pain blossoming in my arm to understand why on earth she would be knocking at a time like this. For a moment, my ears ring, and the voices in my head come roaring to the surface. I'm left pinned to the wall, choking for air while Natalya releases my wrist, exchanging words through the door that I can't make out.

Abruptly, Somnus releases me with a sharp swear just as Engela moves for the first time, throwing the office door open and storming out. Del Mar, Somnus, and Natalya follow her, leaving me blinking in confusion as I'm alone in Hearst's office with a burning wrist and the prophetess standing nearby.

The white-cloaked figure's head turns in my direction.

"You're bleeding," she says quietly.

I fight for breath as I stagger to my feet, gripping my burning wrist. Natalya is a vampyr, meaning unlike legacy vampires, her venom has the ability to turn someone into a vampire…if they die with the venom in their system. As I do now.

But they're gone, so I have no plans to die.

"Where did they go? What's going on?" I ask hoarsely.

The only thing I can think of that would draw their attention away so quickly would be if Pia announced that someone had tried to escape the wards. What if she was reporting Maven's attempted escape? What if my keeper is about to be caught and killed at any moment?

"Your keeper is perfectly safe, Silas Crane," Pia replies, reminding me that she's clairvoyant and quite possibly a mind reader. "She is currently outside the wards surrounding Everbound."

That only adds to my panic, though. "Are they looking for her? Did you tell them?"

The prophetess shakes her white-robed head. "No. I merely came to report to them that a swarm of wisps broke out of Limbo and are ripping to shreds anything and everything they come across within the western wing. Without the Nightmare Prince, it will likely take them a couple of hours to trap and fade the wisps."

Why is she mentioning Crypt? Her words spin in my head, not making sense. Between the earlier blood loss and the vampyr venom pulsing through my system, I can't seem to focus on anything. The ringing in my ears is getting worse.

"I need to get to Maven," I mutter. Only too late do I realize I spoke in fae.

But Pia must understand because she hums. "So loyal. Just as we had hoped."

That statement also makes no sense, but I'm far too exhausted and pain-riddled to ask follow-up questions as Pia supports me and helps me leave Hearst's office. But when we arrive at my quintet's apartment and not an exit, I blink blearily and scowl.

"*Maven*," I repeat emphatically. "I must get to my keeper."

Pia doesn't even acknowledge my protest as she knocks on the door. A moment later, Baelfire opens the door and stares at us. His eyes are wild in the way that tells me he's struggling with his inner dragon. The scratch marks around his neck, as if he's been trying to pry off his collar, further prove that he's struggling.

"Where were you?" he snaps, dragging me inside and slamming the door without so much as a hello to the mysterious prophetess. "Maven left an hour ago. Why the fuck didn't you get here sooner to go with her outside the wards?"

I squint at him through the blurriness crowding my eyes, determined to make his three heads converge into one. "I was preoccupied. But why the fucking hell didn't *you* go with her?"

He swears and yanks hard on the leather around his neck again. "She pointed out that we don't know whether this motherfucking collar has a tracking spell woven into it. It might've tipped off the Immortal Quintet if I left, and then we would've been fucked."

"You're saying she's alone out there?" I snap, storming toward the kitchen to get spell ingredients to null the venom.

At least, I *try* to storm into the kitchen. But my equilibrium has started to spiral, and I smack right into the wall, falling on my ass and hissing at the pain in my leg.

Everything spins as the edges of my vision darken, but I can make out Baelfire standing above me with a frown that almost looks *concerned*, of all things.

"Shit. What the hell happened to you, Si?"

I'm about to black out, but I can't let myself go unconscious with this venom in my system. What if I somehow die while unconscious and come back as a vampire? I wouldn't have my magic anymore, and my powerful line of blood magic is utterly invaluable. I refuse to ever give it up.

So I try to focus on Baelfire's six pairs of eyes and grit out, "Wyvern blood."

"Come again?"

"In thekitchen. Labeled bottle. Ten dropsinmy mouth."

My words slur together, my eyes sliding shut without permission as the vampyr venom continues to burn through my system. I'm lying supine now, and everything is starting to fade.

Please come back to me, sangfluir.

The last thing I hear before blacking out is, "Hell no. I am not fucking with wyvern juice, you blood-guzzling freak."

22

MAVEN

FRESH-FALLEN snow crunches under my boots as I walk into Halfton at two in the morning. It took more of my magic reserve than anticipated to break out of Everbound's wards. But so far, none of the Immortal Quintet or their henchmen have jumped from the shadows and attempted to kill me.

Which is disappointing.

But at least it means I can get Kenzie back quickly.

A thick, ominous chill hangs in the wintry night air as I stroll down the middle of Main Street toward the inn at the very end of the small town. The street lights are dim. The only humans who might be awake in Halfton would be on the other side of town, but otherwise, all humans are resting in their beds in this sleepy little town.

Occasional flurries of snow fall while the breeze rustles dead tree branches. Sinister-sounding wind chimes hanging outside dark storefronts toll softly. The ambiance is so eerie it makes me smile.

And then I sigh, wishing my quintet was here with me. Gods, I'm such an idiot for them.

But it's safer for them that I'm alone tonight to get Kenzie.

I pass by a cemetery before finally reaching the Black Wing Inn. The massive brick building was probably built a hundred years ago, and the owners haven't renovated since then. A broken porch swing hangs crookedly beside the front door, creaking loudly whenever the cold wind blows. None of the lights are on in the three-story building. A feral calico cat hisses when it sees me and hides in the nearest bushes.

Charming.

Quick and silent as a shadow, I pick the lock of the inn's front door and slip inside, ascending the stairs until I finally stop at Room 17. Holding my breath, I use a simple common magic unlocking spell, step inside, and turn on the light to find that—

Thank the fucking universe.

Kenzie lays on the bed in suspended animation, paused in time, staring sightlessly at the ceiling while pale green light shimmers around her from the stasis spell.

Holding my hands over her, I draw from what little remains of my magic, whispering various incantations until, finally, one of them clicks.

The changeling's lingering spell shatters. Kenzie gasps and scrambles back on the bed, her blue eyes wild and disoriented as she grabs the nearest pillow and holds it like a weapon.

"Unless you plan on asphyxiating me with that, it's useless."

Kenzie blinks, focusing on me. For a moment, my throat tightens painfully as I wait to see whether she'll remember me or not. She might be looking at a total stranger. The changeling was feeding on her memories, so there's a good chance that she has no idea who I—

"Maven!"

I'm yanked onto the bed, and Kenzie sobs into my shoulder as she hugs me tight, her body shaking. I shut my eyes, relieved that she didn't forget me.

It's still fucking uncomfortable to be around someone who's crying. Still, I ignore the apprehension dancing along my spine and the cold sweat that starts to prickle my skin to hug her back.

"O—oh, s—sorry," she hiccups, pulling back and mopping at her face. "I know you don't like touching. I didn't mean to grab you like that. I was just so relieved to see you and—and, *oh my gods*, there was a ch—changeling who looked just like Harlow, and it was *inside my fucking head* and…I'm sorry, I know you can't stand crying, but I just—"

Determined to comfort her even if it feels entirely unnatural to me, I re-wrap her in an awkward hug and clench my jaw against the way my nerves tighten in horror at all this extended contact.

"Cry if it helps. I don't mind."

Kenzie takes me up on the offer and cries for another couple of minutes, mourning her lost memories. She finally pulls away and swipes at her eyes again. Her face is splotchy, but she straightens and blows her wild, pale curls out of her face like she's determined to move on.

"So, um…how long have I been here?"

"A few days. In stasis."

Her lower lip trembles. "And my quintet? Are they—"

"They're safe," I assure her.

I've kept my eye out for them at the dining hall and around the castle, and they haven't been hurt or picked off. It helps that their emphasis isn't combat, and they're not a highly ranked quintet, so they don't make for a large target compared to many others.

"I remember them, but…I can't remember much else. I can't remember my childhood at all." Kenzie's eyes water again, and she swallows hard. "It's like I know what's happened over the last year or so, but anything before that…"

I keep my voice gentle. "Changelings feed on memories."

"But can't I get them back?"

I shake my head, wishing I could offer more comfort.

"That stupid fucking bitch," she huffs, wiping away more tears. "If I could shift, I'd rip its stupid fake face off."

"If it's any consolation, I already killed it. After some mild torture."

Too mild, in my opinion.

Kenzie pauses. "Huh. Actually…that kind of does make me feel better. Is that bad of me?"

"In my book, not even remotely." Then I pause. "We need to get back to the university immediately. But first, you should know things changed while you were under."

Kenzie listens with wide eyes as I quickly explain the precarious situation at Everbound, including the hired legacies keeping an eye on the grad students and the Immortal Quintet's presence. I don't explain *why* they're there, but I add that they've been killing off students.

When I'm done, she takes a moment to absorb all of it. Then she frowns. "Okay, but did anything *else* happen while I was a stupid snack for that changeling bitch?"

Anything else? "Is the Immortal Quintet hijacking Everbound not enough for you?"

"I mean, that sucks, but did anything happen with your guys?"

"That is such a Kenzie question," I inform her.

"And that is such a Maven *non*-answer," she shoots back. "Hello? I just went through something really fucking traumatic. The least you could do for me is offer some steamy, nitty gritty relationship details to take my mind off things and make me feel better!"

I snort and stand from the bed, looking around the room for anything else the changeling might've left behind, but it's empty. "I promise we'll talk more, but later. We need to get back through Everbound's wards well before dawn."

Kenzie tries to stand but slumps back with a pained grimace. "Ugh, I feel like shit. Hang on, do I look like shit? Oh, gods, I don't want to see my quintet if I look gross. I mean, I *desperately* want to see them...but I want to be my typical, unbelievably sexy self when I do so they won't be too concerned about me. I mean, I'm supposed to be their brave leader, and we're all still in that honeymoon phase, so I don't want to ruin it all by looking like one of the Undead when I return—"

"Kenzie."

"Right, sorry. Okay, I hereby put my vanity on hold for at least an hour. Here I go."

I try to ignore the way my anxiety spikes as I let her lean on me while we quietly leave the inn and make our way down the street. But soon, I have to step away while she braces herself on a tree so I can swallow down the rising bile and get a grip.

Stupid fucking body. It didn't seem this bad when I was with Baelfire earlier, so why now?

I'm considering using a forbidden transportation spell to get Kenzie just outside of Everbound's wards when, abruptly, all of my senses fly into high alert. After years of honing my instincts in the Nether, my senses developed a hair-trigger response to shadow fiends. I can sense whenever they're nearby...

Like I do right now.

I turn in a circle, searching for any sign of the impending threat.

"May?" Kenzie whispers. "What's going on? What are you—"

"Shh."

For another moment, we stand in silence...until I catch the slightest movement in my periphery, near the cemetery I passed earlier. Under the faint light of the waning moon, I can just make out a hulking humanoid figure hunched over what I can only assume is one of the fresher graves.

A ghoul.

That particular kind of shadow fiend is common in the Nether. They feed on newly deceased, unanimated corpses. While they're fast and dangerous when angry, they rarely make it past the legacies guarding the Divide due to their unintelligent nature.

At first, I think it's odd to see one here in Halfton so far from the Divide. But then I remember kneeling on the stone floor, playing the part of the obedient, subservient weapon as Amadeus sat on his macabre throne, explaining his plan.

With each member of the Four Houses you dispose of, our foothold in the mortal realm will grow. For it is their life force holding us back, nothing more. I will track your progress according to how weak their precious Divide becomes. End them. That is your purpose, my daughter. And when you have ended each of those fools...

I shake my head to bring me back to here and now. Of course. Since Hearst's death, there must have been far more surges and far more escaped shadow fiends than ever. The Legacy Council and all other legacies must have their hands full with that—but obviously, this ghoul slipped away unharmed to feed on dead humans.

Kenzie sees where I'm looking and inhales sharply. "Oh, my *gods*. Is that what I think it is?"

"Yes. But don't worry. It will ignore the living."

The ghoul straightens to its full ten-foot height and starts sniffing the air, which makes Kenzie make a strangled sound.

"You sure about that? Because it seems like it's scenting us!" she hisses, backing away.

Not us. Just me. Since, strictly speaking, I'm not entirely part of the living anymore.

Glancing over my shoulder at her, I offer a tiny smile. "I'm going to lure it away from town so it doesn't linger in Halfton and hurt humans. Stay here."

Kenzie scowls. "Um, May, please don't take this the wrong way, but…you're an asscaster. My absolute favorite asscaster of all time, but still, that is a fucking *ghoul,* and there is no way I'm about to let you deal with that thing by yourself. I'm helping."

"You're weak right now," I point out quietly.

She puts her hands on her hips. "Excuse me, did I stutter? Just tell me how to help, my overzealous little monk savior."

My lips twitch. I've missed her. And even though I work best alone, it can't hurt to have her help ever so slightly.

"Fine. But follow my instructions exactly."

"Roger that."

Five minutes later, I approach the cemetery where the ghoul has returned to digging up a grave. Luck is on my side tonight, and the wind is blowing in the perfect direction, so when I'm standing at the fringes of the forest outside of Halfton's cemetery, the ghoul is downwind from me. I reach into a concealed pocket where my favorite adamantine dagger awaits me. Baelfire gave it back to me before I left the castle, but not before pleading with me to not use it in front of anyone who could trace it back to where I come from.

As soon as the wind blows and it catches my scent, the shadow fiend straightens, dropping whatever it had in its mouth. It turns to look directly at me, its tusks protruding from its hideous mouth. It takes one step in my direction, then another.

Then it bolts toward me.

Game on.

Turning, I take off into the forest as adrenaline pumps through me. Darting around trees and jumping over a small creek, I head toward Everbound. I'll have to kill this thing before I get anywhere near the school, or it might be sensed by the magic wards.

I'm fast over short distances, even faster than shifters on a good day. That was something Amadeus's chief necromancer, Dagon, had insisted on perfecting when they were altering the fabric of my being. I'm patterned after a monster that existed long ago—only it was slower and less efficient.

I'm the experimental new and improved version.

Just as we planned, I climb swiftly into a tree just as Kenzie darts out from another place in the woods, distracting the ghoul. Though ghouls don't usually pose a danger to the living because they don't see them as food, they get distracted easily.

As soon as the shadow fiend is turning toward her, I drop from the tree branches, straddling its shoulders just as I drive my adamantine dagger through its skull—twice, then three times. It roars and flings me off, and I slam into a tree with a grunt. That'll leave a bruise.

Kenzie dodges when the fiend launches toward her. Then the creature crumbles to the ground, twitching a few times while the power of the adamantine works its way through the creature's system. It finally goes slack, its veins bulging through purplish skin.

I feel the exhilarating rush of power cloud my veins as I brush myself off and walk over to yank my dagger out of its skull.

Good old Pierce.

Kenzie watches me with wide eyes as I wipe my blade clean on the mane-like tuft of fur around the dead ghoul's neck. "So, um…you said you were raised by humans."

"Actually, I didn't. You assumed it."

"Huh. I guess that's true." She makes a face at the dead shadow fiend beside us. "And you never ever corrected me, but now I get the feeling that's not right. I mean, you were *fast*, fast. And this ugly thing didn't scare you at all."

"They look far worse than they are." I turn to go. "Come on."

"Hey, May?"

The vulnerability in her voice makes me pause.

"You can trust me, you know. With whatever. Like, I'm not going to go blabbing to anyone about anything you tell me about your past. Not even my quintet. You're like a sister to me."

I tuck my dagger away again and turn to face her.

"I know."

And I do know. Kenzie is like Lillian, and Lillian would die for me if I let her. Which is really damn annoying, considering how I revive in the blink of an eye. But then, I understand since I would do the same even if I couldn't revive.

"Thank you for the dress, by the way."

Kenzie's face lights up. "You actually wore it? Yay! Oh my gods, I can't wait to see the pictures!"

Oops. "Right. Pictures..."

She gasps in theatrical outrage. "You seriously didn't take any pictures for me? Maven Whatever-Your-Middle-Name-Is Oakley, you're in so much fucking trouble. Once we survive all the weird stuff happening at Everbound, I demand you get dressed up in that again so I can take pictures retroactively and pretend I was there the first time, okay?"

I grimace. "We'll have to get another dress. My guys ripped that one."

One second passes. Then two. Then she lets out a shrill, giddy shriek so ear-splitting that I flinch, glancing around for any other threats she may have just alerted to our position.

"*Yes!* I fucking *knew* it! They're your guys, and you totally drove them wild with how gorgeous you looked in that dress until they couldn't take it anymore! Did they rip it off you and ravish you right in the middle of the dance floor? Have you been having wild group sex out the wazoo ever since? Tell me everything. *Everything*."

I fight a smile and roll my eyes as we continue through the forest. "Tomorrow. Tonight, you need to rest and comfort your quintet because they think you've been dead for days."

That sobers her up immediately. "They have? Oh, gods. I can't wait to see them."

"Good. Then you won't mind if I use some magic to transport us there?"

Kenzie blinks at me in surprise, smoothing her pale curls away from her face. "You can do that? I thought...I mean, you were supposed to be an atypical caster before, but now I'm starting to doubt everything I know about you, May. Everything except the fact that you're my bestie," she corrects with a wink. "Sure. Transport me away, mysterious little no-longer-a-virgin."

I smirk. "Be warned. Transportation magic is a bitch."

"Nah, I'm sure I'll be totally fine."

Kenzie is not totally fine.

The moment we appeared outside of Everbound's wards, she keeled over and vomited, apologizing in between gagging and groaning. I felt bad enough for her that I awkwardly patted her shoulder while explaining that her system is probably particularly sensitive after coming out of a stasis spell.

I used up almost the rest of my magic reserve slipping back through the wards, and Kenzie was too queasy and dizzy to even ask how I managed it. Now, I'm supporting one side of her as we hide in one of Everbound Castle's many alcoves, waiting for one of the Immortal Quintet's hired legacies to walk past on their nightly patrol.

As soon as their footsteps fade, I peek around the corner to double-check before we move down the hall, turn a corner, and stop in front of her quintet apartment. I don't want to knock because that will alert any nearby lackeys about us being here, so I mouth a quick goodnight to Kenzie before she slips through the door.

I turn and move on through the halls, quiet as a shadow once again. It's beyond relieving that she's alive and safe with her quintet.

Not that Everbound is the safest place for legacies in general right now, but still. If the Nether has grown stronger after Hearst's death, I'm sure things have grown worse for legacies outside the wards.

Exhaustion weighs heavily on my eyelids as I pause at the end of one particularly dark hallway to listen for anyone on patrol. Depleting my magic like that and the late hour means I'll probably be tired tomorrow, too. But a small smile curls my lips as I remember that at least I won't be waking up in a cold sweat due to nightmares.

I wonder where Crypt got that totem, anyway.

As if my thoughts summoned him, my pulse triples when that alluringly dark presence tickles at the edge of my awareness. I halt and turn around, expecting him to step out of Limbo any moment.

He doesn't, which makes me frown. Is he not in this hallway after all? Did I imagine it?

"Crypt?" I whisper.

A hand goes around my throat, and I'm slammed against the stone wall, the air knocking from my lungs. A vampire hireling hisses down at me, barely visible in this unlit hall.

"What's this? A student breaking curfew?" she asks, baring her fangs threateningly. "I'll be taking you straight to—"

Before she can finish speaking, something blurs into existence beside us. There's a flash of silver, and the vampire vanishes before she can even cry out. I blink rapidly as I realize that the flash of silver was a blade of some kind because the vampire's hands *didn't* vanish. They fall away from my neck, flopping onto the marble floor.

My lips curl up.

That was the work of my Nightmare Prince. I still sense him nearby, so I just wait.

Finally, he emerges in front of me in the darkness, kicking the hands aside before reaching out to twist his fingers through the ends of my ponytail. I can't see him well because of how dark it is, but I'm beaming now.

"You're back."

"You're smiling," he rasps. "You've no idea how much I've missed your face, darling."

"Just my face?"

Crypt moves closer, and I feel his warm breath against my lips, but he's careful not to touch me. "All of you. Every beautifully broken piece that completes whatever is left of my soul. Tell me, were you harmed at all during my absence?"

I squint, trying to make out his face better. Is that...

"Do you have a black eye?"

He ignores my question and gently brushes aside some of my hair to check my neck, where the vampire's harsh grip probably left a mark. Of course, the darkness isn't impeding this incubus's vision like it is mine.

But who the fuck cares if my neck is bruised because now I'm positive that he's missing an ear.

Gritting my teeth, I risk the odds of another hireling finding us and raise my hand to call up a common magic light spell. As soon as I do, I swear viciously.

Crypt *is* missing an ear. He *does* have a black eye. In fact, he looks like he just went through hell. His clothes, including his leather jacket, are ripped and burnt, and bruises darken one side of his jaw and cheekbone. He's also hiding one hand behind his back, which means he's trying to hide another injury from me.

He's a siphon, and they have accelerated healing and regenerative abilities. That means if he looks like this now, he must have looked far worse earlier.

When I give him a silently furious look, he sighs and looks away.

"I was going to stay in Limbo and see you safely back to the apartment without you seeing me like this, but that vampire chose death by touching you."

Scowling, I reach behind him and pull his hand forward. His

hand is extremely burnt, to the point that I can count bones. If he were human, it would probably need amputation—and it's healing far too slowly.

Why do my matches keep getting hurt?

I fucking *hate* it.

I'm so mad I can't even form words as I put out the light spell and grab Crypt's unburned hand, marching toward the quintet apartment. He wisely says nothing, but I know we're both checking corners for any signs of more legacies patrolling for students.

As soon as we step through the front door, Baelfire leaps up from the couch, relief shining on his handsome face.

"Thank the fucking gods you're—oh, yikes. Crypt looks like shit."

"I noticed," I snap, the raw fury breaking my voice. Then I pause when I see Silas asleep on the couch in the nearby TV room. A blanket is haphazardly tossed over him. "Why is he sleeping here? I thought his paranoia prevented that."

Baelfire looks at me, then Silas, then back at me like he's trying to decide whether to tell me the truth. "It's nothing. He's fine."

"Why wouldn't he be?" I ask more menacingly than I intended. Because if another one of them is hurt, I'm going to snap.

Bael glances behind me at Crypt, and I look back just in time to see Crypt shaking his head. He quickly gives me an innocent smile as if he wasn't just telling the dragon shifter to shut up.

Obviously, they don't want me getting any more pissed off than I already am.

Smart legacies.

But I still want the truth. When I turn back to Baelfire, he gives me a soft smile.

"Don't worry about Si. It was fucking nasty to touch his mouth, but I force-fed him a shot of wyvern blood because he told me to, and he's fit as a fiddle again. Just sleeping. So you can go take care of your psychotic incubus. Even if he doesn't deserve it because he abandoned you like an absolute fucking jackass," he adds, shooting Crypt a savage glare.

"Don't ever accuse me of leaving her willingly," Crypt warns darkly.

Baelfire huffs, but I ignore both of them as I gather a wide range of ingredients from Silas's stash in the kitchen. As I walk past Crypt toward the hall, I speak in a voice that leaves no room for argument.

"Come with me."

23
CRYPT

AFTER DAYS of being deprived of the only thing I want, I desperately drink in everything about her.

Maven's anger is evident as she tells me to sit as she prepares her tinctures. I perch on the end of her bed, lost in the quiet pleasure of watching her. Her movements are as bewitching as always while she skillfully combines ingredients I know little about.

My darling shoots me a sharp look that has my heart thrumming. "Enough of that dreamy look. I'm pissed at you."

I know she is. She's unhappy with me for getting hurt.

My chest swells, knowing that she was worried about me. No one has ever fretted over me before, and if they had, I would have broken their face. But knowing *Maven* is upset on my behalf is damn near giddying.

I don't know what to do with a feeling like this.

But I do know that I'm going to make her my muse. I want her ingrained in my subconscious just as deeply as I plan to be permanently woven into hers.

Maven brings over three bowls of different poultices and sets them on the bed beside me. She reaches out to gently but firmly turn my head to one side so she can study the spot where a shade bit off my left ear.

It will grow back faster once I've consumed more dreams to cull my exhaustion. I mean to tell her that, but she's standing between my legs, and when she presses the tiniest bit into me, I bite back a groan. I want her far closer.

But pulling her into my lap the way I want to is out of the question. I'll mind Maven's aversion to touch until she wants more.

And she *will* want more. I can't be the only one dying for a mere touch.

She dabs some of the poultice on my bruises before using small bursts of warm magic on my ruined hand. I've been tuning out the pain of that particular injury for several hours ever since a swarm of wisps caused it.

"Where were you?" she finally asks, meeting my gaze.

I study her beautiful eyes. I'm not a forthcoming person and never have been, but I need her to understand that I would never willingly leave her side. Perhaps some context is in order.

"The curse I was born with is unique," I begin quietly.

"Aren't they all?"

"Not always. Some are hereditary. Other legacies sometimes have curses similar to one another. But mine is only found about once every century, and it can't be broken."

Maven's brow furrows. "Explain."

"It's more a state of being than a curse," I clarify. "As I understand it, when the gods divided the Nether from the mortal realm many thousands of years ago, Limbo was an unintended side effect. It was a living echo between planes of existence, and humans began to dream for the first time as their subconscious naturally reached for that echo. And because souls first pass through Limbo and then the Nether as they sink to the Beyond, they leave more echos behind."

"Wisps and shades," she guesses.

I nod, watching her smooth hands hover around where she begins healing one of my fingers. "But the reverse is also true. When anything passes from the Nether into the mortal realm, it creates a ripple in Limbo. Those ripples allowed wisps and shades to run amuck. The gods quickly realized how chaotic and dangerous the dream plane was if left unchecked, and they assigned a steward—an incubus marked from birth, equipped to manage Limbo and all its dangers. Time after time, random incubi have been born with this unique curse. I'm the latest."

"You…manage all of Limbo?"

I hum in agreement, distracted when she begins dabbing the poultice around the damaged stump of my ear. It's slightly numbing and feels nice, but not nearly as nice as her touch.

Then I notice how tightly her lips are pressed together.

"Something bothering you, love? You don't have to touch me. I can apply that to myself."

"No. I'm annoyed at the gods. They're assholes for giving you that curse."

I smile. "On the contrary. They saved my life by marking me. My curse was the only thing that kept those immortal halfwits from killing me when my mother announced that her mysterious baby was Somnus's bastard child. Natalya was livid, and Somnus wanted to kill me on the spot, but killing the designated steward of Limbo would have offended the gods. Not to mention, since the steward comes around so sparingly, the Immortal Quintet must deal with the extreme repercussions whenever a steward dies young. Which happens often."

In this one thing, I don't offer Maven the whole truth: that stewards always die before the age of thirty, some even younger. The strain of plane-walking is just too much to live long. Even though I'm half-monster and more powerful than the stewards who came before me, I doubt I'll last many more years.

But I won't stain what precious time we have together with that knowledge.

She studies me, reaching up to brush some of my hair away from my forehead. I close my eyes in pleasure when her fingertips trace along the swirling patterns in the skin of my neck.

"This is how you were marked from birth?"

"It makes the chosen steward impossible to miss."

"Are the markings all over you?"

I open my eyes to give her a seductive grin. "Ask me to strip and find out."

Maven gives me a deadpan look. "Are you really trying to instigate something when your hand is covered in fourth-degree burns?"

"Why not? It's not my hand I intend to use."

Her lips twitch, and I go perfectly still when she leans forward to press her mouth against mine.

I mean to be good. Truly, I try not to escalate it.

But then she gently nips my lower lip, and all sense leaves my body. I kiss her back hungrily, relishing the way she opens for me and the tantalizing exchange. When she bites teasingly on my still-tender tongue, I tense and pull back with a breathless laugh.

"Careful, love, I've just got that back."

I can tell she wants to ask what I mean, but I kiss her again, addicted to the softness of her lips. My cock is stiff as steel, the piercings around the head creating extra friction against the inside of my pants, but I dutifully ignore it.

But when I start trailing kisses down her jaw and neck, I can sense the subtle shift in her demeanor. Though she tries to hide it, her muscles tense, and her breathing increases. Not in an excited way. This skin contact must be bothering her.

Once again, I wonder about that subconscious therapy idea.

I quickly pull away and smile apologetically. "Forgive me. If I'm ever pushing things too far with you, hurt me any way you like. I'll have earned it."

Maven snorts softly, shaking her head. "I can handle kissing. I'm not made of glass."

"Believe me, love, I know you're not."

She tips her head, eyes narrowing. "How much *do* you know?"

I wrap some of her hair around my uninjured hand because it feels like I'm anchoring her to me. "I know you're from the Nether. I saw you come back not once but twice, so I would venture to say you're no longer human. And based on where I found you, I believe you intended to kill Melvolin, so I assume the rest of the Immortal Quintet is fair game for you, as well."

Maven doesn't deny any of it. "I'm going to kill your father next. Does that bother you?"

I adore how blunt she is. "Quite the opposite. Tell me any way I can help."

"I see the burning hatred is mutual."

"More than. Morals have never influenced me much, and I have enough blood on my hands to paint a continent, but compared to Somnus, I'm a saint. He's the reason I've spent much of my life hunting down predators to dish out my own form of justice."

Maven traces the piercing in my eyebrow as if lost in thought. She's touching me so freely tonight, and each time she does, my heart rate doubles.

"Sexual predators, you mean," she clarifies finally, then starts healing my hand once more. "That must have something to do with you slaughtering all those humans in court."

"They were all complicit in allowing a serial rapist to go free. Many were bribed, others acquiesced. I decided to rid the world of that level of cowardice."

"Good. And the rapist?"

He's the reason I came to Halfton in the first place weeks ago. I received a mysterious, anonymous tip that the man who walked free, who I was so looking forward to torturing, would be in the area. And while I didn't find him in Halfton, I did come across the faint, lingering remnants of the most uniquely stunning aura I'd ever seen —Maven's aura.

After that, I'd been searching for her. I returned to Everbound and attended the Seeking, hoping to see who that beautiful, shimmering dark mauve aura belonged to. And the moment I saw her standing on that stage, everything ceased to exist for me beyond her.

"Not yet," I reply softly, barely resisting the urge to kiss her again. Instead, I touch the softness of her dark hair again, toying with it.

She studies me. "I heard you also killed Silas's parents' keeper. And his uncle."

"Technically, they killed themselves," I muse. "I only planted the seed in their minds. Constantly."

"You must have had a reason."

My lips twist up. "Must I have?"

When she raises a brow expectantly, I sigh and release her hair. This is something I never intended to tell anyone. Still, I'm thoroughly enjoying this openness with my dark little darling. If I'm an open book for her, perhaps she'll return the favor one day.

"Omar Crane, the keeper of Silas's parents' quintet, was a wolf shifter with a sickness. The kind of perverted sickness of the mind that I hunt down at every chance. He enjoyed taking advantage of children, especially the children of powerful legacy families."

Her face darkens with the same wrath I feel every time I find one of those disgusting bastards.

I look away. "Unfortunately, I had to become intimately familiar with that sycophant's mind in order to more effectively break it, so I know that for him, it was a power trip. Ruining the heirs of his competitors in secret, hiding his putrid fantasies from the world. And when I was in his dreams, exploring his psyche to find the best ways to unravel him, I realized that he had his eye set on..."

I hesitate. Should I tell her this? It may only upset her.

"Set on?"

"Decimus," I mutter.

Her eyes widen in shocked outrage. I was right. This is upsetting her, so I hurry to finish and get it over with.

"He was eight years old at the time and drew too much attention as the miracle child of the revered Decimus family. Which means he drew Omar Crane's attention, too, in all the worst ways. When I discovered that, I unraveled Omar's mind piece by fucking piece until he craved death more than anything else. Watching him drive that silver through his own forehead was beyond satisfying, and I have never once regretted it."

Maven takes a moment as if trying to compose herself despite overwhelming emotions. Then she whispers, "You killed Silas's family to protect Baelfire."

How utterly soft that makes me seem. I make a noncommittal noise and study my previously injured hand. It still stings like hell, and the gradually regenerating skin is bright red, but at least it's no longer half-melted.

"It was a domino effect," I explain. "I only drove their keeper and Crane's uncle insane because they were involved in trafficking. The rest of the lot killed each other or themselves on their own after that, driven by curses and such. But Crane would never believe me if I told him that. He's much more comfortable hating me for it, so I've never bothered explaining."

She nods and then sits beside me on the bed. "If Baelfire was eight, you would have been…thirteen?"

"Something like that."

"You're very sweet, in a fucked up way," she informs me.

I can't resist leaning over to kiss her temple. "I enjoy being fucked up. So do you. We're rather perfect that way."

Maven nods and yawns, and I realize how exhausted she is. I've been too elated about seeing her again to notice how heavily Limbo is weighed down around her.

"You need rest," I say softly. "It's the wee hours of the morning. I assume things must have only gotten worse here, so you'll need your strength."

"First, I have three more questions."

"Ask anything."

"You never told me exactly where you went. Where were you?"

I stand and take the poultices, setting things out of the way for when she goes to sleep. "Recently, there were three bizarrely large surges of shadow fiends, all within hours of each other. It threw Limbo into disarray, which led to wisps and shades breaking free and demolishing two legacy bases near the Divide. The Immortal Quintet sent me to contain the situation."

I also used that time to get more *reverium*, and I tracked down a strangely colorless plant currently tucked in my leather jacket's inner pocket. I found it in the inner reaches of the Divide. I'll give it to Crane when he wakes up so he can see if it will help Maven's condition, just as *reverium* helps me. And if that one doesn't work, I'll find a way back out of Everbound's wards and keep looking, if necessary.

When I turn back to her, Maven seems deep in thought. I smile. "What is Question Number Two?"

"Sexually speaking, are you interested in men?"

My brows go up. That's quite the subject change. She's always so delightfully unexpected.

When Maven sees my reaction, she clarifies, "I thought Baelfire and Silas showered together. They didn't, but I wondered whether you would want to..."

"Fuck around with them?" I grimace. "Not to insult your taste in men, love, but that's revolting."

She tips her head. "What about other men?"

I can tell she's asking only out of pure curiosity. I opt for full transparency.

"I didn't experience real pleasure with women, so after a while, I tried men. It was equally empty, and I gave up on both shortly after. Until I met you, I felt nothing of substance or genuine attraction toward anyone."

Maven's eyes soften, and then she hums thoughtfully. "But that's not true. You went after those predators out of anger. You protected Baelfire. That had to come from feeling something."

"Rage, apathy, and brief instances of vague purpose when I was destroying whoever I chose to. That's all I had until I saw you, darling."

Now, I feel an extraordinary amount of emotions around her. But especially obsession. I crave tying my soul to hers just as much as I crave the taste of her dreams. I've only tasted her nightmares so far, and their flavor turned my stomach. But I suspect that with the barest taste of her dreams, I'll be well and truly addicted.

"Would feeding on my dreams help you heal faster?"

I jolt, blinking at her in bewilderment. Did she read my mind, or am I finally dreaming?

Maven arches a brow. "That's my third question."

"Yes. Feeding would allow me to heal faster. I haven't fed in days." Hence why my ability to heal is lagging. Everyone was too on edge to sleep in the areas where I was fixing tears in Limbo, so there was nothing for me to devour.

She nods thoughtfully. "I haven't had nightmares with the totem you left. Thank you for that, by the way. Where did you get it?"

"Somnus."

She pauses, and it seems as though gears are turning in her head. Her mind is so beautifully unexpected that I don't even dare to guess at what she's thinking. It could be anything.

But finally, she nods. "Stay with me tonight. You can feed on my dreams while I sleep."

My mouth waters at an alarming rate, but not as alarming as the stiffness surging into my cock. Maven's dreams, I crave.

But Maven *sleeping*…

Gods above. Watching her sleep is going to be the death of me. I can't stop the illicit thoughts now running rampant in my head—thoughts of Maven sleeping while I gently peel off her clothes, baring her to my gaze. The way her peaceful breathing would change if I were to play with her pretty nipples.

Would she make those same captivating, breathless sounds in her sleep that she did at that inn?

I bet she would. I want to make her come in her sleep. With her dream state in my grasp, I could harness her subconscious sexual desires and drive her to such pleasure that she would drench my face over and over. Then I would slide the tip of my cock through all that beautiful wetness and—

"Crypt?"

I look away, internally cursing my painfully hard cock for taking all my blood and leaving me lightheaded with need. She's tired. She needs rest. I must make sure she gets to sleep quickly, and I won't push her when she isn't ready for all the furtive ways I desperately want to worship her.

"You have no water in here," I say, my voice barely a rasp. "I'll bring you some."

She looks confused but doesn't protest my sudden offer as I quickly leave the room to force myself to calm down. I get a cup of water from the kitchen, but when I turn back toward the hall and pass the TV room, I spot Decimus. He's sitting on the far end of the couch where Crane is sleeping. Decimus's head is hanging, but when he looks up at me, I pause.

One thing is clear. He overheard our conversation about Omar Crane.

Damn. I hadn't stopped to think about his shifter hearing.

He opens his mouth, looking as if he wants to say something, but then clears his throat and looks back down.

Good. Anything the dragon has to say about it, I don't care to hear. I was going to kill Omar for his past crimes, anyway. Knowing that he was after Decimus was the last straw, but the last fucking thing I need is for these wankstains to think I'm their friend.

Without a word, I leave him and return to Maven's room. Shutting the door softly, I set the water on the bedside table for her. The lamp is off, but darkness doesn't limit my eyesight, so I can still easily make out the way she yawns and curls in on herself slightly under the blanket.

"Thanks for the water," she murmurs sleepily.

Thank you for existing, my love.

I lay on the bed beside her, careful not to touch her. I try to ignore my pounding heart. I'm nearly breathless with anticipation at the thought of consuming her dreams until morning. Yet I can already tell my cock will be leaking all night. I enjoy edging, but there's a fine line between teasing and torture.

"Darling?" I whisper softly.

"Mm?"

"I have a proposal for you."

I explain my idea for slowly helping her overcome her fear of touch through her subconscious while she's dreaming. By the time I'm done speaking, she's turned to face me, a thoughtful expression on her tired face.

"Let's do it. I suggested exposure therapy with the others as a remedy, and I'll continue that. But your method might work."

"You won't mind my being in your subconscious all night?"

"Anything to help me not be so fucking pathetic about touch."

"Don't call yourself pathetic in my presence," I warn her. "You're a masterpiece."

She closes her eyes. "That's what the chief necromancer used to call me. His masterpiece."

He probably considered her an object to perfect instead of a person. I glare at the ceiling. "I'd like to kill him."

"Me too."

Maven drifts into sleep a moment later, and Limbo clouds with her subconscious. I slip into Limbo to taste her dream and instantly find that I was right.

I'll be addicted to her until the day I die.

24

EVERETT

I watch the winter dawn rise outside my office window, the falling flurries of snow swirling over the fields surrounding Everbound Castle. It should be peaceful, but all I can think about is whether Maven is lying lifeless on the cold ground somewhere out there.

That mental image makes it impossible to breathe right. My chest aches.

Walking to their quintet apartment to see if she's there would be easy. If she is, I'll act like a curt asshole as usual and hurry back here to sulk some more.

But if Maven *isn't* there...

I realize the window I'm staring at has completely frosted over as my panic spirals and glazes my office with a thin layer of ice. Taking a deep breath, I begin to pace.

I didn't sleep last night. I stared wide awake at the ceiling, overthinking every possible way my keeper could have been hurt in her mission to get her friend back. Since sleep wasn't an option, I eventually went to patrol the halls like some of the other faculty members have been doing, just to see if I was lucky enough to find her coming back.

Instead, all I found was a creepy-ass pair of dismembered hands. So there's luck for you.

Walking to my desk, I straighten what little is on it. I organize it again and again, and then I pace some more before finally dropping into my chair and rubbing my face.

How the hell am I supposed to get through today? How can I keep resisting every single instinct I have toward her? I was dangerously close to snapping yesterday. And feeling Maven's warm, strong, incredibly fucking *perfect* body pressed so tightly against me when I rolled her out of the way of Baelfire's dragon...

Nope, don't go there. Don't even think about it.

Too late. I glare down at the erection that's trying to strain through my pants.

"You're a helpless fucking idiot, you know that?" I grumble.

"I'm going to pretend you didn't just talk to your own cock," Silas's voice says from the entry to my office.

I startle and scowl viciously. He must have used magic to silently open my door to keep anyone outside from hearing him knock. My face is probably bright red, but I turn back to the few papers on my desk like that's what I've been focused on instead of losing my fucking mind with worry for our keeper.

"I'm busy. Get out."

"No, you're not," he scoffs, sitting and lounging in the chair across from me as he glances at the ice covering almost every inch of my office. "Tell me, why exactly do you even *have* an office? I haven't figured out why you came back here."

"To teach."

"Bullshit."

Yes, it is.

I came here for three reasons. First, I wanted to take a break from modeling for the first time in over thirteen years. Second, there was the whole debacle with keeping Heidi out of Everbound. My parents would only heed my demand that they keep her away from here if I acted as their point of contact at the university.

They were desperate to have someone at Everbound in their pocket after receiving an anonymous tip that the rumored *telum* would be found here.

I've tried to distance myself as much as possible from the Frost family's shady dealings and dirty money. But when they mentioned the *telum*, it created my third reason for coming here. I wanted to know if the rumors were true.

After all, the *telum* is mentioned in my personal prophecy. I hoped learning more about it would shed some light on the disheartening prophecy I received from the temple of Arati so long ago.

But now that I know *Maven* is the Entity's weapon, I'm more confused than ever. And as usual, my family complicates things.

Silas picks up the glass of water on my desk which has been frozen solid. He ignores the way I scowl at him as he turns it over curiously.

"Is there a reason you barged in?" I huff.

"The Immortal Quintet almost killed me yesterday."

"What stopped them?"

Silas's glare is as scarlet as ever. "You're an insensitive prick, you know that?"

"I meant, why only almost?" I clarify. "I've seen how they work. They never change their minds while executing someone, sanctioned or not."

"That prophetess stepped in with peculiarly *serendipitous* timing and got me out of there. But I came to tell you about this because before Natalya sank her teeth into me, they asked some questions about our keeper. Specifically, where she's from and whether she's ever been through the Divide."

My blood runs cold, and ice fractals drift in the air around us. "They're looking for the *telum*."

He nods, examining one of his wrists for whatever reason. "Maven has brilliantly downplayed her abilities since arriving. If she continues to act like an atypical wallflower, perhaps they won't bat another eye in her direction. But now that we've seen her lose her temper…"

Watching Maven demolish the rival quintet, it was obvious that she's a living weapon.

The same one my parents are so desperate to find.

But I see where Silas is going with this. "We can't let anyone else see how powerful she is."

"She had a dangerously strong response to Baelfire getting hurt," he goes on, and then something like affection crosses his face as he smiles at his own wrist. "And according to Bael, when Crypt came back injured last night, Maven looked like she was going to kill the first person who so much as breathed wrong in his direction."

The idea of anyone being protective of the Nightmare Prince is laughable. But if she was that mad, it must mean she's…protective of us.

Well, of them.

But still. Maven tried so damn hard to deny the quintet entirely, so the thought of her getting pissed off for any of us has my chest warming. The ice on the window starts to thaw, dripping steadily as I look away from Silas.

"And she came back safely from that little rescue mission?" I ask tightly, trying to act nonchalant.

"She did. I wanted to give her more time to sleep, so I haven't had a chance to ask her about it this morning." He pauses and then grumbles, "I also didn't want to walk in on the off chance Crypt is naked in there."

Dear gods. She actually *slept* with that unhinged freak in there?

"He better not be messing with her head."

"We'll remove his if he does."

Silas finally stands and then pauses, staring at something on my wall. I realize it's the portrait I decided to finally hang up recently. The blood fae's face darkens with warning.

"Who is that?"

He's deeply annoyed at the idea of me hanging up a picture of some random girl, which makes sense. If any of the others were pining after someone who wasn't Maven, I would be beyond irritated.

But it's a picture of Heidi, my half-sister. Of course, Silas doesn't know that because he's never heard of her. No one here has. She was kept hidden away by her dad and my mom, who both deserve gold medals for being the most uncaring, negligent parents in the universe where Heidi is concerned.

Heidi turned twenty-one last summer, but I would rather sell my soul to Sachar, judge of the Beyond, before I ever see my sister set foot in this school. My parents were all for sending her here to let her sink or swim alone. They had the gall to remind me that weak legacies aren't *"meant"* to survive. It was a godsdamned miracle that I convinced them to let me be their point of contact here in exchange for keeping Heidi hidden safely away in the rural town she's grown up in.

Because we all know she wouldn't survive a day here. Heidi is a shifter, but she's one of the few remaining who isn't an apex predator of any kind. I've kept her at a distance all our lives for her own good, but I still know what my sister is like. She's sunshine personified. She'd probably let a fellow legacy stab her and then apologize for spilling blood on their shoes.

"I saw how Maven looked at you yesterday," Silas murmurs dangerously. "She doesn't hate you, not even with the shit you pulled to hurt her at the inn. It's possible she might even care for you. And if she does, and you're in here drooling over some tramp—"

I freeze his mouth shut before he can unwittingly say another word against my sister, giving him the same withering look I used to use on photographers who tried to get handsy.

"I don't drool over anyone because, in case you forgot, my curse would fucking kill them. Now get the hell out of my office."

Silas uses magic to unfreeze his mouth. He moves toward the door but sighs and looks over his shoulder. "I mostly came to assure you that she returned safely last night. I know I would be spiraling if I couldn't check on her. None of us envy you."

His expression is almost…*kind.*

Which is way too fucking weird. If he and Baelfire hadn't told me all about Maven killing the changeling, I'd be positive this wasn't the real Silas Crane.

"If you're even thinking about pitying me, I'm going to give your dick frostbite," I warn. "Just get out."

He snorts in amusement and finally leaves me alone.

The Immortal Quintet are like helicopters today, watching all legacies. They hover in the halls, check into classrooms, and in general, freak everyone the fuck out.

Their hired hands are equally annoying, and when I see one of them staring at our quintet from beside the doorway during Fiend Studies, I stare them down until they get the shivers and leave.

The only thing worse than being watched so closely?

Baelfire Decimus and Crypt fucking DeLune.

I don't know what the fuck happened to them, but the dragon is panting after Maven even more ridiculously than he has to date—which shouldn't even be possible. If this were a children's cartoon, his eyes would be hearts popping out of his head every time he looks at her.

In the hallways, he tries to hold her hand. And citing "exposure therapy," she lets him for a little bit before slipping her glove back on and returning to the careful act of being a wallflower.

Meanwhile, whenever Crypt isn't haunting us in Limbo, he's looking at Maven like he wants to devour her. And I mean more than usual—which, again, should not be possible.

Then there's the dynamic between Crypt and Baelfire. It's weird as hell. I don't know why they seem so off around each other, but it makes me think I've missed something. Again.

I make the mistake of staying with them for the first time during lunch in the dining hall. When Baelfire tries to get Maven to sit on his lap during lunch so he can hand-feed her, I finally can't take it anymore.

"That's it. Why the hell can't your lovesick lizard keep it in his pants today? What, did you finally decide to fuck him or something?" I snap.

Maven takes another bite of steamed carrots. "Yep."

Oh. I'm an idiot.

Silas chokes on his water, and Baelfire looks smug as shit. Crypt's eyebrows raise, and he tips his head. I can't help noticing that he removed all the piercings from one of his ears. Weird, but then his fashion choices have never made sense to me.

"That explains why he popped into your dreams so damned much last night," he drawls. "I don't mind your sex dreams in the least, but I must say the collar and leash were an interesting addition."

Now it's Maven's turn to choke on her food. Bael gives her bedroom eyes while Silas offers her his water. Crypt leans over and kisses her cheek, laughing.

They're all getting closer to her.

And I'm not. I *can't*.

I knew it would hurt to be left out, but this is fucking unbearable. I stand up and walk away quickly, ignoring how Maven's gaze follows me as I leave the dining hall.

Combat training is less brutal today than it was the last two days. Instead of fighting in Everbound Forest, we run defensive training drills instructed by an air elemental named Agatha Angely. She's one of the few fellow instructors I actually respect. During the training drills focused on evasive maneuvering and ways to break out of holds the Undead typically go for, the others make sure I'm never paired with Maven. I appreciate that and hate it at the same time.

But she notices.

I know she does because when the others aren't looking, she arches a brow as if expecting me to explain why we're all working to keep distance between her and me.

I just act like an asshole and ignore her completely.

But when combat training is over and we make our way back into the castle, Maven stops us from turning down the hall toward the quintet apartment.

"We're not done training. Where are the private exercise rooms?"

Damn it. I forgot that she thinks we're all sloppy and told us we needed more training.

"I have shit to do," I mutter, turning to leave because I'm pretty sure I can't take another few hours of watching all of them together.

It's not jealousy, and it's not that they're so obsessed with her that bothers me—it's that I can't join them. I keep trying to find something about her to hate to delay falling for her, but there's *nothing*.

Not even the fact that she's the Entity's weapon bothers me. It just makes my stomach clench with dread at the idea of my parents finding out.

But before I can leave, Maven's gloved hand slips around mine, and she pulls me back.

Immediately, my heart begins pounding with erratic excitement, the traitorous little bastard. I pull away with a scowl.

"I don't need more training."

"Tell that to your hands."

Damn it. As usual when I'm struggling to control my emotions, they're covered in frost. I can't formulate an argument, and the others also can't seem to think of an excuse for me to get out of this. So, I grumble under my breath as Silas leads us down several flights of stairs. When we descend past the point where regular mage lights are stationed, he calls up a fae light to illuminate the way.

We reach an area that clearly used to be dungeons. But instead of iron-barred cells and rats, Silas opens a door at the far end, and I find that we're looking at a large exercise room full of training mats with a large mirror along one wall of the room. Silas sets up more fae lights in the room, and Maven nods approvingly, shutting the door behind us.

"Perfect. Let's start with Crypt."

The Nightmare Prince flickers into existence right beside her with a twisted smile. "And what exactly are we starting, love?"

She looks him over analytically. "I saw the others in action," she says as if that explains everything.

"Dreadful, aren't they?"

"Fuck off," I say at the same time as Baelfire.

"I haven't had a chance to see how you are in combat," she goes on, folding her arms as she glowers up at Crypt. "But if you can lose an ear, you can lose much worse."

I must be missing yet another thing because I don't get the ear comment at all, but the Nightmare Prince just waggles his eyebrows. "Like my cock? You wouldn't want me losing that, hmm?"

"I was thinking your head, but feel free to prioritize the much, much smaller one," she shoots back smoothly.

I cough, Baelfire bursts into laughter, and Silas smirks. Crypt just looks delighted.

"Did you just trash-talk me, darling? Hardly fair, considering you haven't seen it. Ask nicely, and I'll show you how very not little it is."

I hold up a hand. "Nope. Everyone needs to keep their fucking pants on."

Crypt grins. "Unless we want to use this room for an orgy instead."

"My vote's with him," Baelfire says, raising his hand.

Maven looks slightly flushed as she rolls her eyes and turns to Silas. "Never mind. Let's start with you."

He folds his arms defensively. "The others need training far more than I do."

"Oh, my gods. This is like dealing with four butt-hurt toddlers," Maven huffs. I can't drag my eyes away as she ties her hair into a high ponytail, exposing her very kissable neck. "Look. Obviously, you're all powerful legacies, but you can't rely on your abilities alone. That's where your blind spot is and why we're here. So in this room, there will be no magic, no ice, no shifting—"

"It's not like I can right now, anyway," Baelfire injects.

"—and no slipping into Limbo during combat or whatever other shit you can do," she adds, glancing at Crypt. "In here, it will be pure, physical combat. I'm going to kick your asses until you all stand a better chance of making it out of First Placement and future combat alive. I'm not losing you guys."

My protest dies on my tongue with her last words, and my heart sort of melts into a gooey puddle of mindless warmth.

I'm not losing you guys.

Meaning…me included?

I swallow and look away. "Yeah, okay."

The others mutter their agreements, seeming equally flustered.

"Good. Then let's begin."

25

EVERETT

Arati save me.

She's trying to fucking kill us.

Baelfire slumps to the ground beside me when his turn on the mat ends early. His turn has ended early every time because, apparently, the oversexed idiot gets too aroused every time Maven pins him, and he has to tap out early to cool off.

He wipes the sweat off his face with a grimace and leans back against the wall like I am. "How does such a tiny person put me in a fucking headlock? I'm like three times her size."

"Try ten times, you behemoth," I fire back, watching Silas take a defensive position on the opposite side of the mat from Maven with a determined set to his jaw.

The only one of us who hasn't been brutally taken down repeatedly by Maven has been Crypt. She's pinned him a few times, but the asshole refuses to play by the rules and keeps slipping into Limbo to pin her down from behind and whisper what I assume are filthy things into her ear.

The last time he did it, Maven had enough and head-butted him, and we haven't seen him since. I'm pretty sure he's letting his nose heal in Limbo while he enjoys watching the rest of us fail.

I watch as Silas rushes her and tries yet another tactic. Maven easily outmaneuvers him before he ends up pinned to the ground with his leg stuck in an incredibly uncomfortable-looking position. He swears and taps out, and the pure amusement on Maven's face has me smiling.

She really likes combat, doesn't she? And she's insanely good at it. I know I should be using that as a reason to convince myself I don't want her...but godsdamn me, I love that look on her face. She can win as many sparring matches as she wants with me—I don't mind the sore muscles and bruises if she's happy.

Baelfire elbows me hard, knocking the wind from my side. I shoot him a glare. "What the hell?"

He just shakes his head. "Cockblock curse," he whispers. "Stare at Silas instead. Pretend you like his ass more."

I really hate him so much.

Silas gets to his feet and tips his head. "Why is it that touching during combat isn't a trigger for you?"

"Touch is an entirely different beast during combat. I was never conditioned against fighting. In fact, it's what I was turned into this for," Maven shrugs as if it's that simple.

Immediately, my mouth tastes like bile. I can only assume that the Entity is the one who *conditioned* her and...

"Turned you into what, exactly?" I manage to ask through clenched teeth.

She ignores the question and nods to Silas. "They're still licking their wounds and egos. Get back into position."

But he has his scheming face on, the same one that used to make me anxious as fuck when we were kids. "No, I want to know, too. What are you, Maven?"

"The girl who's about to kick your ass. Again."

He smirks. "Goading me won't work."

She stretches as if to work out a kink in her shoulder. Again, I can't look away, and my hands itch with the urge to rub out whatever discomfort she's feeling. If she let me, I would massage her entire body. She must get really worked up and sore—after all, if she's pushing us this hard, I can only imagine how hard she pushes herself.

I don't like that. I want to see my keeper comfortable and content. I want to spoil her in every possible way.

My mouth goes dry when she abruptly strips off her oversized, baggy shirt, leaving behind a form-fitting black undershirt. Silas and Baelfire stare hard, too, and Crypt finally reappears in the mortal realm to check her out as he leans against the wall.

"All right. I'm officially ready for another round," he says too eagerly.

For once, I agree with him. But Baelfire must notice how much I enjoy seeing her in something tight because he elbows me hard again. This time, a grunt escapes. The sound draws Maven's attention to us.

As soon as her eyes are on me, I dutifully look away like this is the most boring experience of my entire life. But I can still admire her in the reflective glass she's standing in front of.

That tight shirt shows off a bit of her midriff and lower back. I'd like to kiss all of it. I know my cheeks are turning red the longer I can feel her studying me.

"Fine. That's the prize," Maven says finally. "You're all in desperate need of motivation, anyway."

"Not anymore," Crypt smiles. "That's a lovely shirt."

She rolls her eyes. "Here's how it works. If any of you beat me on the mat, I'll tell you what I am."

That has all of us hooked. I can see the resolution set in as Silas rolls his shoulders back and retakes his stance. "You'll keep your word?"

"I always do," she says sweetly, then pins him again in less than two minutes.

Only the gods know how long our private training lasts. It feels far too long before Maven calls it and says we'll do this again tomorrow. Apparently, she thinks this torture is valuable, but I decide I won't protest because she might wear another tight shirt tomorrow. I might pray to the gods for that tonight.

As we emerge onto the main level of Everbound Castle, the others automatically head toward the quintet apartment. I turn down the hall that will take me to my office, which has a passable faculty apartment attached. But it's like the gods cursed all of today for me because I hear Silas calling Maven's name and realize she's walking right behind me.

I halt in surprise, scowling down at her.

She keeps her poker face. "We need to talk."

"Not happening. I need to shower. I'm sweaty."

It's the lamest possible excuse, but there it is. My strongest defense, ladies and gentlemen.

"Maven," Silas says again, stopping beside us and frowning at her. "Curfew starts soon. Let's go."

"I'll stay with Everett."

My heart lurches right up into my throat, and I snap, "No, you most certainly will fucking *not*. I don't want you anywhere near me."

"Agreed. Come on," Silas insists. "Baelfire's making dinner, and I'm sure Professor Frost needs to…grade papers."

I've never graded a paper in my life, but I nod.

Maven fixes us both with a look. "Cut the shit. I know you're all keeping me from being around Everett. You think he's a danger to me. Tell me why, or he and I are going to have a talk."

Silas looks at me accusingly, like this is somehow *my* fault. I just look heavenward, hoping whatever god gave me this curse will see what a dickhead they are. Respectfully, of course.

"Oakley, just go with Silas."

"Pass."

Okay, I have to push harder if I'm going to keep enough distance between us. "You think I want to fucking talk to you? You just abused and annoyed the hell out of me for hours. I'm exhausted, and I'm going to bed. So go run along with your pussy-whipped groupies and take a shower while you're at it because you smell."

It's a lie. She barely broke a sweat. It's fucking aggravating how good she looks right now.

Silas's jaw clenches at my words, but Maven holds my gaze. "Sure. I'll use your shower."

Why, gods, *why* did she have to be this stubborn and attractive? It's ludicrous. I rub the back of my neck, exhausted, confusingly horny, and extremely done with having to ignore her all the damn time. Deep down, I'm aching for her.

But I need to keep up the arrogant asshole front that will keep her at arm's length. This is the best way to protect her from my curse.

"I am not doing this right now," I grit.

"Great. Then I hope you have an extra blanket. I'll sleep on the floor."

She brushes past me toward my office. I debate running away to hide somewhere pathetic, like one of the school's public restrooms. But finally, I sigh and follow her.

"If anything even remotely unpleasant happens to her, I'll kill you," Silas warns from behind me.

Very helpful. "You missed your calling as a fucking cheerleader. Now go away."

If Maven insists on talking to me, I'll just have to be as unpleasant as possible and get her out of my space quickly. Maybe if I can get into a big fight with her, that might help me stop thinking about her so much.

It's pathetic, but it's all I have.

By the time I reach my office, Maven is waiting. I try to give her a death glare, but I'm sure it looks more like I'm pouting as I unlock my office to let us inside. The automatic mage lights built into every faculty office glow softly, dimmed slightly for the nighttime.

Maven pauses to take in my office. "Tidy."

"I hate messes. I also hate pushy keepers who can't mind their own fucking business."

She turns, smirking. "Nice try, but you don't hate me."

"How would you know? You're too busy bouncing between the three other dicks in your happy little harem to give a shit."

Saying stuff like this to her makes my stomach clench—but if I'm crude and bitter enough, hopefully, she'll dislike me enough to want to leave.

Maven rolls her eyes. "You're not going to get me to hate you, either."

Damn it. Why does she have to be so perceptive?

I turn my back on her and straighten the things on my desk out of nervous habit, even though I organized them before I left earlier. When I grab my glasses case to slip into the desk's top drawer, Maven circles around and tips her head.

"You wear glasses?"

"Only for reading," I grumble, acting like I'm busy and she's a nuisance.

When she boosts herself up to sit on the edge of my desk, the slight bounce of her tits under her tight shirt sends a bolt of longing through me. I whirl away from her again, clearing my throat and staring hard at the calendar on my wall as if it's far more interesting than the incredibly sexy enigma perched on my desk.

Don't think about her tits. Don't think about her ass on your desk where you work. Don't think about her body at all, you ridiculously horny pervert.

"I want to see you in your glasses sometime, *Professor*."

"Just spit out whatever the fuck you had to talk to me about," I huff, rubbing my face.

She's silent for so long, I worry I've finally hurt her feelings. But when I turn, bracing myself to face the horror of seeing Maven hurt again, I find that she's quietly studying the few things I have on my walls and arranged decoratively on shelves. When she sees the shard of nevermelt on the end of one shelf, she turns with a surprised look.

"Where did you get that?"

"I made it," I admit, folding my arms to look surly.

Nevermelt is rare. A diamond-hard substance, it's far colder than regular ice and, as the name suggests, can't melt due to the sheer amount of elemental power it's created with. Only ice wielders of the highest caliber can forge it. When I made the rookie mistake of revealing to my parents that I had the ability, they tried to ship me off to work directly for the Immortal Quintet.

I was sixteen at the time and used the money from my modeling to file for emancipation instead. My family used their extensive resources to keep that juicy bit of family drama out of the media, and they threatened to never give me my trust fund as if that would somehow change my mind.

But after a while, they pretended like it was their idea that I leave home early so I could "focus on my career in the world of humans." They still granted me access to my absurdly large inheritance when I turned twenty-four, which I haven't touched with a ten-foot pole.

Maven studies the nevermelt with an expression I don't understand. Then she moves on, raising her brows at the picture of Marshmallow and Blizzard.

"You have dogs?"

The two Great Pyrenees are practically the size of polar bears. They would love her. I have no idea if Maven even likes animals. Still, I can easily imagine them here, rubbing up against her with their tongues lolling out in delight if she decided to pet them.

Instead of giving in and telling her all about them, I scowl. "Can you get out already?"

Maven ignores me, tipping her head at the picture of Heidi.

"Pretty. I didn't know you have a sister."

I tense. "How did you…"

"She looks different from you, but you have the same nose." My keeper makes a face. "I only noticed because I'm trying to break a bad habit."

"What habit?" I frown.

"Killing the relatives of people I know before I even know who they are."

Oh. Wow, I…don't even know what to say to that. "Again, *why* are you here?"

"Take a seat. I know you're nervous."

Before I can ask how she knows that, she glances pointedly at the windows, which are once again icing over. I clench my teeth and sit in my office chair, intending to get this conversation over with so I can regain some illusion of control.

But all ideas of getting myself under control fly out the window when Maven straddles my legs to face me.

My mouth goes dry. "W—what are you—"

"I made a decision about our quintet. You're all mine, and I'll fight for you until the end. But if we're going to work out in the short amount of time we have, then I can't let this thing between us drag on. So I'm going to give you a very simple choice. Hold out your hand."

My heart is hammering hard, but I hold out my hand, looking away because I'm pretty sure staring at her this close will hypnotize me. My cock is torturously hard in my pants, the fucking turncoat.

But when the cold handle of a small dagger presses into my hand, I startle and look at her sharply. "Why are you making me hold this?"

Maven smirks and taps the end of the knife until it barely touches her shoulder. "If you hate me as much as you say you do, then hurt me. Should be easy."

My stomach lurches. *Dear gods, no.*

When I just stare at her in indignant alarm because there's no way she can be serious about this, Maven moves until the knife is pressing against the side of her neck. And when she leans into it—

I drop the knife as fury flashes through me. It clatters to the ground.

"Stop it. I'm not going to fucking hurt you. That's never happening, Oakley."

"You hurt me in Pennsylvania."

I flinch, my stomach churning at the memory. "I…I'm sorry," I whisper. "You have no idea how sorry. I get it if you never want to forgive me for that, but I had to do it because…"

"Because you care about me, and you thought that was the best way to protect me. We both know it's true, so stop feeling guilty."

I clench my teeth, desperate. Do I have to find something genuinely horrible to say to her? Could I even manage to say something to hurt her again? This is absolute hell.

"No. It's just that you're my keeper," I try to insist. "I don't even remotely like you, I just—"

Maven leans forward and kisses me.

Oh, holy gods above.

Her lips are so fucking warm.

Suddenly, I can't seem to pull her close enough. Her fingers tangle in my hair, and I moan when I feel her slide closer, her chest pressing against mine. She's like a fucking heater compared to me, and it feels insanely good. I've never held someone like this, but I know I'll be panting after Maven's warmth for the rest of my godsdamned life.

I've never been so turned on. She can probably feel that my heart is crashing hard enough to bruise my insides, but I can't focus on anything except her *fantastic* mouth and the way her tongue drags gently against my lips until I part them. When she winds her arms around my neck and deepens the kiss, making a soft sound of pleasure, I get lightheaded.

But then her fucking perfect hips roll so she can grind against my throbbing erection—

And I come in my pants.

Fuck. Oh, dear gods, no.

Kill me now. This day really is fucking cursed.

I pull away stiffly, my face burning a thousand degrees as I squeeze my eyes shut.

"Maven."

She must hear the strain in my voice because she starts to ask what happened…but when she inhales slightly, I know she can feel exactly what happened through my pants.

I'm begging you, Syntyche, I pray to the goddess of life reaping. *Just take me now. Right now. Please.*

I clear my throat hard and mutter, "Can you, um…could you get off for a moment? I'd like to throw myself out the window now."

To my shock, Maven's lips press against mine again, and I can feel she's smiling. "So, you *do* like me."

Way too fucking much. The evidence of that is all over in my pants.

"Wonder where you got that notion from. Maybe the fact that you barely touched me and I lost control like a damn teenager?"

I cover my face again, mortified. *Anytime now, Syntyche. Please.*

Maven pries my fingers away until I'm forced to look at her and see the breathtaking smile on her face. There's no amusement or mocking—if anything, she seems extremely happy.

And dear gods, I like seeing her happy. She's just so *pretty*.

"Good. Then we're on the same page."

"Is that the page where I fling myself off the balcony?" I grimace.

"It's the one where we both accept that we like each other, and you tell me what your curse is. It can't be worse than my reasons for rejecting all of you."

I study Maven, my heart still hammering as I drown in her soul-stirring eyes for a moment. Finally, I can't take it anymore.

"Arati's high prophet told me that my curse will kill anyone I fall in love with," I whisper. "I've been a complete asshole because I can't afford to fall for you. And if we can't be bound to break our curses, then…damn it, Maven, I just—if I'm around you, you'll end up fucking dead. I can't do that. I can't lose you before I even get the chance to love you. Losing you would shatter me."

I take a shaky breath. There, I just bared it all. She has to leave now, knowing how much danger she's in because I'm already a fucking goner for her.

But then she…snorts in amusement.

I gawk at her. "Excuse me? What the hell is wrong with you? Did you even hear what I said?"

Maven tries to tame her smile and clears her throat. "I did. And you should know that's not an issue with me."

Did she hit her head during training or something? "What are you talking about?"

Her smile is something twisted halfway between wistfulness and dark humor. "It's complicated, but you don't need to worry about killing me by accident. Or even on purpose. I promise."

I shake my head. "Again, what the fuck are you talking about?"

She starts to respond but then clamps her mouth shut and removes her hands from me, rubbing one arm hard. Her breathing picks up, and she clears her throat again, glancing around the room.

"Where's your bathroom?" she asks hoarsely.

Oh...fuck. Is all that touch bothering her now?

My chest constricts as I realize that Maven might be silently panicking. Without another word, I pick her up and carry her through the small, half-hidden door in one corner of the office that leads into my attached apartment. I set her gently in front of the bathroom.

She slips inside quickly, and I hear the shower turn on. While she's in there, I change as swiftly as possible out of the clothes I just embarrassed the fuck out of myself in.

When Maven finally re-emerges from the bathroom, she looks fine. Her hair is wet, and she's wrapped in a towel that doesn't make it past her thighs, which makes my stupid cock twitch with renewed excitement. But I can't help the questions that bubble up as I fumble, reaching for her and then stepping back and rubbing my neck.

"What can I get for you? Would sparkling water help? I have Tums. And some other human medicine that might help. Or if you want something else, like a potion, I'll go find Silas and—"

"Do all faculty apartments look like this?" she interrupts, brows raised at my apartment.

"No, I paid for professional designers to come in and modify this space." I realize I'm compulsively fidgeting with my clothes and force myself to stop. "Don't worry, I know it's over the top. I might be a trust fund baby, but I'm self-aware. I've seen plenty of normal rooms."

She eyes the full glass wall etched with intricate gold leaf designs, the minimalistic, tastefully abstract decorations and plush rug, and the massive bed with the chandelier made of countless swirling strands of nevermelt overhead.

"If you say so."

I fidget again. "You're killing me here. There has to be something I can do to help with your…"

I don't even know what to call it.

Maven's lips twitch. "It's not as bad as usual. Maybe touch therapy is actually working."

"But why the fuck did you kiss me if you knew it would end up being uncomfortable for you?" I stress, frustrated at the thought.

"Someone had to break the ice," she grins playfully.

She's joking around about this? I scowl. "You know how many times I've heard that joke in my lifetime?"

"Noted. I'll find a better one. Now, about that extra blanket," she says, glancing at my closet like there might be one there.

Before I can tell her that I'd rather kiss Baelfire's scaly ass than ever let her sleep on the ground, I hear a knock on the door in my office and leave my apartment to go answer it. It's Crypt, and he glares at me like he's envisioning ripping my head off.

Pretty run-of-the-mill for him, honestly.

He glares at the expensive-ass dreamcatcher hanging just inside the threshold of my office before he holds out a backpack and a strange, round object.

"She sleeps with this under her pillow."

"What is it?"

"None of your damn business, Frost. Just give it to her and know that I'll make you pay later for taking our keeper and her dreams away from me tonight."

I glare at him, taking the amulet and the bag, which must have clothes and shit for Maven. "What, you think this was my idea? I just spilled my guts to her about my curse because she knows how to play me like a fucking fiddle."

He stares, then smirks. "Good."

"No, it's not."

"It certainly fucking is. I never wanted us to keep secrets from Maven. Plus, as I said, I doubt that your curse ever hurt her, anyway."

I grit my teeth. "We don't know that. What if I end up being the death of her?"

"Then I'll shred your psyche and piece it back together over and over until we both die. Sleep tight."

Then he just vanishes away, leaving me to gawk at nothingness.

Fucking insane incubus.

26

MAVEN

I open my eyes in the morning and stare at an angel.

It's tragically unfair how beautiful Everett Frost is. His flawlessly chiseled face is relaxed in peaceful sleep, one arm crooked behind his head while the other rests on his chest. He's in silk pajamas because, of course, the wealthy elemental professor prefers silk. I study how strikingly light his hair is, though his brows and eyelashes are much darker.

I sigh, relishing the soft scent of mint clinging all around.

I don't regret pushing his boundaries and subsequently kissing him yesterday. For one thing, that kiss was incredible, and it was unexpectedly flattering that he lost control so quickly just because he was so aroused by me.

But for another, now I know what his curse is and how little I need to worry about it compared to their other curses.

It's not like I *can't* die permanently. It's just highly improbable.

Knowing all of my matches' curses means I now know which are the biggest threats. I dislike all of their curses, but Silas's is particularly concerning.

There has to be some way I can ease it.

But before I can explore ideas for helping him, I need to move on to the next target: Somnus DeLune.

I've killed incubi before, in the Nether. There are still old-world monsters there, after all. They're just not immortal like the Immortal Quintet. After Amadeus took my heart and declared me his *telum*, my training sometimes consisted of being chased through the deformed woods surrounding Amadeus's kingdom while two or three monsters competed to see who could kill me first.

So, I know how to take down a strong incubus. I just have to get the right weapons and lure him away from the others where no one will see or suspect it was my doing.

And I also have an unexpected advantage over him. Something I hadn't even considered. Sitting up, I remove the totem Crypt left last night from under the pillow. I examine it, ignoring the strong smell of the *calea ternifolia*.

This is an old totem. Very old. It's no coincidence that Crypt's immortal father has been carrying it around. After all, what use does a nightmare-stopping totem have for an incubus who doesn't even sleep?

I have a theory, but I want to be close enough to kill Somnus before I give it a try.

I get ready for the day and slip into Everett's office. But before I can touch the door, ice completely encapsulates the handle. I glance over my shoulder and smirk.

"Not an early riser?"

Everett rubs his face sleepily, leaning against the doorway into his apartment. "Normally, it's no problem, but it's kind of impossible to sleep with a boner from hell."

I blink. He never came close to touching me again after that kiss last night, so I had no idea he was still turned on. My neck feels warm, and Everett must realize he blurted that out loud because his cheeks flame red. He clears his throat.

"Can you wait a second? I'll be right out. I just don't like the idea of you alone in the halls. There are too many psychopaths wandering Everbound right now."

Why do they keep saying shit like this? They saw me fight. By now, they should know I'm the biggest danger in this castle.

"I'll be fine on my own. Plus, I'm sure the others are already waiting outside."

"Exactly. Psychopaths," he huffs, walking into his room. "Hang on."

A few minutes later, we leave to find that all three of my other matches were waiting like I suspected. My stomach sinks when I see that Baelfire's neck is covered in fresh scratches, Silas has deep dark circles under his crimson eyes, and Crypt…well, he's fine, but I'm pretty sure that's fresh blood on his jeans. He's also wearing a new leather jacket he probably stole from someone else.

Baelfire surrounds me immediately in a big, warm hug, but when he picks me up, I let out an embarrassing squeak of surprise. He buries his face in my neck and inhales.

"There's my little Raincloud," he says roughly. His gravelly voice rumbling against my ear sends prickles of awareness down my spine.

Then he yelps, and I drop back to my feet. Silas just stabbed Baelfire in the shoulder with his bleeding crystal. The blood fae's expression is vicious.

"She didn't want to be picked up, you ass. We're helping her with light exposure therapy, not manhandling her. What the hell were you thinking?"

"It's fine," I insist when I see Baelfire's eyes shift into a dragon's momentarily.

Tendons bulge in his neck, and he growls, scratching at his neck around the collar again. I quickly grab his hands, forcing him to stop and look at me.

"It's your curse," I surmise quietly.

My poor, sunshiney shifter looks miserable, his shoulders slumping. "My dragon is fucking *awful* right now. I don't even know what thoughts are mine and which are his. I just…"

His nostrils flare, his gaze darting down the hall. We all follow where he's looking and see a random group of legacies chatting and heading our way. One of them, a shifter, glances over and waves at Baelfire, obviously another friend.

He turns back to me, shrugging off his brown jacket. "Wear this. I need my scent on you. *Now.*"

Did he just growl at me? I fold my arms. "Let's try that again."

He steps closer until his singed cedar scent envelops me. I'm an average size, but I feel dainty next to his brawny mass. He lowers his voice so only I can hear him.

"After we fucked, I thought my dragon would start to calm down. But it's gotten so much *worse*. It's like now that I know exactly how perfect my mate is, I can't think about anything except someone trying to take you away from me. I swear on all six gods, Maven, I will lose my fucking shit and kill the first person who so much as breathes in your direction if you're not wearing my scent today."

His voice is strained and dangerous. This new display of angry possessiveness does something to me on a primal level that's difficult to ignore.

I swallow and slip on the jacket before looking up at him. "There. Better?"

Relief mixed with satisfaction sweeps over Baelfire's features as he takes in the sight of me in his jacket. It puts him at ease enough that he cracks a smile. "Damn, that could be a dress on you. You're so little."

"I'm normal. You're huge," I correct.

"All over, baby, and you loved it."

Well. He's not wrong.

But I'm not about to draw attention to comments like *that* when they're all present. I've learned that their hive mind gets activated really damn fast, so if one of us, including myself, brings up anything sexual, there's no way I'll be able to focus all day.

Now that Baelfire is no longer on edge, I glance at Silas. "You look awful. Did you even sleep?"

"No."

"Join the club," Everett grumbles as we start down the hall.

Crypt smirks. "I never sleep, so this club must be named after me."

"You don't *need* sleep, you monster sperm," Silas snaps.

They continue to trade barbs as we head to class. Baelfire is annoyed at Everett for not waking me up sooner so I could eat something for breakfast, Crypt lights another of his strange cigarettes and blows smoke at any other legacies who pass us too closely in the halls, and Silas keeps glancing between Everett and I as if he's piecing together what may have happened last night based on how we interact.

And being with all of them like this…

How did I ever think they were only interested in the bet? If anything, they're all getting more obsessive and over the top with every dark secret I reveal. And it's extremely possible that I'm getting obsessed with them, too.

Huh. Maybe the gods picked out people who complement my broken, twisted soul after all.

In Fiend Studies, which has dwindled a bit in size thanks to how brutal the legacies with an emphasis on combat have been, Mr. Crowley announces that we'll study in the eastern library today. Our assignment is to find a book about creatures of the Nether to study in our quintets and present it in a few days.

As we walk to the library, Crypt leans over and whispers, "Does studying *you* count for filling this assignment? Because I'm becoming rather an expert on all things Maven Oakley."

I smirk. It's cute that he thinks that when they don't even know my last name isn't actually Oakley.

Not that it matters, because I also don't know what my real last name once was. I'll probably never know, since my family is long dead. Amadeus told me they were brutally killed off, just like the families of every other child taken into the Nether.

We finally reach the library and I'm surprised and a little on edge to see that we're not the only class here. Plenty of other legacies, both matched and unmatched, are mulling about in their quintets or allies, eying others warily as they go through the motions of studying. Several of the Immortal Quintet's hired hands scan the room from various perches, looking for trouble.

And Engela Zuma sits at one table, reading silently while also keeping watch.

"Babysitters. Big surprise," Bael huffs, tugging at his collar again.

I hold his hand as an excuse to stop him while everyone else in our Fiend Studies class scatters, moving to various library aisles for research. I notice someone waving frantically at me from across the room and light up when I see Kenzie's halo of hair. She's sitting with her quintet at one of the massive, old mahogany study tables beside a long row of tall, arched windows.

We join them. As soon as I sit down across from Kenzie, Luka, who's sitting beside her, clears his throat.

"Hey, I owe you an apology, Min—Maven," he corrects, glancing at Kenzie to make sure that was right.

She covers her mouth to stop from laughing and nods. Luka looks back at me, and the earnest gratitude in his eyes is honestly a bit much.

"I didn't think you'd actually help us, but...thanks. You have no fucking idea how much I owe you for getting her back. I—" He clears his throat and looks back at Kenzie. His features soften like he's looking at the most precious thing in the world. "How can I thank you for saving the best thing that's ever happened to me?"

Vivienne nods in agreement, sniffling. Dirk is equally emotional and getting teary-eyed despite scratching at his elbow.

Oh, gods. I had no idea I was walking into *this* again.

I realize I must look mildly horrified because Crypt starts shaking with silent laughter on the bench beside me, looking away to hide his amusement.

Asshole. He must know public displays of emotion freak me out.

"It was nothing," I grumble, opening a random book to avoid their earnest stares.

Kenzie snickers, too. "Aww! Are you getting embarrassed? Who knew you were so bashful, May?"

I kick her under the table, only I miss and kick Dirk instead. He jerks, looking at Crypt suspiciously. My unhinged Nightmare Prince takes full credit, grinning nice and creepily slow so that everyone across the table immediately busies themselves with studying.

Baelfire sits on my other side while Everett and Silas leave to look for more books. As we sit in the quiet library, I once again study the countless bookshelves and the hallways leading into the restricted areas and wonder…is there anything archived away about what I am?

When I arrived at Everbound, I spent exorbitant amounts of time in its two libraries. I've read through their collections about the five planes of existence, human and legacy history, the Great Wars, the six gods, theories about what afterlives await in the Beyond, and all their records about the shadow fiends and monsters that legacies fight at the Divide.

But there are gaps in their knowledge about what else lurks in the Nether. Which is disappointing since I'd hoped to find something about my condition. I'd even hoped there might be an antiquated, long-forgotten method of how to reverse what they turned me into.

Alas, hope is a cold-hearted bitch. There's no fixing what they made me.

I'm pulled out of my thoughts when Luka clears his throat and glances over my quintet. "So, are our quintets like…allied together? None of us are going to harm each other, right?" He glances at Crypt warily.

"We don't need allies," Silas drawls at the same time Baelfire says, "Sure, why not?"

Kenzie grins. "Pretty sure that's left up to the keepers, guys. And since Maven and I are the keepers, we officially say we're allied as fuck. Right, May?"

I nod.

"Very convincing," Luka mumbles.

Dirk gently swats at his shoulder. "Stop being a brat. They're our friends, so of course, none of us are going to cause problems for each other."

I notice when Baelfire tenses beside me. He's glaring daggers across the library…at Harlow Carter, who's watching me.

Finally.

She's been like a splinter in my brain ever since the changeling mentioned her last name. I didn't have time to track her down, so it's awfully nice of her to show up on a silver platter like this for me.

"I don't like Carter staring at you, Raincloud," Baelfire growls.

I guess Raincloud is the new Mayflower. Maybe nicknames are my curse.

Kenzie looks up with a grin. "If someone's staring at Maven, it's probably because she's so pretty."

Luka makes a face. "I can't tell if you're kidding. No offense, it's just she's kind of bland and—"

"Close your mouth. If you ever open it around me again, you'll learn what your innards taste like," Crypt drawls.

Vivienne hiccups in fear. I bury my face in the book to hide my wicked amusement. I don't care much what anyone outside my quintet thinks I look like since, apparently, my appearance is so divisive. But it's fun to see how easily my match frightens people.

"She's still staring at you," Baelfire grits. "If she knows what I think she knows…"

"I'll talk to her," I decide.

Crypt vanishes immediately, so I know he'll be listening in on my conversation. Baelfire looks at me pleadingly. "I might end up losing my shit and killing someone if you look even slightly upset while talking to her. I'm that far on edge. Fair warning."

Kenzie looks at me wide-eyed. "Oh, my gods. And I thought your matches were insane *before* my little hiatus. This is so cute!"

I admit, their violent tendencies *are* pretty cute.

I leave the table, ignoring the legacies who watch me from all over the library, including Engela Zuma, who glances up as I pass by. There's something unsettling about her that I can't put my finger on, but I ignore it as I reach the corner table where Harlow sits alone.

Her hair is still spiked, but it's hot pink now instead of purple, and she pops gum as she pulls out a seat for me. "Been looking for you, Oakley."

"Not hard enough. I would have preferred to kill you sooner."

She smirks, her voice dropping until it's practically inaudible in the hushed murmurs that make up the atmosphere of this library. "Should I be shaking in my boots, *telum?*"

Well, then. The changeling obviously got too chatty with her.

I sit and fix her with my Nether-perfected thousand-yard stare. "You have two minutes to plead for your life. Call me that out loud again, and you'll be down to one."

Crypt's unseen presence moves closer to me, but I ignore it.

Harlow's brows bounce up. "Shit, they were right. You *can* be scary when you're not pretending to be a little bitch. Smart move, by the way, blending in with the asscasters here. Wolf in sheep's clothing and all that."

"Don't pretend to care about your little support group. Your changeling put Monica in danger."

Harlow's face darkens, and she leans forward. "I didn't hire that fucking changeling. My parents did and told it to take my appearance while I was away for a day. And it only picked Monica because she approached it thinking it was me. She was an easy target—but in case you were wondering, *I* was the one who found her naked in a courtyard and got her to safety. So don't accuse me of not fucking caring because I—"

"Spare me the altruistic posturing. Why did it take Kenzie?"

"My dad probably did that out of spite," she grumbles, folding her arms as she leans back again. She drops her voice down to barely a whisper again. "My parents have beef with Kenzie's parents, the Bairds. See, my parents and hers are both involved in this anti-legacy movement. Only, mine think legacies need to go back to you-know-where."

I arch a brow. "Your family are Remitters? That makes them idiots."

"You're telling me," she grumbles before scratching at her nose piercing. "Look. I know you probably want to kill me—"

"Correction. You have thirty-nine seconds before I slit your throat without anyone noticing and leave you to rot." I slip a small knife from my sleeve and spin it on the table like I'm bored.

Harlow looks uncertain, for once, and then sighs. "The changeling told me what you are, and it's not hard to guess why you're here. But ask yourself, why haven't I told anyone else?"

"Blackmail, obviously."

"No. I want to see *them*—" She nods vaguely toward Engela Zuma, still keeping her voice barely audible. "Dead. Gone. And I doubt there's anyone who can do that except you. So, if you want a reason to keep me alive, how about using me as an ally?"

I twirl the knife around my fingers as I examine her, considering that. She was obviously involved in the anti-legacy fearmongering before the Immortal Quintet got here. She comes from a twisted family background where they are woefully mistaken in thinking the Nether is the best place for legacies.

All of that is shit I don't want involved with.

But maybe I'll keep her alive for just a bit longer. If it was really her parents who hired the changeling and not her, then I guess I'll just have to kill them later to avenge Kenzie's memory loss.

"Bring me liquid bronze before midnight, and I'll consider you an ally."

She huffs, resting a hand on the table. "Liquid bronze? That shit's hard to find or make. Doesn't your blood fae prodigy boyfriend have some?"

I stab the knife into the table right between her index and middle finger, nicking the interdigital webbing on purpose. It makes her hiss in pain.

"So what if he does? That's not what I asked."

He doesn't. I know because I already asked him about it, but that's not the point here.

"Gods! Fine. I'll find some, you hard-ass," Harlow mutters, standing from the table and tucking her bleeding hand into one pocket. Then she smirks bitterly. "By the way, my family's been whispering about you showing up in the mortal world for as long as I can remember. I just hope you don't disappoint."

I smile sweetly. "I just hope you don't find any liquid bronze because I've missed playing with my adamantine dagger."

Harlow's eyes widen slightly, and she hurries out of the library. Crypt materializes beside me a moment later, one elbow resting on the table while he gazes at me dreamily.

"Have I mentioned I adore you? I could watch you bare your claws all day."

I tuck away the little knife and sigh. "I'm worried I've gone soft. I should probably just kill Harlow before she snitches. Was it a mistake to let her go?"

"She could've snitched up until now and didn't," the Nightmare Prince points out, shrugging one shoulder. "But if she does, we can torture her together."

He looks so excited at the prospect that I grin back at him.

Once again...maybe the gods didn't do too bad of a job with this whole perfect-soul-mates thing.

27

MAVEN

It's official. I really am going soft because I take it easy on my matches in our private training after combat class.

I'm a big believer in training like your life depends on it, since mine always did, but my quintet is in rough enough shape as it is. As we take a water break in the training room in Everbound's dungeons, Baelfire tugs at his collar and paces like a trapped animal, Silas glares at the giant mirror as if he might attack his own reflection, and Crypt…

Once again, he seems fine. But he's smoking that strange herb again.

Meanwhile, Everett keeps bringing up the little heart-to-shadow-heart we had yesterday.

"I'm going to need an actual explanation, Oakley," he mutters from beside me as I set down the water bottle Kenzie bought me weeks ago. "What the fuck did you mean?"

"Exactly what I said."

He shakes his head. Gone is the aloof professor. Right now, Everett's ice-colored eyes are soulful and earnest. "You said I didn't need to worry about my curse killing you. But since the moment I first saw you, that is *all* I've worried about. Hell, my entire life, I've been terrified of exactly this happening—of falling in love with my keeper too soon and fucking ruining everything."

Yikes. The *L*-word.

Wait. Did Everett just insinuate that he's...falling in love with me?

I stare at him, unable to process that. The others have said they want me, crave me, need me...all of that, I can approach practically or at least from a carnal standpoint, and it makes sense.

But this? I'm lost. I'm too fucked up to know what to do with tender, romantic feelings.

Growing up as an isolated, experimental living weapon, I never showed my true feelings to anyone but Lillian. Sometime after I turned sixteen, Gideon started saying he loved me whenever he got the chance. I brushed it off for months since it didn't seem relevant, but he grew more aggressive and frustrated, claiming I was his reason for living and he would end himself if I didn't say I loved him back. Of the thirteen kids taken from the mortal realm, he was my only friend. I cared for him, so I finally gave in and said I loved him, too.

That lie tasted like shit.

Honestly, the idea of love puts me on edge. It's too vague, too soft. It brings to mind flowery nonsense, empty promises, sweet nothings, and other useless bullshit.

Obsession, on the other hand? That's dark and twisted. It's real. I'm much more comfortable getting unhealthily obsessed or borderline manic over someone else. Anything but *falling* for them. That sounds awful.

"Why does our girl look like a deer caught in headlights?" Crypt asks, stopping beside Everett and me with his hands tucked in his leather pockets. He hasn't bothered removing it for training practice, probably because we've done very little actual training today.

His words make me realize I've been staring wide-eyed at Everett for too long. I quickly look away and clear my throat, noticing that Silas and Baelfire are watching, too. I'm tabling this topic with

Everett because there are only two hours before curfew, and I want time after this to stop by Kenzie's apartment.

"One more round. Then we'll call it."

"Thank gods," Baelfire groans. "I'm starving. Hurry up and let her beat you like a drum, Si."

But when Silas takes his turn opposite me on the mat, he looks more focused than he did earlier, determination making his handsome features more severe. "If I beat you, will you truly tell us what you are, *sangfluir?*"

"Cross my absent heart."

That makes Crypt snort. Everett pipes up from the side of the room, folding his arms as he narrows his eyes at me.

"Will you be evasive about it, or can I expect an *actual* answer from you this time?"

Testy, testy. Obviously, he doesn't like that I've sidestepped his questions yet again.

"Win, and I'll tell you what I am, all about my magic, and the handful of ways I can *actually* die."

That makes all of them gawk at me. Although, that could also be because I finally strip off my top baggy shirt, leaving me in nothing but an exercise bra and pants. I haven't broken a sweat today, but the way they all devour my appearance as if I'm posing in lingerie makes me suddenly feel flushed.

"Nothing you haven't all seen before," I remind them brusquely, folding my arms to cover any hints of the ragged scar on my chest that I'm still iffy about showing. "Let's do this."

"Hang on," Everett mutters, waving Silas over.

I raise a brow when they convene—all four of them. It's practically a huddle, and that makes me grin. Are they going to try teaming up against me? That could be entertaining.

My smile widens when they prove me right, all moving to the mat and surrounding me in a circle. "Disregarding the rules, I see."

"What rules?" Silas counters. "You only said to keep it strictly combat."

"Fair enough. I'm going to enjoy taking you all on at once."

Baelfire winks. "Yeah, you will. But as fucking hot as that'll be when it happens, you should get your mind out of the gutter and focus, Raincloud."

The gutter? How was I...

Oh, I see. Double entendre. Took me long enough.

Silas launches toward me first, and just like that, my senses sharpen into needle points. I block his attempt to grapple me and sidestep Everett, twisting around Baelfire when he makes the next move. It's adorable that they want to fight me all at once, but without the cohesion that I'm trying to teach them so they can move as a team, they're even sloppier than usual.

But they also seem ten times more motivated than usual.

Soon, all of my dodging, blocking, and ducking grows old. I kick my leg out to tag Everett. He sees it coming and changes direction but crashes into Baelfire, who swears viciously. I can tell Silas is about to attack my other side, yet I'm thrown off for a fraction of a second because...where did Crypt go?

Too late, I realize he's tripping me from behind, working in tandem with Silas until suddenly, I'm pinned beneath the blood fae. He grins victoriously down at me, his red irises bright with excitement as he leans down to brush a kiss against the side of my neck.

That sends a shudder through me. We're both breathing hard, and suddenly, my body is hyper-aware of the way he's pinning both my wrists over my head as he straddles me. Gods, why does he have to be so handsome? Especially all worked up like this, his chest heaving and the veins bulging in his arms as they flex above me...

Baelfire chuckles darkly beside us, no doubt scenting my arousal. "On second thought, dinner can wait. Our keeper wants something else."

Silas hums in agreement. "And then we'll get our *other* prize."

I quirk a brow. "You didn't win the other prize."

Everett scowls, brushing off his hands as he gets up from the mat. "You're literally pinned. We won."

Well, if they're willing to fight dirty, so am I. So I lean up to lightly bite Silas's throat, not even drawing blood. When he startles, I take advantage of his moment of surprise. Tucking my elbows down in a sharp movement to break out of his hold, I simultaneously thrust my hips upward. When Silas falls forward, trying to catch himself, I twist and dig a savage elbow into his gut, making him drop to one side.

From there, it's child's play to pin him down. I smirk when he scowls.

"No dice. Crypt slipped into Limbo to trip me, and that's how you took me down. He broke the rules, so it doesn't count."

Crypt stands with his hands laced behind his head like he has no care in the world. When the rest of them shoot him murderous looks, realizing I'm right, he grins unapologetically.

"We didn't agree with that," Everett huffs. "He acted out of line, but that should still count."

"Popsicle Prick is right for once," Baelfire nods, ignoring how Everett looks like he wants to freeze his head off. "We've been training our asses off. Crypt was a dick all on his own, as usual, but the rest of us gave it our best. Can't that count for something, baby?"

I release Silas and stand, shrugging back into my baggy shirt, which earns a surprisingly heavy sigh from Everett.

"I'll catch up with you guys later. I have plans to visit Kenzie," I inform them.

Silas gets up. "We'll walk you there."

Usually, I would protest. But considering the current mental state of my quintet and how they're all looking at me like they'll murder even a fly for daring to land near me, I decide it's more time-efficient to just go along with it.

And if I'm candid with myself...I don't mind that they're so protective of me.

Aside from occasional help from Lillian or Gideon, I've been watching my own back my entire life. I can handle shit, but it turns out I kind of like how these four gorgeous legacies flank my sides and guard my every move.

When Kenzie opens the door of her apartment, she grins. "They all escorted you here? That's so freaking cute! I mean, it's also probably necessary because I totally saw two legacies killed when they weren't watching their backs right before class today, which was awful, but I mean—still. So cute. Hey, have you guys taken a picture of the Oakley quintet all together yet? You should! Hang on, I'll grab my phone."

Everett turns and storms away before she can even think about getting a picture. Crypt vanishes, probably to stand guard outside this door until I come back out. Silas eyes Dirk suspiciously through the doorway, but Baelfire brushes off the offer for a picture and turns on his typical charm that's been missing for days to ask Kenzie how she's feeling and how their quintet classes have been.

They chat briefly about a shifter professor who apparently went missing in Everbound Forest before Baelfire and Silas leave so I can follow Kenzie into her room. Like mine, it's the largest room in her quintet apartment. I guess that's a keeper thing.

She rushes to shove a couple of what I assume are sex toys under the bed and then hops onto it with a wide grin. Her hair is in a messy bun that's almost the size of her head, thanks to all the curls.

"Oh my *gods*! I didn't want to say anything out there, but is Professor Frost, like…*with* you now? I mean, obviously, he was always in your quintet, but he was all standoffish and uninvolved, wasn't he? But I saw the way he was looking at you earlier in the library, and holy *wow*. That is dead-ass, the exact kind of pining, starry-eyed, melt-your-panties hero stare that love interests always have in romance movies when they secretly can't live without the heroine. So, did you finally get to sample Frost's popsicle, or what?"

Gods. She said all of that in under twenty seconds. Her lungs are beyond impressive.

"I slept in his bed," I admit.

"And?"

"And we didn't fuck, so don't get too excited."

Kenzie pouts. "Monk."

"Slut."

"Guilty as charged," she nods and then sobers a little. "So, you talked with Harlow Carter earlier. Did it have anything to do with… you know. The changeling and yours truly?"

I suppose now is as good a time as any to ask her about this. "It did. She mentioned your families are both involved in the anti-legacy movement but on opposite sides. Her parents are Remitters who think all legacies should return to the Nether, so I want to know. What does your family do in the movement, and why didn't you tell me about it sooner?"

Kenzie stares at me wide-eyed. "Whoa. Hang on. My family is part of the anti-legacy movement?"

Shit. I forgot about her memory loss. She doesn't remember anything from before the past year or so.

"Forget I asked," I say quickly.

But she's in full-blown spiral mode now. "Holy shit. Holy *shit*, May—they might be. They're way friendlier with humans than most legacies because they work in human relations, but last summer, I noticed that they were going to meetings at weird times and were constantly calling unmarked numbers and…oh my gods. They even talked shit about the Immortal Quintet. They don't like how things are run—maybe they never did, but I don't remember. I—I kind of don't even remember who I *am* anymore, much less anything about my family, and…"

She covers her face as emotion overwhelms her, and I once again wish I had killed that changeling far slower. My drama with my quintet members cut that pleasure short.

"You'll learn more about your past when you visit your family for the holidays," I offer gently. "Rediscovering your past will help you discover any missing pieces about yourself."

Kenzie nods, wiping at her face. "Yeah. Yeah, you're right. Gods, I was really looking forward to taking my quintet home to meet my family. I was calling my moms about them all the time and making plans. Fuck the Immortal Quintet for canceling that," she huffs.

Then she pales and looks at me.

"Oh. Um…you're not a fan of the Immortal Quintet, are you? It'd be pretty awkward if you were after I said that."

I smile grimly. "Not even slightly."

"Oh, good! Because the way they're running Everbound right now is fucking *insane*. Right? Like, no contact with the outside world? No fucking *WiFi*? And the faculty isn't even allowed to send out student death notices to their families. This is all giving me the willies. What even is going on?"

I hesitate and then look at her thoughtfully. "You're good at keeping secrets."

"Unless it's a surprise party, yes. Why?"

"The changeling killed Headmaster Hearst."

Her eyes bug out. *"What?* But he's supposed to be unkillable! How is it more people aren't talking about this?"

"No one but myself and my quintet know, but that's why the Immortal Quintet came here. Don't tell anyone else."

She blinks. "Oh. Okay. Wait, but how did you find out?"

I almost give her a non-answer but I pause and consider my options. I've decided to fight for my quintet and spill my secrets to them, but I've known Kenzie longer. She's been so patient with me, and she deserves answers. I still can't say she's my friend out loud, but I seriously don't know what I would have done without her when I first came to Everbound.

She said I could trust her, and all my instincts say that's true—even if she decides she hates me for who I am.

There's only one way to find out.

After double-checking to make sure the rest of her quintet can't overhear us, I brace myself for the worst and spill my guts. I tell Kenzie everything. How I was brought to the Nether as a toddler, was raised fighting for my life to become Amadeus's weapon, was experimented on by necromancers until they turned me into exactly what they wanted, and how I was sent into the mortal realm weeks ago on a mission to slowly kill off the Immortal Quintet.

Hence why I ended up in Hearst's office when he was murdered.

I don't go into detail. I also leave out that the only thing keeping me "alive" is the shadow heart that Amadeus crafted, pulsing steadily with untraceable magic within my scarred chest.

And when it's all said and done, I wait.

Kenzie stares at me for a long time, and then, to my horror, her eyes fill with tears.

"Oh my gods, Maven."

Is she disgusted by me? Afraid? I shuffle and straighten the gloves on my hands, worried that I'm about to lose her for good.

But then she wraps me in a gentle hug, careful to only touch my clothes. "I figured you came from a tough background, but...that sounds like it was beyond brutal. Most people would never believe that someone could survive there, let alone be *raised* there, but...oh my gods, I can't even imagine what you've been through."

Something about her tone of voice is exactly like Lillian's. I miss her so fucking much, and I'm mortified when my eyes start to well with hot moisture. I close them and clear my throat.

"It doesn't matter. I survived."

"Don't you dare minimize your own trauma. If you ever want to heal from it, you can't pretend it doesn't exist."

I sincerely doubt there will be any healing in my future. But I say nothing because my emotions are too out of control, and even if I trust Kenzie, I'm not about to fucking cry in front of someone else.

Finally, she pulls back so I can see the warm, honest affection on her face. "Do your guys know?"

"Yes."

She nods. "And they're still obsessed with you. Good. If they'd changed their minds or had a problem because of something so wildly out of your control, I would have clawed their eyes out."

The mental image of Kenzie trying to scratch any of their eyes out makes me snort. "I would pay to see that."

"So...what happens after?" she asks, frowning.

"What do you mean?"

"Once you get rid of those immortal fucking jerks who are letting Everbound cannibalize itself. If you were trained to be a weapon and you finish your mission to get rid of them, what happens after that?"

I look away. Kenzie found the key question there, the one that not even my quintet has thought to ask. And there's no way I'm giving her the answer. It's too bleak.

"After that, I guess we all live happily ever after."

She squints. "You're deflecting."

"I've overshared enough as it is."

Kenzie snorts. "You, overshare? As if that's even possible." But then she smiles. "So...you're not trying to make your guys hate you anymore, right?"

"Right."

She elbows me, waggling her brows. "So maybe the gods were right about them being perfectly matched to your soul, huh?"

I know what she's after. She pushed so hard for me to just give in to my matches, and now she wants me to confess she was right. She's looking for a sickly-sweet confession of how swept away I've been.

"They're gorgeous idiots. But now they're *my* gorgeous idiots." I hesitate and then clear my throat. "I have a question for you. Several questions, actually."

She squeals and claps like her day has just been made. "Okay, shoot."

My face feels hot, and I fidget with my gloves. "Don't laugh at me."

"I'll totally laugh if it's funny."

That's fair. "Is it normal to want to lick abs?"

Kenzie blinks. Then she bursts into the dreaded laughter. "Oh my gods! Maven fucking Oakley, you're so cute. Lick all the abs you want, and I promise they'll love it. Are your other questions about sexy stuff? Are you finally having your sexual awakening? Girl, if you're asking for a crash course in sex education, I'm *so* down to help! Keep the questions coming."

I do, and our visit lasts far longer than I expected. But half of the time, I'm distracted by Kenzie's earlier question about whether or not my guys know.

I have a delicately balanced plan for how the rest of my mission is supposed to go. Now that I've decided to stop fighting my quintet and give in to temptation, I should include them in those plans and explain my blood oath.

And then, before all hell breaks loose, even if they can't bind their hearts to mine...we'll find a way to offset their curses together.

28

CRYPT

I'VE CONSUMED COUNTLESS DREAMS, but never have I been so sated.

As daylight dawns outside the drawn curtains, my keeper's room is dim and quiet aside from her soft breathing. In Limbo, I lay on the bed beside her and savor every second I can soak in her stunning aura like it's the only balm for my shredded soul.

Knowing what little I do about her background, peace must have been virtually nonexistent in Maven's life, as evidenced by the night terrors that cling so tightly to her psyche anytime they can. With the totem and my presence, she's finally resting.

And *gods above*, she's utterly fucking delectable in her sleep.

I sigh as I adjust my inappropriately hard cock for the hundredth time. If she knew how deviant my desires for her are, I wonder how she would react. She might be disgusted.

But then, my beautifully twisted little darling is always taking me by surprise. So perhaps if she knew...

Maven's dream that's been perfuming Limbo around me for the last couple of hours fades abruptly, and she opens her eyes to squint at the window. She glances in my general direction as if to acknowledge that she can sense me before rolling out of bed and dropping into a set of wide push-ups.

She did this the last time I fed on her dreams all night, too. I admire how driven she is, but I also must assume this is a habit she was taught in the Nether. She's so on edge in the mornings. Decimus gave me an extremely fast rundown of what Maven shared with them about her past while I was away, and if I ever meet the bastards responsible for making her feel like nothing but a weapon, I'll hang them with their own intestines.

I'm also quite petulant that I missed out on seeing her torture a changeling. It must have been quite the sight.

Finally, I slip into the mortal realm, ignoring the familiar flare of pain in my limbs that says I'll need to smoke more *reverium* soon.

But it's far easier to bear than usual, thanks to feeding on my keeper's dreams all night. I grin down at her.

"Hello, love."

She finishes her last reps of lunges and stretches, giving me a mouthwatering glimpse of her lower stomach before she moves toward the large bathroom. "How did my dreams taste?"

"Heavenly."

Not to mention, I spent quite a bit of time gently detangling touch from panic within her dreams. Maven's psyche is irreversibly scarred from trauma. I suspect she will never willingly share a lot of her dark past, but even if I can't see what memories are hurting her, I can try to ease the pain in her dreams.

"Care for a hand in the shower?" I ask, trying to keep my voice light and teasing. Not pushing is difficult, especially when my cock has been achingly hard all night.

My heart flips in on itself when she smirks over her shoulder. "If you're offering."

Gods save her from me.

I'm immediately at her side, enraptured as she strips out of her pajamas and steps under the water. Watching how the moisture flows over her perfect, naked skin, curling over her curves, trailing over her breasts, dripping between her thighs…

It's beautiful. I envy that water far more than I'm proud to admit.

She tips her head back to wet her hair, arching a mischievous brow at me. "Are you watching or joining?"

I remove my clothes and step under the warm spray of the shower with her. Maven's eyes widen, and I laugh as her gaze slowly moves over my heavily patterned arms, chest, and legs. She seems fascinated by the extensive, swirling markings I've never been without—but it's glaringly apparent that she's avoiding looking at my cock, which is jutting out like a steel pipe.

Instead, her attention catches on the diagonal barbell piercing in my left nipple.

She tips her head. "May I?"

"Never bother asking to touch me, darling. I always want your hands on me."

Gingerly, she reaches out and traces the piercing. When she twists it ever so slightly, I shudder as it sends a spike of pleasure through me.

"Intriguing," she murmurs.

Yes, it is. I grin. "And how do you feel about the rest of them?"

My words have their intended effect, and eager need rushes through my veins as Maven's eyes finally settle on my cock and the three dydoe piercings around its head. Her gaze heats, and she swallows hard.

"That's…"

"It's called a king's crown. I thought it befitting my royal status since evidently, I'm the Nightmare Prince," I manage to joke despite the arousal making it impossible to tear my attention away from her extremely fuckable body.

I got the piercings years ago after hearing the moniker. I'd hoped they would finally make sex pleasurable for me, but it was useless. But now, when Maven trails her fingers over the piercings, a shudder wracks my spine. It feels unbelievably good, to the point that my cock head already beads with precum.

Still, if Maven doesn't like them, I'll have them removed. Anything for her.

"I like them," she murmurs without me having to ask a single thing.

Thank the gods. She's painfully perfect for me.

Leaning down, I capture her lips and groan when she immediately presses against me. In two steps, I have my obsession pressed against the shower wall as our mouths tangle and my tongue brushes teasingly against hers. She makes a soft sound of pleasure, and I smile against her lips before letting my hands wander down her devastating body.

Her grip twists into my hair, adjusting my head's angle as she kisses me back. The exchange is making me dizzy because I need her more than I need oxygen, but finally, she breaks away to gasp for air while I kiss down her jaw and neck.

But before I kiss lower, I pull back and gently trace the pale scar between her beautiful breasts with my fingertips.

"What happened to your heart after it was taken from you?" I murmur out loud...

Like an absolute fucking imbecile. Less than a second later, it registers that asking her this just ruined any chance of delicious shower sex. The question just slipped from my tongue before I could help it, and now I want to kick myself.

My keeper looks away, her hands sliding from my neck. "It doesn't matter."

I take her chin to make her look at me because this is the second time she's uttered that bullshit in my presence. I won't stand for it.

"Try that again, darling."

Maven's dark eyes flash, and for a moment, I'm certain she's going to tell me to go fuck myself. But instead, she slips out from between me and the wall and begins shampooing her hair. She speaks nonchalantly.

"Amadeus preserved it with magic. It sits on display on his mantle."

On display.

Like a damned trophy.

Fury floods my system, and I spend the next five minutes lost in especially violent machinations within my own head. I've never seen the Entity, and I have no reason to believe I ever will—but imagining skewering eyeballs and carving skin slowly calms me down until the water droplets from the shower are no longer hovering around us from lack of gravity.

Someone knocks on Maven's bedroom door. "You ready, Raincloud? Class starts soon. Tell Stalker Boy to back the fuck off so you can eat before we go."

I sigh wistfully when Maven dries off, dresses, and leaves without a word. I know she's not mad at me for asking, but she loathes talking about her past. Not a wonderful way for me to start her day.

Thirty minutes later, we take our typical seats in Fiend Studies. Frost was already waiting, as usual, and stubbornly looks out the window despite Maven giving him a curious look. They still haven't found their footing after exchanging secrets the other night.

Probably because Frost is a fucking idiot.

Meanwhile, as the professor waits for everyone else to take their seats, Crane rocks slightly and pulls at his wild hair, eyeing everything around us as if it's all crawling with ghostly spiders. I can sense the heaviness in Limbo around him. He isn't sleeping, and there's no fucking shot in hell that he would ever accept if I offered to help with his parasomnia.

I pause, frowning. Was I actually just considering helping Silas fucking Crane with his sleep troubles?

Good gods. This camaraderie is like a disease. I must be more careful, or we'll all be braiding one another's hair and getting matching tattoos.

I shudder at the thought.

But I reconsider offering my help to Crane when I see Maven's face fall as she notices his struggle. She's careful not to show emotion or weakness around people outside our quintet, though, and merely looks forward with her lips pressed tightly together.

I can't stand knowing that she's unhappy.

Finally, the professor clears his throat and announces that First Placement has officially been rescheduled and will take place in three days. Whispers immediately fill the room as students turn to each other with wide eyes. Aside from Decimus flirtatiously asking

Maven if she wants to sit in his lap for exposure therapy, our quintet remains relatively silent.

Maven rolls her eyes but takes Decimus's hand under the desk, resting it on her thigh. I'm on her left side and rest my hand on her left thigh, curious to see if she'll push me away or tense up even minutely as she always does, regardless of who is touching her.

But this time, she doesn't.

Whether it's the subconscious therapy or her attempts at exposure therapy…it's working.

Decimus must think the same thing because he catches my eye over her head and grins. I'm beyond pleased, too, but I opt to flip him the bird with my free hand.

There will be no brotherly bonding today, thank you very much. Not on my watch.

After the rest of the classroom calms down, the professor clears his throat. "Now, then. We've gone over all known monsters and creatures found in the Nether, and you will be presenting what book you studied. But before we get to that, did anyone find anything of unique interest on this subject while browsing Everbound's wonderful libraries?"

A few students raise their hands and share tidbits, but Maven looks at Crane again with a puckered brow. Finally, she sighs as if she's made a decision.

Then she raises her hand, which takes the rest of us by surprise. Even Crane glances over with a perplexed frown.

"Yes, Miss Oakley?" the professor calls on her. He looks equally surprised, which makes me think she's never raised her hand in a class at Everbound.

"I read something that mentioned revenants."

The professor's eyes widen into saucers and his brows nearly reach his hairline. "Did you, indeed? Dear gods, this is exciting! I'm sure none of you are aware of this, but I have quite a love for learning about extinct monsters. I actually studied this particular being extensively many years ago. Which book did you find that in, may I ask?"

Maven impersonates a shy wallflower, feigning a timid shrug. "I don't remember the title."

Her performance makes me grin, but then she glances at me and the others in our quintet meaningfully. As if she's telling us to pay attention.

"No matter," the professor says, beaming at the rest of the classroom. "Well, what a treat. Since Miss Oakley has brought it up, I may as well indulge all of us. You see, as with every type of extinct monster, revenants have ceased to be taught or written about. They were all wiped out during the Great Wars hundreds of years ago. Here, let me just—"

The overly excited professor moves to the chalkboard and begins writing notes to accompany his lecture. Meanwhile, Crane is now entirely focused, and Decimus, Frost, and I are riveted to the spot.

If Maven wants us to hear this, does that mean…?

"Trapped between life and death, a revenant was a uniquely powerful reanimated being which quite infamously used a now-defunct form of magic called *terai per vitam*—or "weapon of life." In other words, through slaying the living, it could siphon a life force and use it to wield unspeakable levels of highly destructive dark energy, an unholy subset of dark magic all its own."

No wonder Maven wanted us to pay attention. My dark little obsession is keeping her promise of telling us what she is.

Namely, a revenant.

"These were powerful aberrations," the professor goes on. "Especially considering they would reanimate as many times as necessary to fulfill their given purpose. You see, at their creation, these beings would be assigned one objective to fulfill, typically one of vengeance or justice. And once they fulfilled their purpose, their soul would immediately pass on to the Beyond."

The temperature of the classroom drops, which means Frost is just as agitated as I am hearing that Maven might die as soon as she fulfills some unknown purpose. My hand tightens on Maven's thigh, but when I look at her questioningly, she stares forward without reacting.

The professor finishes writing on the chalkboard and brushes off his hands. "There are also ancient accounts of revenants which describe them as deathly berserkers—for once they reached a certain level of feeding, they fell into a trance-like state and would hunt down and kill any living thing within miles. Likewise, their unique magic had a terrifying snowball effect, for the more they slaughtered, the stronger they became, creating an unstoppable, formidable cycle. As a matter of fact, the Entity used a group of revenants to kill the goddess Reniah during the Great Wars."

A shifter in another quintet pipes up. "Wait, if these things were strong enough to destroy a fucking *goddess*, then how the hell did they go extinct?"

"Excellent question. Despite their immense power, they were rather slow beings, so it wasn't difficult to hunt them down after the kill order went out following Reniah's murder. And though they would reanimate much of the time, there *were* ways of permanently destroying them even before they fulfilled their purpose."

There's a menacing edge to Crane's voice when he asks, "What ways?"

The professor tips his head back and forth. "The most effective methods are debated among scholars, but as I understand it, these monsters could be permanently killed through full dismemberment or by being burned to death. Records also say either blessed bone or nevermelt through a revenant's heart worked quite well."

Nevermelt?

Crane, Decimus, and I all glance at Frost simultaneously. He's pale as snow. Probably because when we were young kids, he'd proudly bragged that he was the youngest ice elemental to ever craft nevermelt, and when Crane dared him to prove it, he did.

Precious few other ice elementals have that ability. If Frost's rare ability is one of her few weaknesses, maybe I should kill him as a precaution after all.

"In any case," the professor keeps droning, "these beings had to be destroyed completely, or else they would inevitably rise again. Quite fascinating monsters, though it was never clear how they were created or how they multiplied in the first place. Luckily for us, they haven't existed for hundreds of years," he smiles. "And, since you will never have to fight those evil beings at the Divide, let us move on to a presentation of something you *will* need to be prepared for. Fulton quintet, you're up."

A group of legacies begins talking at the front of the room, but I pay no attention as I absorb everything I just learned about my keeper. I'm so distracted that Maven has to gently nudge my hand on her thigh to get my attention when class ends.

But as we leave the room, instead of heading toward lunch, Crane takes Maven by one gloved hand and storms toward the private alcove where we first met her after the Seeking. She keeps up with him easily, as do Decimus, Frost, and I.

As soon as we're alone in the space where we won't be overheard, Crane whirls on Maven, his jaw clenched and crimson eyes severe.

"Tell us your purpose."

She pauses. "If you're mad because you're stuck with a monster—"

"That's not why he's mad," Decimus snaps. "I'm fucking pissed, too, Raincloud, and it's not because of what they made you. All I want to fucking know is what your purpose is so we can stop you from fulfilling it because you *passing on* is not an option. It's just fucking not. Okay?"

Maven looks dubious about answering, so I offer my two cents. "Ending the Immortal Quintet is your purpose, is it not?"

"It is."

"And once they're dead?" Crane asks impatiently. "Will you die? Permanently?"

"Yes."

My chest hollows into that same feeling of abysmal nothingness that I used to exist in until I met her. I can't lose my reason for being. Even if it means that fucking prick Somnus lives forever, I refuse to let this happen.

Frost swears viciously, covering his face. "Okay, then we're leaving Everbound. Immediately. I don't care if we have to go on the fucking run. I'm not letting you stay anywhere near them."

"It's laughable that you think you *let* me do anything. But you don't have the full picture. Remember, I also made a blood oath."

That shuts us all up as we realize the distinction. Maven has some revenant-focused purpose...*and* a blood oath. Two separate things to worry about, both of which could take her from us forever.

Decimus growls, "Okay, then who did you make the blood oath with if it wasn't that Undead king-of-the-assholes wannabe father of yours?"

Her lips twitch. "Very apt description."

"This isn't a joking matter, darling," I warn.

Maven nods. "You're right, it's not. I'll tell you the truth. There are humans in the Nether. And I don't mean humans that were stolen away to be raised there like me and the twelve others," she clarifies.

Crane frowns. "Other humans? How do they survive?"

"They don't. They're kept, just like cattle. Bred, fed, sacrificed, eaten. They're even used for entertainment," Maven adds bitterly, shaking her head as stark disgust eclipses her features. "You have no idea the hell they're living, but I do. And I'm the only one who can help them."

"How?" Frost demands. "I don't get it. How did the humans get in the Nether in the first place?"

She glances at the hallway behind us. "We'll miss lunch if I share everything."

The rest of us make no move to stop her, not even the bottomless pit of a stomach that is Baelfire Decimus.

"All right." Maven lifts her chin. "Then you should know something that the Immortal Quintet has carefully removed from history. They made everyone believe they saved the mortal realm hundreds of years ago by valiantly driving back Amadeus and his forces and creating the Divide." She rolls her eyes. "The truth is, they took the coward's way out. The fight against the forces of the Nether was killing off the Four Houses, so the Immortal Quintet tricked an army of human warriors, both male and female, into going into the Nether as a diversion. Then they begged the gods to create the Divide. The gods obliged and fortified it by tying it to the life forces of the Immortal Quintet."

Crane considers all of that. "Then, if you kill the Immortal Quintet…"

"I'll unleash the Nether on the mortal realm," she says in the same tone one might say they're thinking of planting a garden.

My brows go up.

"Fucking fuck," Decimus grimaces.

Articulate to a point, that one.

"I'm not finished. The Immortal Quintet thought that the monsters and creatures of the Nether would devour those humans and then shrivel away without anything left living to feed on. They failed to take into account that the Entity has the powerful advantage of foresight. Amadeus captured that troop but allowed them to live. They were fed and contained, and they naturally started to multiply over time. Hundreds of years passed, and now the Nether is the way I know it: absolute hell, but with thousands of humans who are kept in compounds and treated exactly like animals. They're seen as a resource—the life to feed the death that rules there."

Maven looks out the nearest window, but her mind appears far away. "The first time I stumbled across one of the human compounds, I was on the run during a training exercise. Their condition was sickening. But even though they were worse off than me, the humans tried to help me. They were…kind. Horribly beaten and hopeless, but kind. Years later, when Amadeus turned me into this and gave me my purpose, I realized that if I was fated to die anyway—"

"Please don't fucking say that," Decimus grits, squeezing his eyes shut.

"Then I may as well take advantage of Amadeus's scheme and use it to save them," she finishes, looking at each of us. "I have a plan. I'm compelled to end the entire Immortal Quintet to unleash the Nether since Amadeus made that my purpose…but I'm going to leave one member of the Immortal Quintet alive. I'm going to weaken the Nether just enough for the humans to escape."

I consider this and put the pieces together. "Your blood oath is with those humans. You promised to free them from the Nether, didn't you?"

She nods, her jaw set in determination.

And just like that, my consuming obsession only doubles.

I knew Maven must have a strong reason, but knowing that my keeper has leveraged her terribly dealt hand in life in a gambit to save thousands from the king of the Undead...

I'm in awe of her.

And yet, at the same time, I can't bear knowing this.

"I see what Pia meant by your nobility now," Crane murmurs as if to himself, his expression softening. He leans against the wall, rubbing his temples. "But what happens once the humans escape, Maven?"

"If you're worried about the Nether consuming the rest of the world, I have a plan for—"

Silas huffs. "What I'm worried about is *you*. If you don't fulfill your purpose as a revenant, what will happen to you?"

Maven adjusts her gloves and smiles at us. "Nothing. I told you, I have a plan. I'll be fine."

Crane's jaw clenches tightly before he looks away. "Professor Crowley explained your unique magic, but what about the necromancy? How can you use that *and* common magic? Necromancy doesn't play nice with other magics. It shouldn't be possible."

"I agree. It shouldn't, but there were unintended side effects to their methods of making me into this. And before *you* start spiraling," our keeper goes on, raising a knowing eyebrow at Frost. "Nevermelt stabbed through a heart only works when there's an actual heart to stab. You aren't going to be the death of me."

He flinches, looking positively miserable. "We don't know that."

Decimus starts to say something else, but I'm distracted when I feel a sharp, painful ripple in Limbo from somewhere nearby.

Several markings on my hands and neck light up. The severity of the ripple tells me that it has something to do with wisps.

Maven sees the markings light up and catches my eye. "Go. We can talk more about this later."

I don't want to go.

As the steward of Limbo, I always knew my time with her would be limited, but knowing Maven is in such peril...now even the idea of being apart from her for a second pains me almost as much as my curse.

"Crypt. Go." Her eyes are gentle.

I'm loathe to leave her, but with a sigh, I slip back into Limbo to handle it.

29

MAVEN

When Crypt disappears, I'm left with Baelfire dragging his hands through his hair anxiously, Everett, who has frost up to his elbows and refuses to look at me, and an inexplicably frustrated blood fae.

"There. Now you guys know everything," I offer.

Silas gives me an acerbic look. "If you say so."

Damn it. He somehow knows I lied there at the end.

But when he asked what will happen to me, I couldn't find the words to explain that even if I succeed at killing most of the Immortal Quintet, saving Lillian and all the Nether-born humans, and find ways to break my matches' curses...

There's still no way this can end happily for me. I came to terms with that long ago.

It's shitty, but there it is.

Before any of us can say anything else, footsteps sound nearby, and several seconds later, Professor Gibbons pokes his head into the alcove, blinking in surprise. I know he didn't overhear us, thanks to the special acoustics of this alcove, but he still looks flustered.

"Oh, my," he grimaces, looking between the four of us. "Miss Oakley, as the keeper of your quintet, you should ensure that you're all abiding by the rules set forth by our leaders. That means eating lunch during the scheduled block, not canoodling in the hallways!"

Canoodling?

I make a face. "Don't repeat that word around me."

Baelfire folds his arms. "I wish we *were* canoodling. Would've been way more enjoyable than that emotional fucking roller coaster."

Gibbons starts to fret. "Please, won't you all come along to the dining hall? You're breaking the rules, and the Immortal Quintet has been extremely intolerant of those who cross them lately. Speaking of which, all legacies and faculty are mandated to stay inside the dining hall during the next hour."

"Why?" Everett asks.

"I…well, I don't know," the warlock grimaces, rubbing one bushy eyebrow. "Asking seemed unwise."

I'll bet it did. At what point will the Immortal Quintet give up all pretenses and start killing legacies left and right while they look for their mage's murderer? They're fucking tyrannical, and it reminds me too much of Amadeus.

"As unwise as canoodling?" Baelfire suggests, earning an elbow to the side from me, which only makes him grin.

Great. Now he's going to keep tormenting me with that stupid word, isn't he?

If the Immortal Quintet is forcing everyone to stay in the dining hall, I assume it's either to keep us away from something else shady happening within Everbound Castle. That, or they want to sift through students there more effectively.

There's only one way to find out.

When we reach the crowded dining hall, a veritable feast is laid out on individual tables already set with plates, eating utensils, and napkins. Legacies eat and chat in groups, sticking to their quintets or those they have agreed-upon allegiances with. It takes me less than ten seconds to pinpoint Kenzie's pale corkscrew curls.

When my quintet and I sit at the table with Kenzie's group, she leans forward with large, animated blue eyes.

"Okay, this is so fucking weird. What do you think is going on?"

"Perhaps they're trying to distract us," I mutter, reaching for an odd-shaped food item on the platter at the center of the table.

"Oakley, wait. That dumpling has meat in it," Everett cautions. "Try this spring roll instead."

He sets two rolls on my plate and begins picking other non-meat things out for me to try, arranging everything meticulously and even pouring a glass of some kind of juice for me. When he realizes I'm side-eying him, and so is most of our little table, his cheeks pinken. He clears his throat, standing and adjusting his blazer three times in a row.

"I'll talk to other faculty members to figure out what's happening."

As soon as he leaves, Baelfire shakes his head. "Poor Frozen Blue Balls."

That makes Kenzie choke on the water she's drinking, spraying some of it on the table. Vivienne pats her back, looking concerned. Luka gives Baelfire a dirty look as he sips on a blood bag, but then he squints across the table at me.

"What exactly do you think they're trying to distract us from, Mable?"

"Maven," Kenzie corrects, looking at me supplicantly. "I promise he doesn't mean to be a jerk."

I believe her. It comes naturally to some people and apparently to most vampires.

"Right, Maven. Sorry," Luka grumbles.

I shrug in reply before digging into the food Everett got for me, quickly finding that there's not a single thing on my plate that I don't like. I've been getting hungrier more often now that my quintet members have started introducing me to new foods they think I'll enjoy.

Turns out, food can be enjoyable instead of just for function. Who fucking knew?

From a table across the room, I spot Amelia Lykoudis staring longingly at the back of Silas's head. When she sees me looking, she glares fiercely.

Too bad, Angry Girl. He's mine now.

Typically, I'd flip her off, but I still feel kind of bad about the fact that she doesn't know her dad is dead yet. Or that I assassinated him.

Speaking of assassinations, Harlow dropped off the liquid bronze just before curfew set in last night. Which means I need to start crafting it into the bronzeblend spell I intend to use while killing off Somnus DeLune once I find a chance to isolate him.

I'm drawn out of my homicidal scheming when I sense Crypt's presence a second before he ripples into existence on the bench beside me. His sudden appearance makes Luka flinch and Vivienne yelp.

I quickly scan Crypt for any signs that he was hurt while tending to Limbo, but he winks and leans forward to kiss the tip of my nose.

"All's well, love."

"I doubt that. The Immortal Quintet has us corralled in here."

He hums. "I overheard them. This is merely an extra precaution while their hired casters adjust the wards to set something up for First Placement in the forest."

Dirk grunts at the end of the table, absentmindedly scratching his elbow. "That's a relief. Not to get into politics or anything, but I was worried they were keeping us here because of another anti-legacy thing like those burning pyres."

"Unfortunately not," I sigh. Those burning pyres were less of an issue than I expect First Placement will be under the direction of the Immortal Quintet.

Dirk guffaws. "Damn, Maven! Have a heart."

A laugh rips from my mouth. It makes Vivienne and Luka jump, and they both look mildly concerned to see me laugh for the first time. Silas and Crypt are both fighting dark smiles of their own, and Baelfire just shakes his head at me, sighing, "Fucking morbid as fuck."

"Inside joke," I explain to Dirk.

The lunch break goes on, and I listen to Baelfire make effortless conversation with Kenzie and her quintet while I eat. Even though I notice him tug at his collar and occasionally wince like his dragon is bothering him, he still comes across as a charming social butterfly.

Even Silas makes small talk with Luka when he isn't zoning out and spinning his bleeding crystal on the table.

Even after weeks of being here, it's strange to me how easily people converse. They just open their mouths and chat like it's second nature. I rarely spoke at all for most of my childhood, and the conversations I did have with other people as I got older mainly consisted of threats or warnings. I suppose that impacted my social development.

Except for with Lillian, of course. Gods, I miss her. If only there were a way to contact her directly in the Nether.

Crypt studies me and leans close to talk so we won't be overheard. "Something wrong, darling? You look unhappy."

I quickly compose my expression and stab at the remaining bits on my plate with my fork. "It's nothi—"

He tips my chin toward him, his silver-speckled violet gaze filled with warning. "None of that. Tell me."

It's odd, but his touch on my face doesn't send any pang of alarm through my body. It's just a warm, pleasant touch.

Perhaps my haphephobia is making progress.

"Just missing someone," I mumble, feeling weak for admitting it.

"Who?"

"Lillian. She was my caretaker. She…kept me sane."

She did a hell of a lot more than that. Lillian was my teacher, guardian, confidante, and the only person I had in my life for a long time. Amadeus put her in charge of my upbringing when I turned five years old, and she was the only stable thing I had to anchor myself to. Without her, I would never have made it this far.

Not seeing her these last few weeks has been weird as fuck. I worry about her, especially because Amadeus knows he can use her to threaten me.

Crypt starts to say something, but a sudden burst of splitting pain in the center of my chest makes me choke, squeezing my eyes shut as I grip the edge of the table. I try to keep myself composed, but I can barely breathe as the familiar agony starts to expand in my chest.

Fuck.

Horrible timing, as usual.

But unlike usual, I'm not dealing with this alone. A warm, gentle hand squeezes my thigh.

"Crane," Crypt rasps. "Get her out of here while we create a diversion. Come on, dragon."

"On it."

"Maven?" Kenzie says, worry coloring her tone. "Is she okay? What's going on?"

What's going on is that my insides are imploding, and oxygen has ceased to exist.

I'm abruptly in someone's arms. Blinking my eyes open, I can vaguely make out that Silas has me in his lap, his jaw clenched tightly as he appears to be waiting for something.

"May, are you—"

"Don't draw attention to her," Silas warns Kenzie quietly.

I hear Baelfire snarl nearby and blink blearily over Silas's shoulder in time to see the dragon shifter send Crypt flying into a table. Food flies everywhere, and glasses shatter. Students yelp as they try to get out of the way.

"Fucking asshole!" Bael roars dramatically, effectively drawing the attention of every legacy in the dining hall.

Crypt picks up the nearest chair and throws it at Baelfire. It smashes to pieces against his back, but the dragon shifter is barely fazed as he tackles the Nightmare Prince, destroying another table while nearby legacies scramble away. Several pissed-off hirelings approach, shouting at them to knock it off.

In the chaos and destruction, Silas lifts me up and races from the dining hall, taking the nearest exit. Two legacy hirelings posted outside the door yell after us, telling him to stop. But a blast of white fills my vision before suddenly, Everett is right behind Silas.

"Do you have it?" the professor demands as they turn a corner.

Have what? My world is turning watery.

"Yes. Let's pray this works."

Silas shoulders his way into one of the school bathrooms, his panic-stricken scarlet eyes dropping to me. I want to tell him to calm down since this happens all the time, and it's really not that fucking big of a deal, but the acute pain is making my vision darken, and I have no air to speak with.

He passes me to Everett, who cradles me like I'm made of spun glass. Silas reaches into a pocket void, a common spell that strong casters use as an invisible storage space. He withdraws an elixir bottle full of colorless liquid and...a giant fucking needle.

Oh, joy.

In general, needles don't bother me because they're too much like miniature rapiers for me to not like them—but I was constantly injected with experimental magical mixtures for months on end while Dagon was toying around with my biological makeup. If Silas plans on sticking me with that thing, I'll make sure it ends up in one of his gorgeously taut ass cheeks instead.

One of them says something, but the words are too warped to make out. Finally, everything fades away as my soul falls out of this plane of existence.

There are no images sent from Amadeus this time. Just cold oblivion.

My condition made itself known immediately after I entered the mortal realm. The first time I expired and revived like this, I assumed it had something to do with the necromancers getting too ambitious when creating me. There's only so much a human body can take when being turned into a monster, so I decided it was just a fluke in my design.

And ever since that first time, my revival times have varied. So I can't tell if it's minutes or hours later when I'm violently returned to my body, jolting awake with a gasp.

"Shit! Are you in pain? Is she in pain? Do something," Everett says frantically from somewhere beside me.

Someone shushes him and adjusts a blanket over me. "*Sangfluir?*"

Opening my eyes, I find that we're in my room. Silas takes one of my hands and kisses my fingertips, his crimson gaze trained on my face.

"How do you feel?"

Weak. I try to sit up, but as usual, my bones are like cold lead after reviving, so it takes a couple of tries. Once I'm propped up against the headboard, I squint out the window. It's dark outside.

Fuck. How long was I out?

And even more importantly…

I look back at Silas. "Tell me you did not inject me with that shit while I was unconscious."

He looks down at my hand, still grasped between both of his. I expect my body to start breaking out in hives or a cold sweat, but there's nothing besides a slight curl of apprehension in my gut. In fact, something about it is…comforting. His fingers and hands are covered in countless little scars from casting, and I'd like to kiss every single one of them.

"I did. But there was a good reason for it."

Silas explains how *reverium* helps Crypt and how Crypt brought a colorless herb back from the Divide that Silas has since been developing into an elixir to help me with my episodes. But then he sighs heavily, pulling at his hair as if the voices in his head are tormenting him.

"I'm a fool. It didn't work on you—of course it didn't, because I developed the elixir with blood magic and not necromancy."

Everett does a double take. "Necromancy? Why would you have to…"

When understanding crosses his face, I nod. "Only death magic can heal the dead."

"You're not dead," he snaps, his arctic blue eyes penetrating.

"I'm not exactly alive, either," I mutter, then frown. "Where are Baelfire and Crypt?"

They exchange a glance that I don't like. Immediately, I try to get out of bed, gritting my teeth against the lethargic heaviness of my limbs. But Silas gently grips my upper arms to keep me in place, shaking his head.

"They knew causing a scene would get them in trouble. As I said, Crypt is as invulnerable as a cockroach, and even if the Immortal is pushing things, they wouldn't dare kill Brigid Decimus's youngest son. It would cause too much of an uproar. They'll both be fine, and getting you out of there was worth it."

I stare at him, then at Everett. Then I squeeze my eyes shut and rub my temples. I'm exhausted from that episode, but now all I can think about is how Crypt returned in such terrible shape and the look of agony on Baelfire's face when he was hit by the silverblend spell.

If either of them comes back hurt...

My throat tightens.

Caring about others leads to pain. That's another thing I learned early on when I grew attached to my first caretaker. She was killed in front of me for saying the wrong thing to one of Amadeus's favorite necromancers, and at only four years old, I became terrified of experiencing that loss ever again.

So when Lillian was brought in to meet me six months later, smiling gently and speaking sweetly, I refused to talk to her. I pushed her away. I was a brat to her for months, hoping she would stop coming to take care of me every day so I wouldn't have to be afraid of losing her, too.

But no matter what I did to repel her, she always returned. And years later, when Amadeus thought I'd outgrown a caretaker and decided it would be amusing to make Lillian fight in his arena, I took her place every time. I took any beating or punishment they thought she deserved for simply existing. I did anything and everything I could for her because how the fuck else could I possibly repay someone for loving me when I make it so hard?

It's no different here. These legacies are mine, so I have to protect them.

Even if that means facing the entire Immortal Quintet at once.

But when I try again to get out of bed, Everett places a cool hand over one of mine, catching my eye. "I'll go. I can get answers quickly."

"I don't want answers. I want to kill anyone who touches any of you four that isn't me."

His face softens into something tender, and he scoffs softly. "So territorial. All you need to do is rest, Oakley."

"But if you get in trouble, too—"

"Then I can get right back out of it with my pretty face."

He smiles at me reassuringly, and with a start, I realize this is the first time I've ever seen Everett Frost smile.

And he has *dimples*.

Fuck. Seriously? This is not fair. His looks were already catastrophically perfect, and now this? The gods really don't know how to rein themselves in, do they?

I want to protest more, but Silas gently presses my shoulders back into the pillows. It's like I'm half-melted in this state because I immediately feel sluggish and drowsy, my eyes drooping.

"Rest, *sangfluir*."

"No."

"Such a stubborn keeper," my blood fae laughs lightly, kissing my fingertips again. "As I've told you, I have no issues with being an asshole. Fighting dirty is my forte. Please don't make me mix a sleeping draught for you, Maven. You know I'll do it."

I glare at him. But then, just like when he was threatening the changeling…I understand him on a level others perhaps don't. He's just doing whatever it takes to accomplish what he thinks is best. I do the same thing, so I must begrudgingly respect his cutthroat ways.

"Fine," I mutter finally. "But only if Everett kisses me before he goes."

Everett's cheeks turn pink immediately. His smile is long gone. "Maven," he warns. "I still can't risk killing y—"

"Don't flatter yourself. Your curse will have to take a ticket and stand in line behind a dozen far more likely ways I'll die permanently," I inform him, arching a brow. "In fact, maybe the gods really did know what they were doing, matching us together since I'm essentially immune to your curse. So stop tormenting yourself."

The ice elemental professor fidgets with one sleeve of his blazer, rolling and unrolling it several times as he silently panics.

"I, um...but, what if..." He scowls, glancing at Silas. "Are you going to help me out here?"

"And subject myself to watching even more of your sad attempts? I'd rather poke my eyes out. Kiss our keeper already and get out so she can sleep."

"You really are an asshole," Everett mutters, looking every kind of flustered as he moves closer to where I lay. He begins fidgeting with his other sleeve, pauses, and shoots a fierce scowl in Silas's direction. "Are you at least going to look away?"

"No. Why would I? She's mine, too." Silas folds his arms, his scarlet irises striking as he watches us.

When I glance at Everett, his face burns a brighter shade of red. Am I reading this wrong, or...does the ice elemental *like* others watching?

Kenzie mentioned something about her own flare for exhibitionism to me once before I yet again threatened to shun her forever. I make a mental note to ask her more about it later.

Finally, Everett grumbles under his breath before leaning to place the gentlest kiss in the world against my mouth. His lips are soft and slightly cool to the touch in the most pleasant way possible.

Before he can pull away, I tangle my hands in his hair and kiss him back hard, slipping my tongue into his mouth to tease him. He groans, and suddenly, I'm being pressed back into the pillows as he traps me with his body, his mouth working fervently against mine as both our breathing ratchets up.

Everett has given up any resistance, and now he's trying to fucking devour me. He tastes like the same subtle, cool mint scent that wraps around him, and I can't get enough of it.

When his hands bracket my face so he can angle my head exactly how he wants, I arch to press against him more fully, feeling the deliciously hard length of him rubbing me through the blankets. He breaks away with a rough swear, squeezing his eyes shut as he tries to breathe and regain control. His cheekbones are pink, his chest heaving.

I *love* seeing him on the brink like this.

"Nearly made a mess of yourself there, professor?" Silas taunts, smirking.

"Fuck off," Everett mutters, but I don't miss the way he also shudders.

Interesting.

When he finally looks at me, there is absolute reverence in his soft blue eyes. It makes my already-racing pulse spike.

"You're too good for me, Oakley," he whispers.

"That's ironic since I'm literally a monster sent from hell. Just how lowly do you think of yourself?" I ask, tracing his perfect features.

My ice elemental closes his eyes. "I don't like you calling yourself a monster. Dear *gods*, you're so warm. It feels so damn good."

My stomach flutters, and I'm wet as hell as I lean up to whisper against his ear so Silas won't overhear. "Actual fucking would be even better."

Everett groans and buries his face in my neck. He grinds against me ever so slightly, sending a jolt of need up my spine—but suddenly, the professor pulls away. He gets off the bed and presses the backs of his hands against his flushed cheeks as he shakes his head, backing away.

"Stop torturing me, Oakley. Now isn't the time for…" He clears his throat and opens the door. "You need to sleep off that episode. I promise I'll get the others back here."

He leaves before I can say anything else.

Once we're alone, Silas moves to lay beside me on the massive bed, adjusting the pillows and blankets to his liking with magic.

"I know you don't believe his curse will actually harm you, but just be warned that the rest of us will kill him if it does."

So dramatic. "No, you won't."

"You doubt me?"

I smirk, letting my eyes drift shut from exhaustion. "You all say you hate each other, but actions speak louder than words. If you were all such enemies, why did none of you kill each other sooner?"

He's quiet for a moment. "If we weren't in a quintet together, I wouldn't hesitate to kill Crypt."

I open my eyes again to study him. Of course, he's not lying. He really hates the Nightmare Prince for what happened to his family. He also doesn't know *why* Crypt killed some of them, but I don't think it's my place to say anything. I'm not about to start playing referee to these legacies' many issues with one another.

So, instead of addressing that honesty, I glance at his arm resting in front of him. "You could hold me if you want."

His eyes flare. "Want is an understatement where you're concerned, but would it bother you?"

"Not really. Touch is becoming...tolerable." Honestly, it's becoming more than tolerable where they're concerned. "I want this."

He wastes no time wrapping his arm over me, pulling me close until I'm against his chest. Even though my insides clench, expecting the nausea and panic to cripple me, I find that I can breathe just fine, even if my pulse is faster than usual.

"I'm so glad to hear that, *ima sangfluir,*" he breathes against the top of my head, laying a kiss there.

It's so warm and fucking nice being held like this. My eyes grow so heavy that they refuse to open the next time I blink, but I still mumble, "Stay with me."

"I will."

"Good. And Silas?"

"*Tha, imo ghrài?*"

Which means, *yes, love of mine?*

He used the *L*-word, too. In fae, but still...that word haunts me as I slip closer to sleep.

"If they come back injured, heal them. Even if it's Crypt."

He kisses my head one more time. "Anything for you."

30

SILAS

HOLDING Maven in her sleep is an intimate pleasure unlike anything I've experienced. She breathes softly, her soft hair brushing against my chin as I wish this moment would never end.

But the voices in my head have been getting so strong lately that they ruin even this for me.

You're letting her waste your time. Useless boy. Utterly useless, my father whispers.

One of these days, she'll pass out and never revive. Let her go. She's dangerous for you.

Leave me alone, I think back, pulling Maven tighter as my ears ring.

I should have realized my blood magic would nullify whatever effects Crypt's plant would have had on Maven. I need to find someone whose magic *will* work with her. Perhaps she must make the elixir for herself with her necromancy, or...maybe I need to find Pia. After all, the prophetess mysteriously healed my keeper after the Matched Ball.

Someone needs to ask that prophetess questions. I'm suspicious of her, but I won't know any peace until I help Maven fend off her condition.

You want true peace? You only get that one way, another voice sniggers.

She can't break your curse. She is a waste of time. You know what you must do to escape us.

"Shut up," I whisper miserably, squeezing my eyes shut to bury my face in her dark hair.

The ringing becomes unbearable, and my vision darkens as the madness takes hold. And this time, when I shake off the insanity, I'm straddling Maven with my hands around her neck.

She stares up at me with wide eyes, her hands poised and surrounded by dark magic, but she's not moving to stop me as this situation smashes into me like ice water.

I'm…hurting my keeper.

I'm strangling her.

I cry out in horror and break away from her, bile burning its way up my throat before I lurch away from the bed to expel anything left in my stomach. I fall to the floor, tugging at my hair as the voices' mocking laughter echoes in my head.

I was just hurting my blood blossom because of them.

They're right. There's nothing left of my mind, anyway—I'm absolutely fucking insane, so if I'm hurting my keeper, I can't let myself exist. I can't keep posing a threat to her.

The ringing hasn't subsided, so I can't make out whatever Maven is trying to rasp from the bed. I stagger to my feet, trying to get to the door. I can't even fucking look at her. If I see marks from my hands around her neck—

Just like the marks that Gideon probably left, a voice in my head crows.

She'll look at you like you're him now.

More nausea threatens to escape. The voices in my head were just taking advantage of Maven's most traumatic memory. And *my* hands were around her neck.

What have I done?

What have I fucking done?

"Silas!"

A flare of dark magic slams the door shut just as I open it, and then Maven grasps my arm and turns me around. I was right. She has bruises around her throat. A sound of devastation breaks from me, but she stubbornly grips my jaw to force me to meet her gaze.

The moment I see her determined, beautiful eyes, free of the hurt and hatred I should see there, I drop to my knees to bury my face against her stomach.

"*Sangfluir. Sangfluir, im altha echair a—*"

I'm babbling nonsensically in fae, but she starts stroking my hair.

"Shh. Breathe."

Maven stays in place, fixing my hair while she waits for me to calm down and stop shaking. How vulnerable I must seem right now—how absolutely fucking *weak*. She should be ashamed to have me in her quintet. Why is she comforting me? I just hurt her despite promising I never would.

I cannot fucking believe I hurt her. The shaking gets worse.

"I can't live with myself," I whisper brokenly. "I can't live with the voices anymore, Maven. They're right. I can't—"

As the voices' laughter and ringing fade from my ears, I go silent when I realize my keeper is singing softly. It's an old, traditional fae lullaby I heard constantly as a very young child. It warms my chest immediately.

She's incredibly off-tune, yet I've never heard anything more beautiful.

"How do you know this?" I manage.

"Lillian used to sing it to me."

I don't know who Lillian is, but hearing the rough scratchiness of her voice makes me desperate to fix what I just did. I reach for the bruises on her throat, determined to erase them, but despair fills me again when I remember I can't even fucking heal her.

Am I truly so useless to the woman I love?

She frames my face with her hands. "It wasn't you. It was your curse."

"That's no excuse. You just woke up to your greatest fear. I deserve death—no, death would be far too merciful for me now," I grimace.

"First of all, that is hardly my greatest fear. If someone *did* strangle me, I'd revive and gladly repay the favor. Second of all, this isn't a big deal. Some people enjoy choking. Kenzie says it's kinky."

Gods above. How is she joking at a time like *this*?

I cover my face. "Don't make light of this. Please."

"If you insist. Come here."

She leads me back to the bed. I don't want to sit down with her. What if my sanity ebbs again, and I do something far worse? I should retreat to my private dorm and wallow in self-hatred, where I pose no risk to her. There's plenty of hard liquor there I can try to drown my sorrows in.

"Silas. Sit."

"I need a drink."

Maven considers that. "Okay. Sit first."

I do, but I keep an arm's length between us. I feel wretched. Haunted. I will never fucking get the image of me choking the life from her out of my broken head. I always knew what my curse would be and always anticipated hating the feeling of slipping away, but this is far more torturous than I ever could have imagined.

I'd loathe the gods for doing this to me…but then again, they gave me my blood blossom.

So, even if I hate them right now, I'll always be in their debt.

Maven huffs and scoots closer to me on the bed. At first, I think she's going to offer sweet words or offer empty assurances that she's all right, even though I can see the motherfucking bruises.

Instead, my soul nearly leaves my godsdamned body when my vicious little keeper withdraws a concealed knife from her pants and drags it across her palm. I shout in alarm, but then the intoxicating scent of her blood slams into me, and I go dizzy with hunger.

Her dark eyes sparkle with daring. "You said you needed a drink."

"I—I can't…" My mouth aches. My chest is on fire, my heart

thrumming with desire and terror. She can't let me do this. "No, I just hurt you. I won't do that again."

Maven's hand is now dripping, and she rolls her eyes before raising a red finger and wiping it gently across my lips. My tongue darts out on instinct, and—

Holy gods above.

I'm on her in an instant, my fangs burying into her hand as lust and cavernous hunger roar through my veins. I immediately have her pressed against the bed beneath me, trapped. Maven's sharp inhale vaguely registers, but I'm too far gone from her breathtaking flavor to do anything except feed.

All magic tastes the same to me.

But not hers. No, Maven tastes like she's *mine*.

It's beyond all description as her magic lights up my entire system beyond any other power I've ever experienced. I moan and grind desperately against her. All of my instincts are dialed up to ten as I lose control.

When she groans and bares her neck, I eagerly sink my teeth there, eyes rolling back as her flavor floods my mouth.

I could live like this.

I could die like this.

She could control me with just one drop. I'm utterly captive to my need for her and wouldn't have it any other way.

"Silas," Maven breathes finally, the soft rasp of her voice cutting into my frenzied state of heaven-struck bloodlust.

I force myself to unlatch from her neck, lapping gently at the puncture marks left behind as I try to catch my breath. I can barely speak.

"Godsdamn you."

"They already have, but what is it for this time?" she laughs breathlessly.

I groan and continue licking and kissing down her neck. Feeding has never aroused me before, but my cock is throbbing in my pants as I try to come down from that overwhelming experience.

"Why would you reward me for hurting you by allowing me to hurt you further?" I demand, finally looking up at her.

But there's no sign of hurt or even discomfort on my blood blossom's face. Instead, she looks nearly blissed out. For vampires, pleasure feeding is typical, but it occurs very rarely in blood fae. We feed for magic, which is usually very painful for anyone we bite.

Yet, in some cases...

I lick my lips of all traces of her, needing every last taste. "It didn't hurt?"

Maven's smile is wicked. "Maybe slightly. But I prefer it that way."

Then her expression sobers, and I immediately realize I've been all over her without checking in to see if her aversion to touch was bothering her. I apologize and try to remove myself, but Maven wraps her arms around me and shakes her head.

"I was just thinking. How can we fix your curse?"

"There's no cure." Aside from breaking my curse by binding my heart to hers...but hers is in the Nether.

She seems thoughtful for a long moment before tipping her head. "Would Baelfire's dragon scales help somehow? Is that why you wanted them so badly?"

The reminder of how terribly I'm failing at getting those scales makes me sigh. I move to lay beside my keeper, pulling her close again. It's selfish, considering everything that just happened, but I need her close.

"No. The dragon scales aren't for me. I want them for two things."

She waits expectantly.

I study her and sigh. "The main reason, I'm not at liberty to say. I promised to keep it a secret."

But Maven is exceptionally sharp, so it only takes her a moment of thought. "You have no close family left. The closest person in your life is most likely...the Garnet Wizard, your mentor. Are the scales for him?"

I can't say a word, but I can nod.

"His quintet died," she goes on. "I overheard that weeks ago when I was studying in the library, and two faculty members mentioned him in passing. So, if his keeper is dead, then his curse returned. It must be a nasty curse since he's believed to be very powerful. Do you want scales to help him with easing his curse?"

I nod again. "I'm running out of time to help. He's been my only semblance of family for ten years, and his last letter read like a goodbye. If I don't get scales to him soon, he—" My voice cuts off as my fae promise keeps me from saying anything else about it, and I sigh. "By the way, you would make a decent detective."

"Just as you make a *decent* caster," she snarks, the same insult she used after seeing me fight for the first time.

I narrow my eyes at her, trying not to smile at her playfulness. "Minx."

"I take it you promised him not to tell a soul, which must be why you resorted to betting on my pussy just to get what you want from Baelfire."

I flinch. Fucking hell, I've been the worst match in the world to her, haven't I?

"I'm sorry for that. I'll *always* be sorry for that."

She shrugs and examines her hand, which is still bleeding lightly. "It's in the past. I forgive you. But I'd like to know the other reason you want dragon scales."

The sight of her injury turns my stomach, despite how my mouth waters again at the sight of her blood. It's such a paradox.

"I'll get bandages," I say hoarsely.

But when I try to move, Maven again stops me and seems almost…nervous. I realize why when she softly chants in necromancy. Just like when we were searching for the changeling, the air chills and my own magic tingles with wariness in my veins at my proximity to such a twisted, dark craft.

I watch in fascination as Maven's skin starts to heal and the bruises fade. But her fingertips blacken, and her skin becomes paler than its usual olive-toned hue.

When she's done, she looks at me. "Well?"

"Forbidden though it may be, I find your necromancy beautiful."

Her lips twitch. "Thanks. But I meant, what's the other reason?"

Ah. I grimace. "Don't tell Baelfire. Or the others. They'll think I secretly have a bleeding heart."

Again, she waits, and finally, I huff and sit up to magically clean up the mess I left on the floor earlier. As my magic works, I mutter, "The last family of dragons are infertile. In another generation or two, they'll go extinct. I'm developing a potion to reverse their troubles, but it requires golden dragon scales."

Maven stares at me before sitting up and tilting her head. "You're...trying to help Baelfire's family procreate?"

I wrinkle my nose. "Phrasing it that way makes it sound obscene. But yes, basically."

"But why wouldn't you tell Baelfire?"

"The Decimus family is extremely proud. They get unbelievably testy about the fact that none of his siblings has had children if it's brought up. Baelfire would probably rather eat shit than ever ask for help, let alone from me. If I told him I wanted scales for that, he would think I was freakishly invested in his pedigree, which I'm not." I shrug. "Also, I was going to sell the fertility potion to his family at a ridiculously high price."

"Because why be altruistic when you can be rich instead?"

"Precisely."

She snorts and shakes her head. "You idiots are all so determined to pretend you hate each other."

I lean forward to kiss her. "We're your idiots."

She smiles back at me, which twists my heart into delighted little knots, but then her expression shifts quickly to something heartbreaking.

"You deserve to have your curse broken. I want to find a way to help, but..." She clears her throat and looks away, seeming pained. "It's not too late for you to find a different keeper—"

"Not this again," I sigh. "The answer is no, Maven. Absolutely fucking not."

"But if someone else who has an actual fucking heart can keep you from going insane—"

I kiss her again, forcibly this time to keep her words from coming out. Pulling away, I shake my head. "My curse isn't your burden. If it goes unbroken, then that's my fate. I still want *you*, *ima sangfluir*. The descent into madness will be much sweeter with you at my side."

Maven looks as if she's about to argue more, but we both hear the sound of a door closing somewhere else in the apartment. Her face lights up, and even though I can't stand the rest of our quintet half the time, I swear on the gods, I could hug all three of those bastards for getting that pained expression off our keeper's face.

Before she can try to leave her bedroom, I quickly stand and hold up a hand to stop her. "Let me check on them first, *sangfluir*."

She goes very still. "You think they're injured."

"Possibly."

"And you don't want me to see it, snap, and slaughter everyone I pass on my way to the Immortal Quintet."

"Again…possibly." The whole truth is, I don't want to see her more upset than I've already seen her tonight.

Maven grumbles but agrees. As she waits in her bedroom, I slip out and find Crypt and Everett in the TV room. Everett's perfectly fine, of fucking course, but Crypt's face is slowly healing from several bruises. I watch as he rebreaks a bone in one of his fingers so it will heal correctly.

"Enjoying the show, Crane?" he drawls.

"Very much. Where's Baelfire?"

Everett loosens his tie ever so slightly, looking exhausted. "He didn't want Maven to see all the blood."

Damn it. "How bad was it?" I ask Crypt.

"If you're offering to kiss my boo-boos away, you can go fuck yourself instead. Frost told us the elixir didn't work on Maven." He stands and goes toe to toe with me, his violet eyes murderous. "For your sake, you'd better hope the next draught works. If you're useless to her, I see no reason to keep you around."

Everett rolls his eyes. "Back off, dream eater. We all know you won't hurt any of us because it would upset Maven. Your bark has lost its bite."

Did Everett Frost just *defend* me? I make a face. "Just because I'll watch you kiss our keeper doesn't mean I want your friendship, you frozen ass."

The elemental's face turns bright red, and he mutters something under his breath about my creepy-ass red eyes before storming toward Maven's room.

"I'm not covered in blood, so I'll be with her. Crypt, wash that shit off of you."

Her door closes, and the Nightmare Prince looks at me. "Did fucking *Frost* just try to give me an order? So much for him not being covered in blood."

Before he can move to go after Everett, I hold out an arm to stop him, shaking my head. "Don't stir up shit tonight. Maven is tired. We're all fucking tired."

"Especially you," he smirks cruelly. "How many days has it been since your insanity last let you sleep? Three? Four?"

I grit my teeth, my freshly-powered magic tickling at my fingertips. I'm always on edge around Crypt, and if he keeps insisting on needling me, I'm going to end up hurting him and upsetting Maven.

Just a little murder won't hurt, a voice in my head insists.

He'll kill you if you don't get to him first.

Avenge me. Do something useful for once, my father hisses.

Baelfire steps out of the hallway shower wrapped in nothing but steam and a black towel. He doesn't bat an eye at the standoff between me and Crypt. He just shoves us apart so he can walk through the hall to Maven's room. Obviously, his inner dragon is making him moody.

When her door opens, I can hear Maven's sigh of relief, and then she pokes her head out into the hallway to look for the rest of us. I quickly step in front of Crypt to hide his bloodied clothes from her.

She's too smart for that and rolls her eyes. "As long as no one is hurt, blood on clothing won't bother me. Both of you come here. I have a request."

We exchange one more glare before walking side by side to Maven's room. Crypt shoves me into the wall to go in first, and I repay him by discreetly kicking him in the shin when I pass by him on the way into the room.

Baelfire, the big brute, immediately picks up Maven and sits on the edge of the bed with her in his lap, burying his face in the crook of her neck. The rest of us scowl and glare at him for not even asking first, but she gently traces the collar around his neck as she glances over the rest of us. I notice that she's put gloves on again, to hide her blackened fingertips from the others.

"What did you want, love?" Crypt asks. "Anything, and it's yours."

She squirms a little, and Baelfire promptly takes her off his lap and sets her beside him. At the very least, I can be glad the assholes I'm in this quintet with know how to sense when Maven's haphephobia is acting up.

"Don't be too sure. It's a weird request," she mumbles.

She's usually so confident. Seeing her unsure makes me move to sit on her other side, smiling gently. "There's remarkably little the lot of us wouldn't do for you."

Maven fidgets, clearing her throat. "Would you all sleep in here tonight? With me? I just…" It seems to take effort for her to get the next words out. "I need to know that you're all safe. And close. If you don't mind."

I blink. Everett and Crypt look equally surprised, but Baelfire's face lights up like the sun.

"You want a sleepover? Abso-fucking-lutely, Mayflower. Also, that's not a weird request at all. Most fully fledged quintets sleep in the same room, you know."

Our keeper looks between us and arches a brow pointedly. Her meaning is clear: most quintets aren't *us*, with all our ongoing squabbles.

We all exchange looks and come to a silent agreement: if Maven wants us to play nice and stay in the same room, we can manage it.

"Truce," I mutter to Crypt. "Just for one night."

"In your fucking dreams," he murmurs back. "But at least you'll be *having* dreams tonight. Feel free to thank me in the morning."

He slips into Limbo without another word to me, but his meaning is clear: he'll make sure I sleep tonight. But sleeping near the Nightmare Prince without a dreamcatcher to protect me is out of the question. Paranoia crawls over my entire body like leeches, sapping away my control until my ears start to ring again, my eye twitching.

Before it can get too far, Everett spots a small spill of blood on the bed and the air in the room plummets. Our breaths plume before our faces as the sudden cold snaps me out of it.

The professor glares at me. "Want to explain this, bloodsucker?"

Maven doesn't miss a beat. "I offered Silas a snack."

Baelfire chokes, and Everett recoils.

She rolls her eyes. "Stop clutching your pearls. I enjoyed it. Now, if you don't mind…" She waves her hand and turns off the lamp using common magic. "I'm exhausted."

We remain quiet as we all settle into bed with her. When reserving this apartment, I had the bed in the keeper's bedroom custom-made to be larger than an Alaskan king, so it's not a tight fit, even despite Baelfire's overbulked frame.

Maven curls up in the middle of the bed, and Baelfire is quick to press against her left side, nuzzling against her neck. I lay beside her on the right, not surprised when Frost lays at the very edge of the bed on my side, still wary about getting too close to Maven.

But apparently, no matter how conflicted he is, he's too far gone for her to try to leave tonight.

"Night, Mayflower," Baelfire yawns, and I hear him kiss her cheek.

She hums, obviously already drifting off. But I have no hope in hell of going to sleep anytime soon. I'm still keyed up from feeding, and having Maven's body so close to mine is keeping my cock hard as fucking steel. I shift slightly under the blankets, gritting my teeth as I stare at the dark ceiling. The voices in my head are whispering, chills slithering over my bones at the idea of resting anywhere near the rest of these legacies.

I think I'm in for a long, miserably hard night.

So I'm not expecting it when a brush of incubi power sends a flood of fatigue through my system, sending me into a deep sleep within seconds.

31

CRYPT

THOSE THREE DOLTS thought it would be just one night.

But two more days have passed full of classes, tense hallways, intensive combat training followed by far more exhaustive personal training sessions under Maven's orders, brief casual touching for Maven's exposure therapy, highly monitored lunches and dinners, etcetera, etcetera—

And each night, they all end up resting in the same bed as my dark little darling.

After that first night, Decimus insisted that sleeping near Maven had helped him deal with his pissy inner dragon, and she hadn't argued when Crane and Frost somehow wound up in there with them. Yesterday, after Maven put us through a ruthless training in the dungeon exercise room, Frost had showered, changed into ridiculous silk pajamas, dragged himself into her room, and passed out on the bed before they even discussed it. Crane and Decimus followed suit.

I grin to myself as I watch all of them sleeping deeply. I can hardly blame them. They now know as I do that a night spent *not* at Maven's side feels utterly empty and cold.

Perhaps I would find it annoying, keeping Crane's dangerously unraveled psyche in such a deep sleep every night...except I've found that sleeping so close to all of her matches naturally gives Maven constant wet dreams.

I live for the pleasure she finds in her dreams.

Though to be fair, they *all* get wet dreams sleeping so close to her. It's been absolutely fucking hilarious to watch Maven wake first every morning and pretend as if she doesn't have to crawl through a veritable forest of morning wood just to get out of bed and go to the bathroom.

We've all been too busy and exhausted for the last few days as we prepare for First Placement for anything else to happen in bed besides sleep. Not to mention, none of us wants to push Maven. She's barely getting used to not being petrified of physical touch, so we've all come to the unspoken agreement not to pounce on her at night. We're waiting for her to take the lead since she does it so naturally.

But all this sexual torture isn't good for them. Or me.

I think it's past time for everyone to blow off steam. It'll do the entire quintet good and offer some postcoital clarity before we face whatever horrors the Immortal Quintet decides to lob at us today in First Placement.

With that thought in mind, I tiptoe mischievously through Limbo, passing through Decimus's dream first to get to Maven's. Decimus is dreaming about her, of course. His projection of what she would look like clad in lace lingerie is mouthwatering. Perhaps almost as good as she'll look actually wearing it in the real world.

But when I slip into Maven's dream space, my heart sinks. It isn't a nightmare—at least, not yet—but this isn't a pleasant dream. I spent too long working to protect everyone else from Crane's utter insanity by keeping him fast asleep. I should have returned to her subconscious sooner, but now I watch as Maven singlehandedly slaughters five ghouls in her dream.

She's standing in the center of a stone arena, wearing leather armor and splattered with blood, as she demolishes the creatures. It's not even a fair fight. She moves so beautifully as she kills that it's hard to pull my eyes away. Undead watch in chilling silence from the sidelines, hideous visages of rotting flesh and eyeless sockets that are unable to make a sound. Everything is nearly colorless, and the sun overhead is so dim that it may as well be a full moon.

Once the ghouls are dead, a banshee is brought out. Then a strange, bony monster I've never heard of. Then another. On and on the bouts go, and Maven's face is unlike I've ever seen. It's as if she's in a trance, utterly lost in the bloodshed.

Even when a wendigo finally manages to sink its claws into her back, ripping through her skin until she's a bloody mess, Maven has no reaction. She's mindless with the need to kill.

I change her dream quickly, weaving and adjusting until she's in this same exact room, in this same situation. All her matches are at her side—only in this dream, I lay wrapped around her. And, of course, she's entirely naked because I'd always have her naked if it were possible.

My keeper blinks as she gradually adjusts to the new surroundings. She kisses my jaw. "You're changing my dreams again."

"I only want you to rest peacefully, love."

"Resting in peace is for other dead people. It's okay to let my dreams be."

"You're not dead. If you were, I would be haunting you in the Beyond instead."

Maven begins kissing her way down my jawline, turning in my arms to press herself against me. I shut my eyes, enjoying every one of her touches. Still, it's difficult to be much more engaged than that when I'm also carefully unraveling the tendrils of panic and anxiety that start to unfurl from her psyche with all of this contact.

Maven grinds against my straining erection, humming thoughtfully. "Someone's excited."

"How can I help it when you sleep so beautifully?"

She pulls away slightly to study me. "Are you this hard because of the dream, or…"

"Or?" I prompt, distracted by the tantalizing friction of her squirming against me.

"Or is it because I'm asleep?"

Godsdamn me, is it that obvious? I look away, toying with the ends of her hair.

"Anytime I'm near you, I'm desperate, but your sleeping body is a temptation that I would gladly sell the remaining fragments of my soul to worship. Does that bother you?"

She turns my chin to make me look at her, and the sultry, curious sparkle in her dark eyes makes my heart stutter.

"No. Actually, I'm…intrigued. Is this something most people do?"

I swallow. "No."

Maven considers that and returns to kissing my jaw. "Their loss. Like you said, I think we both enjoy being fucked up. So you have my full permission."

Gods above.

I exhale slowly, trying not to frighten her by showing how desperately I want that. But what if I'm influencing her dream to make her say this? I hesitate, checking to make sure that's not the case.

None of my power is seeping into her subconscious. This is all Maven.

"You're sure, love?" I rasp, my cock aching as excitement pulses through my veins. She has no idea how much I want this or all the fantasies she's giving the green light for. "You're giving me permission to take your gorgeous body when you're asleep?"

She kisses me in her dream. "Yes. Fuck me while I dream about you, Nightmare Prince."

I moan at the unfiltered arousal perfuming her entire dream. I could feed on this every single damned night, and having her explicit permission to adore her sleeping body to my heart's content is the single greatest thing I've ever been given.

But the first time I fuck Maven, I want it to be in the mortal realm and not in her pretty dreams.

"Hold that thought, darling," I whisper, kissing her before slipping back out of her dream.

From Limbo, I watch as she makes a soft sound of need in her sleep. It makes Decimus roll over, his own dream wavering as he nearly wakes.

I roll my shoulders back and pop my knuckles. It's been a while since I've intertwined dreams. And never sex dreams.

But like a maestro, I grasp Frost's vague dream about kissing and interweave it with Maven's. Then I work at Decimus's and finally Crane's. By the time I'm done merging their dreams, all of Limbo around me is thick with want and desperation. Silently, I check back into the conjoined dream and find—

Fuck me. She's taking two of them at once.

I gaze in awe, palming my rock-hard erection through my pants as I watch Maven moan and rock between Crane and Decimus in her dream. Decimus is rutting her pussy from beneath as she rides him, and Crane swears in fae as he fucks her ass with a vengeance. There was no need for buildup or lubrication in a dream like this—because sensations are different in the dream world. They're heightened, unhindered by real-world troubles.

They're all panting, gasping, coming undone. Frost kneels beside them and whispers for Maven to open up. She moans when he slides his cock into her mouth—the collective dream ripples as Frost nearly wakes at the dreamy pleasure. There's a dream projection of me, too, approaching on Maven's other side.

But I don't care to keep watching. I'm too ravenous for her.

Stepping out of Limbo, I slip under the blankets at the foot of the massive bed and crawl until I'm between Maven's legs. My breathing is labored, desperate, as I gently pull her pajamas off. I press my face against the thin panties between her thighs and inhale, stroking myself as I obsess over how utterly perfect my darling's pussy is.

I kiss up her thighs, licking and tasting until I finally pull aside her panties and lap at her entrance. *Gods,* she's so wet and sweet and fucking heady. It's the first time I've tasted her gorgeous cunt, and I can do nothing but groan and devour the ambrosia that is her arousal. I slip one finger inside of her and gently circle my thumb around her clit, kissing and licking as I relish every clench of her dripping cunt.

Obsession beats in my veins like a drum, growing more intense with each passing moment. I want to breathe her, taste her—wrap myself in her twisted, beautiful mind and etch myself into her bones until every move she makes, I make with her.

When I make her my muse, my dark little darling will discover how utterly obsessed I am. She'll see inside my head and learn just how unhinged I become at the very thought of her.

And she'll love it. Of that, I'm certain.

As I devour Maven, I'm vaguely aware that their combined dream is ripening as they no doubt approach climaxing in their sleep. Some people wake from such intense sensations—and if one dreamer wakes from a combined dream, they all do. So I'm not particularly surprised when, a moment later, I hear Frost's sharp gasp before the dream ruptures, all four of them snapping awake.

I grin against Maven's thigh, placing a kiss there. Time to see if my meddling worked.

I don't have to wait long. Decimus moans and rocks his shorts-covered erection against Maven's thigh, which is obnoxiously close to my head.

"Godsdamn, baby, you smell so fucking *good* when you're wet for us," he whispers.

Maven is gasping as she pushes the blanket back to look down at me. She doesn't quite see my eyes in this dark room, but I have the glorious ability to see how flushed she is as she bites her lip and lifts her hips, grinding slightly against my face.

"More," she whispers, squeezing her eyes shut. "Please, I'm so close already, just—"

Crane licks a path up her neck, his hand slipping up beneath her shirt and the other tugging off his clothing.

"I need you. Now, *sangfluir*," he pants.

Our keeper makes a delicious little sound that goes straight to my cock. I move out of the way, watching in open-mouthed anticipation as Decimus starts quite literally ripping the rest of her pajamas off of her as if they've personally offended him.

As soon as her tits are free, Decimus sucks one of her nipples into his mouth as Crane moves on top of Maven. Frost is at the edge of the bed near me, and I hear him swear quietly when Crane thrusts home as Maven cries out, arching off the bed with pleasure.

Crane fucks her mercilessly while I stroke myself to the exquisite sounds Maven makes as she comes. When the blood fae finishes several moments later with a harsh swear, she squirms and whispers, "Fuck me. I need all of you to fuck me."

Without wasting another moment, I shove Crane aside and lean down to capture Maven's lips with mine. Dragging the pierced head of my cock through her sopping entrance, I savor the way her breath hitches and her fingernails drag down my back when she feels my piercings dragging against her sensitive clit.

"Crypt," she whispers, arching against me. "Gods, I need—"

I know exactly what she needs. Thrusting forward, I grit my teeth when her tight, hot pussy squeezes all of me. Fucking hell, I can barely breathe through how good she feels.

Sex was never like this before. It was empty and lacked much sensation, just like the rest of my dismal existence without Maven. But now I pound home, the blinding pleasure almost too much. I pin her down so I can fuck my darling hard and rough like we both need.

"Listen to how wet she is," Decimus breathes. "You're doing so fucking good for us, baby."

He leans down and kisses below our keeper's ear, whispering filthy things—things my darling certainly likes, judging by the way she suddenly comes again, gasping and arching her back as she gushes around me.

It's too much, and I hiss in pleasure as euphoria barrels through me, my cock jerking and pulsing inside of her.

"Fuck. It's my turn. I need that pussy," Decimus groans raggedly. As soon as I pull out of her, dizzy from the force of that orgasm, he grabs Maven and maneuvers her until she's straddling him. They both moan as she sinks onto him, and my cock twitches in appreciation when I see our keeper's head thrown back in pure ecstasy.

"Gods, fuck, gods," she chants. "Harder."

"She's so perfect," Frost whispers.

Crane moves behind Maven, and for a moment, I'm worried he's going to try their little dream fantasy before she's prepared—but then his fangs are in her neck, which makes Maven gasp and writhe with pleasure.

"So fucking needy for us, aren't you?" Decimus murmurs. "Gods, baby, you're so fucking gorgeous."

"I—I want Everett, too," Maven pants. "Now."

I'd almost forgotten about Frost. He's still at the edge of the bed, gazing at our keeper with hooded eyes. Poor sap must think he's still dreaming.

"Don't keep my mate waiting," Decimus growls, leaning up to nip at one of her nipples. That makes her cry out, and I begin to stroke myself again because how could I not be hard as fucking steel, watching all of her glorious pleasure?

Frost swallows hard. "Maven, I—I don't…I haven't, um…"

She has no idea he's a virgin. I could laugh at how nervous he sounds.

"I want to taste you," Maven whispers.

Lucky bastard.

Frost shudders, and for a moment, I think he's going to run from the room to avoid embarrassing himself. But finally, the ice elemental crawls to Maven as Crane moves out of the way. He brushes a chaste kiss against her lips.

"I can't just…" he trails off uncertainly.

Maven makes a sound of frustration, and then I have to grip my throbbing erection tightly when she sticks two of her own fingers in her mouth, riding Decimus as she sucks on herself so fucking sensually, it may as well be a godsdamned cock.

"*Fuck*, baby," Decimus grits out. "You're so damn hot. You just need something in that pretty mouth so fucking bad, don't you?"

She hums in agreement, reaching up with her other hand to pinch one of her own nipples. Gods above, I could watch her like this for eternity.

"If Frost is refusing you, let me—" I begin.

As I expected, Frost immediately shoves me away, swears creatively, and kneels beside Maven, ripping down the front of his pajama pants to feed her his straining cock.

"Fine. You fucking want this? Open."

Maven eagerly sucks his cock into her mouth, and he makes a strangled sound, his head thrown back as he clearly is already on the brink of losing control. Since Decimus and Frost are keeping her occupied, I move to her other side. Leaning over Decimus to suck one of her pretty nipples into my mouth, I bite it playfully.

The added stimulation makes Maven moan around Frost's cock. That sends him over the edge, and he gasps as he comes in her mouth. The fact that she swallows it without hesitation makes us all groan—and Decimus swears before thrusting hard up into her one last time, his thick cock pulsing inside of her.

We all slump onto the bed, trying to catch our breaths for a long, rapturous moment. Crane gently brushes Maven's hair out of her face, kissing her temple and forehead. His voice is full of concern.

"How do you feel so far, *ima sangfluir?*"

"Fucked up, but in a much better way than usual."

Decimus laughs, rubbing his face. "He means, do we need to rush you to a toilet and hold your hair out of the way?"

Our keeper pauses as if she's taking stock of her body. She rubs one of her arms and clears her throat. "No. I'll shower in a moment."

I close my eyes, basking in the knowledge that all that fuckery I instigated isn't going to end up with her suffering as much afterward as she did in Pennsylvania.

Progress is progress.

"Hang on. *So far?*" Maven sits up and squints through the darkness down at Crane.

Decimus hums. "We have hours before sunrise to kill with more *canoodling*, Boo."

"Not Boo," she mumbles. "Maybe I should punch you again."

"Right, sorry. *Not*-Boo," he grins. "So, now that you've sampled all the cocks that matter in this quintet—"

"You're such a fucking dick," Frost scowls, covering his face with one arm.

"—feel free to tell the rest of these fuckers that you like mine the most," Bael finishes.

I mime gagging myself, and then realize my theatrics are lost on everyone except perhaps Baelfire, and even the shifter's night vision isn't nearly as good as mine.

"If you'd like, love, I'll knock out the dragon so he sleeps during this next round," I offer.

"All this talk of a next round is…" Maven sighs, rubbing her arm harder.

Frost's voice is soft. "Ignore them. We'll all leave you alone so you can sleep if you're tired, Oakley."

"Actually, I was going to say it's making me horny as fuck again. But if we don't stop, we'll all be exhausted tomorrow—"

My cock is once again painfully hard. I quickly offer a solution so I can get my hands on her beautiful body again.

"I can make sure you all rest extra deeply for the last hour or two before we need to leave. An utterly dreamless, restful sleep."

"How bizarre. The incubus is useful for once," Crane muses, kissing Maven's neck. "We'll help you shower."

When he licks where he bit her earlier, she inhales sharply and squirms. Decimus groans again about how delicious the scent of her arousal is. Frost is already kissing her again as he lifts her to take her into the bathroom for a shower.

I grin to myself as I follow. I'll have to meddle like this more often.

32

MAVEN

THE NEXT TIME I wake up, I'm surrounded by three gorgeous, naked legacies, all fast asleep around me with their delicious muscles on display.

I'm turned at an angle on the massive bed. Everett is on one side of me, looking utterly angelic as my head rests on his subtly rising and falling chest. His heartbeat is a steady thrum under my ear, and the steadiness of it makes me sigh softly.

Despite what I told Silas, I miss having a heartbeat.

Silas's face is nuzzled against my neck on my other side, one arm thrown over me, and Baelfire has my naked legs flung over his, snoring softly near the foot of the massive bed.

Even in their sleep, they can't seem to let go of me.

Woe is me.

Grinning, I carefully leave the bed without waking any of them. As soon as I'm standing, I notice how sore I am between the legs. My body isn't used to oodles of sex, so going a few rounds with four ravenous legacies in the wee hours wasn't my best idea ever.

Or was it? No regrets here.

Crypt slips out of Limbo to hug me from behind, kissing the back of my neck. "Morning, love," he rasps. "No wake-up exercises today?"

"First Placement will be enough of an exercise."

Plus, oddly enough, I didn't wake up feeling like a wired bomb. I feel almost relaxed.

Glancing at a clock on the wall, I realize it's only an hour and a half away before the assembly that marks the beginning of First Placement. These guys are all still sleeping off our intense sex romp, so I should really get them up and going.

But first, I pause to gauge my body's reactions once again. I wouldn't put it past my stupid fucking body to have an extremely delayed response to all the touching from last night. Yet I still don't feel nauseous or like my nerves have been dipped in acid. Beyond feeling sexually sated and sore, I feel...mostly normal.

Crypt seems to sense my shock and hums against my neck. "You're getting used to our touch."

Not breaking out into a cold sweat at the slightest touch will be really fucking nice. I turn my head to kiss my Nightmare Prince, but when he immediately reaches down to slip his fingers through my bare pussy, I jolt and shake my head.

"That needs a break."

Crypt frowns, and to my mortification, he turns me around and crouches directly in front of me. I jolt again when he reaches up to spread me open, scowling softly at how reddened I am down there. The rest of me is covered in Baelfire's love bites, tiny puncture marks from a handful of places Silas fed, and dried cum.

"We were all too fucking rough," he mutters. "Are you sore, darling?"

I ignore the question and bat his hands away, my face a thousand degrees from his thorough examination when I must look like a fucking mess.

"I'm going to get ready. Could you wake them up for me?"

He smirks and slips into Limbo. Half a second later, all three legacies on the bed wake in a blind panic. Everett shouts as spikes of ice bloom around him, Baelfire falls off the bed, and Silas's red magic flares through the room, crashing into one of the walls and knocking off the clock.

When Crypt reappears with a wicked smile, I give him a sardonic look. "I meant *nicely*."

"That was me being nice."

"Fuck you," Baelfire groans, throwing a pillow at the Nightmare Prince.

Twenty minutes later, I'm dressed and sitting at the kitchen table while Everett and Silas take showers. Crypt sits across from me with wet hair and not one stitch of clothing on as he twirls Pierce around on the table where I set it earlier. The swirling markings on his arms, sculpted chest, and neck are mesmerizing, and I find myself staring again at his nipple piercing.

That had been *very* useful in working him up into a frenzy last night.

Baelfire, who showered with me and failed epically at keeping his hands to himself—not that I minded getting the life fingered out of me while he begged me to come for him—sets a bowl of mushy something in front of me with an unhappy sigh.

"It's just oatmeal. Basically adult baby food. You're going to fucking hate this shit, but we've run out of all other food here. The university stores are closed, and we don't have time to go to the dining hall. But I swear that as soon as the Immortal Quintet lifts the wards, I'm going to Halfton and buying you a shit ton of different ice cream flavors. Any flavor you want, Hellion—especially anything you'll want to lick off my body," he winks.

I tip my head. "Hellion? What happened to Raincloud?"

"You're a hellion in the sheets, so it's what I'm calling you now," he grins, sitting beside me.

Silas sits at the head of the table, and Everett joins us. We're all an odd mix of extremely satisfied from our early morning shenanigans and nervous about what today holds.

I notice that Everett's subtle, compulsive habit of fixing his clothing is far worse than usual this morning. He's not looking at me again. Last night, he was incredibly sweet, but he never fucked me. He seemed to enjoy watching and kissing, aside from when I demanded to suck his cock.

Was he so hesitant to join because he's still wary of his curse, or was it something else?

Silas is stirring his food around with a heavy frown. He's quieter today, and when I see the flash of guilty misery cross his face, I know he's still beating himself up over his curse getting the better of him yesterday. I'll have to reassure him later, yet again, that I'm perfectly fine.

Everett glances at the front door with a huff. "Faculty members are supposed to drop off the standard combat uniforms for each quintet to wear into the test today. They're running late."

They seem to be getting more and more on edge, so I decide to change the subject and glance at Crypt. "I know you eat dreams, but I've seen other incubi eat normal food."

"They do, but I've got more monster in me than most."

"So you don't eat, or you can't eat?"

"I can and I have eaten your pretty cunt," he smirks. Then he surprises me by reaching out to dip his finger in Everett's oatmeal, licking the food from his finger. "Mortal food is tasteless and offers no nutrition, but I can eat it if the fancy strikes me."

Everett looks revolted as he pushes his bowl away. "I fucking hate you."

"Yet you didn't hate watching me spread Maven's legs for Baelfire to take her last night."

Heat suffuses my neck and cheeks.

Baelfire grins. "Nope, Snowflake liked that. We all did. Especially our little Hellion. She just *loves* canoodling with all of us."

Oh, my fucking gods. "New rule. No sex talk for the rest of today. We can't afford to be distracted."

"She's right," Silas sighs, rubbing his temples. He looks much better after the last couple of nights of sleep, but I've seen how severe his curse is getting now, and I know he's just trying not to show how much the voices in his head are bothering him. "We need to have a strategy."

"How can we strategize when we have no idea what First Placement will be like under the rule of those immortal motherfuckers?" Bael asks, making a face at his own oatmeal.

I'm not sure why he hates it so much. It's basically what I ate my entire life until the last couple of months.

I turn to Everett and Crypt. "What was First Placement like when you were here before?"

"Hellish," Everett grumbles. "Unmatched legacies fought to the death. But the quintets had a different test, so I have no idea what it'll be like today. Even the faculty hasn't been let in on the Immortal Quintet's plans for today, only their hirelings."

"I skipped mine," Crypt shrugged. "Seemed boring."

Silas squints. "Now that you mention it...did you ever officially graduate Everbound?"

"I attended very few classes and spent my time tormenting instructors," the Nightmare Prince grins. "They gave me official legacy documentation anyway because the Legacy Council didn't want their bounty hunters chasing someone they knew would be a perpetual drain on their resources."

Why am I not surprised?

The more I learn about Crypt's past, the clearer it becomes that he's never given a fuck about anything. Since he's already sharing, I decide to ask something I've wondered about ever since hearing all the rumors about him.

"All right. I'm finally going to ask," I say, setting down my spoon. "Why the fuck is your name Crypt?"

"Don't!" Baelfire's exclamation startles me, and he shakes his head in warning, his golden eyes comedically wide. "Do yourself a favor and don't fucking ask that, Boo."

I scowl at him over that nickname, but Crypt tips his head. "If you don't like it, I'll change it, darling. We wouldn't want you cringing every time you cry my name in pleasure, now would we?"

Silas snorts, and Everett rolls his eyes so hard I'm sure it hurts.

I take another bite of oatmeal. "It was a simple question."

"I was named after where I was conceived."

Oh. Shit.

"Not this again," Baelfire grimaces. He turns to me. "I asked him this question when I was five. *Five*. And five-year-olds don't need to fucking hear this kind of story, but he didn't leave out *any* details."

"It's not my fault they were explicit when they told me about it. I merely passed it on the way I heard it," the Nightmare Prince shrugs nonchalantly. "Anyway, Somnus—"

Baelfire holds up a hand. "Shut up before I puke. Here's the *highly* edited short version, Hellion. Crypt's jackass father has a thing for not-very-alive people, okay? He thought this one succubus chick was dead in a crypt when, really, she was just super passed out from crying over her newly deceased husband. She woke up later, and *bam*, preggers—and nine months later, Somnus got in hot water when a really fucked up stork dropped Crypt into the Immortal Quintet's lap and everyone found out he was running around doing...*that*. Big scandal. Extremely gross and not at all PG-rated. Got it?"

The story isn't funny, but the way Baelfire looks at me like he's silently begging me not to ask any follow-up questions makes me laugh. Crypt grins at my amusement and winks at me.

A moment later, faculty members knock on our door and drop off the official combat uniforms Everett mentioned. They look similar to soldier's uniforms, only since we're in a quintet, they're color coded. Everett's uniform is light gray, Baelfire's is a burnt orange, Silas's is a forest green, and Crypt's is maroon. Each uniform has its House emblem embroidered on one shoulder, underneath a number I'm sure will appear under the Legacy Council's records reflecting our names.

My uniform is green, too. Keepers aren't specially marked in combat to avoid drawing attention to them. But when I walk out in my uniform and combat boots, all four of my matches stare at me.

"Don't take this the wrong way, but it's honestly kind of...weird to see you in a color," Everett ventures.

I couldn't agree more.

"But you're hot as fuck in that," Baelfire adds with a smile. "You look ready to kick ass."

Probably because I am. I made the bronzeblend potion one day ago using the rest of my magic reserves. It's now tucked securely into one of my pockets in case I get a chance to get Somnus DeLune alone today. Pierce is concealed in one of my boots, so I'm prepared even if they don't allow us other weapons today.

During First Placement, I'll certainly have to kill to defend my quintet. Which means I'll have plenty of fuel to slowly pick off the rest of the Immortal Quintet.

"Kenzie was right," I muse, studying the four of them. "Men are sexy in uniforms."

Silas's scarlet gaze grows sinful, and he steps up to kiss my temple, whispering, "Don't tempt me right now, *sangfluir*. I know Baelfire got to play with you in the shower, and I'm trying to behave so you'll let me have my turn next."

Crypt uses Limbo to appear suddenly at my back, hands on my hips as he tuts softly. "Weren't you paying attention to her dream last night, Crane? She doesn't want turns. She wants to take all of us at once."

Gods. I almost forgot about that dream. Baelfire underneath me, Silas behind me, Everett down my throat while I stroked Crypt's cock and toyed with his piercings until he came all over me…

My thighs clench. Damn it. Who cares about being sore when they're all so fucking attractive?

Baelfire growls. "I smell that, Mayflower. And I'm not about to let you go into combat smelling like that pretty pussy of yours needs another good, long fucking."

Everett surprises me by striding over and scooping me up, talking over his shoulder to the others as he marches toward my room. "The lizard's right, for once. Our keeper needs us. Come on."

Yes, please.

Now that my body is starting to accept that their touch is safe, how the hell am I supposed to pry myself off of them all the time? Even though I should point out that we need to get going, I just close my eyes and enjoy Everett's cool lips dancing along my jaw as he carries me toward my room.

But we're all stopped cold in our tracks when someone bangs loudly on our front door. Baelfire growls and storms toward it, his inner dragon's moodiness on full display.

"Whoever this is, I'm going to fucking kill them for interrupting."

It's Mr. Gibbons, who is oblivious to the glares he's getting from the rest of my quintet as he explains that he wanted to make sure his *favorite* quintet got to the assembly on time since it's starting very soon. It's a very effective mood killer.

Everett sets me down, grumbling unhappily about it as we follow the mage through the halls of Everbound. Surprisingly, he leads us outside to the training fields where I see that a makeshift stage has been set up in the snow-dusted grass near the dark, misty forest. Lined up in clean rows in front of the stage are formations of quintets, all dressed in their new combat attire. Some are shivering since the uniforms didn't come with jackets and winter is finally starting to deepen.

Onstage, Iker Del Mar and Natalya Genovese stand observing the final legacies trickle onto the field. I can feel their immortal gazes burning into us—into *me*—as we line up behind another relatively highly-ranked quintet. Crypt and Everett flank my sides, with Baelfire standing in front and Silas behind me. It's standard for quintets to stand at attention like this, with their keepers central to the group.

I can feel how tense every legacy here is. It's not just the matched legacies emphasizing in combat who are lined up, so I can't help searching for Kenzie's quintet in the crowd. I finally spot her standing near the front, fidgeting nervously while Dirk comforts a terrified-looking Vivienne. Luka glares at everyone nearby as if he expects foul play during the assembly.

One of the hired legacy minions joins Iker and Natalya onstage, his hand glowing with a simple megaphonic charm. When Natalya speaks, her bell-like voice carries easily over us legacies standing on the snowy field.

"Welcome to First Placement. Many of you will die today."

If she wasn't one of my targets and a selfish monster, I would like her more for leading with that. As it is, her words clearly strike fear into the hearts of the legacies standing around me. Some start crying quietly, while others crack their knuckles or move closer to their keepers. It's obvious which legacies have been practicing combat and which picked other emphases.

As if she can sense that I have no heart for her to strike fear into, Natalya's blue gaze flicks to me. Her eyes begin to glow. Instinctively, I empty my head of anything she could possibly find incriminating or suspicious. Amadeus knew each of the Immortal Quintet's abilities and trained me extensively against psychic probing.

Silas slips something warm into my pocket, and I glance up at him.

"Keeps her out," he mutters quietly.

If any one of us needs help controlling their thoughts, it's not me. I take the talisman and slip it into Baelfire's pocket. He just shakes his head and winks at me.

"Don't worry, baby. I've been thinking about last night on repeat so if that bitch tries to look into my head, all she's getting from me is an endless loop of you coming."

Well. That's infinitely horrifying.

"Just keep it," I mumble, shivering from the cold, which only seems to be getting worse. My dragon shifter automatically steps closer to share his excessive warmth while Everett moves away from me with a grimace.

"Sorry, Oakley. I'm shit at controlling it when I'm nervous."

I frown. How can he struggle with his element so badly after so much training? Didn't he say he even had private combat tutors?

Whatever Natalya was looking for, she obviously didn't get because she pouts and turns to whisper something to Del Mar. While they're conversing, I look for Somnus or Engela near the stage, but they're nowhere to be found.

Finally, Del Mar takes over, his voice booming over the gathered legacies while his forked tongue flicks out occasionally. "We decided to keep First Placement exceedingly simple this year. It is a test of survival. If you escape the maze alive within one hour, you pass. If you fall prey to one of the many shadow fiends on the prowl inside, you die a failure, as weak legacies ought to. Foul play is expected and encouraged. Weapons are welcome, and many may be found as prizes inside the maze. May the gods favor you, or may you die as fate always intended."

Touching.

With that, the faculty members gathered on one side of the stage begin ushering students toward the edge of Everbound Forest. Transportation spells are set up to take us into First Placement. I wince when Kenzie and her quintet step through the tree line and vanish.

Please make it out of there.

If we're not too busy fending for our own lives, perhaps I'll try to track them down. I'm not much for allies, and I won't care much if Luka gets staked, but I don't want to lose Kenzie.

"This is going to be brutal," Everett sighs.

Silas nods as we follow the crowd of uniforms, sticking close together. "Everyone guard Maven."

"No shit," Baelfire huffs. "I just want this fucking collar off. Whatever is in there, I could take it down if I could fucking shift."

"Wait until I make a few kills," I murmur. "Then I can get your collar off."

They all glance at me like they want more explanation, but I'm not about to expound on that when other legacies might overhear. Besides, they should have been paying attention to Professor Crowley's lecture on revenants and the kind of magic I can use. It's nothing but destructive, which means I can shatter powerful spells easily as long as I have enough fuel.

And I'm confident I'm about to get a *lot* of fuel in there.

The thought makes me smile, which makes Everett sigh.

"Please don't tell me you're actually looking forward to this, Oakley."

"Very much." Legacies vanish in droves ahead of us, off into whatever fun awaits. But as we get nearer to the forest's edge, a new concern blooms in my head, and I frown. "If I lose control in there and begin berserking, you four need to abandon me and run."

Crypt snorts. "Good one, love."

"I'm serious. In that state, I have no idea if I'll be a danger to you—"

"There will be plenty of targets in there," Silas says quietly, his crimson eyes darting all over the place as if the voices in his head are working him up even more. "So if that happens, we'll stay out of the way and watch you gleefully slaughter our opponents once again. But we're not leaving you, *sangfluir*. I'm insulted you would even suggest it."

I scowl. "Fine. But if I kill any of you, I'm going to…"

Huh. What's a good threat for after death?

I don't get to think of one because it's finally our time to step into Everbound Forest, and the transportation magic sweeps us into First Placement.

33

SILAS

THE MAZE IS FILLED with the echoes of screams.

As soon as the transportation magic fades, we find ourselves inside a massive stone hallway, the top of which is left open to the dark, cloudy winter sky that lightly scatters swirling snowflakes from above. The hallway is so wide that if we all stood side by side with extended arms, we would barely bridge the length.

"This must have taken their minions days to build with magic," Everett mutters, moving to stand protectively behind Maven as we all take in our surroundings.

Vibrant red magic flares around my hands when we hear a scream around one of the nearby corners, but Maven shakes her head.

"Wait. That wasn't from a shadow fiend."

Everett frowns, his glacial eyes sweeping over the empty maze hall we're standing in. "How can you tell?"

"I can sense them. That was probably a rival quintet."

A rival quintet to finish the job for us, one of the voices in my head coos.

One to slit the pretty revenant's throat.

"Shut the fuck up," I grit.

Maven is also analyzing our surroundings. "Fine, I will. Gods."

Damn it. "I wasn't talking to you, it was—"

I'm interrupted when an incomplete group of matched legacies round the corner and charge toward us. Some of them are bleeding heavily, but their keeper refuses to back down even after she sees who they're up against.

Soon, we're locked in combat—only this time, Maven's personal training has paid off because our quintet works together far more smoothly.

We've knocked out a siren, and things are going well until the remaining two get too close to Maven. As soon as they do, Crypt's markings light up, and suddenly, the rival legacies turn on each other, brandishing fangs and magic. The rest of us watch in surprise as they tear into each other, and soon enough, they're both dead.

Maven tips her head, looking far more curious than alarmed. "What was that?"

"Mania," Crypt shrugs. "It's useless against shadow fiends or monsters and does little against powerful legacies, but it's quite fun whenever weaker legacies are in question."

"I can see that." Then she turns her face to the sky, shielding her eyes from the falling snow. "If you can fly in Limbo, can you get above the maze to look for a way out?"

The incubus tries Maven's idea but returns a moment later, explaining that they have magic wards in Limbo to keep all incubi within the maze. He's barely had time to report back before a fucking wendigo rounds the corner, its howl splitting the air when it sees us.

I've only seen wendigos in pictures. For a moment, I gawk at how intimidating they are in real life. This malevolent, insatiable monster has a huge, skeletal wolf body, bony human-like arms and legs, and a ram's skull for a head with the horns twisted at odd angles. Its eyes glow green as it launches toward us, snarling.

Turn and run like the coward you are, a voice in my head whispers.

No, fight! Cranes do not run, my father's voice snarls. *Fight and die. Do not shame our family even more than you already—*

"I said *shut up*," I snarl, pricking my finger to draw from the magic in my blood.

Everett throws up an ice shield while I send a wave of malicious magic toward our fiendish foe. It howls in pain but leaps over the thick ice shield, whirling to bare its sharp teeth. Bloodied saliva drips steadily from its hideous snout.

As Everett and I continue to fend off the wendigo, Maven shouts a warning that more shadow fiends are coming. We barely have a moment to process that before a group of vile-smelling, moldering Undead are suddenly upon us, launching themselves with gaping jaws and jagged teeth. Pain flares in my shoulder as one of the fiends digs its broken, rotting teeth into my shoulder.

Before I can even cry out, Maven beheads it with her dagger.

She moves with blinding speed, and as Everett manages to trap the wendigo in an impressively strong cage made of ice, Baelfire and I gawk as we watch Maven in her element. With perfected agility, she slashes, kicks, snaps necks, and leaves the ground littered with the remains of our Undead enemies.

Crypt is enjoying himself, too. He pulls a godsdamned *sword* out of Limbo and uses it to cut through several of the Undead horde.

When they're all dead on the ground, with nothing remaining but twitching limbs and severed body parts, Baelfire grimaces. "Those things are fucking nasty."

I glance at Maven with an inkling of suspicion. "You killed those all easily."

"It was fun."

Still…

"That time when we all sparred you at once. You weren't even giving it a real shot, were you? You were taking it easy on us."

She shrugs almost sheepishly. "Sue me. It was just fucking adorable that you all wanted to fight me at once."

Baelfire lights up, turning to Maven. "Hey, if you killed a lot of them, does that mean you can break me out of this collar so I won't be a fucking deadweight?"

"Unfortunately, no," she sighs, kicking aside a twitching leg. "I can only wield life forces. The Undead have already died once, and they're only kept alive by necromancy, so they're useless to me. Aside from them being fun to take out," she adds.

"Agreed," Crypt grins.

"Where did you get that thing?" Everett frowns at the gleaming sword in the incubus's hands as he seals the wendigo's cage. The creature is trapped in a solid block of ice, still howling and clawing to get out.

"This? I've always got it with me. It's enchanted to be both a sword and a lighter, whichever I need more."

We follow Maven's lead further into the maze. She pauses occasionally to determine whether she senses shadow fiends before proceeding down each new path. Screams still resound throughout the sprawling maze, and various roars and inhuman shrieks join the chorus now and then.

It's positively spine-tingling, which is probably why my morbid little blood blossom is smiling to herself as we walk.

Baelfire huffs. "Damn. Where did you get a weapon like that, Stalker Boy?"

"I stole it from Melvolin when I was eight."

Everett snorts. "Melvolin Hearst was an asshole to all of the faculty whenever he was around, including me, so knowing that almost makes me like you."

Crypt gags. "Never say that to me again, Frost."

The screams of legacies punctuate the air nearby, and we all step into formation around Maven as another group of legacies rushes toward us. No—I realize it's several quintets, and they're not running toward us but away from something else. They pass by, shouting and darting in different directions to scatter away from whatever horror is slowly approaching.

We're all confused, but then a strangely lyrical, otherworldly screech fills the air. Maven tenses, her eyes widening slightly.

"A harbinger," she breathes. "Fuck."

I frown. "A what?"

She grabs Crypt's and Everett's hands, turning to lead us in the opposite direction of the unfamiliar shadow fiend. She mutters something under her breath that I don't catch—but it must piss Baelfire off because he grabs her arm to stop her with a growl.

"Hell, no. You are *not* going after that motherfucker alone."

"Try and stop me," she snaps back.

Let her go.

This is how we'll get rid of her, another voice in my head agrees.

Death to the revenant.

I shake my head hard to clear the aggravating echoes. "Why the hell would you want to fight it alone? What is a harbinger?"

In all my studies of monsters and fiends, I've never heard of it, and clearly, neither have the others. But the way Maven's gaze darkens as she looks behind me, toying with her adamantine dagger, makes it clear she's come across this kind of fiend before.

"Harbingers are incredibly rare because Amadeus drove them to near extinction. He enjoyed using them in his arena because there was no winning for anyone who fought this creature. Either it kills you, or you die when you kill it." She looks at us seriously. "Anyone who hears a harbinger's song and slays it immediately dies with it. Which means if it attacks any of you and you kill it in self-defense, you'll be dead. I'll take care of it."

What she means sinks in immediately, and I snarl. "Absolutely not. You're not going to fucking sacrifice yourself to take down that thing."

"It's hardly a sacrifice since I'll come back," she rolls her eyes. "I'm literally the only person in this maze who can destroy it and make it out alive."

"Just let someone else kill it so it thins out our potential enemies," I growl, grabbing her hand to pull her away.

Maven snatches her hand back, shaking her head as she glares at me. "What if Kenzie's quintet runs into that thing? They don't know how it works. They would die trying to take it down."

She has that same determined gleam in her eyes that she did when she told us about her promise to free the humans in the Nether. Godsdamn it, why must my keeper be so unfailingly selfless when all I want is to keep her out of harm's way?

"Too bad for them, then," Crypt drawls. "It's not worth having to watch you die again, so let's get on with it, shall we?"

When he, too, makes a move to grasp our keeper's arm, she moves so fast that we're all left blinking in shock when she brutally twists Crypt's arm behind his back and pins him face-first against one of the massive concrete walls with her uncanny revenant strength.

"You all really need to stop trying to fucking manhandle me," she warns darkly. "It's getting on my nerves."

Crypt exhales roughly, resting his forehead against the concrete. "Now isn't an ideal time for you to give me a boner, love."

"Right, because that was obviously her intention just now, you fucking deviant," Everett huffs, repeatedly adjusting the pocket zippers on his uniform. The frost coating his hands has crawled up past his elbows, and I'm fairly certain most of the snow coming down now is his fault. "Oakley, no one needs to kill that thing. Let's just focus on getting the hell out of here."

She grits her teeth before releasing Crypt and adjusting her gloves.

"Fine. I'll leave it be. Let's go this way," she nods down another pathway in the maze.

We obediently move down that pathway as she walks behind us, all of us on high alert as we wait to encounter even more threats. The screams and wailing have reached a fever pitch, echoing around the maze—but abruptly, I realize I don't hear Maven's footsteps behind me anymore. I halt, closing my eyes.

"Gods-fucking damn it," I curse.

Maven adjusted her gloves. That's her tell.

My blood blossom was *lying*.

Yes, she's a liar. Let her die, a voice in my head urges.

Another giggles. *No more keeper*.

Sure enough, when I turn to glare over my shoulder, our keeper is nowhere to be seen. Baelfire notices, too, and halts, ignoring how Everett swears when he walks smack into the back of the hulking dragon shifter.

"Wait, what the fuck? Where's Maven?" Bael demands.

"She went to take down the godsdamned harbinger," I seethe, turning to run back in the direction we just came from.

Moments later, Baelfire, Crypt, Everett, and I come to a screeching stop and shout in alarm when we see Maven race up the arm of a massive, ghostly white, disgustingly spider-like creature. She uses her momentum to leap into the air, and a moment later, the harbinger's fanged mouth closes around her.

At once, the voices in my head burst into applause and cheers of approval. I cry out at the deafening commotion, covering my ringing ears and staggering.

It's difficult to perceive much outside of my damned curse. Still, I see Everett drop to his knees, ice spreading everywhere he touches the ground. He chokes out a prayer to Arati, goddess of battles, that Maven will still somehow win. Baelfire roars, sounding like his inner dragon as he claws at his collar and races forward.

Crypt vanishes and reappears a second later on the top of the massive, terrifying shadow fiend. His face is a mask of fury as he lifts his sword, ready to drive it through the creature's skull in violent vengeance—

But just as he does, it shrieks horrifically, and Maven's blade pierces it from the inside out, slashing a gaping hole across its bulbous stomach.

The harbinger screeches one more time before slumping to the ground, its legs twitching and blackening as foam fills its fanged mouth. Baelfire gasps and catches Maven just in time as she falls out of the belly of the terrifying monster, its dark innards gushing around her.

"Maven!" I shout, hurrying to her side.

Her skin is red and steaming from stomach acid, her arms and legs are cut up, and I watch in horror as her eyes white out precisely at the same time the harbinger goes still. She goes slack in Baelfire's arms. He chokes, muscles in his neck bulging while his eyes shift to those of a dragon's. Crypt rolls away from the dead creature, dropping to his knees beside Maven.

"She'll come back. Her deaths don't stick," he rasps, but the frantic terror on the Nightmare Prince's face tells me his thoughts are spiraling in the same direction mine are.

What if this is an unknown way in which revenants can be killed permanently? What if she doesn't wake up? What if…gods above, what if I just lost my keeper?

The voices in my head cheer harder. The ringing in my ears increases until I grip the sides of my head, gritting my teeth against the darkness creeping at the edges of my vision. The fact that I can't even fucking think straight in a moment like this curdles my gut.

But then I see that Maven's skin is healing. Any sign of damage disappears, and she finally jolts awake, catching her breath as she frowns up at us.

"Did someone just scream? What's going on?"

Baelfire's head drops forward with relief. "Oh my fucking gods. Maven. You can't do that to me, baby. Please don't ever fucking do that again."

"So dramatic," she grumbles. "I'm clearly fine, so let's…"

Her gaze latches onto Crypt's sword, barely protruding from the harbinger's head since he didn't have time to properly stab it. Her face darkens with wrath. She's on her feet in a split second, gripping Crypt by the front of his leather jacket. Her voice is deadly.

"What the *fuck* were you thinking? If I hadn't gutted it in time, it would have killed you!"

"It *ate* you," he snaps back, parts of his hair drifting aimlessly as his anger seeps into the mortal world. I've never seen Crypt express much emotion over the years, aside from unpredictable anger and taunting—but now he looks both livid and tormented. "How the fucking hell could you think I would just stand by, waiting on nothing but a godsdamned prayer for you to emerge? I told you not to make me watch you fucking die again!"

"And I told *you*, death is part of my nature," she seethes, more upset than I've ever seen her. "I'm the fucking scourge, so I can walk it off, but I swear, the next time you put yourself in danger for no fucking reason when I *explicitly* told you—"

A laugh rings out over us, and we all stiffen. "My, my. Trouble in paradise, whoreson?"

Somnus DeLune strides into this portion of the maze with Engela Zuma and two dozen powerful-looking hired legacies at their side. His lips turn up cruelly when he sees the dead harbinger, and then he looks meaningfully back at Maven, and I tense.

He knows, a voice in my head taunts. *He was watching. They were all watching.*

Here comes her reckoning. Run and save yourself.

My eye twitches as Somnus sneers at Maven, who releases Crypt with a clenched jaw.

"So. The prophesied *telum* truly has left the Nether. Good old Amadeus sent a revenant after us, did he? Ridiculous. How he could ever think you could be a match for us is beyond me," the immortal scoffs, approaching painfully slowly. "Though I must say, it is poetically fitting that this worthless bastard should wind up with a homely bitch from hell."

We're all tensed, but none of us move as the experienced hirelings surround us, standing at the ready. Engela Zuma makes a motion with her hand, and all the exits are suddenly blocked off with stone.

They have the *telum* trapped.

But Maven doesn't look nervous. In fact, she's glaring back at Somnus so murderously that some of the hired legacies standing behind him start to look nervous.

"Apologize," she says in a flat voice.

He scoffs. "As if I would ever apologize to a reven—"

"Not to me. To Crypt."

Crypt wipes some of the harbinger's black blood off his face. "Darling, I don't want his apology. I want his head rolling on the ground."

"You'll get both."

Somnus's nostrils flare with rage, and he motions at his hirelings and Engela. "Enough of this. Kill them all, but I'll be the one to end this arrogant little cunt."

Things happen all at once after that. While Everett launches spikes of ice at the nearest hirelings and I prepare a powerful spell to hopefully wind Engela, Crypt launches toward his father. But Maven...reaches up and grabs onto Baelfire's collar.

Right. Since she killed the harbinger, her magic now has fuel.

The collar crumbles in a flare of smoke-like black tendrils, and Baelfire darts into the midst of the hirelings just before he shifts for the first time in days. Blinding royal blue fire explodes around him, and the rival legacies shout in alarm. Some of them summon shields of fire or magic or manage to leap out of the way, but others aren't so lucky. Others begin hurling countless deadly attacks at the massive beast, but his scales take most of the brunt as he roars and snaps at our foes.

I deflect a deadly hex from one of the hired casters and prick another of my fingers to send a devastating attack toward Engela. A solid slab of stone shoots up from the ground, shielding her from my magic, but it rebounds and hits another one of their hired hands.

Where is your precious little keeper, little Crane? a voice in my head mocks.

I do a double-take. Damn it. Where *is* Maven? This fight has dissolved into deadly chaos, and I startle when I see Crypt unconscious on the ground, his own sword impaled through his right shoulder as a severe injury to his head heals slowly.

When did that happen?

Another attack spell careens toward me, but I counter it in time. Flashes of deadly light and smoke from Baelfire's dragon fill this section of the maze. Meanwhile, Everett is fighting off a trio of vicious wolf shifters, bright flares of his white magic creating a haunting glow to the smoke filling the air.

These hired legacies are powerful and have more experience than we do. I roll out of the way of a fire elemental's attack before throwing out enough magical attacks to give myself cover as I strain to see where Maven could be.

From the corner of my eye, I finally see Maven reappear—hanging onto fucking Somnus DeLune's back as she wrestles him into a headlock. With a start, I realize that he's covered in thousands of tiny, bleeding piercings that look extremely painful. She must have used her bronzeblend spell already, but…how is she surviving when he took her in and out of Limbo?

"Get *off!*" the immortal roars, slamming his head back into Maven's jaw.

I hear a crack, but she just grunts in pain and tightens her hold.

I can sense the angry surge of his incubus powers all the way from where I'm standing. Several hirelings fighting closer to him drop to the ground in a deep sleep as they're affected—but a flare of Maven's dark magic shatters through his power. She twists hard to one side, using her momentum to slam the immortal into the ground.

Somnus cries out. He pulls an obsidian dagger from his waist and tries to jam it back into her side, but she twists out of the way, grapples his hand, and uses it to plunge the blade into his back instead.

Somnus howls. "You fucking cunt! Zuma! Help me!"

Baelfire's dragon roars in pain, the sound deafening, and I look up just in time to see Engela drive a thick spike of rock up through the beast's stomach. Alarm courses through me—shifters are hardy but not invincible. That could be fatal if he doesn't heal quickly. I send another blast of magic toward Engela to drive her away from my quintet member.

She again blocks it with stone. But then, as if in slow motion, I see her look over at where Maven now has Somnus flat on his back, screaming in pain as her magic courses through him, dark shadows writhing around both of them.

"Zuma! *Now!*" he screeches. He manages to finally drive his obsidian dagger into Maven's thigh. She barely reacts, as if she's entranced by her dark magic, eager for his death.

The immortal earth elemental has no expression. She waves her hand, and one of the other pathways of the maze opens up again—and then Engela Zuma simply walks out of the fight unscathed without a single look over her shoulder at her dying quintet member.

I don't have time to linger on how strange that is. Instead, I race toward Baelfire, who has shifted back into his human form and is wrestling with another shifter despite the gaping wound still trying to mend itself on his stomach.

As I run to him, a sharp cry from Somnus draws my attention. I dodge another magic attack and see Maven carving the immortal up with her adamantine blade. Neither of his arms seems to work.

One moment, he's cursing her out and promising her an agonizingly slow death—but then she pulls something out of her pocket. I realize it's the totem Crypt left her, and she sets it on Somnus's chest.

And when Somnus sees that, his threats turn to pleas for his life. He begs for mercy, screaming and thrashing. His power lashes out again, and the caster launching another attack at me drops into a dead sleep.

But Maven's dark magic once again deflects his attempt to stop her. I watch her whisper something to the immortal right before she drives her adamantine dagger through his heart—and, simultaneously, through the totem.

He goes still immediately.

Gods above. Somnus DeLune is dead.

A small, practical part of me was dubious about Maven's knowledge and capability of bringing down the untouchable, centuries-old monsters who have been tyrannizing legacies, but now...

My awe is cut short. Everett cries out, and I whirl to see that he's pinned by the only wolf shifter remaining. It's clawed up his entire chest and is biting one of his arms, trying to rip it off. He's covered in blood as he blasts the animal away with ice using his other arm, but then he goes slack.

Damn it. *Damn it.*

They're all injured. Which one do I try to heal first? Who needs it the most? My head is pounding, and the ringing in my ears isn't going away.

Let them die.
They were going to betray you anyway.
Their blood will free you, little Crane.

"Silas!"

Maven's voice barely cuts through the encroaching madness, and when I look at her through the smoke and snow, the ringing in my ears softens ever so slightly. For a moment, I'm desperate to make out what she's shouting at me to do. She's motioning toward Everett, then toward Baelfire, and then—

An elemental hireling tackles her and bursts into flames.

My keeper's agonized scream pierces through everything in my head, shattering through my curse. My world is nothing but sharp, cold hysteria as I race toward her, throwing out spells to kill the elemental and extinguish the raging fire. Somewhere in the background, I can hear Baelfire roaring as a dragon again, and I know the fight is raging on, even if Crypt and Everett are still down. I have no idea whether we're winning or losing right now.

But I don't care. Because when my magic douses the fire, and I drop to my knees beside Maven, she's burnt almost beyond recognition.

She's not breathing.

She's…going to die.

And if she dies this way, I'm going to lose her for good.

Without thinking, I begin chanting a healing incantation, drawing from the blood on my shoulder where the Undead bit me earlier. Red light glows around me, but nothing happens to Maven's motionless, smoking body.

Let her go, a voice in my head whispers.

You're useless to her anyway, my father's voice whispers.

She's dying, and your blood magic can't heal her. Useless boy.

My hands tremble, and I can't breathe as I crouch over her, my tears splashing and sizzling against her charred skin. For once, the voices are right. If my magic can't save her…then what is the point of it? Was I always meant to fail my keeper this way?

No. I refuse to lose her. If my blood magic can't help Maven, then it needs to change.

I need to change.

My heart thunders as my entire world narrows in on this moment. In the Garnet Wizard's library, there were many books forbidden to the rest of the world. But under his tutelage, no magical knowledge was off-limits to me. He was proud of my unparalleled gift for remembering countless spells, charms, hexes, incantations…

And amid those ancient tomes, I found spell books written in the language of the Nether, outlining the path to wielding death magic—the initiation, the sacrifice, the price.

I memorized those spells, too.

Which is why, when the blood magic fades around my fingertips, I squeeze my eyes shut and begin uttering the forbidden words. They taste acrid on my tongue, and a cold, greedy, malicious energy sweeps through me. It clings onto my existing magic, twisting it and reshaping everything I've ever learned. Everything I've ever been.

It feels as if I'm being consumed alive.

But this time, when I chant the words of a healing ritual, dark magic surges through the air and wraps around Maven. It seeps into her body, and her skin begins to heal. Her chest rises and falls with new breath.

She'll survive. Thank the fucking gods.

But the moment I finish uttering the powerful words, I collapse beside her. The world blurs around me as the voices in my head whisper nothing but truths for once.

You've lost it.

Only a fraction of those who attempt to take up dark magic survive the transition.

Was she really worth losing yourself, you useless boy?

"Yes," I whisper, closing my eyes and letting the madness have me.

If I survive this, I'll be a necromancer.

If I die, I die saving my blood blossom.

Either way, I regret nothing.

34

MAVEN

It's a shame I didn't kill Hearst. If I had, I would have already known the incomparable surge of power that comes from killing off a member of the Immortal Quintet.

That heady buzz is humming in my veins, so rich and promising in its destructive capabilities that it almost lulls me to sleep. I'm groggy, and for some reason, I feel like I should be in a shit ton of pain.

But I'm not.

Why am I not?

My skin is tingling, not in a pleasant way, but it's not bad either. Weird. This is the same sensation I used to experience whenever Amadeus would have his necromancers patch me up instead of simply letting me expire and come back. Did I somehow manage to heal myself after Somnus hurt me?

No, wait. Somnus didn't hurt me.

It was fire.

Oh, fuck. Am I truly dead this time? Did I fail Lillian and the humans in the Nether?

But no. Even if I'm struggling to open my eyes, the air is still thick with smoke and the titillating scent of battle. Someone shouts nearby, and I hear a dragon growling—*my* dragon. Is he okay? Are any of them hurt?

Warm hands brush against my face, and someone lets out a breath of relief. Soft lips brush against my forehead.

"Thank the gods. I can sense you're awake, love. Open those beautiful eyes for me."

I do, and then I squint. "You're covered in blood."

"Most of us are. But not to worry, you look good as new," Crypt smiles, but it's weak. He looks exhausted.

Despite how tired he sounds, I realize he's scooped me up off the ground, and we're leaving the maze. My eyes flutter as I try to keep up with our surroundings. Why the fuck am I so out of it? How did I survive that fire? It hurt like hell, and then everything went black. I thought I was finally slipping away for good, but now...

I focus on Crypt again. "What do you mean, good as new?"

"Silas was finally useful. I'll have to thank him, for once."

Crypt...thanking Silas? It's like I woke up in an alternate universe. What happened?

I stare at the beautiful swirling markings on Crypt's neck. "I killed your father."

"I know, darling. I left his corpse in Limbo for the wisps."

Oh. Then I frown, noticing how silent it's become. We're out of the maze now, and the incubus's boots crunch across the dead grass and snow of the training fields outside of Everbound Forest. Something gleams in the sky overhead, and I hear Baelfire's roar distantly.

"Is First Placement over?"

He hums. "Let's assume so. Many other legacies are still trying to get out, but I suspect the Immortal Quintet is long gone, along with all the wards. That's how we got out so quickly—I was able to fly up and finally see the way out. I know too well how the Immortal Quintet works. If Engela left the fight and told the other two about you winning against Somnus, they'll be trying to get as far away from you as possible."

Damn. Hunting down moving targets will be a pain in the ass.

But the more important thing to worry about is...

"Are any of you hurt?"

Crypt's violet gaze flicks to mine and back up as he steps into Everbound Castle. It's still eerily silent, as if we've left one storm and are in silence before another approaches.

"I won't lie to you, love. We're all in poor shape. Your professor and your fae are unresponsive. Baelfire flew them back to the castle to get them to the apartment faster."

Oh, my gods.

I push at Crypt's arm, and he sets me down on my feet with a soft sigh. That's when I realize I'm stark fucking naked—but with the way my throat is seizing painfully at the idea of any of my matches being hurt, I don't care if anyone else sees me naked.

Crypt shrugs out of his bloodied, charred leather jacket and wraps it around me. He doesn't let go of my arm, and we end up supporting each other as we hurry back to the quintet apartment. In the halls, we pass a few whispering faculty members huddled off to the side of the hall, wide-eyed as they watch us.

Then we pass Pia, the prophetess. She's staring sagely out a tall stained-glass window, and I halt in my tracks.

"You. You can heal people even when they can't be healed."

Her white-cloaked head tips slightly. "Everyone can heal, my fearless one."

If she's trying to be profound, I don't give a fuck. "Come with me."

"What's the magic word?" she asks softly.

Seriously? She wants a fucking *please* when my quintet member's lives are at stake? I'm far too emotional and on edge at the moment, not to mention brimming with fresh power from such a big kill. Lucky for this prophetess, I'm really fucking good at composing myself.

Unfortunately, I'm not so good at stopping myself from using my *I'm going to kill you* voice right now.

"My bad," I smile dangerously. "Let me try that again. Come with me, *now.*"

I expect her to be annoyed, but the prophetess laughs softly.

"I should have known you would take after her," she murmurs.

...What?

No. Whatever cryptic shit she's trying to pull, I still don't give a fuck. I'm relieved she finally follows Crypt and me until we reach the quintet apartment.

As soon as we get inside, panic claws at my insides. Baelfire is slumped in one of the dining room chairs, his skin beaded with sweat as he wraps bandages around a still-healing injury on his midsection. Everett is a bloody mess on the kitchen floor, and Silas—

"Where's Silas?" I ask thickly as Pia crouches and begins healing Everett.

Baelfire gives up wrapping himself and stands to wrap me in a hug. He inhales by my neck as if my scent is all he needs for a moment. "In your room. He's still breathing, but..."

I take over wrapping his injury, blinking through the moisture in my eyes, desperate to keep anyone else from seeing them. Crypt has also sat in one of the dining room chairs, his forehead on the table. He needs to feed to recuperate—especially if all that blood is his.

"But?" I ask Baelfire.

"Um...what does it mean when a caster's fingertips turn black?"

I freeze. "What?"

Bael must be too tired to stand anymore because he lowers himself back into the chair, wincing with every movement. "Fuck. I don't know. He has this gods-awful fever, and his fingers are all charred. Maybe he just touched you when you were still..." He swallows hard, his voice breaking as it turns into a whisper. "Still on fire. Oh, fuck. I almost lost you, Maven. Fucking gods, I almost—"

"Don't blaspheme, please," Pia chides quietly, straightening and turning to the dragon shifter. When I see that Everett's chest is no longer a bloody mess and he's now in a deep sleep, I start to feel like I can breathe again.

"Hold still," the prophetess instructs, her hands hovering over Bael's midsection.

Baelfire waits while Pia heals him, but I can't take it anymore. I hurry into my bedroom, and when I see Silas on the bed, I feel like I'm choking.

I can sense it even from here. The change in his magic.

How dare he do this? I might've been fine. If I had died from that fire, I...

Fuck. No, I would have died permanently. He knew that.

I sit on the bed beside Silas, wiping any remaining moisture from my eyes. The light outside is well into the afternoon. Other legacies are still in the maze or dead—I can only pray to the universe that Kenzie and her quintet are all right. And if the Immortal Quintet dropped their wards and ran at the first sign of the *telum*, things are about to get a lot harder.

I'll be hunting them. They'll be hunting me.

It's going to be a viciously bloody mess.

But even that knowledge doesn't cheer me up as I stare at Silas, lying unconscious on the bed. His dark curls are damp with sweat, clinging to his forehead as he fights the fever. His breathing is labored, and his slender fingertips are, in fact, blackened from necromancy.

Pia knocks softly on the door. Despite all the healing, there's not even a spot of blood on her white head-to-toe ensemble. "I can heal him, too."

"But you can't heal the fever," I mutter.

She shakes her white-veiled head. "No. That was his choice."

I watch as she heals Silas. Then she pauses by the door on the way out. "Many of the Immortal Quintet's hired hands escaped with them. Rumors will spread, and it's only a matter of time before bounty hunters and others arrive. Everbound won't be safe for you."

"No shit." Safety is an illusion.

It almost sounds like she's smiling. "Is it? Perhaps you should pray to the gods for their aid."

"Or perhaps I should stick my thumb up my ass and spin around three times while reciting poetry. That's just as likely to help me face what's coming next. The gods forsook me a long time ago."

Pia is quiet for a long moment, then leaves without another word.

Offending a prophetess is pretty damn far down on my list of sins, so I pay her no mind as I continue to stare at Silas.

After a moment, I feel Crypt's presence in the room, but he doesn't leave Limbo. It's as if he's just checking in on me, and then he leaves again—maybe to shower.

"You all right, Boo?" Baelfire murmurs, walking into the room and taking my hand in his. His injuries are gone. He still looks exhausted, and he's still covered in ash, dirt, and black harbinger blood, but he's okay.

When I nod and continue observing Silas, he glances down at the blood fae.

"Silas has never gotten sick. Not even when we were kids."

"He's sick because of the necromancy," I say quietly. "It's a transitory phase. Sort of like turning into a vampire through vampyr venom, only with magic. It's excruciating."

I would know. I felt much of its effects before I learned I had access to necromancy.

Baelfire's eyes flash to mine as he puts two and two together. "You mean...he's becoming a necromancer. For you."

That sets another emotion off in my chest. I swallow, nodding as my vision blurs slightly. Knowing Silas sacrificed his blood magic for me...

"He's such a fucking idiot," I whisper.

"Always has been," Bael sighs, "but I get why he did it this time. Even if he can't use his oh-so-special prodigy magic anymore... you're worth it, Maven. You're worth everything."

He leans over to brush a warm kiss against my forehead, his face softening when he sees the moisture trying to escape my eyes. "I'm gonna go shower all this shit off of me, so you can keep staring at your pointy-eared, sweaty nerd for a bit. But when I get back..."

"We need to decide where to go next. I still have to hunt down the Immortal Quintet."

He snorts. "You just killed Somnus fucking DeLune. I know we'll have to leave Everbound, but you deserve a small break. Wherever we go, we can lay low and take time to recuperate. But before we go...I'll need you."

I give him a sardonic look. "Such a one-track mind."

"It's not sexual. Not unless you want it to be," Bael adds with a weak smirk. But it fades quickly, and he shakes his head. "I just need to hold you for a while. Even if my curse is appeased from everything that happened today, my dragon's still on edge, and so am I. My mate just survived getting eaten by a monster and then burned to a crisp. You probably just shaved twenty years off my life through trauma alone, you know that? I have to covet you now and make sure you're taken care of. It's a dragon thing."

He places a sweet kiss on my forehead again and leaves the room.

My gaze falls back to Silas, and my fists clench when I see his brow furrowed slightly in pain. He really shouldn't have done this. Sacrificing his powers just to heal me. This damn cutthroat blood fae does whatever he thinks it takes to get what he wants, but I'm going to give him hell for ruining himself for me when he wakes up.

"You *will* wake up," I warn him, moisture crowding my eyes as I reach out and run my fingers over one of his soft curls.

After all...most casters don't survive the transition into necromancy. Even really powerful casters don't always have the best odds.

When my emotions become too much to handle, I finally stand and exhale harshly. I should get all this blood and gore off of me, too. Sitting here getting misty-eyed isn't helping Silas. I need to come up with our next plan of action and get my quintet to safety before—

Stay with me, sangfluir.

I freeze, staring down at the gorgeous blood fae. He hasn't moved.

But I heard him in my head clear as day.

Which should be impossible for unbound quintet members. That level of connection only happens with powerful quintets—ones that have already received the blessing of the gods, broken their curses, and had their hearts bound together.

And I don't even have a fucking *heart* right now, let alone the blessing of a god, so this can't be happening. It's just in my head.

Silas? I think, concentrating as I try to push the thought to him. *I'm here.*

His brow smooths out slightly as he slips back into a deeper rest. The room is quiet as I try to decide whether I imagined that. One of my bare hands absentmindedly slips to my chest, rubbing the stinging sensation lingering there.

Then I blink.

Silas healed me with necromancy. I was burned to a crisp, and every other injury vanished without even a fresh scar. So why is my chest still stinging?

Glancing down, I gasp at the straight, thin, rune-like line emblazoned directly over my scar—the quintet emblem for the House of Arcana.

Somehow, without a heart and without the blessing of the gods...

I've been bound to Silas Crane.

ABOUT THE AUTHOR

Morgan is a certified nerd who loves long bubble baths and big, bad, sexy cinnamon roll book boyfriends. When she's not busy reading spice or lint-rolling cat hair off of her yoga pants, she works a day job while daydreaming about the before-mentioned cinnamon roll book boyfriends.

To find out about upcoming releases or signed copies, join her mailing list at https://prodigious-knitter-8903.ck.page/48d02b6fe8.

Printed in Great Britain
by Amazon